'A rich and wonderful tale of high
fantasy to be read under the covers
with a torch ... and the doors
deadlocked. Twice!' GARY CREW
FOUR TIMES WINNER, AUSTRALIAN CHILDREN'S
BOOK COUNCIL CHILDREN'S BOOK OF THE YEAR

The BOOK *of* LIES

JAMES MOLONEY

Angus&Robertson
An imprint of HarperCollins*Publishers*

A NOTE ON THE COVER: The pictures on the cover are steel engravings, the
most efficient way of printing images in the nineteenth century, which have been
made into a collage using the computer technology of the twenty-first century.

Angus&Robertson
An imprint of HarperCollins*Publishers*

First published in Australia in 2004
by HarperCollins*Publishers* Pty Ltd
ABN 36 009 913 517
A member of the HarperCollins*Publishers* (Australia) Pty Limited Group
www.harpercollins.com.au

HarperCollins*Publishers*
25 Ryde Road, Pymble, Sydney NSW 2073, Australia
31 View Road, Glenfield, Auckland 10, New Zealand
77-85 Fulham Palace Road, London W6 8JB, United Kingdom
2 Bloor Street East, 20th floor, Toronto, Ontario M4W 1A8, Canada
10 East 53rd Street, New York NY 10022, USA

National Library of Australia Cataloguing-in-Publication data:

Moloney, James, 1954- .
    The book of lies.
    For children aged 8-12.
    ISBN: 0 207 19831 4.
    I. Title.
A823.3

Cover by This Is Ikon Pty Ltd
Internal design by Jenny Grigg & Louise McGeachie, HarperCollins Design Studio
Typeset by HarperCollins in 13 on 16 Historical Fell Type Roman
Printed and bound in Australia by Griffin Press on 70gsm Bulky Book Ivory

10 9 8 7 6   06 07 08

For Charlotte and Sydney.
Welcome to the world.

Contents

Part Three

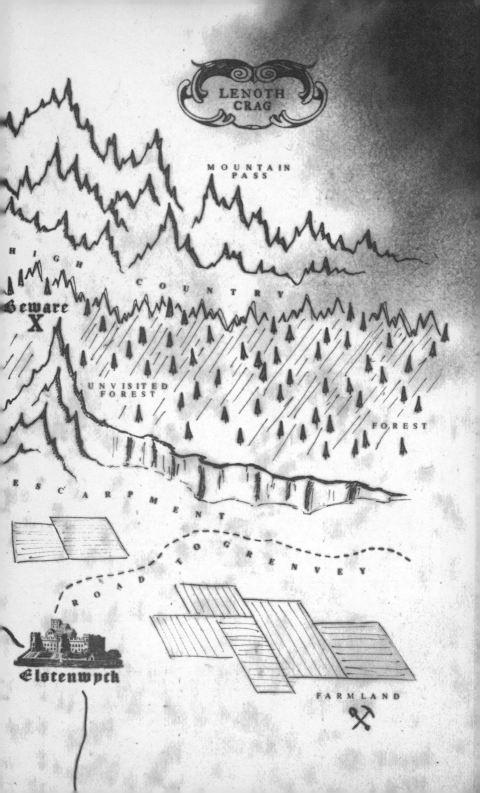

Prologue

O N A NIGHT WHEN angry clouds boiled and
burst overhead and the people of Fallside
prayed by their fires that the storm would
soon pass, four men emerged from the forest that
surrounded the village. None spoke a word, and even
their footsteps were unnaturally silent as they
splashed through muddy pools. They wore heavy
robes, their faces shrouded in cavernous hoods like
damned monks cast out into the night and driven to
this remote corner of the Kingdom by their deeds.
Between them, they carried a bundle wrapped in a
sodden blanket, the coarsely woven cloth straining
under the weight of their load.

The village lay on the other side of a stone bridge
across a stream. It was no more than a handful of

wretched houses, really, all clustered around the main street between the inn at one end and the church at the other. But these men were not heading for Fallside. Before they reached the bridge they turned and hurried towards the waterfall that gave the village its name. Here, where a stream suddenly plunged into the valley below, they found their destination.

A house stood alone, only fifty paces from the cliff's edge, two storeys of grey stone with a single-roomed tower rising, like a grim warrior on guard, from its centre. As the men approached, a yellow light flickered in the two narrow windows of this tower, watching them like eyes.

They passed silently through the gate and across the cobbled courtyard to the kitchen. The blanket was placed carefully on the stoop and once it was settled their leader rapped three times on the heavy door. His hand paused for three counts, then knocked again, once, twice, three times, beginning a strange and ghostly rhythm that would continue until the door was opened.

Upstairs, a woman stirred in her sagging bed. She hoped that the knocking had been in her dreams, but there it was again. One, two, three. Slowly — for she was worn out after a hard day's work — she lit a candle, and pausing only to gather her patched and mended dressing gown around her, she hurried into the corridor.

Her son was already waiting. 'The knocking,' he whispered. 'Another one has come.' He towered over his portly mother, the candlelight picking out the ugly spots that marred his cheeks and left him feeling awkward in front of the village girls. 'Should I fetch His Lordship?' he asked.

The woman shook her head briefly, which made the fleshy folds beneath her chin jiggle and sway. 'He will know already. Our job is to get the poor thing inside,' she said, as she led him down the staircase and into the kitchen.

The knocking continued relentlessly. One, two, three. The sound sent a shiver through the woman's body. She had been listening out for it, but she prayed that the noise had not woken anyone else. She mustn't lose courage now. Steeling herself, she drew back the bolt and pulled open the door.

A gust of misty rain greeted her, snuffing out the candle and obliging her to take a tighter grip on the folds of her dressing gown. Here were the hooded figures she had seen before, but she forced herself to ignore them and let her eyes fall quickly to the shape wrapped in the saturated blanket. 'Is this one even breathing?' she gasped.

The faceless figures made no answer. Nor would they carry the blanket and its hidden cargo across the threshold. Together, she and her son had to step into the rain and drag the heavy load from the paving stones themselves.

Finally they released their burden and the woman relit her candle. Holding it close, she reached out tentatively to turn back the blanket. 'A boy,' she said, adding, as she touched his forehead, 'Oh, and he's as cold as ice.'

'He's not dead, is he?' asked her son anxiously. He could cope with his fear of the silent visitors, but the body of a dead child ...

'No, and he'll live a long life yet if I have anything to do with it. We'll soon put some colour back into those cheeks. Quickly now, upstairs with him,' she said briskly.

But her son didn't move. Instead, he stared over her shoulder, which made her turn around. The kitchen door was still open to the rain and the four strangers huddled under the eaves.

'Will you not come inside and warm yourselves while we tend to the boy?'

Such kindness came naturally to her, but this was not the first time the strangers had come and she guessed her offer would not be accepted. When the hooded figures remained silent and still, she sighed and told them, 'Your job is done, then. You may as well go.'

She could only watch as they turned quickly and began the long journey back to wherever they had come from. When she bolted the door, she caught a last glimpse of the four silhouetted forms as they marched through her gate and disappeared into the darkness.

THE WOMAN DID NOT realise it, but above her in the tower another figure stood watching. With his eyes on the departing travellers, he passed a hand before his face in a single sweeping movement. Suddenly, the men stopped and stared about them, as sleepwalkers do when awakened from a dream. Their first tentative words escaped into the rain-swept night and one of them pushed back his hood to reveal a bewildered face. He pointed the way uncertainly and led them towards the village and the dark forest beyond. In the morning, they would forget they had ever come to Fallside or brought a sleeping boy to a house near the cliff's edge.

IN AN UPSTAIRS ROOM, a little girl lay straining her ears for every sound. She had struggled to stay awake, hoping to hear an entirely different noise, but tonight it had not come. Instead, the ominous knocking had started up, frightening her, and she had buried herself deeper under the blankets. But it had stopped now, and only moments ago she had heard the bolt snap back into place on the kitchen door.

Someone was coming up the stairs — two people, she guessed, when the footsteps passed her door. They continued down the hall to the small guest room at the end. Her curiosity had been roused and she felt she would never sleep until she knew why. She slipped out of bed, then, sure-footed and without a sound, she crept to the door at the end of the hall. It had been left ajar, just an inch, but enough to let the pale candlelight spill into the passageway.

'He's a fine-looking boy,' said a woman's voice, one she easily recognised. 'We'd better get him out of these wet things.'

The girl heard muffled sounds, then at length the two sets of footsteps came towards the door, leaving her just enough time to step aside before it opened wide to reveal the woman's familiar figure, with a bundle of damp clothing under her arm, and her son close at her shoulder. He held a candle for them to see by, but neither noticed the girl even though they passed close enough to touch her. She was not surprised; in fact, her face creased into a satisfied smile.

When the light had disappeared altogether, she tiptoed inside and closed the door behind her. With the candle gone, she had to wait while her eyes adjusted. After a minute or two she could see that the room was simply furnished with a bed, a roughly made table and stool and a battered wardrobe. The room was so small that there was little space for anything more.

The boy was sleeping deeply. She poked him gently on the shoulder. No response. She poked harder and still he didn't stir. She shook him vigorously and even pulled his ear, but he slept on. Surely such slumber wasn't natural. Distracted by these efforts to wake him, she didn't hear the footsteps in the corridor until they were right outside the door. With only a moment to hide, she flicked the wardrobe latch and stepped silently into the shadows behind the door. There she waited, as still as a stone.

Her heart beat frantically as she watched a man slowly walk across the room, carrying a candle. He held it away from his face to protect his eyes and so she could not see his features, but his movements were stiff and stern. He might once have been as tall as the doorway itself but now old age made him stoop at the waist. Robes of the darkest green and black fell loosely from his pinched shoulders, pooling untidily where they touched the floor.

He carried something heavy in the crook of his arm, hugging it tightly to his chest like a young mother holds her new baby. A book, the girl realised, when he placed it carefully on the table. Free of his precious burden, he went to stand over the sleeping boy, lingering there for some time. Then, releasing a deep and weary sigh, he stretched his hand out over the boy's face and began to mutter words she couldn't hear.

'No! No!' the boy cried immediately. With his eyes still closed, he thrashed wildly under the blanket until the man pressed one hand firmly on his shoulder. At the same time, he continued to sweep the other over the boy's face, palm turned downwards. The boy lay still, but his resistance was not over. In a much calmer voice now, he recited a verse that seemed to come from a part of him that the old man could not reach.

My fate is my own, my heart remains free

But before he could utter any more words, long and aged fingers touched his lips. 'Be still now, Marcel. Your magic is no match for mine.'

The boy cried out, a loud and desolate sound of loss as though his very soul had been wrenched from his grasp. But that hand remained over his face and he settled again into a fitful sleep.

Now the man dragged the table to the bedside and laid the book on top of it. He straightened his back painfully as he sat himself on the stool, and after a moment's reflection he began to speak.

Before she died, my mother told of her last wish. She had chosen a name for her newborn baby, the name of a favourite uncle she had known as a child.

As he spoke, the book opened of its own accord and the pages began to fan first one way then the other. When this frantic shuffling ended and the open pages lay still, a second voice joined in, an identical voice, repeating his words at the very moment he uttered them.

Where had this second voice come from? There was no one else in the room, the little girl was sure of it, though this didn't stop her from glancing around fearfully. Her eyes turned back in time to see the dark

8

figure pass his hand over the book. The second voice continued freely now, even though the old man himself had stopped speaking.

And so it was that after my mother was laid to rest in the graveyard, my father announced that his new son was to be called Robert.

On the bed, the sleeping boy stirred once more. His face grimaced into an agonised frown as he rolled his head back and forth. 'It's not me, it's not my life!' he wailed. But then that wrinkled hand was extended again and he lay still.

Not his life! What did he mean?

The girl heard the desperation in his cry and sensed his pain. She had never seen the boy before, knew nothing of him except for his name, but if he was suffering, how could she not help him? If only she could get closer …

Without thinking, she nudged the wardrobe door just enough for it to creak. The man stood up instantly and took a step in her direction. This man was a sorcerer. Just the thought of the enchantments he might work upon her chilled her bones to the marrow.

What could she do? In the shadow of the wardrobe's door she could stay undetected, but not if he pushed the door aside and let the candlelight pick her out. He came a step closer. One more and he would be able to swing the door out of the way. The girl drew back, but that was all she could do. He would surely find her.

But before he could take that final step, the old man faltered, and for a moment it seemed he would fall. He staggered sideways, groping desperately for the edge of the table to support himself. Finally, he turned his back to the wardrobe and hunched over, exhausted and fighting for breath. By the time he had recovered, a full minute later, he seemed to have forgotten the creaking wardrobe door. Behind that door the little girl finally dared breathe again.

The wizard turned back to the boy. 'I will leave you while my magic takes hold,' he muttered, then shambled out into the passageway and shut the door behind him while the voice of that strange book continued its story.

Slowly, cautiously, the girl emerged from beside the wardrobe and stood watching the magic at work. Now she could see that the words the sorcerer had spoken were written in a black, spidery hand on the pages of the book itself. The story droned on while the boy listened through his sleep. He was frowning again. A low groan broke from his lips as the name Robert was repeated.

No, this wasn't right. He wasn't Robert at all. She had heard his real name just now: Marcel. She knew she must stop this magic somehow ...

The book, perhaps that was the key. She leaned over the stool, and with a quick flick of her hand she slammed it shut. The voice continued, though muffled now so that the words could not be heard. That should do it, she thought with a smile of satisfaction.

But the smile was soon wiped from her face when the book opened again by itself, at exactly the same page, and the story continued. She tried again, this time sitting on the front cover. It worked for a moment, then she gave a little shriek as the book bucked her off and left her sprawled painfully beside the table.

If she couldn't stop the telling, then she would have to stop the boy from hearing. She grabbed the candle and began to search for something that could block up his ears. But apart from a few threadbare blankets in the wardrobe, she found nothing, while behind her the storytelling continued, every word searing itself into the boy's mind. Candlewax dripped onto her hand, hot and runny. She picked it off, moulding its softness between her fingers before she flicked it aside. Then her fingers stopped suddenly. She realised she had found just the thing.

Working quickly, she melted a pool of wax into her palm, and while it was still warm she worked it into two lumps and pushed them into the boy's ears. There, it was done. His face became less troubled and his slow, gentle breathing told her he was drifting into a calmer sleep. She sighed with relief and withdrew into the shadows beside the wardrobe once more in case anyone returned.

After the first telling the book began again, and after the second came a third, but just as this was starting there were more footsteps in the hall outside and the door opened to admit the woman and her son. They stood listening without a word until the story reached its tragic conclusion.

When I was twelve years old, my father cut his leg with a scythe and the wound began to fester. After struggling desperately for over a week, he died, and because there was no one to care for me I was taken to a home for orphans in Fallside.

Finally the voice ceased and the book closed without the touch of a hand.

'Your new name is Robert, it seems. It's as good a name as any.' The woman touched the palm of her hand to the boy's face. 'He's warmer now,' she said to her son, tucking in the blankets where the boy's twisting and turning had torn them free.

Watching from nearby the little girl held her breath and hoped they would not see the wax in his ears. But there was no need to worry, she soon discovered. 'Come on, Lord Alwyn will be waiting for his book,' the son said quickly, and taking the candle with them, they left the room.

Even when the house grew quiet, the little girl hesitated. She was still terrified of being discovered.

At last, when her fears had calmed a little, she returned to the boy's side and removed the wax from his ears. Even this intrusion did not wake him, and she guessed that the old man's magic was still at work. Then she returned to her own room and climbed into bed. The night had many hours still before dawn, but she didn't sleep a wink.

Part One

CHAPTER I

Mrs Timmins' Home for Orphans and Foundlings

DAYLIGHT FRINGED THE CURTAIN of the tiny room, then when the sun had climbed high enough, arrows of sunshine broke around the edges, finding targets on the table, the chair and the gaping wardrobe. At last, one golden beam touched the boy's face, and he awoke.

Staring down at him was a pair of kindly green eyes. There was a mouth that quivered uncertainly between a smile and a frown, a bulbous nose to match the round and reddened cheeks, and above those eyes, wisps of greying hair that refused to stay in place under her cap.

'Who are you?' he asked weakly.

'I'm Mrs Timmins,' she said softly. 'You've been brought here to live with me and the other children. Counting you, that will make thirteen altogether.'

'To live ... other children?' he murmured, closing his eyes again. Sleep began to welcome him back into its drowsy folds but he fought his way free, opening his eyes a second time. 'Where am I?'

'You are in a home for orphans and foundlings. From this window, you can see the village of Fallside,' she told him, sweeping aside the curtain with a plump hand. 'Such as it is,' she added without enthusiasm as she glanced briefly at the village. Then she tried to reassure him. 'Don't worry. You're quite safe here.' She helped him sit up, wedging pillows behind him.

'Orphans and foundlings,' he repeated under his breath. He pushed aside the blankets and tried to stand up.

'My, you're almost as tall as I am,' exclaimed the woman. 'You won't be with us for long, that's for certain. Any farmer in the district would be pleased to have a fine lad like you working his fields.'

This made no sense to the boy at all. Work in a farmer's field? He couldn't remember ever doing any such thing. In fact, he couldn't remember much at all. Whose hands are these? he thought, looking down at his body. They must be his feet, because he was standing on them.

A small mirror hung from a hook on the wardrobe. He went closer but he was only certain that this was really his face when a pair of wide blue eyes blinked back at him. What else could he see? There was brown hair, almost black really, and pale skin, as though he had been kept out of the sun for some time. He worried for a moment that he was a ghost, but then wouldn't this woman have been afraid of him? What had she called herself? Mrs Timmins, wasn't it? There she was, watching him with friendly amusement. No, he wasn't a ghost.

He took another look in the mirror. That mouth drooped a bit. Perhaps it came from feeling so dazed. Now that he'd seen it he decided that, as faces went, it could have been worse, and the thought brought a smile to his lips.

'Can you tell me your name, then?' Mrs Timmins asked.

'Name ...' the boy murmured. He opened his mouth quickly but no words came out, causing him to frown in confusion. 'Name ...' he said again. Why was it so hard for him to say it? Wait ... he did know, after all. 'I think my name is ... Robert.'

'Ah, you do remember,' Mrs Timmins said brightly. 'Welcome to my orphanage. There's always room for one more in this house.'

She left him alone to dress in the clothes she had brought for him. 'Robert,' he said to himself when he was finished. He knew he had been born with that name and he sensed somehow that his mother was dead. Was it ... yes, when he was a baby. If he was an orphan then his father must be dead too. Shouldn't he feel sadness? With a shock, he realised that all he could feel was emptiness and the few things he could remember rattled around inside his head like peas in a kettledrum.

He was still grappling with these thoughts when Mrs Timmins returned. 'It's time you met the others,' she announced briskly. 'Come with me.' She led the way out of the tiny room, along the passage to a flight of stairs. There she paused. 'We have few rules in this house, Robert, but one is that you be as quiet as you can just here, outside the entry to the tower,' she said, nodding towards an imposing oak door set into the wall opposite the staircase. He glanced at it, but for now he didn't give it a second thought.

'Come on, the girls are rather keen to see you — though they're *meant* to be working in the kitchen.' They started down the stairs, but after three steps the boy stopped, startled by the gang of five girls that had gathered at the bottom.

'It's a boy,' said a voice rather dismissively.

'Quiet, Dot,' hissed one of her companions, but Dot wouldn't be silenced.

'I wanted it to be another girl,' and with this announcement she led the posse of girls away, disappointed.

One of them seemed to linger for a moment. Was she smiling at him? It was difficult to tell, because the girl herself seemed no more than a shadow.

'Am I the only boy, Mrs Timmins?'

'No, no, the boys are outside, doing their chores.' She looked pointedly towards the girl. Then she led him down the remaining stairs and through a large kitchen. 'Come on, Robert,' she called when he lagged behind.

Robert? Yes, of course, that's me, he thought. He stepped into the sudden brightness of a cloudless day. The sunshine felt good on his skin and he turned his face towards it, hoping that the sun, at least, would recognise him.

A tall boy, almost a man, came striding towards them. 'This is my son, Albert,' said Mrs Timmins. 'He's in charge of all the outside work that's usually left to our boys.' Albert was rather proud of his role, judging by the grin that filled his face, a face already crowded with an unsightly rash of pimples. 'He'll give you jobs to do as well, but not today, since you've only just joined us.' She glanced at Albert to be sure he had understood.

'No, not today,' he agreed readily enough. 'Come on, I'll gather all the boys to meet you.' He walked to the well in the middle of the courtyard and shouted, 'Boys, boys, come here!' Before long, half a dozen boys had joined them in the courtyard.

'This is Robert, everyone,' called Mrs Timmins. 'I hope you'll make him feel at home.' She picked out two of the older boys. 'Hugh and Dominic, I'll leave him in your hands, so you can show him around.'

After an awkward moment or two, a boy stepped forward. One of his legs was shorter than the other, making him limp noticeably as he moved. 'I'm Dominic,' he said, offering his bony hand like a man. The boy shook it warily, but the hand was warm and the gesture friendly.

He relaxed a little as a second orphan introduced himself. 'My name's Hugh.' He put his hand to his mouth to stifle a sickly cough. Hugh didn't have a limp but he didn't have much else either. His arms and neck were skinny, the bones visible beneath the skin. His face was painfully narrow too.

'Do you want to join them, Fergus?' Mrs Timmins added, bringing a sterner tone to her voice. 'It's not so long ago that *you* were the new boy.'

This Fergus was a head taller than the rest and broad-shouldered. He nodded politely to Mrs Timmins but then turned to the younger boys around him, rolling his eyes in mockery. They sniggered uncertainly. 'What's your name again?' he asked bluntly.

The new boy hesitated, as though even this simple question were too much for him.

'You *do* know your name, don't you?' Fergus urged him.

'Robert,' he answered finally, not sounding quite convinced.

'Of course it is,' said Mrs Timmins a little too eagerly. 'Well, come on, Dominic, introduce the others. I have work to do if you lot expect to be fed.' She bustled off towards the kitchen. Albert lingered a moment, but he didn't seem one for words and soon he had disappeared as well.

Dominic turned to the waiting circle and fired off names faster than they could be matched to faces: Watkin, Oliver, Jonathan …

'Where do you come from?' asked Hugh.

Where *do* I come from? he asked himself. He wished he could remember.

Hugh tried again. 'What happened to your mother and father?'

'I'm not sure. I think my mother's …' Something held him back. It was in his mind, yes, as hard as a stone. His mother was dead, but still he didn't feel it.

When he said nothing further, Fergus wandered away, uninterested, and the younger boys went with him, leaving only Dominic and Hugh.

'I suppose we'd better start showing you around,' Hugh said. 'That's the stables over there.' An arm waved vaguely towards the low, ramshackle building that faced them across the courtyard. 'Old Belch lives in there, in one of the stalls.'

'A horse?'

'No, a man,' Dominic said with a laugh, 'but he smells like a horse. Worse, really.'

'Why's he called Old Belch?'

They glanced at each other, smirking. 'You'll find out when you meet him,' said Hugh.

While they were talking, a tall girl had walked past them to the well in the middle of the yard, where she filled a bucket with water. Now she sloshed that water heedlessly over the sides as she returned to the kitchen. She was much older than the girls he had seen near the stairs — older than he was, he guessed. She was brushing the end of her long ponytail with her free hand as she went, paying more attention to this than the bucket. He said hello, but she didn't even look at him.

'What's she being so high and mighty for?' he asked.

'She's always like that,' said Hugh. 'Did you see the way she was spilling the water? She'll have to go back for another load.'

'What's her name?'

'Nicola. Only been here a few weeks. No one likes her much.'

'She was sent back,' said Dominic. There was something about the way he said this that made the newcomer raise his eyebrows, puzzled.

Hugh tried to explain. 'A family in Fallside wanted someone, a bit like a servant, but more like a daughter really.'

'Except she was hopeless. Too proud to do anything useful so they sent her back,' Dominic continued bitterly.

Hugh dropped his voice to a whisper. 'It's a terrible thing to be sent back.'

'She lost her chance,' said Dominic, and suddenly the new boy understood why he spoke so savagely.

Dominic's limp meant *he* would never be offered a home.

After Nicola had disappeared haughtily through the kitchen door, the tour continued. They headed for the back of the house, past a vegetable garden, and beyond it a field with two well-fed cows. They rounded a pond where ducks quarrelled and a family of geese strutted proudly at the water's edge.

'This is the orchard,' Dominic said as they walked between rows of apple trees that ran all the way to the stone wall bordering the orphanage. 'Albert and Mrs Timmins sell the fruit in the village. That's how we buy the food we need.'

They showed him the rope they swung on and their favourite climbing tree among the oaks on the other side of the house. But since the conversation about Nicola the new arrival had sunk into a reverie, and no matter how hard Hugh and Dominic worked to make him feel at home, he remained distant.

'Will we show him the waterfall?' asked Hugh.

'We're not supposed to cross the wall,' Dominic replied cautiously.

'Oh, come on, Albert's not watching,' Hugh insisted. The gleam in his eye showed a spirit far stronger than his withered body. It was enough to carry Dominic along.

The three boys clambered over the waist-high stone fence and a minute later arrived at the cliff's edge, or at least, as close to it as any of them dared go.

'It's massive,' the newcomer breathed in awe, becoming more enthusiastic now. From the waterfall at his right, the craggy cliff continued as far as his eye could see. He inched closer to the edge, feeling the fine spray from the plummeting water, cold against his face.

'It's straight down, all the way,' said Hugh. 'How far, do you think?'

'A thousand feet.'

'More like two thousand,' Hugh corrected him. 'It's like the earth broke itself in two and pushed one half straight up into the sky to make these highlands.'

The boy looked out over the cliff's edge to the enormous plains below. They seemed to flow in a shimmer of midday heat all the way to the horizon. 'Perhaps I come from down there,' he whispered, too softly for his companions to hear. Then he asked, more loudly, 'How do you get down into the valley?'

'There are paths down the rock face in places,' said Hugh.

'Or you can jump!' Dominic laughed at his own little joke but a shudder ran through each of the boys all the same.

They headed back through the stand of oaks and then Hugh and Dominic left him so they could catch up on their chores. The boy drifted aimlessly through the orchard to a place where the ground disappeared under a wild mess of brambles and blackberry canes.

There was a well-worn path at the edge and an opening large enough to crawl through. He dropped to his hands and knees and found himself under a tightly woven archway of thorny vines that formed a sort of cave. The ground had been hollowed out, except for a few small boulders, to form a snug hideaway. Best of all, it was peaceful and he could be alone. He found a seat on a rounded granite boulder.

'You can't remember, can you?' said a voice.

The boy stood up sharply, bumping his head on the thick canes that formed the roof. He looked around him but he couldn't see anyone. 'Who said that?'

'You've lost your memory,' the voice said again.

'Who is it? I can't see you!' He whirled around frantically, stopping to stare at the place where the voice seemed to come from. To his amazement, a figure emerged from the shadows where it had been standing unnoticed even as he gazed at it. It was one of the little girls, the one who had smiled at him.

Her face was bordered by swirls and ropes of brown hair growing wild, like creepers around a statue. Her skin was dark, which helped her stay unseen in the shadows. Perhaps she kept her dress dull and dusty for the same reason. But she wanted to tell him something, and while the eagerness gripped her, her eyes sparkled and he could see her clearly.

'Who are you? And why were you hiding there?'

'I wasn't hiding,' she said defiantly. 'Not on purpose, anyway.' She hesitated a moment then seemed to make up her mind. 'Your name,' she said softly. 'It's not Robert at all.'

'What do you mean, not my name? But Mrs Timmins, she called me ...' He didn't say it. 'If my name's not Robert, what is it, then?'

The girl hesitated.

'Tell me, please!'

At last she spoke. 'Your name is Marcel.'

'What did you call me?'

'Marcel,' she said again, more confident now.

He felt his heart leap at the sound of this name and he braced himself to remember who he was and all that had happened in his life to this day.

Nothing came.

'You've told me my name, but ... but who am I?'

She shook her head sadly. It was a simple thing to tell him his name, but the rest ...

'You *must* know. Why did I think I was called Robert?'

'It came from a book.'

'A book!'

The girl told him then of all that she had witnessed the night before, of the old man in the dark robes and the heavy book he had brought to the room at the end of the hall, of the voice and its story and how it couldn't be stopped. He listened, wide-eyed. Finally she told him how she had plugged his ears with wax.

'You saved me,' said Marcel, for he had no doubt now that this was his name. 'You're much braver than girls are supposed to be. How can I thank you? If there is anything I can do for you, you only have to ask. That's a promise,' he added slowly. But the girl just smiled uncomfortably.

A hundred questions were swirling through his head. 'Do you think my real life is still inside that book? If I could get hold of it, maybe my life would be in there for me to find.'

The emptiness he felt round his heart was swept aside by a sudden fury. 'Who was this man? Where did he come from?'

'I heard them call him Lord Alwyn, but I can't tell you any more than that. He just arrived one night, while we were all asleep, like you did. He lives in the tower above us. There's a door across the stairwell now. It has no lock, not even a doorknob.'

Marcel's eyes widened. 'Mrs Timmins pointed the door out to me, but I didn't pay much attention to it. Have the other children seen him?'

'No, he never comes out. But we … hear things.'

Marcel didn't like the sound of that, especially the way she had said it. What things? he was about to ask, when a voice echoed faintly through the little hideaway. 'Robert, Robert! Come and eat.'

It was Dominic, calling him by a name that meant nothing to him any more.

'I have to go,' said the girl. 'It's my turn to set the table.' She was already on the move and again so hard to see that if he hadn't known she was there he would have missed her.

'Quickly, tell me your name.'

She spoke a single word, softly, so softly that he could barely make it out. It sounded like 'bee'. Had he heard right? But before he could ask her to repeat it, she had disappeared altogether.

He crawled under the archway of thick vines and out into the light. As he blinked and straightened up, he found himself facing the house. There was the tower, brooding and ominous, staring down at him. For an instant he thought he saw a hand and part of a face at one of the windows, but when he looked again, they had gone.

'A book,' he murmured to himself. 'A sorcerer's book.'

Lord Alwyn

MARCEL WAS STILL THINKING about the strange little girl when he entered the kitchen with Dominic, and even after Mrs Timmins had given him his first job. 'Robert, would you take those jugs of milk into the dining room?' she asked.

Hearing that false name made him hesitate, but he wasn't sure what to do about it yet. Dominic was carrying a tray laden with freshly baked bread and the aroma reminded him of how hungry he was. He followed Dominic into the dining hall, where other children were already busy setting out plates and arranging a motley assortment of chairs around the long table. He looked for the girl among them but couldn't see her. Had he imagined the whole thing?

The dining room was dark and cool after the sunny courtyard. A fireplace, freshly cleared of last night's ash, was built into the far wall. Its homely scent of wood-smoke hung in the air. The high ceiling and bare stone floor made the room rather noisy, but it was the happy noise of children eager to fill their growling bellies.

All the children seemed to have their own place to sit around the table and Marcel was left out until Hugh and Dominic made room between them. Mrs Timmins took her place at one end of the table and Albert at the other. They all lowered their heads and recited a simple prayer, but as soon as the last word died on their lips, hands shot out to the plates of bread.

Marcel wasn't the only one to hold back. The tall girl he had seen spilling the water watched the snatching hands all round her. There was something proud about her, as though she were waiting to be offered the plate. Finally she took a piece and bit into it delicately. No wonder she had been sent back by the family in the village, Marcel thought. He watched her for a moment and saw with a grin that hunger made her dainty bites come a little too rapidly for good manners.

She might be careless with a bucket, but not with her appearance, he noticed. Her long tresses, now loosened from their ponytail, stretched almost to her waist and she had stroked them to a brassy sheen. Pale freckles from working in the sun dotted her nose and cheeks, but they couldn't hide what a pretty girl she was. How much prettier she would be if she didn't spend so much time scowling.

Meanwhile, Mrs Timmins began listing names around the table. 'I don't think you met the girls before. That's Sarah and beside her is Dorothy. We call her Dot because she's small and round.'

'I am not,' the girl retorted, but the others only laughed. They seemed to do that a lot around this table.

More girls' names followed, Kate and Lizzy. When it was her turn, Marcel was officially introduced to Nicola. She offered him a stiff smile, said, 'How do you do,' and went back to her delicate eating.

He barely noticed her rudeness, because he was looking for a particular face, and so far he hadn't found it.

'Oh, and I shouldn't forget Beatrice, wherever you are, little one,' said Mrs Timmins.

'Here she is, next to me,' called the girl named Sarah, and at last Marcel spotted her. 'We call her Bea,' Sarah explained to him.

'So now you've met us all, Robert,' said Mrs Timmins, taking charge again.

But his name wasn't Robert. The little girl from the hideaway under the vines was real after all and so was the name she had given him. His head was spinning. He felt like he had been born only an hour before.

'No, my name is not Robert.'

The frantic eating slowed as every eye turned first towards him and then to Mrs Timmins.

'But only this morning you told me it was,' she said, alarmed.

'I was wrong.'

'You're playing tricks with us,' said Mrs Timmins, forcing a smile. 'That's it, I'm sure. You're playing a little game.'

'No, it's not a game, and I think you know my real name already. It's Marcel, isn't it?'

If the eating hadn't entirely stopped around the table, the low murmur of talking certainly had. The faintest blush of self-reproach touched Mrs Timmins' cheeks. There was fear in her face too. 'How did you come by this new name?'

'I can't explain,' he said. It shouldn't be Marcel who had to explain at all. How could she help this sorcerer to steal away his life with a sweep of his hand?

Mrs Timmins rose from the table. 'Come with me,' she ordered. He followed her into the kitchen, where she sat him in a chair and drew another up close. 'Now, tell me. How did you hear this name? Did you find it written somewhere?'

He shook his head.

'Did someone tell you?'

He didn't want Bea to get into trouble. 'No,' he

assured her. 'It just came to me, from inside, as though it had always been my name.'

The concern in her features deepened. She looked perplexed, but more than anything she seemed afraid for him. 'What do you remember?' she demanded. 'You must tell me how much you can recall of your life before you came here.'

'Nothing,' he answered honestly. 'I can't remember a thing.'

The sadness in his words seemed to convince her. 'I believe you, and thank heavens for it.' She took his hand and squeezed. 'I'm sorry,' she whispered. 'It's not my doing that this has happened. But there's something I have to do now. Someone you have to meet. Stay here.' She swallowed hard and set off towards the stairs.

Some moments later Marcel heard a distant knocking and knew it was the woman's hand on that forbidding door set so impregnably into the wall opposite the stairs above. Her knock was answered by a savage growl, muffled by the door but loud enough to fill the entire house and send a blood-chilling terror through everyone who heard it.

Albert appeared at the door of the kitchen with a large chunk of bread and a wedge of cheese for Marcel. He couldn't swallow a bite. 'That ... noise,' he managed to say. 'What kind of beast ...?'

'Don't be afraid. No harm comes to the children in this house.' Albert seemed to fight off his natural shyness and placed his hand gently on the boy's shoulder. That touch alone eased the boy's fear. 'I'll stay here with you until my mother comes back, if you like.'

Marcel looked up gratefully and nodded. He was glad to have a companion in the anxious minutes ahead. They stretched on unbearably, until at last he heard the creak of wooden boards on the staircase. He traced the slow approach of footsteps before Mrs Timmins appeared in the doorway. When she moved aside nervously, a second figure came into view.

Just as Bea had described him, this stooped old man was hidden in the many folds of a black robe edged with the deepest green. Around the hem, two odd shapes had been embroidered in gold thread, the same combination repeated many times. The folds made it difficult to see what they were, until the wizard moved slightly and Marcel realised that one of the outlines was certainly a dragon with vicious talons open and grasping on its feet. What was the second shape beneath each dragon? Were they bats, with wings outstretched, golden bats flying on the night sky of that black robe? Before he could decide the man came closer, and now Marcel saw what Bea had not been able to describe. His face was deeply lined with age, long and sorrowful as though it had never known laughter in all the years it had lived through. Bea had given him a name, too. Despite his terror, Marcel recalled it easily. Lord Alwyn.

Frail though the old man appeared, Marcel wasn't

fooled. This man had worked a cruel magic upon him that had swept away every memory he had. If it hadn't been for Bea, even his name would be gone.

'You are the child who calls himself Marcel?' said the wizard in a deep and weary tone.

Marcel looked for Mrs Timmins, hoping she would answer for him. But, to his dismay, he found that both she and Albert had gone, and he had been left alone with the wizard. He wasn't sure his voice would work, so he offered a weak nod instead.

'Come. I want to speak with you.' Lord Alwyn seated himself at the kitchen table, motioning for Marcel to sit close by where he could watch every muscle in the boy's face. On the table beside him he placed an ancient book almost half a metre long and as thick as a grown man's arm. Its dusty red cover was cracked along thin jagged lines where the leather had dried, giving the book a rough and weathered surface. Marcel eyed it with rising dread. This book had already been used against him once.

'You fear the book? That might be a good thing, since —' The wizard stopped suddenly and turned his body stiffly to the left, peering hard into the gloom where light from the windows didn't reach. 'You there,' he called at last. 'Come over here.'

Bea's tiny figure appeared from nowhere and came to stand beside Marcel. She was shaking through every inch of her body. 'Excuse me, sir. I was caught in here by mistake.'

As she spoke, the book opened of its own accord and riffled from page to page, until on one of its last leaves it found a space not covered by words. Marcel watched in amazement as new words began to appear, the very words Bea had just spoken.

I was caught in here by mistake.

The wizard stared harshly at her for some time. 'Your lie has been recorded in my book. In fact, those who don't know any better call it the Book of Lies. Now, tell me the truth. You hoped to hear what I said to this boy, isn't that so?'

Bea hesitated, but she had no alternative now. 'Yes, sir.'

This time the book closed quietly and lay motionless on the table. Watching it, Marcel thought he saw the faintest glow rise from the cover, until his attention was drawn again to the old man.

Lord Alwyn's lips had curled into a brief smile. 'What is your name?'

She told him.

'Well now, Bea,' he said, 'you are braver than your friends but you will have no gossip for them. Go,' he commanded, 'and tell the others in the dining room to stay away.'

He turned to Marcel. 'Tell me about yourself,' he said, with less threat in his voice.

'I can't remember anything, sir.' As Marcel spoke,

Lord Alwyn stared at the book, which remained still and silent on the table, though this time there was no doubt that it glowed a rich reddish-gold to match the sunlight outside in the courtyard.

'I believe you,' he said at last. 'But tell me: how did you come by your name?'

'I don't know. The name simply came to me, as though it had always been there, in my —' He stopped talking and turned in horror towards the book. It had opened again, hurrying to that same page, where it began to write everything he had just said.

'Now I *don't* believe you. Someone told you.'

'No, sir!' Marcel insisted. 'It's true. I would never forget my real name.'

There was no quill, no pot of ink, but the book recorded his words again. Lord Alwyn eyed him impassively as the book worked its telling magic. What could he do? The book knew he was lying, yet to tell the truth would betray Bea. He stayed silent and closed his eyes, waiting for a harsher magic to strike at him. The next few moments seemed like hours.

Then he dared open his eyes and found the old man staring at him thoughtfully. 'You need not be afraid of me,' he said, though that voice remained as hard as steel. 'Not as long as you do what I say.'

He turned slightly and called out to Mrs Timmins and Albert, who came scuttling through the doorway. 'Listen to me, all three of you,' he said. 'What I intended has somehow been foiled. All of the other children have heard his name now, and to alter the minds of so many would be too much for me. There is nothing else for it. You, Marcel, are to live here in this foundling home until I say otherwise. When people come looking for children to adopt they will not choose you. They will not even see you. No one must know there is a child here by that name. Do you understand?'

He paused, considering whether words were enough to ensure obedience. Then his face became even harder. 'If you take one step beyond the boundaries of this orphanage,' he told him ominously, 'I will know and I will send my companion in the tower to fetch you.'

He thrust his arm upwards, and at that moment a terrible growling erupted above them, building relentlessly until it exploded in a furious roar that turned their blood to ice.

The old sorcerer did not wait for their promises. He rose from his chair and shuffled to the stairs, leaving Marcel to ponder what was so special about his name that it needed a savage beast to keep it secret.

CHAPTER 3

Old Belch

ALL THE BOYS SLEPT in one room, and since there were seven of them, it was crammed with two large beds that could fit three boys in each, and a narrow cot for the seventh. The room at the end of the hall, Marcel learned, was reserved for sick children or for new arrivals who came in the middle of the night. Marcel found he was to share a bed with Hugh and Dominic, and though it was a squeeze he was too exhausted to care.

In the morning, he was just another of the orphans who had to dress quickly when Albert called them and hurry down to breakfast before it was all gone.

'I want you to help Old Belch today,' Albert told him. 'Hugh and Dominic can take you along to the stables.'

When the three boys reached the well in the middle of the courtyard, Marcel looked up again at the tower that brooded over them. The sight of those two small windows set in the stone put him on edge. Though he tried to shut it out, he heard that vicious roar again in his head and it sent a shudder through his entire body.

'Have you ever seen it?' he asked.

'Seen what?' responded Dominic.

'The creature he keeps up there. The one that made that terrible noise.'

'Never. We've heard a few strange things but nothing like yesterday.'

In the silence that followed, each boy conjured a picture of the beast in his mind. They were about to walk on when Hugh let out a rasping cough, then asked, 'What do you think he feeds that thing?'

The other two stared at him. What kind of a question was that? They didn't even want to think about it. But Hugh had a point to make. 'It sounded pretty big, don't you think? It'd need quite a bit to eat, but all Mrs Timmins ever leaves outside that strange door is a small tray for the old man.'

'Maybe he lets it out at night, to go hunting in the forest,' suggested Dominic.

'How does it get out, then? We've never heard it going though the house.'

'There's a tunnel,' said a voice.

They spun around, all three of them trying to find who had spoken. Marcel was the first to see her. 'Bea,' he breathed in relief when the girl appeared from the shadow of the well where she had just filled a bucket. 'How do you know there's a tunnel?'

'Because I've heard strange noises in the wall beside my bed. They started soon after that man came to live in the tower.'

'But where does it come out then? I've never seen a hole in the wall,' said Dominic sceptically.

'It's on the other side of the house, where we don't go very much, near the orchard. There are bushes up against the wall, that's why you haven't noticed it. I've seen some tracks there — giant paw prints, they looked like — but the opening is hidden somehow. I need to take another look.'

'No!' blurted Marcel, horrified. 'Don't go near those bushes. Whatever's up in that tower, well ... I don't think any of us wants to meet it face to face.'

Before they could say another word, little Dot called from the kitchen door. 'Bea, Mrs Timmins is waiting for that water.'

Bea hurried off, easily visible to them all now in the sunlight. Very strange, Marcel thought to himself yet again.

Though they were meant to be on their way to the stables, the boys couldn't resist detouring to the far side of the house, where they stayed well back from the overgrown bushes that hugged the walls. 'In there somewhere, eh?' said Hugh.

None of them went in for a closer look. They could still see that tower from here, though. There was only one window on this side. Marcel scoured the glass for a glimpse of Lord Alwyn. 'Why does a sorcerer live *here*?' he wondered aloud. 'A man like him would have a house of his own, don't you think?'

'Or a whole castle.'

'If you ask me, he's here because of you,' said Dominic. 'You heard Mrs Timmins at dinner last night. We're not even supposed to mention your name over in the village.'

'And if I go there myself, he'll send that beast after me.' I don't think I'll ever find out who I really am, Marcel added to himself.

Hugh broke into his thoughts with another loud cough. 'Come on,' he said to Dominic, 'Albert'll be wondering where we've got to.'

They walked silently back into the courtyard and to the stables, where they parted company. Marcel pushed aside the groaning door and called tentatively, 'Hello, anyone here?'

When there was no answer, he sank down on a saddle in the darkness to wait for Old Belch. He hadn't laid eyes on the man yet and didn't know quite what to expect.

Soon he heard heavy footsteps on the cobblestones of the courtyard, then the stable door was swept aside to reveal the silhouette of a man as wide as he was tall. 'Now then, where's this lad who'll be helping me with my horses?' he called.

Marcel scrambled to his feet, but no sooner had the man shouted into the narrow confines of the stables than a loud gurgle exploded from his throat. He slapped a hand over his mouth. 'Er, sorry, my boy,' he muttered, but it did him no good, as his stomach immediately erupted again.

No need to ask how he acquired his name then, thought Marcel. 'Albert said I'm to work with you today, sir,' he said, as he reluctantly moved closer. Despite the gloom of the stables, Marcel could see the man better now, his little pig eyes squeezed above hearty cheeks. His beard was nothing much to speak of, just a few gingery wisps that had no chance of hiding that series of bulging chins. Lower down, he just got rounder, his stomach most of all. It rumbled as Marcel's eyes rested on it, but this time the man managed to suppress his burp.

'They tell me I shouldn't eat so many onions,' he said apologetically. Then his face broke into a wide grin. 'But I like 'em too much,' and to show it, he fished an onion out of his pocket and munched on it like an apple. 'I've got an empty stall that needs cleaning out. Come on, put a shovel in that wheelbarrow and follow me.'

After doing as he was asked Marcel was led to the last stall along the row. 'I had a horse in here until last week. You see all this straw and what the horse added to it? Take it all to the vegetable patch, then fill the stall with clean straw. And mind you do it properly, not like that

Fergus. He disappeared before the job was half done,' Old Belch explained, doing his best to look serious, though the face he made was more comical than gruff. Then he burped. 'Oh, excuse me,' he said, and promptly burped again. The pungent odour of half-digested onions wafted heavily through the stables.

Marcel started in with the shovel. It was easier work than he had expected and he was finished long before Old Belch came back and told him he could leave.

'Could I stay and have a look at your horses?' he asked.

Old Belch looked surprised. 'No harm in that, I suppose. Come on, I'll show you around.'

There were seven stalls, counting the one Marcel had cleaned out. The first contained no horse but a thick bed of straw, a blanket and a book. Marcel remembered what Hugh had told him about Old Belch's sleeping habits, but the book was a puzzle. How did someone like Old Belch learn to read? Then he realised that he could ask the same question about himself.

A fine chestnut horse poked its head out of the second stall, hoping they had brought it a treat. 'He cut himself badly jumping a fence,' Old Belch explained. 'All better now though, so he'll be heading home soon.'

As they stopped at each stall, Marcel soon realised that all of the horses suffered from an ailment of one sort or another. One trod gingerly on its foreleg; there was a plough horse recovering from ulcers where the heavy yoke had rubbed against its shoulders; and in the stall beside it another withered beast stared at him, sad-eyed and listless.

Old Belch answered Marcel's question before he could even ask it. 'People send me their horses, to heal them.'

'What's wrong with this one?' Marcel asked, looking into the next stall, at a horse with rather spindly legs and a long neck hidden beneath a matted mane. This mane was black, but as for the rest of the horse, name a colour and it was there: earth-brown, grey and plenty of dirty white with flecks of a lighter brown on its rump and face. 'This one's an ugly thing,' he commented bluntly.

Immediately the horse snorted and threw back its head as though it protested at these words. Old Belch went into the stall and spoke to it in whispers that Marcel couldn't hear, but they had an immediate effect and the horse settled down. 'There's nothing wrong with her,' he said in a voice that seemed far too soft and friendly for a man whose hair looked like a grizzled nest of snakes. 'She's just a bit wild, that's all, too wild for her master — he didn't want her any more. So now she's mine.'

Marcel took another look at the mare. She was no beauty, that was certain, but she was alert and eager to be free of the stall that confined her, no matter how well Old Belch cared for her. Wasn't that just how he felt about Mrs Timmins and her orphanage?

The last stall was the one Marcel had cleaned out. Old Belch was impressed with what he saw. 'You worked hard. A proper young Hercules — but I suppose you wouldn't know what I'm talking about, would you?'

'Hercules,' Marcel repeated. 'Yes, I know who he was: a great hero who cleaned out the dirtiest stables in the world.'

Old Belch's eyebrows shot up. 'So he did. Now, where would a simple boy from the high country hear that story?'

Marcel shrugged his shoulders. 'Someone must have told me.' This puzzled him. He couldn't remember a name or a face or a single day of his life before yesterday, yet he knew the tale of Hercules. There was more he remembered too, and the excitement of such memories made him eager to repeat them. 'Didn't Hercules have a horse, a special horse with wings?'

'Ah, now you're thinking of Pegasus. It wasn't Hercules but another great hero, Bellerophon, the only man who could tame such a wild beast.' Old Belch's face glowed proudly as he glanced over at the speckled mare. 'The poor fellow came to a bad end, though. Pegasus was stung by a gadfly and bucked him off while they were high in the clouds.'

Marcel had followed Old Belch's eye back to the ugly mare. 'Does she have a name?' he asked.

'Name! Not that I know of. I'll ask her, if you like, to see what she wants to be called.'

Marcel laughed, thinking this was just a joke, but his smile slipped a little when Old Belch entered the stall again and put his lips to the horse's ear. What was more, when he was finished the horse did the same, pushing her long snout close to the man's own ear.

'She was listening to my story about Pegasus but she doesn't want the name of a horse that was tamed. She would rather be the gadfly.'

'Should we call her Gadfly, then?' suggested Marcel.

'Why not!'

The horse reared her head away and turned a stern eye on both of them. Could she really understand them? Marcel was beginning to wonder, but Old Belch was unconcerned. 'I prefer these animals to the well-bred beasts I looked after in the Army,' he confided.

'You were in the Army?'

'Not as a soldier, no. Fighting's not for me. I cared for the horses. In fact,' he said, standing a little straighter and pulling back his shoulders, 'I was once in charge of the *royal* horses. Had my own room in the palace, no less.' He looked down in mild embarrassment at his huge stomach, which he patted gently. 'Of course, that was in my younger days. But it's true. You can ask Lord Alwyn if you don't believe me.'

'Lord Alwyn! You know him?'

'A little, but then everyone round the palace knew Lord Alwyn. It's a great surprise to see him here, in

Fallside, I must admit. Most brilliant sorcerer of his age, they say. He's served our kings and queens for as long as I can remember. Master of the Royal Books, he was. Still is, I suppose, since I haven't heard tell of a new one.'

Books!

'Belch,' Marcel interrupted anxiously, 'Lord Alwyn came down to … er … meet me yesterday. Just me. He brought a special book with him. It knew whether I was telling the truth.'

'Ah, the Book of Lies, it sounds like. He created it long ago, to help judge matters in the royal court.'

'But how can it tell who is lying and who is telling the truth?'

'Well, only Lord Alwyn himself could tell you that for sure. It seems he managed to bind up all things, past, present and future, into that book. It knows it all. More than that …' Old Belch's face became mischievous, like that of a little boy who knows a secret, and bending forward as much as his belly would let him, he said softly, 'I heard talk at the palace. It's said that book can look deeply into a man's mind and discover what he's thinking. Who could keep a lie hidden from such a thing, eh?'

'So powerful,' Marcel whispered in awe.

'Yes, and unpredictable too, even in Lord Alwyn's hands.' He dropped his voice even lower. 'There's a story about the first time the Book was used. It was in the time of Queen Madeleine, as good a queen as any kingdom could ask for, and a wise woman, too. All the great lords and ladies were there, with the Queen on her throne and the Book on a table before them all. No one even saw the little sparrow.'

'Sparrow! What's that got to do with —'

A loud burp interrupted Marcel, giving Old Belch a chance to go on. 'The tiny thing had flown in through a window above them. It landed on the Book's cover and started to chirp away, loud as you please. Then, as the whole court looked on, that sparrow became a mighty eagle.'

'That's impossible!'

'Not at all. It was the Book, don't you see? Even animals lie to themselves and pretend they are mightier than they are. I know that better than anyone. The Book of Lies discovered that little bird's deepest secret and showed it to the world. In its heart, it wanted to be a mighty eagle, but as soon as it flew away from the Book it changed back into a harmless sparrow. Since that day, Lord Alwyn has kept his book well clear of animals. It's no surprise he's brought it here with him.'

'But what's he *doing* here? Why did he leave the palace?'

'If you ask me, he's come here to die.'

'Die!'

'You've seen him, haven't you? Old and weary. He's been Master of the Royal Books longer than most of us have been alive. But even great sorcerers are human beings. He can't live forever.'

Just then Albert's voice called through the doorway, 'Belch, Mum wants you to go with me into the village. As for you, Marcel, go and ask my mother if she has anything for you to do.'

Moments later, Marcel found himself standing alone under the eaves of the stable roof, trying to make sense of what he had just learned. One thing troubled him more than anything else. Yes, Lord Alwyn was old and weary, but he was sure Old Belch was wrong about why he was here. Dominic's words echoed in his ears. *He's here because of you.*

He shut the stable door, and was crossing the courtyard, hoping Mrs Timmins would have no more jobs for him, when he heard angry shouting coming from the direction of the orchard. Turning, he saw Dominic squaring off against another boy who already had his fists raised.

'Fergus,' he murmured. He hadn't taken to the boy from the moment they were introduced, and every time he had seen him since, he had liked him less. Already his legs were running. He hurried into the trees, where he found Hugh trying to pull Dominic away, but behind the solid figure of Fergus were the three smaller boys, eager for the punches to start.

'What's going on?' Marcel demanded as he caught his breath.

'He called me a cripple!' Dominic shouted furiously.

'Well, that's what you are,' Fergus goaded him. 'Look at you. You can't even stand up straight.'

Dominic advanced an unsteady step and swung wildly.

Fergus ducked under it easily then pushed him lightly. It was enough to make Dominic fall backwards. 'There, what did I tell you?' crowed Fergus, enjoying the adulation of the little boys.

'Stop it, Dominic! You can't fight him!' Hugh insisted.

Dominic stood up again as quickly as he could. If anything, the push had made him angrier than ever. 'I'm sick of the names he calls me! "Lame Duck", "Limpy". I've had enough! I'm going to knock his tongue down his throat and then he won't be able to talk at all!' He shaped up, his bony fists at the ready, though he was clearly no match for the lithe and muscular Fergus.

'If anything's going to get knocked, it's your head,' Hugh tried to persuade him, but Dominic wasn't listening. Watching from close by, Marcel could tell this wasn't the first time his new friend had been stirred up like this. This time, he'd clearly been pushed too far.

'I'm going to get Albert,' said Hugh, disgusted.

'He's gone into the village with Old Belch,' Marcel told him.

'Mrs Timmins, then.'

Fergus snorted rudely. 'You lot are always running off to her. I say we work out who's boss, here and now.'

Oliver, Watkin and Jonathan all cheered at this, and Marcel could see that Fergus wouldn't back down, not with these three for an audience.

'We don't need Mrs Timmins,' seethed Dominic, too enraged to see sense. 'I'm ready, Fergus.' His fists were still in position. 'You think you can lord it over the rest of us, well now's your chance.'

The trouble was, as Marcel could see, that was exactly what was going to happen.

'Wait!' he shouted, stepping between the two boys as they stared at each other menacingly. 'If you're going to fight someone, Fergus, it should at least be a fair fight.' He put up his own fists to show that he was taking Dominic's place.

'But he'll make a mess of you instead, Marcel!' cried Hugh, behind him.

Oh, great. Even Marcel's new friends thought he would lose. In fact, now that he was here, facing Fergus, he wasn't so sure he had done the right thing. Fergus suddenly looked a lot bigger.

He glared at Fergus, whose round face was bloated with arrogance, as though he had won the fight already. Marcel would love to bring him down a peg or two, tussle that woolly brown hair and iron out those thin little lips so that they couldn't curl into a permanent smirk. So what if he's got shoulders like a plough horse? If I'm fast on my feet, he told himself, he'll never land a punch.

Hugh was looking at those shoulders too. 'It's still not a fair fight,' he cried. 'If this is some kind of challenge, then neither of you should have the advantage.'

'What are you talking about?' asked Fergus, dropping his fists.

'What about a race?' suggested Hugh.

But Fergus sneered at the idea. 'That's for babies.'

'A horse race, then,' said Marcel, as he recalled his morning's work.

Fergus eyed him cautiously, but there was no doubt he was interested now. 'A steeplechase, you mean, like the way cavalrymen race?'

Marcel wasn't sure what a steeplechase was, but if it meant he didn't get beaten up … 'Yes, all right. When Old Belch comes back we can ask him if he'll lend us two horses.'

'I'm not waiting for *that*,' Fergus announced impatiently. 'If we're going to have a steeplechase, then let's have it now.'

CHAPTER 4

The Race

FERGUS AND HIS LITTLE band of followers hurried off towards the stables. Marcel found he had his own troop close on his heels. 'We're coming with you,' said Dominic, keeping up as best he could.

'Maybe you two should race as well,' said Marcel. 'To tell you the truth, I don't know if I've ever ridden before.'

They stopped in their tracks, staring at him dumbfounded. 'Well, you're about to find out, then,' Hugh commented drily.

They dragged open the heavy door of the stables and crammed inside. Fergus headed the march past the stalls. 'I'll take this one,' he said almost instantly.

Marcel was not surprised when he led out the splendid chestnut stallion and began to strap a saddle onto its back.

Then it was Marcel's turn. Forget the lame horse and the dispirited one, he thought, and no plough horse was going to win him this race. That left only the dappled mare.

At least she looks up to a race, he thought, as he took her outside to where Hugh and Dominic waited with the saddle. Fergus was standing ready beside his chestnut mount, but each time Marcel and his friends tried to heave the saddle onto *their* horse's back she shimmied sideways.

Marcel wondered whether she'd respond to her new name.

'Stand still, Gadfly!'

The mare flared her nostrils and threw her head about wildly as though she were thinking of escape.

'Hurry up, or I'll start without you,' Fergus threatened.

Marcel left the saddle to his companions and turned to confront him. 'We haven't decided on the course yet.' He looked around the grounds of the orphanage, planning a route in his mind. 'What about twice round the inside of the orphanage walls?' he proposed.

'No, that's not a real race,' said Fergus. 'We'll go through the orchard first, then follow the stone wall around past the blackberries and the oak trees, but once we reach the gate it's out onto the road and across the bridge into Fallside. See the steeple of the church?' he said, pointing in case Marcel was left in any doubt. 'That will make it a real steeplechase,' he joked.

'Into the village!' cried Marcel. He turned and found his own alarm mirrored in the faces of his friends.

'Marcel, you can't ride into Fallside!' Hugh reminded him in a whisper.

Marcel ignored him, just as he was trying to ignore his memories of yesterday and that fearful roar from the tower. 'We can't let Fergus get the better of us,' he declared, clamping his teeth together. He hoped this made him look determined, because inside he was quivering like a leaf in a gusty breeze.

Fergus saw their indecision and seized his chance. 'I'm not waiting any longer. The race has started.'

'No!' Marcel shouted angrily, but Fergus had already spurred his horse away from the stable and all he could do was stand and watch as it galloped towards the orchard. How would he ever beat Fergus now? They still hadn't managed to get a saddle onto Gadfly.

'It's all right,' he cooed, hoping to calm the restless mare. He tried to stroke that proud nose but she pulled her head away and shot him an exasperated glare, as though she were growing impatient with the boys' ineptitude. 'You know this is a race, don't you,' he said to her, 'but until we can get this saddle on your back, we can't go anywhere.'

The mare rolled her eyes again and walked a few anxious paces in the direction of the orchard. Was it his imagination, or was she looking for Fergus to see how much ground they would have to make up? 'Hugh, Dominic. Help me up.'

'You can't ride her bareback! It'll be hard enough with a saddle!'

He ignored them, and this time Gadfly seemed ready to oblige. After a little heaving and grunting, he was on her back, but before he had a chance to catch his breath she lurched into a gallop. He held on to her matted mane as if he were clutching at life itself. If he fell, it would be the end of him.

They charged towards the orchard, scattering aside the ducks and geese near the pond, then followed the chestnut stallion's path between the wall and the blackberry canes, until they were climbing a gentle slope. Marcel began to get the hang of things, working into the rhythm of Gadfly's movement instead of against it. Exhilaration replaced fear and he told himself, I can do this! Maybe I *have* ridden a horse before.

Was that Fergus in the distance, approaching the gate? Certainly they were closer, much closer than when they had first set out after him. They passed the two cows, who looked up, startled, from their grazing.

'Come on!' he shouted to his mount. 'We can win this yet.'

A stand of oaks swallowed them up but Gadfly showed no signs of slowing down, not even for these thickly growing trees. Unfortunately, the same couldn't be said for her rider. He had grown more confident now, and sitting up to look for Fergus, he didn't see the low branch reaching out through the shadows until it swept him from the horse's back.

Marcel found himself on his bottom amid a cloud of dust and despair. He heard hooves trotting towards him and wondered if Fergus had come back to gloat, but when he looked up he saw Gadfly glaring down at him in disgust.

That look alone spurred him to his feet. This was a race, he reminded himself, and if he didn't win ... He couldn't bear to think of Fergus holding sway over the rest of them. He scrambled once more onto that twitching, restless back and the horse did the rest, charging off again as she had from the start.

They galloped across the grass in front of the house until the stone wall loomed ahead once more. He expected her to turn and follow the wall to the gate — but not Gadfly. There was no time for Marcel to think. The horse simply launched herself into the air, clearing the stones easily, then crashed back to earth, front legs first. Marcel was catapulted high onto her neck, but she simply flexed the muscles of her shoulders and threw him back into place.

Up ahead, Fergus was crossing the stone bridge that led into Fallside. By the time they reached it, he had galloped to the church and begun his return, the thunder of hooves drawing people out of their houses and several men from the tavern, one still holding his pint of ale.

'You'll never catch me, Marcel!' Fergus cried, passing Gadfly as he galloped back to the bridge.

Marcel. The name tumbled free, the name no one was meant to hear. Just once he called it, but Marcel dared not imagine the consequences. For now, he just raced, his mind locked onto the same goal as Fergus: to be first through Mrs Timmins' gate.

Brave Gadfly kept up her punishing pace, but was there enough of the race left to catch Fergus? They thundered on, the villagers standing wide-eyed, some throwing themselves off the road to get out of the way. Marcel caught sight of Albert and Old Belch, but they barely had time for an angry shout. Beneath the steeple, he finally turned Gadfly for home, although by then Fergus had already crossed the bridge with only the length of the road to the finish line.

Suddenly Gadfly changed course, galloping wildly between the houses until she sighted the open fields. Then she set off directly towards the side gate, where Hugh and Dominic and the rest of the boys had gathered to judge the winner.

'The stream!' Marcel cried, as though Gadfly could understand him. 'You'll never get across the stream!'

She ignored him, charging on towards the finish line, the stretch of swiftly flowing water in view now. It was ten metres across, at least, with high banks on both sides. More worrying still, much more worrying, was the waterfall itself, only another hundred paces away. If Marcel found himself in that water, he would surely be swept over the falls before he could reach the safety of the bank.

He gripped Gadfly's mane harder than ever and pushed his chest down onto her neck. Here was the stream, only two strides ahead. If he'd had any energy left he would have screamed. Gadfly took one last stride to gather herself then leaped into the air, sailing upwards like a bird, her legs stretched out beneath her, that dappled brown and white and black body tracing a magnificent arc against the sky. As the stunned children watched from the distant gate, she crashed onto the steep bank on the other side, the hooves of her front legs biting into the grass of its rim. With a mighty grunt, she hauled her hind legs up and onto level ground and raced on towards the finish line.

Fergus was still closer to the gate than they were, but with every stride the gap narrowed. It was impossible to guess the winner now. The last few strides would settle it.

Then, with both riders only a pace or two from the gate, the race was suddenly over. Gadfly was the bravest of horses, but even she baulked at the sight that confronted them. She slammed her front legs into the dirt and sent Marcel hurtling forward, his arms locked around her neck until he fell painfully to the ground.

He sat up quickly as icy terror gripped his heart. A fearsome beast was circling him, a snarling, spitting creature with claws like knives. It had all the stealth and pose of a cat — yet what cat was ever this size? Its head loomed high above Marcel's. Its body was covered in glistening black fur and its cruel mouth was drawn back to reveal a row of savage teeth. A leather thong was laced around its neck, and dangling from it was a pouch large enough to hold a dozen gold coins. Could there be any doubt? This was the beast he had heard in the tower.

The world had gone silent except for the growls of this beast. All other things around Marcel had become invisible. He wondered whether his heart was still beating.

Fergus too had been thrown from his chestnut stallion, which bolted, whinnying loudly, back towards Fallside. He rose to his feet unsteadily, but when he saw the beast he froze in fear.

'Termagant, bring them both inside the gate,' cried a deep voice nearby, laced with fury.

The beast stopped its circling and came towards Marcel, who was still lying prone on the ground. A gasp of horror rose up from the boys huddled together beside the gate. One or two screamed.

But before the beast closed in, a desperate wail broke the silence. 'No, Lord Alwyn! You mustn't hurt him!'

It was Mrs Timmins. She had rushed from the house when she heard the sounds of the beast, followed by the girls, who had all been working indoors. She reached the gate and kept coming until she stood bravely above Marcel, shielding him from the beast with her stout body.

'Stand aside, Mrs Timmins. I told this boy to stay inside your boundaries. Instead, he rides a wild horse through the streets of Fallside.

'You disobeyed me,' Lord Alwyn said to Marcel, his voice low and threatening. 'You showed yourself in the village. Worse still, your name was shouted out for all to hear.'

'But, Lord Alwyn,' Mrs Timmins interrupted, 'the people of Fallside are simple folk —'

'Enough!' he cried fiercely. Turning back to the boys, his eyes blazed, and he focused on one of the pair in particular. 'I blame you, Marcel. Didn't I warn you to stay inside these walls? You can't imagine the misery this day could bring upon you, and many others as well.'

'Don't hurt him!' came an anguished cry, though which of the little girls had dared speak no one could tell.

The wizard ignored this pleading. He considered the boy before him, his face darkening. To Marcel, it seemed that not just the old man's face but the whole world grew blacker. This is his magic working on me, he decided, and braced himself for what was to come.

But his concentration was quickly shattered by Fergus's voice. 'What's happening?' he asked, looking around him in alarm. 'Everything's getting darker.'

Sure enough, it was not just Lord Alwyn who had fallen into shadow. All around them, the ground, the house, the orchard beyond it, everything was becoming dimmer and harder to see.

Now even Lord Alwyn was looking around him for the cause, and moments later they all saw it: a black curtain sweeping quickly over the forest, blocking out the day's bright sunshine. Night had never come like this, marked by a black line across the sky — and it was not even midday.

'What is it?' Fergus cried, but his voice was quickly lost amid the screeching that rained down from that writhing black canopy.

Then Marcel knew. 'Bats!' he exclaimed. 'Thousands, millions of them!' Already the leaders of this mighty horde had reached the village. Any minute now, it would break over the rim of the great cliff and sweep down into the valley below.

But Marcel's attention was torn away from this sight by words, the old wizard's words, though none he could understand. He turned to find Lord Alwyn with his arms outstretched, calling up to the blackening heavens above them. As he chanted his strange verses and swept his arms across the sky with as much grace as his ageing limbs would allow, that great, raucous cloud stopped its progress. More words, more waving of those thin arms, and the tide gradually began to turn back.

It took many minutes, but at last the darkness was repelled and the bats returned to wherever they had come from. Most of them, at least. Some came to earth instead, landing on the stone wall and on the roof of the house, a few hanging upside down from the eaves as though they had come especially to watch Marcel face his punishment.

'What happened?' cried Mrs Timmins in terror. 'Your Lordship, all those bats! Where did they come from? Why would they suddenly appear like that? And so many! They almost hid the sun.'

The sorcerer didn't answer her. He seemed deeply troubled by what had happened. 'It should not be,' he muttered, but slowly he forced himself out of his daze. His wrinkled brows weighed heavily over his weary eyes as he turned them on Marcel.

This made the boy more terrified than ever. He would gladly ride Gadfly over that treacherous stream a dozen times rather than stand here, waiting for Lord Alwyn to unleash his magic upon him.

Suddenly the sorcerer stretched out a hand, not to call down punishment on Marcel but to steady himself. If Mrs Timmins hadn't rushed to his side and taken hold of his arm, he might have fallen to the ground. When he recovered, he threw her hand off petulantly, but it was clear now that the effort of turning back the strange cloud of bats had drained him.

He motioned feebly to Marcel, summoning what little strength he had left. 'You disobeyed me,' he said gravely, his voice quavering. 'If you cannot do as I command, I shall need other measures. Come here, take this.'

Marcel held out his left hand and found a gold ring lying in the centre of his palm.

'Put it on your finger,' Lord Alwyn commanded faintly.

He slipped it loosely onto the smallest finger of his right hand.

'Since you refuse to do as I say, that ring will *remind* you. If you dare cross these walls again, Termagant will come after you, to fetch back that ring and you with it.'

A shudder ran through Marcel's body at these words. He felt the ring, cold and unfamiliar against his skin. His thumb worried at it, trying to push it free, but though it turned easily around his finger, somehow he couldn't get it past the knuckle.

'Try all you like,' said the wizard. 'It will not come off.'

'Never? Not even with your magic?'

Lord Alwyn smiled contemptuously. 'Oh, yes, there is a way.' He looked at the mud-splattered mare, still panting from her desperate gallop. 'I see you dare to ride wild horses, and no doubt these children here think you a brave young man. The true test is whether you find the courage to remove that ring.'

The wizard gazed at Marcel searchingly until it made him uncomfortable. He pulled at the ring openly now, but Lord Alwyn seemed unconcerned. He turned away and spoke harshly to Fergus. 'Don't think I have forgotten your part in this escapade. You would do well to heed Mrs Timmins and become the kind of boy a farmer would gladly take into his home.' Then he addressed Mrs Timmins. 'Send them both to bed hungry.'

Turning back to Marcel, he lowered his voice. 'You have escaped unpunished this time, but disobey me again and Termagant will bring you to me ... in her jaws.'

With that, he turned and made for the house, his faltering steps among the loose stones an odd contrast to his ominous words. In a few quick bounds, the beast he called Termagant was at his heels. The orphans watched as he disappeared around the end of the house, and only then did anyone move or dare to say a word.

EVEN AS LORD ALWYN *delivered his dire warning, it was too late. The name had been heard. In Fallside, when the drinkers returned to their tankards of ale, the landlord soon noticed that one had been abandoned half-full. Where was the traveller who had paid for it? No one had seen him since they had all rushed outside to watch those mischievous orphans race by on horseback.*

And they wouldn't see him again, for at that moment he was already urging his horse along the forest road. By nightfall he would be travelling across the plains below, and in the morning he would gallop on to the capital. He knew a man there who would pay a hefty price in gold to find a brown-haired boy named Marcel.

CHAPTER 5

The Book of Lies

ARCEL'S BODY SHIVERED, HALF with exhaustion and half with fear. Beside him, Mrs Timmins looked ready to faint. 'That beast would frighten the bravest knight. I don't like having it live above us,' she declared, turning to the boy. 'But listen to me, Marcel. Do as Lord Alwyn says. Stay within these walls and you'll be safe. If you leave ...' She hesitated, shocked by what she was about to say. 'If you leave, you may well be killed.'

'Yes, by Lord Alwyn,' he snapped, suddenly infuriated. 'And you're helping him.'

'No!' she cried, hurt to the quick. 'He won't harm you, not while I draw breath.' Then she addressed both boys with all the sternness she could muster.

'The pair of you need a good lesson. Fergus — Albert and Old Belch will be back with a new load of firewood shortly, and when it's here you'll spend the rest of the day with an axe in your hands. As for you, Marcel, you can get onto your hands and knees in the vegetable garden, and there'd better not be a single weed in sight by nightfall. But first you, Fergus, can go and find that stallion, and Marcel, you can put this poor mare back in her stall. Just look at the state she's in!'

Marcel led Gadfly back to the stables where he rubbed down her flanks with a cloth to wipe off the sweat, as he somehow knew he should do. At first his hands trembled after his encounter with Lord Alwyn's beast, but there was something about Gadfly that helped him overcome his fear, and by the time he had finished grooming her his nerves had steadied. She had taken him so close to victory. He could still feel the wind in his face and the power of her galloping body beneath him. Even the mad leap across the stream, with their lives hanging in the balance, had become a triumph now that the real danger had passed. 'For a moment I thought you could fly,' he told her.

Even after the meal that evening the smaller children talked wide-eyed about the race. They gathered around the fireplace with the glow of the flames dancing on their cheeks.

'Marcel's horse flew like a bird,' said Watkin, describing the fantastic jump.

But it was little Dot who turned their attention to the most frightening part of the story. 'What about Lord Alwyn's beast? Did you hear its name? Termagant,' she whispered, sending a fearful shiver through all who were listening.

Marcel wasn't part of the excited circle, but he had crept close to catch a little of the fire's warmth. When he heard those awed whispers, his mouth went dry. He looked for Fergus, who had given him a wide berth since the race, and found him in a corner picking gingerly at his palms, which were blistered from woodchopping. Did those swaggering shoulders droop a little? Fergus was doing his best to hide it. Without realising, both boys stood up together, making everyone in the dining hall notice, when in fact each had hoped to slip away to bed unseen.

Marcel fell into bed drained and desperate for sleep. It wouldn't come at first. The race had been exhilarating and he was a victor of sorts, but in the things that mattered most he had fallen further behind. He fidgeted with the ring that Lord Alwyn had forced him to wear, a ring that tied him to the orphanage more powerfully than ever. When finally he drifted off, he slept fitfully, strange faces filling his dreams, though none showed themselves clearly. A voice began calling to him. 'Marcel! Marcel!' He tried to ignore it but the voice continued, whispering so closely it seemed to echo inside his ear.

Gradually he realised it wasn't a dream at all. He woke with a start to find a hand on his shoulder, and though he couldn't see anyone the voice was one he knew.

'Bea!'

'Shh,' she cautioned. She motioned to him to follow her.

He slipped out of bed, careful not to disturb Hugh beside him, and went with her into the passageway. He could only guess what time it was, but the house was dark and surely Albert and Mrs Timmins would be fast asleep. The two of them crept soundlessly along the corridor, but on the stairs Marcel lost his footing and slipped heavily onto the step below.

'Watch your feet!' Bea hissed.

'How can I, when it's pitch-black?' he protested, but he grasped the banister all the same. 'Where are we going?' he whispered.

'The kitchen,' Bea replied. They reached the bottom of the stairs and she pushed the kitchen door gently ajar. As soon as they entered, she lit the candle Mrs Timmins kept on the table and led him into the pantry, a snug little alcove separate from the room itself.

'What's going on?'

'I have something for you,' she told him at last.

'At this time of night!' He watched as she pushed aside some large earthenware jars. Even then he had to wait while she carefully drew back a folded tablecloth. But when finally he saw what lay revealed, he could barely breathe. 'The Book of Lies!'

He reached in and took it down from the shelf, carrying it carefully to the kitchen table, where he stroked the cracked and flaking red leather of its cover. 'What was it doing there, in the pantry?'

Bea sent him an exasperated glance. 'I hid it there,' she said, in a tone that hinted he should have guessed that much for himself.

Marcel didn't notice. He was still trying to grasp the fact that the Book was right here in front of him. 'But how did you get hold of it?'

'I took it from the tower, of course.'

'You can't have! The door is sealed by magic.'

'I told you, there's another way up there.'

Another way. What was she talking about? Then it came to him. 'The hidden tunnel! You mean you …'

'This morning, when you and Fergus were racing into the village, I sneaked away from my chores and saw Lord Alwyn watching you from the window.'

'You guessed he would send Termagant down through that passage to get me, didn't you?'

Bea was excited now. She could barely manage to keep her voice down. 'I hid myself near the bushes and saw where she came out. The opening, Marcel — I found it at last! Now I can go up there any time I like.'

Marcel stared at her. 'Any time you like! Are you mad?'

'No, it's all right. Tonight, I just had to wait until I heard that noise in the wall and then I knew Termagant had gone out hunting. It's so narrow; no wonder Termagant makes such a noise when she squeezes through it. And even in daylight it's impossible to see.'

'But what about Lord Alwyn? I suppose he said, "Hello, come on in, Bea. Let me hold the candle for you."'

Bea made a face. 'Even wizards sleep at night, you know — and besides, even if he had been awake, he wouldn't have seen *me*,' she said confidently. She folded her arms to show she was growing tired of his lack of faith in her.

Marcel made himself calm down. If he had sounded a little harsh, it was only because he was worried about her. Terrified, really. This was the second time she had taken a dreadful risk to help him. 'I'm sorry I questioned you,' he said softly, and to show it he touched her gently on the arm. 'You went up there just to get this book for me. I can't believe it. Bea, that's braver than anything I did today.'

Bea blushed brightly, not easy for a girl who usually faded into the shadows. 'Now we can work out whether your real life is written inside. Quickly, see what you can find,' she urged him. 'Termagant won't stay out all night, and I'll have to return it before she comes back.'

Marcel opened the cover and leaned forward, impatient to read the words inside. There were so many.

Every page was covered from top to bottom and edge to edge with a solemn, flowing black script. The pages were yellowed and furred at the corners, some torn a little in places. Marcel read the first page, but by the second his eyes were growing tired. He began skimming the text quickly, hoping to pick out his name. But even this took an age. Four, five, six pages. He couldn't take them in any faster. 'This is hopeless,' he moaned. 'It would take me a year to read every word in this book.'

He was hardly ready to give up, though. 'Old Belch told me how it works. A little bit, anyway,' he muttered. He had seen Lord Alwyn use it too, at their first meeting in this very room. Closing the Book again, he laid his hand on the rough texture of its cover and said, 'My name is Marcel.'

Nothing happened at first, and he wondered whether the Book would teach him anything at all, but then it began to glow a comforting golden-red. With his hand still in place, Marcel spoke again. 'I am an orphan.'

Instantly the glow ceased and his hand was flung aside. The Book unfurled its pages, fanning rapidly and fluttering the flame of the meagre candle until it reached the second-last page. Here, it wrote his words.

I am an orphan.

Marcel's smile almost split his face in two. 'See how it works?' he said excitedly. 'Truth and lies. I'm *not* an orphan. The Book knows it somehow, even though I don't.'

He didn't bother with his hand this time but simply leaned over the open pages. 'I want to know the true story of who I am.'

The Book closed without delay and sent out its golden glow. They watched expectantly but it did nothing more. Marcel's fingers worked unconsciously at the ring Lord Alwyn had forced him to wear, waiting for a further sign.

'What's wrong?' asked Bea after they had waited a full minute.

'Who am I?' Marcel asked stiffly, but this time the yellowish tinge ceased and the book simply lay there, making no response at all.

He thought back to what Old Belch had told him and slowly he began to understand. 'It can't tell me who I am. That's not what it's made to do. It might contain the most powerful magic in the world, but it can only do one thing: judge what is true and what is not.'

He discovered that he was right when the Book glowed in response.

'Why is it called the Book of Lies, then?'

'You've seen the way it works, Bea. Every word written in this book is untrue. No wonder they call it the Book of Lies! And look at it, almost full.'

Suddenly he realised what this meant, and his heart sank inside his chest. 'It's hopeless. This book doesn't have my life on its pages. It can't tell me who I am or where I come from. That would be the truth, and all of this is …' He flicked his hand disdainfully at the cover. 'You risked your life to get it for me, but it's nothing but lies.'

Bea had stopped listening, to stare intently at the doorway leading into the hall. Then she murmured, 'Someone's coming.'

'Hide the Book!' Marcel whispered urgently, passing it to her and shooing her into the pantry. The sound of slow footsteps grew louder. He expected to hear Albert or Mrs Timmins herself, but instead the silence was broken by a girl's voice. 'Who's there?' she called curtly.

'It's Marcel,' he replied.

The girl came closer until the candle's pale light caught her face. It was Nicola. 'What are you doing down here?' she asked suspiciously.

'I couldn't sleep,' he answered quickly, but to his horror he heard the pages of the Book of Lies flap and unfurl somewhere in the pantry behind him. Nicola had heard the sound too and glanced over his shoulder, looking for the cause.

He distracted her by asking, 'How did you know I was down here?'

'I was awake and I heard someone trip going down the stairs. I waited for a while but they never came back up. I'm surprised that strange old man in the tower hasn't come down to check as well. He's going to make sure you stay here, that's for sure,' she said, rather unkindly. 'Not like me,' she added with a bitter chuckle as she walked to the back door and looked out into the night. 'They can't wait to get rid of me. Already tried once.'

'I heard you were sent back.'

'Sent back!' she snapped indignantly. She spun round to face him again, making no effort to keep her voice down. 'I ran away. They treated me like a slave, those people. I had to do everything, cook and clean and wash all their filthy clothes. And the boys in the family! Stank like pigs, all three of them, and they wouldn't move out of the way unless I kicked them.'

Marcel didn't doubt that she had done just that. The candle threw light playfully onto her long hair, which she had loosened for sleep. It didn't look quite as brushed and perfect now. She looked better this way, he decided.

Nicola noticed him stare at her. 'Is it right what the other children are saying?' she asked, in a more sympathetic tone this time. 'Don't you have any memory at all, not even of your parents?'

'Yes. I mean, no. What I mean is, my life before I arrived here has gone from my head. Vanished.'

She thought about this for a moment, running her eye over Marcel as though inspecting him for the first time. 'That doesn't seem fair,' she said, with an unexpected hint of concern for his plight. 'At least I can remember my parents. Well, my father, anyway.'

Marcel was touched by the melancholy in her voice, and before he knew it he had whispered, 'Not your mother, though?'

Nicola sighed, and her shoulders sagged a little as she told him, 'She died when I was born, so I never knew her. I only have what others told me about her. I've even had to make up what she looked like. Long hair like mine, only the colour of straw and much more beautiful. I've always imagined her like that.'

She stopped suddenly. 'Did you hear something?'

'No, nothing,' said Marcel quickly, though he had indeed heard a sound, not the rustling of pages this time but a muffled voice. It had come from the pantry where the Book was. 'Go on, Nicola. You were talking about your mother,' he urged, hoping that if she kept speaking she wouldn't take any notice.

Nicola seemed eager to tell her story, so she ignored the noise. As she started up again Marcel was surprised at how much her face changed. Her pretty features softened in the candlelight and her voice swapped its sharp-edged hostility for a gentleness that matched her memories. 'My father talked about her all the time. He called her his angel and then he'd say that I reminded him of her. He wanted me to marry a rich landowner when I grew up. He didn't expect me to help around the house, of course. That was for servant girls, he said. He made sure I had everything I wanted.'

'... everything I wanted,' said a voice.

'What was that?' she asked, more certain this time. 'You spoke. You copied what I just said.'

'No, I ...' Marcel didn't know what to say, but he had to keep Nicola from discovering Bea and the Book of Lies.

If Nicola's memories of her parents had opened a door to a different girl, now that door was slammed shut by a new anger. 'You're making fun of me, aren't you, just because I've told you something about myself. Well, if you're going to be like that ...'

Before she could unleash her fury, Bea's little figure emerged from the darkness. She held the Book open in her arms.

'Bea, no!' Marcel whispered.

'It's all right, Marcel,' she said calmly. 'Nicola should see this and so should you.'

'What's *she* doing hiding in the pantry?' Nicola demanded hotly. She would wake the whole house soon, if they weren't careful. 'Don't tell me you couldn't sleep either, Bea. What's going on here, and what's so special about that book?'

Bea did her best to ignore Nicola. With her eyes glued to Marcel's, she said, 'I think we have found a way to use the Book after all.'

'Show me,' he urged her.

As she laid the Book on the kitchen table again, she turned to Nicola. 'Keep talking. Tell us about your father.'

Nicola stared at the Book suspiciously. 'Is this some sort of trick? You haven't got the rest of the orphanage in the pantry laughing at me, have you?'

When neither Marcel nor Bea would respond to her goading, she didn't know quite what to do: stomp away to bed or stay and see what this creeping around was all about. 'All right,' she said finally, and after taking a breath she started up again. 'We had a large house. My father did well, selling fine cloth to rich ladies.'

The Book began to speak in unison with her, matching every word as she uttered it, but they waved her on, and despite a sceptical glare she kept speaking. 'But gradually, the rich women stopped coming to his store. They didn't like the colours and complained about his prices. Father himself became ill, and when he died there was nothing left, no money to support me, no one to care for me.'

The Book of Lies hadn't missed a word. What was more, Marcel and Bea recognised the voice itself. 'It's Lord Alwyn. This was what happened on the night you arrived,' said Bea excitedly.

'What's going on?' Nicola came closer, leaning over the Book, reaching down with one wary hand but pulling it away at the last moment. 'What sort of book is it?'

'It's the Book of Lies,' Marcel told her.

'I don't understand. It said what I said, at the very moment I said it. How could it do that? There's magic here, isn't there? What does it mean?'

Marcel could barely believe it, but he had an answer for her. 'It means this book has your life written in it, or at least what you think is your life. It's all lies, you see. Not your real life at all. Your name probably isn't even Nicola.'

'You're mad, both of you,' but as she spoke she looked directly at Marcel. He had been named Robert, for a few hours at least. Then he had become Marcel, and suddenly that wizard and his beast in the tower had come out of hiding. It was enough to make her ask again, 'What does it mean?'

'It means you're like me. Your real life was wiped from your mind, just like mine was, except that Lord Alwyn gave you a new one in its place.'

'I don't believe it,' said Nicola defiantly. 'My mother. She was beautiful ...'

'Your real mother might still be alive,' said Marcel.

At this, the Book of Lies started to flip and fan its pages, but Marcel wouldn't be distracted. 'Don't you see, Nicola? You're not an orphan after all. You don't have to go to another family, like that one down in Fallside. You have your own family.'

'I don't know what to believe,' said Nicola, putting her hands to her forehead. 'The memory of my parents is all I have now that I'm stuck here, alone, with no one to love me.'

'But don't you understand what I just told you?' Marcel urged in frustration. 'Instead of dead parents you can only dream about, you might have a mother and a father alive somewhere, desperately looking for you.'

It was all too much for Nicola. She turned away abruptly and ran to the darkness of the staircase.

'This book is the key to everything' said Marcel when she was gone.

'Maybe it is, but I have to take it back to the tower tonight,' Bea insisted. 'If I don't, Lord Alwyn will know it's gone and he'll send Termagant to find it.'

Marcel tried to imagine Bea crawling back through that pitch-black tunnel alone. 'I'll come with you, then,' he told her, swallowing a hard lump in his throat.

'You can't.'

'But Termagant …'

'You can't come with me because you smell,' she told him bluntly.

'What do you mean I smell?'

'You'll leave a scent and Termagant will pick it up.'

'What about you, then?'

She thrust her arm under his nose. 'I have no scent.'

Marcel pulled his head back awkwardly. No scent! There were so many strange things about this little girl. 'Bea,' he whispered uncertainly, 'why is it, well … sometimes I can see you plain as day and other times it's as if you're invisible. Is it magic, like Lord Alwyn's?'

She shook her head. 'No, not magic. I've always been like this. I don't know why.'

The hint of pain in her voice told him it was a touchy subject. But it had been a night of strange discoveries, and now Marcel's mind was working fast. Didn't Bea seem special, like Nicola and he did? What if Lord Alwyn had stolen away *her* life too?

'Where are you from?' he asked her. 'How did you come to live here with Mrs Timmins?'

'I don't know where I come from.'

'You mean you're like me? Did you come here in the middle of the night as well?' he pressed hopefully.

'You think my life is hidden in the Book too,' Bea guessed.

'If you are, then we can soon prove it.' Marcel was excited now.

'No,' she said sharply. 'I don't want the Book to hear my story.'

Marcel couldn't work out her reluctance. Why wouldn't she want to know the truth, just as he did? 'Are you afraid of something?'

She nodded miserably, and suddenly he understood. 'You're not afraid that it will find you *are* like me and Nicola, you're afraid that it *won't*.'

Bea looked up, her eyes glistening in the candlelight and clearer than ever before. 'If I'm not like you, then I'm truly a foundling after all.'

Marcel slipped her hand into his. 'There's only one way to know for sure, isn't there? You have to tell your story.'

She shifted herself closer to the Book, and with a last glance at Marcel, she began.

'A baby girl …' Her mouth had become dry and her throat suddenly hoarse. 'Abandoned,' she tried to say, but she needed a moment to calm herself.

'As a baby girl I was abandoned on the steps of a church. The priest found me there in the morning, blue with the cold and almost starved.'

The pages hadn't moved, but she wouldn't give up now. 'He took me to a convent where the nuns fed me and kept me warm. They named me Beatrice after their patron saint. I could grow up and become one of them, they said, and they took good care of me. I liked it there.'

Still no response from the Book. Bea closed her eyes and Marcel guessed her story was about to change. 'But after a year or two, when I could walk and talk, the nuns became afraid of me. If I stood perfectly still in the shade of a tree, it was like I'd vanished into thin air. They thought I was bewitched and complained to the priest about the child he had brought them. The priest had no answer for their questions, but it was clear the nuns didn't want me among them, so he brought me to Mrs Timmins.'

Now that she was finished, she dared to open her eyes and look at the Book. It cast a golden glow into the kitchen's dim light. Her story was not in Lord Alwyn's Book of Lies. It hadn't given her this life to replace her own. What she had just spoken aloud was the truth.

Bea sat before the silent, unmoving Book and the hope seemed slowly to leave her body. 'I'm not like you,' she sighed.

They could not delay any longer. It would soon be light, and they had to return the Book. Bea shook herself free of her sadness and ventured out into the damp night air, making her way to the far side of the house. Marcel followed Bea as best he could, using his ears more than his eyes. Then she disappeared altogether into the overgrown shrubs beside the house.

He waited anxiously, scouring the darkness, expecting to see Termagant at any moment, until suddenly Bea was back beside him and he could breathe again. Then they crept noiselessly into the house once more, up the stairs and into their beds.

CHAPTER 6

Whispers in the Orchard

AS EACH DAY PASSED quickly on to the next, Marcel soon found he had been with Mrs Timmins for a week and the routine of life in the orphanage had begun to settle around him. That was the strange thing about routines. After seven, or was it eight days — he wasn't sure — he felt as though he had been there for a year.

Nicola wouldn't speak to him the morning after they had huddled together over the Book of Lies, and she seemed even more wary of Bea. Marcel could hardly blame her, and in fact he was quietly pleased. It seemed to have brought her down a peg or two. She might have gone back to her haughty ways, but he detected an uncertainty behind her sullen glares.

'She's confused,' he whispered to Bea. 'I'll bet she doesn't know what to think.'

He felt sorry for her too, because he knew what misery she was going through better than anyone. 'It's even harder for her than it is for me. I've got nothing to remember, but the life Lord Alwyn put into her head must seem pretty real to her.'

'Yes, you're right. If she's going to believe us, then she has to forget the life of the pampered girl that she remembers. That must be a hard thing to do,' said Bea.

Marcel noticed the sympathy in her eyes. It was when her face warmed like this that she was easiest to see.

But if Nicola was avoiding *him*, Marcel couldn't seem to avoid Fergus, no matter how much he wanted to. Mrs Timmins threw them together at every opportunity, whether it was chopping wood or hauling water from the well. Perhaps she thought they might come to like each other.

When she sent the older boys into the orchard with Albert to collect apples one day, Marcel and Fergus competed to see who could retrieve the highest fruit. But apple trees aren't much good for climbing. It was clear that one of the pair would come crashing to earth sooner or later. The younger children gathered to see who it would be.

Marcel felt a branch straining under him. He didn't know whether he had been afraid of heights in

89

his earlier life, but as he swayed precariously in the apple tree, he certainly knew he was now.

He was saved when Albert came looking to see where all his workers had gone. 'Get down from there, you fools!' he bellowed angrily. 'I don't know what it is about you two. First you ride wild horses like a pair of madmen and now you're determined to break every bone in your bodies. Seems I'll have to keep you apart until you learn some sense.'

He ordered Fergus off to the woodpile. 'As for you, Marcel, there are plenty of apples down the end of this row.' He tossed two empty sacks at his face and waved him away, calling to the rest of the boys to follow him back towards the house.

Marcel wandered miserably towards the stone fence. It was the limit of his world and a reminder of what Lord Alwyn's powerful magic had done to him. On the far side of the wall lay a stretch of tall grass and blackberry bushes that separated the orphanage from the dense green and black of the forest. Even the colours recalled the wizard and his robe, and as Marcel stood staring into the trees, fighting a deep despair, once more he turned the golden ring on his little finger with the tip of his thumb.

He sighed and began to pick apples. He soon had one of the sacks bulging with the fruit he could reach from the ground, then, putting this aside, he climbed into one of the trees. He was still only a short distance from the ground when an odd whooshing noise caught his ear, not loud and lasting less than a second. It stopped suddenly when an arrow thudded into the ground only inches from the sack he had just filled with apples.

The shock made him lose his grip. He fell out of the tree, landing painfully on his bottom, which had only just lost the bruises after his fall from Gadfly. His first instinct was to lie still. His second was to flee. He was about to do the latter when he realised there was something wrapped around the shaft of the arrow. It looked like the page from a book, lashed tightly into place with coil after coil of black twine.

With a desperate lunge, he darted out into the open and snatched the arrow from the ground before retreating like a lizard to the meagre protection of the apple trees. There, he used his teeth to snap the twine, and instantly, the paper spiralled open in his hand. It wasn't a page from a book but a letter.

> *Marcel,*
> *Yes, I know that is your name and that you do not belong in this orphanage. I have horses waiting in the forest. Join me now. Tell no one and be sure you are not seen.*
> *From a friend of your father's.*

My father's! Marcel gasped. It was true, then. Everything he had discussed with Bea, everything he had guessed at and hoped for was real. He had a father and most likely a mother too, both living. He rushed to the boundary wall and readied himself to leap over.

Be sure you are not seen, the letter had warned. He turned back towards the house and to his relief found that none of the other children was in sight. But at the last moment, he caught a glimpse of the grey stones that formed the very top of the tower. Termagant. The enchanted ring. He fell back into the orchard, shoulders slouching helplessly as his eyes scoured the forest with a longing that almost burst his heart.

What could he do? How could he signal whomever had sent that message? All he could manage was to spread his hands wide in futility and wave the letter pathetically.

Minutes passed, and he was ready to turn away, aching with disappointment, when he saw a sudden movement. Someone dressed in black broke from behind a tree. Moments later a second figure emerged. They were in the open for only seconds before they disappeared again behind some sprawling blackberry canes.

'Marcel,' came the call soon afterwards. It was a furtive whisper, pitched to reach his ears and no further. 'Marcel, don't be afraid. Come with us into the forest.'

In the same carefully gauged whisper he replied, 'I can't. If I jump the wall, Lord Alwyn will know straightaway.'

'The great wizard!' came the deep voice again, clearly alarmed now. 'He is here …?'

With a glance over his shoulder, Marcel confirmed it. 'He lives in the tower above the house.'

This news brought silence, a silence so long that Marcel feared the men had backed away into the forest, leaving him to his fate.

'Please, tell me who I am!' he called, as loudly as he dared. 'If you are a friend of my father, then you can at least tell me who he is! Where is he, and where do I come from? Please tell me *something*!'

The men had not retreated — or at least one of them had not, for after a further pause that seemed to Marcel to stretch out for a lifetime, a tall figure all in black stepped out from his hiding place so that Marcel could see him. That is, he let his body be seen, neatly dressed in a stylish woollen cape and splendid leather boots that came almost to his knees. His face, however, was hidden beneath a fine wide-brimmed hat topped by a large and jaunty feather.

The man kept low, but even so, the dozen strides he took to reach the stone wall were measured and confident. A sword slapped against his thigh but the object that caught Marcel's eye was the dagger tucked into his belt, the rich red of rubies glinting on its handle. He halted and asked softly, 'Are you saying that you don't know who you are?'

'Only my name. Lord Alwyn worked his magic on me, on the night I arrived. I can't remember a thing from before then.'

'No memory,' the stranger repeated to himself. Still he hesitated, weighing this startling news in his own mind, as though it were a heavy stone he did not want to pick up. Slowly, he tilted his head back until the face, unseen until now, was finally revealed.

An attractive face it was too, with a handsome nose and chiselled cheeks diminished only by the first shadow of stubble on its pointed chin. Standing to his full height at last, he was taller than any man Marcel could remember seeing. And there was no mistaking the proud bearing. This was a man whose orders were obeyed.

His sharp blue eyes demanded Marcel's attention the very moment they fell on him. He seemed to be looking for something in Marcel's eyes too, and after a moment the boy guessed what it was. Recognition — yes, this man expected him to know who he was.

'Who ... who are you?' Marcel asked tentatively.

The question finally settled the man's doubts and he answered then without hesitation. 'My name is Sir Thomas Starkey, but it was a true queen who knighted me, Madeleine herself. Now that a usurper sits on her throne I refuse to use the title she gave me. People call me Starkey, and nothing more. I prefer it that way, until the false king is overthrown. I have dedicated my life to that end.'

His compelling eyes bored into Marcel as he paused. 'Are you sure you haven't heard of this king? His name is ...' Again he halted, watching Marcel's face while he pronounced the word. 'His name is Pelham.'

'No, I have never heard the name before,' Marcel assured him immediately.

'What of Princess Eleanor, then? Does that name mean nothing to you? Or Prince Damon?'

He was supposed to know them, or why else would the man ask? Marcel's misery narrowed his throat, so that he could answer only with a shake of his head.

'This is an amazing thing,' said Starkey, stroking his chin.

A movement behind Marcel made him spin around, afraid that one of the orphans had strayed into the orchard after all.

'Hector,' Starkey whispered urgently, 'join me here and don't say a word.'

To Marcel's surprise, a man appeared from among the apple trees behind him. This was the second dark figure he had seen scamper from the forest, a much shorter man but strongly built like a fighting dog and, it must be said, with a face to match. Heavy brows hooded his eyes, which were little more than slits, and half of his left ear was missing. A longbow protruded from behind his shoulder, and hanging from his waistband, beside his sword, was a quiver full of arrows, each fletched in the same colours as the one that had so nearly pierced the sack of apples. The man lingered and Marcel heard him take a sharp breath, as though he intended to speak in defiance of his master. But he changed his mind and climbed silently over the wall to stand behind Starkey, scanning all directions at once.

Starkey's hand continued to work at his stubbled chin.

'This is a terrible crime Lord Alwyn has committed against you. I can barely believe it, even of him. Such an evil spell could only have been ordered by Pelham himself, I'm sure of it.'

'But why has he done this to me — and how did you know where to find me?' Marcel pleaded.

'The second part is easy to explain. Rumours of missing children have been whispered for weeks now. Then a traveller sympathetic to my cause heard your name, here in the nearby village. He spoke of a wild horse race, though I hardly listened once he had described you. But enough of this. I will tell you the rest once we are on the road.'

'But I've told you, I can't leave. If I try, Lord Alwyn will track me down.'

'We have horses. With a good start, we can outrun Alwyn's magic.'

'Can you outrun a huge cat, black as coal and more dangerous than a lion?' Marcel demanded.

Starkey's eyes widened in alarm. The bowman, Hector, had listened to the rest stony-faced, as though the wrath of God himself would not frighten him, yet now even his rugged features creased uncomfortably.

'Lord Alwyn calls her Termagant,' Marcel went on. 'See this ring?' he said, holding up his right hand. Once more he pushed and tugged at it with all his might. 'It won't come off, and if I cross this wall, Lord Alwyn will know and send Termagant after me. She would cut you two to ribbons before you could even draw your swords.'

'I don't like the sound of this, Starkey,' said Hector, speaking for the first time. His voice was a low rumble from deep inside his powerful chest.

Starkey seemed thwarted and went back to stroking his chin. 'I'll confess to you, boy, I'd hoped to steal you away from here without any bother. I need you if I am to right the great injustice that has been done. That's why I have come all this way.'

'But what can I do to help you? I don't even remember who I am,' Marcel reminded him.

'It's who you are that matters, not whether you remember it,' snapped Starkey. Suddenly, his eyes brightened and his confidence returned. 'In fact, it might be ...' he murmured to himself, trailing off. 'Yes,' he said, looking across the wall at Marcel. 'You can still play a role, a vital role indeed, and one that only you can perform. If I can just get you away from Lord Alwyn ...'

These words made Marcel's frustration unbearable. He wrenched uselessly at the ring around his finger and felt its curse like never before. What could he do that was so important? he wondered. Only he could do it, according to this man, even though Lord Alwyn had tried to erase all trace of his former ...

'Wait!' cried Marcel.

At this, the two men ducked quickly behind the wall. 'Quiet, boy! You'll have everyone in the place here beside you.'

'I'm sorry,' he went on, in a whisper now. 'There's a girl here, named Nicola.'

'What of her?' said Starkey in an offhand manner as he dared to stand up, though there was no doubting the interest he was already showing.

Marcel hurried to explain. 'Lord Alwyn did the same thing to her as he did to me. I'm sure of it. She doesn't know who she really is either.'

Starkey and Hector exchanged an astounded glance. In fact, Hector was about to put their surprise into words when Starkey held up his hand to stop him. 'This girl. Is she older than you?'

'I think so. Maybe a year older.'

His answer brought rising excitement. 'Describe her,' Starkey demanded quickly.

Marcel did so, and with each feature he named, her hair, the pale skin dotted with freckles, even her haughty demeanour, he saw Starkey's face brighten with glee.

'Yes, it must be her,' he declared at last.

'Can she help you too?' Marcel asked.

'Help us! Why, she can do everything that you were to do.' Then the light in his face died as quickly as it had come to life. 'Does she have a ring like yours?'

'No,' Marcel assured him.

'A stroke of luck at last. We can take her instead of you!'

Marcel's heart immediately sank into his shoes. In a matter of moments he had been cast aside like an unwanted puppy. It wasn't fair. It was *his* name that had brought them here. He was the one — with Bea's help, it was true — who had discovered Nicola's connection to the Book of Lies in the first place. They *had* to take him.

Then things became even worse.

'The third child,' Hector whispered to Starkey. 'Could he be here as well?'

Starkey turned eagerly to Marcel. 'Hector is right. *Three* children disappeared in all. Perhaps all three were sent here, to be watched over together by Alwyn himself.'

'Another girl?' asked Marcel.

'No, a strapping boy, your age but taller, and I daresay somewhat stronger. Thick brown hair, a wide round face — oh yes, and a short temper, by all accounts,' he added with a grin towards Hector.

Marcel was devastated. The description could not have been more accurate. Of all the children in the orphanage, in fact, of all the children there must be throughout the entire kingdom, why did the third child have to be *that* boy?

Could Marcel deny it? He was tempted. These men might never know he had lied. Yes, he was sorely tempted, but he made his head nod all the same, just once.

'He's here,' he said quietly. 'We call him Fergus.'

THE FIRST PERSON MARCEL came across after he had left the orchard was Bea. He felt terrible about deceiving her, but he had already decided to tell her nothing about Starkey.

What could he have told her? That two strangers had suddenly come for him, two men who frightened him as much as they gave him hope? Starkey, especially, was an odd collection of people all bound into one. Fierce determination shone in his eyes, stronger than sunlight through broken cloud. He had set himself a quest to bring down an evil king. Was there any more dangerous task, or any more important? Yet he had shown gentleness and sympathy when Marcel told of what had been done to him.

If only he could go with them!

He pushed such vain hopes aside and went to find Nicola. She was puzzled when he asked to speak to her alone, but she agreed to follow him into the little cave beneath the blackberry bushes. There, she listened, open-mouthed, to the amazing story he had to tell.

'Ever since I found you and Bea in the kitchen with that strange book I've been thinking. My memories seem real but somehow I can feel myself acting like I'm expected to, instead of the way I truly am.' She could barely sit still. 'And now this man Starkey comes along. It's almost too much to believe. He wants me to go with him, tonight?' Nicola asked breathlessly.

'Yes, after Termagant has come back from hunting.'

'How will he know when to come for me?'

'It's all been arranged. I will signal Starkey with a candle when we reach the orchard,' Marcel explained.

It had been his idea entirely. With Termagant loose for much of the night, Starkey and Hector would have been easily discovered. If she had found them lurking near the orchard ... he didn't even want to think about that. But with Marcel acting as a spy inside the house, listening near the girls' room for Termagant's return, they stood a good chance of escape.

'Are you coming too, Marcel?' Nicola asked.

He grimaced and held up his hand, allowing what little light there was in the tiny grotto to catch the gold of his ring. 'I can't leave the orphanage with this on my finger.'

'I'm sorry. I've seen how restless you are here,' she said, surprising him. Since when had Nicola bothered to do more than glare at him, and as for caring about how he felt ...

Fergus was even easier to convince, not because of what Marcel told him but because of what he didn't.

He would simply have assumed it was a trick if Marcel had tried to explain the whole story. Instead, he took Fergus aside and said, 'Some strangers have come to the orchard, a knight and a soldier. They want a brave boy to go with them and be part of some adventure they have planned. If they go to Mrs Timmins, she won't let you go, but you can escape with them tonight, if you dare.'

If he dared. That was Marcel's real trick, just the kind of challenge Fergus could not possibly turn down. 'Where do I meet them?' was his instant response.

Marcel had to smother a smile. Yet no smile could survive on his face for long that day. Nicola and Fergus were about to escape, while he would be left behind.

IN THE EARLY HOURS of the morning, Marcel lay awake listening for sounds of Termagant as she moved through the tunnel. He had heard her leave the house many hours before and now waited anxiously for her return. He fought sleep, raking his fingernails across his thighs to keep himself awake.

Then it came, the familiar sound. The beast had returned to her lair in the tower. It was time to fetch the others.

Nicola was already waiting for him outside the girls' room when he arrived with Fergus. Marcel carried the candle he had taken from the kitchen after dinner, and when they had safely left the house and reached the last apple tree before the boundary, he lit it.

Starkey and Hector joined them three minutes later.

'Yes, I recognise you both. You are the ones we have been looking for,' Starkey whispered exultantly into the darkness, killing Marcel's last hope that Fergus, at least, would not be invited to go with them.

The candlelight caught the fevered excitement in Starkey's face. 'All three of you. I could not have wished for such luck. What names do you two call yourselves?'

Nicola answered, then began to ask Starkey what her real name was, but he cut her off. 'We must get moving. For now, you should keep the names Lord Alwyn gave you. Quickly, climb across the wall.'

Marcel heard the urgency in Starkey's voice and realised they were about to slip away into the night without another word. 'Please,' he begged, 'you haven't really told me much at all. Why were the three of us brought here? Let me know that much, at least.'

'Haven't you guessed?' barked Starkey. 'To keep Pelham on the throne, that's why. He's a usurper, a false king who has stolen the crown from the rightful heirs.'

'The rightful heirs. Who are they?'

'I mentioned their names this afternoon. Damon and Eleanor. With these two to assist me, there is a chance, at least.' He moved to help Nicola clamber over the wall, not an easy task with the folds of her dress catching her knees and feet.

Fergus, however, had already jumped over it in a single bound. He had little idea of what they were talking about but the mention of a quest to bring down an unworthy king was enough.

'I'm coming with you,' he assured Starkey, and because he couldn't give up the chance to taunt his old enemy he turned to Marcel, adding cruelly, 'You stay here with the other little orphans. We'll come back for you when the job is done.'

Marcel felt his heart twist and writhe inside his chest. On any other occasion he might have whacked Fergus on the nose, whatever the consequences. But tonight was too important.

Even in the darkness Starkey could sense the dejection that had all but consumed poor Marcel. He reached across the wall and took him gently by the elbow, whispering, 'I wish I could take you as well, truly I do, but you know yourself what a risk that would be. I promise you, as soon as Pelham is dead, I will come back for you.'

'But it's still so dangerous. Tomorrow, when Lord Alwyn finds out these two are gone, he'll send Termagant along the road after you.'

'Don't fret. Thanks to your warning earlier I have decided not to use the roads, nor even the horses. I sold them in the village this afternoon in exchange for these supplies.' He nodded towards the pack Hector now carried on his back, with a bundle of blankets protruding from the top. 'I know of another way to get to where we are going.'

'And where is that?'

'Best you don't know.'

He was not to know anything much, it seemed, because Starkey turned quickly on his heel and led the other three figures off into the night.

Marcel watched them go, conscious as never before of the crushing emptiness inside him. He still knew nothing of who he was, or of the father Starkey had mentioned. All he had gained were three names: Damon, Eleanor and the man Starkey had sworn to overthrow, King Pelham.

CHAPTER 7

Pandemonium

OR WHAT REMAINED OF that long, long night, Marcel stayed awake listening for the sounds from inside the wall. If Termagant were on the move again, it would mean she knew of the escape and had set out after them.

No sounds came. His fevered mind churned with questions. Where were they going? What role were Nicola and Fergus to play, the vital part that had been his until Starkey learned of the ring and its curse? Damn this ring, he cursed for what seemed the hundredth time since sliding into bed.

Above him in the tower, Lord Alwyn doubtless lay sleeping, unaware of the daring escape. Somewhere in that forbidding room, a room Marcel was afraid even to picture in his mind, lay the Book of Lies. If he could get his hands on it again, he would have so many more questions for it now.

He wondered if it could answer the most important question of all — more important than any question about himself. Would Starkey succeed in forcing King Pelham from the throne, or would Nicola and Fergus die along with him in the attempt? Even if their fate was a heroic death, that fate was his too, by rights, and his soul ached to think it had been snatched away from him like this.

That sounded foolhardy, he realised, but he knew just as strongly that it was not false bravado. He wished the Book of Lies were before him now, because it would certainly glow brightly as he spoke into the darkness: 'I would rather die with them than live here for the rest of my life and never know who I am.'

DAWN FINALLY TOUCHED THE windowpanes and Albert came to rouse them for another day. 'Where's Fergus?' he asked, bemused. At the same time, Nicola's empty bed was the talk of the girls' room.

Mrs Timmins was unruffled at first. They would be in the kitchen, hoping for an early bite of breakfast, she guessed. But they were not in the kitchen, nor were they to be found in the orchard or the stables. The house was soon in uproar.

'Albert! Into the village with you and ask if they've been seen. And Belch,' she called, seeing the stable hand's anxious face appear at the kitchen door, 'search the forest roads, even the forest itself if you have to.'

Old Belch rode off on the chestnut stallion soon afterwards. 'Search the forest,' he repeated to himself grumpily. 'She might as well ask me to sift the entire ocean through my fingers.'

As for everyone else, they ran through the house, in and out of rooms that had been searched five times already, calling, 'Nicola, Fergus, where are you?' until Marcel was ready to scream.

He was the only one who knew that they would not be found, and aware of this, he checked under beds and behind doors harder than any of the others.

He couldn't hide his secret from Bea, though.

'I've been watching you. You aren't really looking for them at all. You know something, don't you?' she challenged him.

Marcel glanced around nervously, in case someone else had heard her accusation, but they were alone in the boys' room. 'Shh,' he said, putting a finger to his lips.

'Only if you tell me what's going on.'

What harm could it do? They were gone now, so he told her everything that had happened since the arrow landed in the orchard.

'Have you heard of this King Pelham?' he asked when he was finished.

'Mrs Timmins has mentioned his name. Or Albert,

maybe. He lives in a place called Elstenwyck, the capital.'

'Elstenwyck,' Marcel murmured, memorising the name. 'What about this Prince Damon and Princess Eleanor that Starkey spoke about?'

But this time, Bea shook her head.

'They're just names to me as well,' he confessed dejectedly. 'How can I be so important to them and to King Pelham? If only I'd been able to find out more from the Book of Lies.'

'I could steal it again, tonight maybe.'

'Don't be silly, Bea. It makes my skin crawl just thinking about how you did it last time. No, it's too much of a risk now that the others have escaped.'

They were disturbed by the sound of heavy footsteps on the stairs. Marcel poked his head cautiously through the doorway. What he saw made him swallow hard. It was Mrs Timmins, climbing one slow step at a time. She did not see him because her eyes were fixed on the mysterious oaken door.

With a face as pale as milk, she knocked three times. 'Your Lordship,' she called in a trembling voice. 'There is something I must tell you.'

A full minute passed before the door drew back to reveal Lord Alwyn in his dark robes. Marcel and Bea could see him clearly from where they stood. 'What is it, Mrs Timmins?' that weary voice sighed.

'T-two of the children are missing, Your Lordship,' she stammered.

'Not Marcel. I would know if he had disobeyed me again.'

'No, not Marcel. It's the other two, the girl and the boy you named Fergus. Please forgive me, Your Lordship. They seem to have disappeared in the night. I have Albert and Old Belch —'

'Quiet!' the old wizard shouted imperiously. 'Disappeared, you say? You're easily fooled, Mrs Timmins.' His anger was growing with every word; his face blazed a bright red, and he raised his arms as though he were determined to punish Mrs Timmins there and then. 'These children haven't disappeared, they can only have been stolen away from under our very ...'

But he never uttered the last word of this tirade. Instead the colour drained from his face as quickly as it had appeared. His arms dropped, one hand clutching at his forehead as the other groped blindly for the support of the doorpost. Moments later he collapsed, and if Mrs Timmins hadn't stepped forward to catch him he would have slumped onto the hard stone of the steps behind him.

Marcel and Bea saw it all. Mrs Timmins was a sturdy woman, but even she struggled with the gangling figure, now as limp and helpless as a rag doll in her arms.

Without a second thought, Marcel rushed to help her. She didn't stop to ask him where he had come from or how much he had heard. 'We must get him upstairs, into his bed,' she gasped.

'Into the tower, you mean?' Marcel was terrified. He knew only too well what lived there with the old wizard.

If Mrs Timmins heard the dread in his voice, she chose to ignore it. 'Take his legs,' she ordered, and slipping her own hands under Lord Alwyn's armpits, she began to back up the narrow staircase. It turned in a tight spiral. If Termagant was waiting for her master at the top, they would not see her until the last moment.

Every nerve in Marcel's body told him to drop the man's legs and scurry back to the safety of the passageway below. Only his respect for Mrs Timmins kept him at his task.

'Get away!' she yelled suddenly, kicking at something beneath her feet. Marcel's heart missed a beat, but it was no more than a half-grown kitten which scampered away with an offended meow. Moments later, they stepped out of the dark, winding stairwell and into the room Lord Alwyn had made his home.

Motes of dust drifted languidly in the musty air, visible only when they strayed into the morning light that streamed in through the twin windows. Eyes, Marcel had called them in his mind. He had never expected to see them from the other side.

But a chilling fear could never be far away now that he was inside the wizard's lair. Where was Termagant? What would she make of her master in their arms like this?

His eyes darted left and right. No sign of her. Was she hiding, waiting to spring out at them if she didn't like what she saw? There was a darkened recess in the corner to Marcel's right, and to his alarm he found they were moving steadily towards it.

'This is his bed,' Mrs Timmins said curtly when she read the terror in his face, and sure enough, once he was out of the two gleaming shafts of sunlight, his eyes let him see a narrow bed.

'Lift,' she ordered. 'Now down, gently.'

Lord Alwyn stirred, suddenly aware of his surroundings. 'What are *you* doing here?' he protested. But he was still too weak to stand, and despite his annoyance, he let them lay him on the bed.

Free of his burden, Marcel turned quickly and searched again for Termagant. On the far side of the chamber a low alcove was built into the wall. A rough metal grate closed it off from the rest of the room. Beyond that grate, bones lay scattered about the floor, animal bones gnawed to the marrow and cracked through in places by immensely powerful jaws. Termagant did not seem to be in residence, but this didn't stop Marcel's mouth from going dry in an instant.

The cat Mrs Timmins had brushed aside pressed itself playfully against his legs, as though it knew him. Hardly the beast he was looking for. His heart settled to a more regular beat now as he gazed round the rest of the room.

The tiny chamber was cluttered with a wizard's paraphernalia: earthenware jars, tiny boxes, some with their lids removed and giving off a strange mixture of scents, both pleasant and disgusting. More than anything, though, the room was stuffed to bursting with books. Row upon row crowded onto the shelves that lined one wall. Still more were piled in stacks on the floor. Where he could, Marcel read the fading words on their covers. Magic lore, enchantments, necromancy — *The Secrets of Thaumaturgy* was the title of one. Old, cracked along the spines, the pages frayed and perishing, they could only remind him of the book he had recently held in his own hands.

Where was it? Could he pick it out among the rest? It was much bigger than these, and its red cover would surely stand out ... But he did not need to search among the others. There, alone on a table by the windows, only a short distance away, lay the Book of Lies.

Mrs Timmins' ample body was bent down over Lord Alwyn, who still kept his eyes closed. Did he dare? What a question! His feet were already on the move.

'Marcel,' called Mrs Timmins.

He spun round in alarm. 'What ... what is it?' he asked, trembling.

'You did well, coming to help me with Lord Alwyn, but you have no place here. Quickly now, down the stairs, and if Albert has returned from the village, tell him what's happened.'

She had turned towards him as she spoke and she would stay watching him until he was gone. His brief opportunity had evaporated, he realised, though to be honest, part of him was relieved.

In three slow strides he was at the top of the narrow stairwell. He turned again for a final glimpse of this room he had feared so much, and he was already backing away onto the first step when he saw it, just the slightest movement. Termagant, he thought at first, but he quickly realised that it was not. He was meant to notice this. It was a sign just for him, a face removed from the shadows for the briefest instant then snatched away. It was Bea, already in place beneath the very table where the Book of Lies lay waiting. She must have crept in while their backs were turned.

Marcel hesitated. Should he stay to distract Mrs Timmins?

Bea herself answered this quandary. She risked another appearance, just her hand this time, but there was no doubt what it meant. She was waving him away, down the spiral staircase, where he would have to wait while she put her own peculiar magic to use.

That was how he hoped it would happen, but he was wrong. It wasn't Bea who came down the spiral staircase a few minutes later. It was Mrs Timmins.

She saw him lingering near the magical door at the bottom. 'Is Lord Alwyn still sleeping?' he asked hoarsely.

'He's stretched out on his bed, yes, but he's not asleep. That was quite a turn he took just now, but he's made a rapid recovery, by the look of things. I offered to bring him some medicines — my own kind of magic, I call it — but he sent me packing with his usual good manners,' she said in a wry tone, crossing the hallway to start down the staircase opposite.

As if the wizard's words needed confirming, the heavy door behind Mrs Timmins now groaned on its hinges, and without a human hand in sight, it slammed shut with a boom that could have woken the dead in their graves.

There was no way in, and just as certainly no way out. Bea was trapped!

Marcel didn't hesitate for a moment. Although he hadn't seen her, Termagant might still be up there. Perhaps she had been watching from the secret passage, and now that Mrs Timmins was gone, she would have come to her master's side. He rushed down the staircase, almost knocking Mrs Timmins over in his haste.

'Mind yourself, you silly boy!' she shouted after him, but by then he was through the kitchen, scattering Dot and Sarah aside in the courtyard like chickens. He sprinted faster than he had ever thought possible, round past the vegetable garden and the duck pond, until he was on the far side of the house.

Where was the entrance to the tunnel? It must be directly below the tower. He dived into the thick tangle of shrubs and, after groping desperately with his hands for some time, found the opening. No time to think of claws and vicious teeth. He scuttled along on hands and knees and bumped his head twice, the second time drawing blood, until he was climbing a rough set of stairs in pitch blackness. What he would do when he reached the tower room, he had no idea.

Then he stopped. It wasn't the narrowness of the tunnel nor the jagged, brittle edges of the bones that he crawled over. (He wouldn't let himself think about those.) He had been careful to remain as quiet as he could, and that was why he'd heard the sound up ahead in the tunnel, a scraping sound.

His muscles seemed frozen. Even if he could make himself flee, he couldn't turn round and he'd never back out of the tunnel in time.

The scraping sounds were nearer now, hurrying towards him. With only moments remaining, sound didn't matter any more. He waited for the touch.

Here it came. Every muscle was tensed, every pore in his skin gushing sweat, every corner of his mind alive to this final moment. Then impact! He was bowled over and lay in the tunnel waiting in terror for the first cruel slash of those claws. Two seconds, three. Why did the beast hesitate?

'Marcel? Is that you?'

Relief flowed through him, warmer than blood. It was Bea!

'Oh God, I thought you were Termagant!' he gasped.

'I didn't see her up there. It doesn't matter where she is, anyway. Marcel, I've got the Book!'

But it *did* matter where Termagant was at that moment. Suddenly, her name filled the tunnel. 'Termagant! Termagant, come here to me!' came the thunderous cry. It was Lord Alwyn's voice, bounding down the black and squalid tunnel, as frightening as the beast herself.

'He knows the Book is gone! Quickly, back up!' Bea urged.

Marcel had barely begun crawling when those fearsome scraping sounds echoed along the passage, louder and more violent this time. She was coming, the real Termagant! In case there was any doubt about her mission, Lord Alwyn bellowed after her. 'Find that little girl! She's the one who's taken the Book. Bring her to me!'

No one has ever crawled backwards faster than Marcel did that day. He emerged into the daylight, scratched and bleeding yet feeling none of his wounds. He dragged Bea to her feet before she was clear of the entry and hauled them both through the thickly matted shrubs.

'This way!' he yelled, pulling her towards the corner of the building.

They had rounded the back of the house and were in the courtyard now. They couldn't go back inside. Where, where could they hide? What shelter could they find with only seconds to search for it?

The first building that caught their eye was the stable. With Bea clutching the Book of Lies and Marcel clutching Bea, they raced across the cobblestones. Marcel wrenched open the stout door and shoved Bea ahead of him into the darkness.

Termagant had already appeared round the corner of the house. She came racing towards the stable, eating up the gap between them with prodigious bounds. Marcel had just enough time to slam the stable door shut before she cannoned into it, shaking the entire building with such force that he worried it would collapse around them.

Termagant would not be defeated by a door — not for long, anyway. She was already scratching and tearing at the planks. The wood began to splinter under the relentless force of her claws. If this wasn't enough to stop the hearts of the two fugitives, the terrible roars she emitted as she pounded and pummelled at the door certainly were.

'She'll rip us to pieces, you most of all!' Marcel shouted amid the din. Then, seeing the effect of his words on poor Bea, he wished he could take them back.

'What are we going to do, Marcel? She'll break her way in here any minute.'

The horses were already spooked by this ferocious onslaught on their sanctuary, and they stamped and whinnied inside their stalls. Even Gadfly tossed her head, her nostrils flaring, her eyes wide and questioning.

Suddenly Marcel had an idea. 'Come on!' he called desperately. 'Into Gadfly's stall!'

As soon as they were beside the horse, Marcel lifted Bea onto her back. 'I'll push the door open, as hard as I can. Termagant won't be expecting that. That will give you and Gadfly a few seconds' start.'

At that very moment, the stable was filled with the dreadful sound of two massive wooden planks splitting apart. Once Termagant had removed a third board in the same way she would be inside and their last hope would be gone.

'But Marcel, I've never been on a horse before!' Bea wailed. 'What do I hold on to? And how can I hold on to anything with this book in my hands?'

He looked around. A leather feedbag hung from a rusting nail high on the wall. With a jump, he managed to unhook it, and slipping the Book of Lies inside it he hung the bag around Gadfly's neck. The heavy book pulled it down until the leather slapped against her chest.

As soon as he did so Gadfly flung her head around violently, and when Marcel led her out of the stall she took command of her own destiny. Far from approaching the splintering door, as Marcel had planned, she backed away towards the opposite wall. With her hindquarters almost touching the warped and creaking boards, she threw her weight onto her front legs and kicked out with her back.

The walls were far more rickety than the stable's solid door, and one well-placed blow was all it took. Several wooden boards exploded free, leaving a gap just wide enough for Gadfly to squeeze herself through.

She turned, ready to burst out into the open, and Marcel placed his hand on her rump to slap her as hard as he could.

Bea saw his hand and grabbed hold tightly. 'No! I'll fall. Come with me, please!' She wouldn't let go. If Gadfly pulled away now, Bea would be tugged from her back.

The decision was made in an instant. He leaped up in front of Bea, contorting his body until he had a leg on either side. No sooner was he in place than Gadfly charged through the gap in the wall, forcing him to clutch her mane simply to stay on her back. At that same moment, Termagant slashed her way through what remained of the door and came after them. Another race on Gadfly's back had begun, this one far deadlier than the first.

'Head for the gate!' Marcel shouted, and before Termagant had taken more than three steps towards them, Gadfly turned on her hind legs, almost spilling her riders before the chase had begun. Moments later, they had galloped free of the orphanage grounds.

Marcel did his best to steer them towards the stream, where he hoped Gadfly would repeat her miraculous leap and leave Termagant to wade her way across. The delay would give them some chance, at least.

That was his vague plan, but Gadfly had other ideas. She veered away from the stream and began to follow along its bank, not towards Fallside but towards the waterfall. The bulky sack tugged and bounced around her neck, the hard corners of the book digging into her chest, distracting her. She threw her head angrily from side to side, but there was nothing she could do.

She galloped on, full tilt, with Termagant behind and drawing closer with every stride. How would they escape now? They were being driven into a wedge of ground where the stream met the frightening drop of the great cliff.

'Turn away!' Marcel shouted. 'The cliff! The cliff!'

Gadfly refused to slacken her stride. What was in her mind? Marcel had no reins to pull, no way to turn her or bring her to a halt. 'The cliff!' he shouted again desperately, but still she wouldn't yield.

Did she think she could leap across a valley a hundred miles wide? *Wild*, Old Belch had called her, but with the fearsome beast on her heels now and no chance of escape, had she gone *mad*?

The rhythm of her hooves faltered in readiness. Gadfly was gathering herself as though it were no more than a low stone wall ahead of her, and with the two riders still on her back, both shrieking now at what lay beneath them, she leaped from the cliff's edge.

Then they were falling, falling like stones among the glistening pearls of the waterfall. Death would be swift, but first they must endure the agony of the fall itself, painless to the body perhaps but torture for the mind.

All the terror Marcel had experienced in his short life at the orphanage — Termagant's snarls, the leap across the stream, the heart-stopping moment in the darkened tunnel — all of it seemed nothing now. This was sheer horror. This was the end.

The up-rushing air snatched away his scream before it could reach his ears. It flooded into his mouth and invaded his churning stomach. It tore at his clothes, which were already damp from the fine spray, and tried to dislodge him from Gadfly's back.

There was no reason to hang on, with death only seconds away, but still he clutched doggedly to the horse's mane. He felt Bea's arms just as tightly bound around his waist. They would die together.

As for the crazy horse herself, she showed no fear at all, but kept her legs outstretched as though she expected to land softly on the plain over a thousand feet below.

Then it began. The most amazing thing Marcel had ever seen. Beneath them, on Gadfly's flanks, lumps started to undulate beneath her skin. Within moments they had broken open like cocoons releasing their butterflies. Marcel's feet were pushed aside by strange legs that seemed to be growing from the horse's side.

But these weren't legs. They grew larger, until at last he could see what they were.

'Wings!' he cried into the merciless wind.

What miracles they were! They were stretched out now to their full size, magnificent in every detail. Marcel looked down, first on one side, then the other, to see feathers fluttering madly in the gale created by Gadfly's descent. But slowly, oh so slowly, their death-fall was changing into a graceful glide out and away from the column of white water, out into the clear air above the plains.

With a lurch of her shoulders Gadfly beat her wings powerfully, as an eagle does. Another beat took them forward and even up a little, until there was no doubt that Gadfly was soaring like a huge bird above the ground. They had fallen almost to the valley floor, the ground little more than fifty metres below them. But now, with every beat of those wings, they were climbing.

Marcel couldn't keep it in. Still bent forward over Gadfly's neck, he began to whoop with enormous cries of relief and exhilaration. 'Flying!' he yelled. 'We're flying like a bird!'

Gadfly calmly turned her head to inspect her wings, as though she found them not the least bit unusual. She flexed the muscles of her shoulders, settling the riders into a comfortable position and taking them higher with every beat. It had taken only seconds to fall, yet their return was oh so gradual. At last they broke over the lip of the great cliff, still climbing towards the sun. Gadfly's wings worked themselves into a slow and powerful rhythm that took the three of them higher still.

Without a word from her riders, the horse banked in a wide arc until they found themselves circling the house. What a strange way to see so many familiar sights: the well, the stable, the orchards, all contained within the stone walls that had once marked the boundary of Marcel's world.

But not any more. Termagant stood stranded at the cliff's edge, snarling vainly up at them as they swept overhead. For now, at least, she would be left harmlessly in their wake.

Gadfly turned again, towards Fallside and the forest beyond. Marcel twisted around for his final glimpse of Mrs Timmins' orphanage. Sunlight caught the eyes of the tower set above its roof. He had explored the wizard's room and looked out through those windows. They did not seem such a threat now.

As he watched, the sunlight faltered for a second and those eyes seemed to blink uncertainly, as though a spell had been broken. Then Marcel turned his own eyes forward as the last of the fields disappeared and a vast ocean of deepest green forest swept beneath them.

Part Two

CHAPTER 8

The Forest

HIGH ABOVE THE TREES, with the ground such a long way below, Marcel and Bea could do little more than hold tightly to the horse's back. Slowly, their fear began to subside, and though they were reluctant to look down, at least their powers of speech had returned.

'How can she fly like this?' Bea shouted against the roar of the wind.

'Who knows? I just hope the magic doesn't stop as suddenly as it started.'

For her part, Gadfly seemed ready to fly to the far side of the earth.

'Where is she taking us?' It was a question either might have asked. They had no way of knowing, and no choice in the matter either, since Gadfly decided their course for now. It was enough that Termagant could not catch them, and this thought, added to the exhilaration of flight, drove all cares from their minds. Marcel even forgot about the ring for a while.

What a sensation, to be so high and to see so far over the forest, dense and dark beneath them! Far to their left, it rose onto the slopes of high mountains until the deep green gave way to glistening snow. Away to their right lay the dramatic edge of the great escarpment. The high country finished abruptly in the cliff's jagged edge, which ran on as far as they could see in both directions. Beyond it, they could make out the soft and blurred colours of the vast plain below.

Dead ahead they could see a single mountain perched on the rim of the escarpment, so high its peak was shrouded in the clouds. Was it near or far? It was difficult to judge, and before Marcel could decide, his mind drifted to more pressing questions.

'Do you think Gadfly will help us find the others?'

Bea took her time before answering. 'That's what you want, isn't it, Marcel?'

Yes, it was, he couldn't deny it. This was his chance to join them and play his part.

Gadfly surged on as though she would never tire, so it caught them by surprise when she suddenly dropped low enough for her hooves to skim the treetops. Then, without any reason they could see, she arced smoothly, swooping even lower over a small lake. The two riders clung like barnacles to her back as she touched down expertly on the stony shore.

Marcel slipped off the horse, then turned to help Bea down. Now at last they could examine those miraculous wings, which she stretched out like a cormorant letting its feathers dry. Marcel marvelled at their size and delicacy, touching them gently to feel the downy softness. 'They're magnificent,' he breathed, receiving a neigh of approval from their proud owner.

The heavy sack was still pressed against Gadfly's chest, so he went quickly to remove it. He had just slipped it free when Bea asked in awe, 'How could that happen? What sort of magic was it?'

She had barely uttered the words when the wings began to shrink, first folding against the horse's flanks, then tucking themselves more tightly against her shoulders, until finally it was as though they had never appeared.

'What did you do?' Marcel demanded, spinning round to face Bea.

'It wasn't me!' she cried. 'It started when you took that sack ...'

Marcel looked down at the bundle in his hands. 'The Book of Lies,' he murmured. What had Old Belch told him in the stable that day? The Book could grant you your heart's desire. A little sparrow had become a great eagle. Gadfly had been listening.

'That's it!' he told Bea in excitement. 'The Book can search our souls. That's how it knows when we're lying. Animals must have hopes and dreams too, deep in their hearts. But for them, it works a different kind of magic.'

He stared with renewed admiration at Gadfly, who seemed to consider it nothing less than she deserved. She moved off nonchalantly towards the succulent green of the forest and began to tear noisily at a tuft of grass.

Their thoughts slowly turned from Gadfly to the world around them.

'I've never been in the forest before,' breathed Bea. She spoke as though she found it as wondrous as Gadfly's wings.

Marcel looked around at the greenery spread out before them in every shade imaginable, from the pale tops of the ferns where the sunlight caught the leaves to the dark velvety moss that hugged the trunks of the beech trees. Some of the trees were young and proudly pointed straight to the sky, while others leaned with age, one at an impossible angle, as though it had started to fall and been frozen halfway to the ground.

'It's beautiful,' whispered Bea, so softly that Marcel doubted he was meant to hear. He watched as she took a few steps, until she was free of the pebbly shore. Then, secure amid the trees and the tranquil silence, she hugged her arms tightly around herself as though she had found her true home at last.

What's so special? he asked himself. Now that he found himself deep within the forest it was not quite the dark and fearful place he had imagined, but to him it was simply where he hoped to find Starkey and the others.

When Gadfly had eaten her fill she led them once more, though she walked as any horse would now, because the Book of Lies hung from Marcel's shoulder and not around her neck. The going was slow until they came across a rough track worn down by the feet of woodsmen and hunters.

Gadfly's ears twitched, and Marcel quickly guessed the reason why. 'Someone's coming,' he murmured.

'Is it them?' Bea asked.

If it was, then it was Gadfly's doing. The Book had given her an eagle's wings: perhaps it had given her an eagle's eyes as well. But they couldn't be sure who it was for now, so they hurried into the trees, hiding themselves easily — even Gadfly — amid the thick growth of the forest.

The travellers appeared soon afterwards, in single file: a tall man in a dashing black cape leading the way, two weary children behind him and a grim-faced bowman bringing up the rear.

'What will we do?' Bea asked when they had passed.

Marcel felt the ring on his little finger. If he appeared now, calling to them, Starkey might be furious and send him straight back to Mrs Timmins.

'I'm not sure,' he confessed sadly. 'We'd better follow them, I suppose, at a distance.'

They trailed behind them, careful to remain hidden. After about an hour, the forest became darker. Had the trees grown taller here, Marcel wondered, or was it those menacing grey clouds that now crowded out the sun? Whatever the reason, it had become a different place somehow. Gadfly's ears twitched again and moments later the howl of a wolf echoed through the trees, bringing goose bumps to every inch of their skin.

A commotion ahead on the track made the others stop, and leaving Gadfly where she was, Marcel and Bea crept closer to see what had caused it. A wolf was prowling in a wide circle around Starkey, Hector and the two children. When it stood still for a moment, Hector took aim and hoisted a stone at it.

The wolf ran off, but Nicola slumped onto a log to show her exhaustion, and even Hector dropped his pack and his heavy sword onto the ground at his feet. Seeing this, Starkey signalled a few minutes' rest.

Not for Fergus, though. As Marcel and Bea watched from a distance, he took the sword Hector had discarded and waited until the others were turned away from him, then slipped silently into the trees.

'What's he up to?' Bea whispered.

'I don't know, but it's a chance to speak to him alone. Starkey might have told them where they're going, or more about who we are.'

'But there's no trail to follow where Fergus has gone. How will Gadfly find a way through?' Bea asked. Marcel had to think quickly before he lost sight of Fergus. 'You stay with Gadfly, Bea. I'll speak to Fergus alone.'

He had already started moving off before he felt the Book of Lies pulling at his shoulder. He could not waste another second; it would have to come with him.

But then he looked back at Bea, standing beside two dappled trees that had grown into one. His face fell and he stayed where he was. She was so small, so vulnerable — and he was about to leave her alone.

She knew what was troubling him. 'Gadfly and I will be all right. I feel safe here, safer than I've ever been. You don't have to worry.'

Marcel headed off quickly, puzzled at Bea's strange confidence. But if he was to find Fergus, he would have to put his mind to the task. There was no track to help him, but it wasn't long before be came across the imprint of fresh footsteps. Soon after that, a mighty war cry sounded through the trees, spurring him to hurry on, until he rounded a huge boulder and found Fergus standing in an open stretch of ground, Hector's sword held in both hands above his head.

Fallen twigs and the crunch of Marcel's shoes on the ground made Fergus spin round.

'Marcel!' He was stunned. 'How did *you* get here? You were supposed to stay behind.' Then his eyes widened in a moment of fear that he couldn't hide. 'Termagant! She'll be after you!'

'You don't need to worry. She's miles behind, and besides, I didn't leave a trail she can easily follow.'

Fergus couldn't make sense of this, and Marcel was quietly satisfied by his confusion. 'I've been following you all for a while now, and when I saw you go after the wolf —'

Fergus cut him off, smiling triumphantly. 'He'd have been in after our food tonight if I hadn't chased him away.'

'But what if he'd turned on you?'

'I'm not afraid of a wolf. And besides, I have this,' he said, brandishing the sword proudly. 'It's Hector's. He's a real soldier, Marcel, a sergeant in the Army — or at least he was.'

Marcel did his best to listen, but he was becoming increasingly distracted by the eeriness of the clearing. Since Gadfly had landed on the lake's shore over an hour ago, there had always been a bird calling to its mate in the trees or the sound of wind breathing under the bracken. Now, there was only an unsettling silence.

Suddenly, he noticed that Fergus was staring towards the huge boulder. When he turned, he found the way he had come blocked by a stony-eyed wolf.

'I thought you'd frightened it off,' he reproached Fergus.

'It's not the same one.'

'What do you mean?' said Marcel.

'Look at it. See the white fur on its belly? The wolf I chased away was black from head to tail.'

Just as he spoke, that same black wolf stalked out from behind the boulder to join the first. Marcel felt a chill in his bones. He backed away, but when he turned to check the ground behind him, he saw that two more wolves were edging their way into the clearing. There was something sinister about their red eyes, almost as though these creatures were more than simply wolves.

Fergus raised his sword and lunged at the closest of them. Beside him, Marcel had nothing to fend them off but his bare hands. He tried swinging the bag with the Book of Lies inside it, but heavy though it was, it wouldn't be enough.

Slipping the strap over his head again, he snatched up a fallen tree branch to make a club of sorts. He struck at the nearest wolf, but his feeble attack brought only a low, menacing growl that turned his blood to ice.

Fergus's sword swung again, making the wolves wary, but they weren't as cautious with Marcel. He struck hard with his club, hitting one on the snout as it backed away. The wolves were toying with them, testing them. Any second now, they would rush in from all directions.

'We haven't got a chance if we stay apart!' Fergus yelled. 'We'll have to stand back-to-back!'

Marcel didn't take this in. Fear made him stare blankly at the wolves and chased everything else from his mind.

'Behind me!' Fergus shouted, with more urgency this time. When Marcel still didn't move, Fergus swore savagely and moved closer himself until he was guarding Marcel from behind.

'Move when I move, and turn when I turn,' he commanded, and at last Marcel understood. The wolves in front of Fergus were kept at bay by his sword, wielded bravely and with a skill that even he couldn't explain. When they circled towards Marcel, who had only a stick of wood to defend himself, the boys turned quickly in unison, bringing Fergus to face them.

The black wolf rushed in, but it fell away sharply, snarling in pain from a blow to its jaw. The pack circled again, closing in on Marcel, and though he fought them off with heavy blows, one grabbed his arm. Fergus swung round with a mighty slash that took the wolf just behind its front leg. Yelping as the blood spilled onto its fur, the beast released its grip.

'Are you all right?'

'There's blood, but I can still move it.'

'Stay on your feet,' Fergus told him urgently. 'If they get us down, we're finished.'

A second wolf sprang at them and this time snared the leg of Fergus's breeches just above the ankle. Despite his own warning, he was dragged to his knees. Marcel swung his awkward club and forced the others away, but there was nothing he could do for Fergus. If he turned on that wolf for a moment, the other three would tear both of them to pieces.

Fergus hammered desperately at his attacker using the handle of the sword, but this alone was not enough. Turning the sword in his hands, he held it like an enormous dagger, and with only a moment to aim, he drove the point into the wolf's side. A pitiful yelping rose up instantly as the wolf slumped to the ground beside him. Marcel watched, his stomach churning as Fergus pulled the blade free. 'Behind you!' Fergus screamed, and Marcel turned just in time to beat off another attack.

Fergus struggled to his feet, dragging air back into his lungs, and once again turned back-to-back with his companion. One wolf lay dying, and a second bled from a shoulder wound, but it circled still with the other two, all twice as thirsty for the kill now that their companion had been slain. Exhausted, and bleeding themselves, the boys might not be able to beat them back this time. The wolves advanced.

Then a noise in the distance made their heads turn. Even the wolves looked away. Running feet, human feet, pounding quickly towards them.

'Here!' shouted Fergus desperately.

Starkey burst into the clearing, his sword whirling ferociously and in his other hand the jewelled dagger. He came at the wolves, catching the weakened one with a second blow, so that now two wolves were accounted for. His terrible blades kept up their savage work until the remaining pair finally backed away to the edge of the clearing.

'Marcel!' Starkey cried in astonishment when he realised there were two boys to be saved. 'What are you —' He broke off. There was no time for such questions now. 'Quickly, there might be others nearby,' he hissed, pushing them in front of him. He kept his sword ready, looking ahead of them one moment and over his own shoulder the next.

No more wolves appeared, and by the time they reached the track, where Hector and Nicola were waiting, it was plain that for now the creatures had given up the attack.

'Marcel! You escaped after all!' cried Nicola, her enthusiasm taking him unawares. But when she saw the blood on his sleeve, her voice changed quickly from amazement to concern. 'What happened?' she asked, looking beyond him as though Termagant herself were chasing them.

'Wolves,' Starkey answered, as he guided Fergus to a fallen log and sat him down to inspect his leg. 'You're lucky,' he said after tearing away the ravaged cloth. 'It didn't get hold of you.'

There was blood dripping onto the soil, though, and it was only then that Starkey realised it came from a deep gash in his own hand. Hector brought him a rag, and after he had dabbed away the blood he bound the wound tightly.

Another was handed to Marcel, who laid the leather sack aside and sat down next to Fergus. When he had wiped the blood away, he found that three teethmarks had punctured his skin.

'You'll live,' Hector sniffed dismissively. He took back his weapon from Fergus, then turned his mind to something that concerned him more than flesh wounds and stolen swords. 'What's this one doing here?' he muttered to Starkey, nodding towards Marcel. 'He's meant to be back in Fallside. How could he have caught up with us?'

Starkey fingered his chin and gazed thoughtfully at Marcel. 'Hector is right. What are you doing so far from the orphanage? How did you come to be in that clearing?'

'I had no choice; I had to escape,' Marcel told them hotly. At the same time he wondered how he could explain about Gadfly. They would think he was mad. A flying horse! Even he could barely believe it. And what would he tell them about Bea and the Book of Lies? He wasn't ready yet to reveal the prize he had brought with him!

But he had brought magic of another kind with him too, and this was all that mattered to Starkey. 'You still have that ring on your finger, I see. What did you tell me back in Fallside? The beast you spoke of, Termagant, you told me it would follow you, it would be able to find you, wherever you went. Wasn't that Lord Alwyn's curse?'

His face grew stony as his suspicions hardened into fear. 'The old wizard has *let* you escape. He has used you, boy, used you to lead his fearsome creature to the rest of us.'

At this, Hector fitted an arrow to his bow and stared into the trees in the direction they had come. Soon they were all looking about them nervously, even Marcel as he worked at the golden ring, tugging vainly.

Starkey rested one hand on the hilt of his sword, ready to use it at a moment's notice, but his eyes settled on Marcel. The fingers of his other hand cupped his chin, stroking roughly through the stubble until he seemed to reach a decision. 'There is only one solution,' he said firmly. 'You must go back to the orphanage.'

'But you've got swords and Hector's got his bow,' Nicola protested.

'Against such magic? Even with a hundred men, I would still send him back. So long as Marcel has that ring on his finger, Termagant can find him and Lord Alwyn will know where we are.'

The terrible emptiness stirred again in Marcel's heart, causing more pain than the teethmarks on his arm. 'But I have some part in what you're going to do,' he pleaded. 'You told me so yourself.'

'I have these two instead. You're nothing but a threat to us,' answered Starkey with a cruel candour. But when he saw how deeply he had cut Marcel, he tried to convince him with gentler arguments. 'You must go back, for the good of us all,' he urged, and coming forward three paces he laid his hand lightly on the boy's shoulder.

Marcel heard the change in Starkey's tone and knew instantly that he was right. For the good of them all, he must go back before the curse of Lord Alwyn's ring led Termagant to this sorry band of fugitives. She could end their flight with a single savage swipe of her claws. Just the thought of it made him wince.

'You're right, there's nothing I can do about the ring,' he conceded, splaying his fingers in front of him to catch the glint of the shiny gold. 'I have to go back.'

'At least give him a sword,' Fergus insisted.

'We cannot spare one,' growled Hector.

'But he must have something. There are wolves out there,' Fergus went on.

'Well, it seems you have an ally, Marcel,' said Starkey, raising a bemused eyebrow. 'He's right, too. Hector, give the boy your sword.'

'But —'

'Do as I say,' Starkey snapped, but he seemed to think better of this approach and immediately dropped the harshness from his voice. 'You're the best archer I've ever seen, Hector, and that will have to be enough. Now, give him your sword.'

Such praise chased the scowl from Hector's face, but he still wasn't happy as he drew his sword and tossed it in the dirt beside Marcel.

'The matter is settled, then. You'll leave as soon as your wound has been seen to,' Starkey declared.

This job was left to Nicola. She had watched Hector tend Starkey's hand earlier, and now she tore the shredded sleeve of Marcel's shirt to get at the wound, just like an expert. 'It's not too serious,' she assured him.

When she had tied the bandage around his arm and knotted it in place, Marcel looked down to inspect her handiwork. Impressed, he touched it gingerly with his other hand, but immediately found himself staring at his little finger. 'Damn this ring. I've tried to yank it free so many times, it's a wonder my whole finger hasn't come off.'

He laughed to himself, realising what he'd just said. 'Now *that* would be a trick to play on Lord Alwyn, don't you think?'

Nicola was puzzled by the odd expression on his face, part grim determination, part bald fear, as he said over and over to himself, 'What a trick it would be ... what a trick ...'

His mind created the scene: a truly horrible picture, he had to admit, but if he could actually do it, if he had the courage, then he'd set himself free.

How could he manage it, though? He'd need something to do it with. His eyes fell onto Hector's sword, so recently laid at his feet. It was *his* sword now.

But he could not do what he was planning by

himself. He would need someone to help him. Nicola would be no use. That left Fergus.

Starkey and Hector were busy separating some provisions for Marcel to take on his journey back to Fallside. There was a chance to slip away. 'I need your help,' he whispered to Fergus. 'Meet me in a minute or so behind those trees,' and he nodded to show the direction. With that, he picked up the heavy sword. Just the sight of its blade so close made the colour drain from his face. No, don't think, he told himself. Get moving.

Perplexed, Fergus watched him slip away, but this seemed yet another promise of adventure so he followed soon afterwards, making sure he was not seen.

'What are we going to do?' he asked eagerly when he joined Marcel behind the screen of trees.

'You'll see,' whispered Marcel, relieved to hear a certain determination in his own simple reply. 'Here, take the sword,' he said, pressing the handle into Fergus's hands.

Marcel led him deeper into the forest until he spotted a tree stump that seemed to suit his purpose. But when he looked back at Fergus, brandishing the sword, his mouth went dry.

'What's all this about, Marcel?'

'I'm going to make sure Termagant can't find me.'

'But the ring, there's no way you can get rid of it.'

'Yes, there is. That's why we're here. We're going to cut it off.'

'But it's a magical ring. Nothing in the world will cut through that metal.'

'It's not the metal we have to cut through.'

This made no sense to Fergus, until he saw Marcel's face and finally understood what he was planning. 'No, you can't do it! The pain!'

'Don't worry. You won't feel a thing.'

'How can you joke about it? You must be mad! Your own finger!'

'It's the only way to get the ring off my hand.'

Fergus had shown his own courage against the wolves, yet now he confessed to Marcel, 'If it was me … I don't think I could do it.' Holding the sword carefully by the blade, he offered the handle to Marcel.

'No, I can't do it myself. That's why I gave the sword to you. You have to cut the finger off for me.'

Fergus's face went even whiter than Marcel's. 'I can't.'

'You're the only one who can. Come on, quickly, before they realise we've disappeared.'

'No.'

Marcel goaded him. 'You're the one who wants to be a soldier. You want to be a hero — well, here's your chance.'

'It's not the same. I'd rather fight a hundred wolves than do this.'

'Do it, Fergus! Do it now.'

With grim resolve, Marcel knelt beside the tree stump and folded back the rest of his fingers. Just the smallest was left, laid out across the rough surface. The ring glinted in the afternoon light that filtered through the beech trees.

Part of his mind screamed in protest. It wasn't worth it. He would go back to Fallside as they wanted him to, then one day Starkey would return to set him free.

No, he told himself. I can't leave the danger to others. This might be the only way I'll ever find out who I am. For some reason, he thought of Bea, and felt that her bravery in bringing him the Book of Lies was greater than anything he was doing now. 'Come on, Fergus, hurry,' he urged.

'I can't do this!' Fergus wailed.

Then, as Marcel watched, he made himself look down at the ring and the blade of the sword and his own trembling hands. 'I'll try,' he whispered hoarsely.

A noise behind them made their heads turn. There was a flash of coloured clothing.

'Now,' Marcel hissed. 'Before they find us. Come on. If you lose your nerve, so will I.'

Fergus hoisted the blade until it hovered above his head. Then it was moving, scything down through the air, the cutting edge hungry for its target. It struck a clean and solid blow. A scream pierced the air, the echoes bouncing chaotically against the rocks and massive tree trunks until the sound oozed around them like blood.

It was Nicola they had seen through the trees. She had spotted Fergus with the sword raised, seen it flash downwards, and it was her scream that had split the silence of the forest.

But Marcel's hand was still pressed against the edge of the stump. The sword's blade was buried in the wood. It had missed his finger by the breadth of a hair.

'What are you doing?' Nicola yelled at them both.

'It has to come off,' Marcel replied, now fierce in his determination. 'It's the only way to get rid of the ring.' He switched his attention to Fergus. 'Again,' he demanded. 'And this time, don't miss.'

'No!' Nicola roared at him. She grabbed Fergus and tried to pull him away. The sword clattered to the ground and Marcel feared his chance had gone. Starkey must have heard Nicola's scream and would surely try to stop them.

Marcel picked up the sword, gripping it tightly despite the pain in his arm from the wolf's bite. He raised it as best he could, moving his other hand into position beneath him and knowing with a steel-hard certainty that he would do it — he would do anything to see that hated ring gone from his hand.

It was at this very instant that the ring moved. Or, at least, he thought it had moved. When he looked down he saw it still gleaming, taunting him to carry out what he had so far failed to do. There was no going back. He took a tighter grip on the sword.

But now he was sure the ring had moved. It had slipped down over the first knuckle. He shifted his hand and saw it fall a little further, until it rested against the second knuckle. He laid the sword aside, poking at the ring with his other hand, and it fell from his finger to lie harmlessly in the centre of the stump.

'The ring has come off!' he shouted, as relief flooded through him. 'I'm free!'

CHAPTER 9

A Verse in Golden Letters

FERGUS AND NICOLA STARED down at the ring in disbelief. 'But all those times you tried!' protested Nicola. 'How could it simply *fall off*?'

Starkey came running through the trees, his sword in one hand and that pitiless dagger in the other. 'What are you three up to? There was a scream.' He followed their eyes and soon he too was gazing down in amazement at the ring.

'It just slipped off, as though it was never meant to be there,' said Marcel, at a loss to explain.

'Oh, it was meant to be there, all right,' Starkey assured him, 'but Alwyn is a trickster, like all magicians. There must have been a key. Some words.'

Marcel looked at him blankly. 'What do you mean?'

'Some magic cannot be undone, but a curse like that ring is different. Such a spell is never cast without some way to unravel it. What did he say to you when he first made you put it on?'

Marcel thought back to those terrifying moments after the horse race when he found Termagant circling him, growling and spitting, ready to snap him in two at the slightest signal from her master. Snatches of Lord Alwyn's goading came back to him. *The true test is whether you find the courage to remove that ring.*

'It wasn't what I *said*,' he murmured. 'It was what I tried to *do*. I was really going to do it, you see. I was going to cut off my own finger.'

Starkey eyed him suspiciously for a moment, though there was an unmistakable gleam of admiration in his flinty gaze. 'You're a determined one, I'll grant you that, Marcel. Well, there's no need to send you back now. You may as well join us after all.'

This was just what Marcel had hoped for. Starkey was inviting him to go with them!

Before any of them could react, Starkey snatched up the ring and hurled it far into the forest. 'Get your things,' he ordered Marcel, 'and you'd better give that sword back to Hector.' He looked up at the fading sun. 'Come on, all of you. We must push on. We have a long way to go before nightfall.'

Marcel went to get the Book of Lies, which he had left back where Hector was waiting for them. His pace had begun to quicken, when he stopped mid-step.

Bea! Bea was still out there in the forest with Gadfly! He was suddenly ashamed that he had not given her a thought since rushing off to find Fergus. Just as suddenly, he was running, anxious to reach Starkey, who was striding purposefully onwards. 'Wait! There's something I haven't told you,' he called.

Starkey turned, folding his arms across his chest impatiently as he waited for Marcel to explain.

'My escape from the orphanage,' he began tentatively. 'I had help. A little girl came with me from the orphanage. We escaped on a horse named Gadfly.'

Starkey didn't like the sound of this. 'Where are they now, this girl and the horse?'

'I left them a little way back on the path.'

Starkey ordered Hector to stay with the other two. Marcel led him to where the two speckled trunks were entwined and grew as one. But there was no sign of either Bea or Gadfly.

'Bea!' he called, expecting her to appear, but the only reply to his cry was the cawing of a crow that flew low overhead.

'Your little friend has run off and left you.'

'No, you don't know this girl like I do. She wouldn't abandon me.'

But where was she? A dreadful thought came to him. 'You don't think that the wolves have ...'

Starkey considered this possibility with a coolness that seemed part of his nature. 'No, not the wolves,' he said after inspecting the ground around them. 'There's no sign of their paw prints. Face it, Marcel, the girl became frightened when she heard the wolves attacking you and she took the horse back to Fallside. Come on, we can't delay any longer. The others are waiting.'

Marcel just couldn't believe that Bea would leave him to the wolves, but at the same time, he wondered how much she had seen. Had she been watching, minutes earlier, when the ring fell from his finger? If she had, then she knew he was free to join Nicola and Fergus now. There was nothing more she could do to help him. Had she climbed onto Gadfly and gone back to face Lord Alwyn alone? He shuddered at the thought, yet Bea was the only person he knew who was brave enough to do just that.

'Well?' Starkey prompted him, impatiently.

He felt his lips move and heard his own voice, fretting already at how much he might come to regret his words. 'I'll come with you,' he said.

They returned to where the others were waiting to set off again, ignoring their quizzical looks. Marcel returned the sword to Hector. The sack containing the Book of Lies lay just where he had left it. When he lifted it to his shoulder, Starkey called out, 'What's in there?'

He had to think quickly. He didn't feel sure enough of Starkey to reveal the prize he had brought with him yet. 'It's food.' Yes, that sounded right. 'It's food I stole from Mrs Timmins.'

Immediately he felt the Book stir inside the leather bag, straining and bucking, trying to open its pages. But to his relief, it settled again before anyone noticed.

'Bring it with us, then; there's little enough food in Hector's pack, what with those blankets,' Starkey growled, and without looking back, he set out after the others.

Minutes later, the party was spread out along the track, with Hector in front at first, until Starkey took the lead. Fergus came next, but Marcel was surprised to see him suddenly drop back, and even more surprised when he found the boy walking beside him.

'That was a brave thing you did just now. With the ring, I mean,' said Fergus, his voice lively and full of feeling. He had never let himself appear excited about anything in front of Mrs Timmins and the other orphans. He leaned closer and whispered, 'I could never have done anything like that. I couldn't even make myself aim properly at your finger.'

'I'm glad you missed,' Marcel joked grimly, and noticing Fergus's face, still solemn and somewhat pale, he couldn't help himself. He laughed at him.

If anyone had laughed at Fergus back at the orphanage, they would have had a fight on their hands. Now, though, he relaxed and joined in. 'I mean it, you know,' he insisted. 'Look at the way you kept your head when the wolves attacked us.'

'That was you, Fergus. You were the hero. If you hadn't made me stand back-to-back with you, those wolves would be chewing the meat off our bones right now.'

Fergus didn't just smile at Marcel's praise, he beamed. 'Were you scared?'

'Terrified,' answered Marcel.

Fergus hadn't expected such a blunt admission, but after a few seconds his face softened. 'Me too. But we did it, didn't we? We fought off those wolves, you and I together.'

They walked on in thoughtful silence until Fergus spoke again. 'I thought you were just another weakling back at Mrs Timmins',' he said quickly, as though he had a lot to say and feared he would forget the words. 'Until the race, that is. You really beat me in that race, you know. That's why I kept fighting with you afterwards. I don't like to lose.'

Yet even this explanation was only delaying what he really wanted to say. He struggled a little longer until finally he said, 'I'm sorry, Marcel. It was just that back there in Fallside I felt trapped, I suppose, like I didn't belong. I hated the place and everyone there. But I was wrong about you.' He slapped a hand onto Marcel's shoulder and shook him in a playful way. It was the action of a friend.

What was going on here? Marcel wondered. Maybe Fergus wasn't so hard to understand after all. His smile seemed sincere. Marcel couldn't help returning it a little, and for an instant he longed to let go, to relax and smile openly.

No, there was so much more he needed to know before he could feel free. He must have been free and content with the world once, in the life Lord Alwyn had stolen from him. He could not really be free until he had won it back.

'Who do you think we really are?' he asked Fergus.

A silent shrug was his first answer. Then, after Fergus had considered for a moment, he answered, 'There's something special about us, something important. I'm sure of that much. Your parents, my parents, Nicola's too,' he added, nodding towards her as she struggled along behind them. 'They must all be important people in the Kingdom, don't you think? We were being held as hostages, most likely, so our parents would do whatever they were told.'

'By this King Pelham,' said Marcel.

'Yes, and Lord Alwyn is probably already on his way to tell him we've escaped.'

'I hope he is,' Marcel responded, drawing a strange look from Fergus. But Marcel was thinking of Bea, on her way back to Fallside right now. If the old wizard had already left by the time she arrived, hopefully she would escape his punishment.

Then a second thought took hold of him. 'Do you think he's sent Termagant after us?'

Every dark shadow could hide her. Despite Starkey's mighty throw, the ring lay only a few miles behind them and their trail was fresh. Termagant could come snarling and spitting from the undergrowth at any moment. He hoped that Bea and Gadfly would be safe from her.

Fears of Termagant seemed to be in Starkey's mind as well. He marched them hard through the forest, sometimes following a trail beaten firm by the forest's deer, sometimes the course of a stream; and steadily uphill.

Even Fergus was soon puffing hard, though Starkey was deaf to Nicola's pleas for rest. 'You can be sure that black beast won't be taking rests.'

In the distance directly ahead lay a solitary mountain, dark and brooding, it seemed to Marcel. It was the one he had seen from Gadfly's back, the peak obscured by a misty cloud, as though, like Starkey, it preferred to keep its face hidden from unwelcome eyes.

The sky became grey and threatening as this mountain grew ever closer. Tree roots snagged their feet, and the clouds thickened and sent down a fine, freezing rain that made the moss-covered stones treacherous to step on.

Nicola slipped on the hem of her dress, landing heavily in the mud, and instantly she became the spoiled princess of the orphanage again. But when her vanity met with nothing but laughter from the two boys she quickly stopped her complaints.

When Starkey noticed her shivering in the thin, mud-soaked dress, he unfastened his cloak. 'Here, take this,' he said, fitting it around her shoulders. But he made no effort to find shelter.

He drove them on relentlessly, and always upwards, until exhaustion seemed too mild a word. They trudged on, wet and freezing, until the last of the day's sun deserted the forest and they could barely see the ground ahead of them.

'We'll make camp here,' their leader announced, as they stood in a small clearing on the bank of a meagre stream which already reflected the early evening stars in its surface. After the persistent drizzle it was difficult to get a fire going. The three children huddled on fallen logs around the flames to warm themselves against the chilly night air.

Nicola sat closest, stroking her fingers through her hair in dismay and trying vainly to comb out the pine needles that had lodged in it during the day. Marcel and Fergus took off their shoes and competed for the honour of biggest blister. When Fergus thought he had finally beaten Marcel at something, Nicola kicked off her flimsy left shoe and showed him one twice the size.

Meanwhile, Starkey and Hector prepared the meal that the children had been dreaming of since early afternoon. Marcel's mind conjured up hunks of juicy meat dripping with gravy, but instead he found himself staring down at a pile of turnips and carrots that Starkey planned to roast in the coals, and a small portion of dried venison so tough that he could barely cut through it with his dagger.

Nicola couldn't help smiling at Marcel's downcast face, having known what to expect. Still, she saw fit to complain, 'Turnips and carrots *again*! Isn't there anything else?'

'Here, bring me that bag of food you've been carrying, Marcel,' grunted Hector.

Food? Marcel wondered. Then it hit him like a stone. 'But it's ... it's mine,' he answered lamely, clutching at the Book of Lies within its protective sack.

'You'll get your share,' Hector growled. 'No room for gluttons on this journey.' He snatched the bag from Marcel's hapless grasp. 'He's been carrying a heavy cake, by the feel of it,' he remarked.

But they were all soon disappointed. 'What's this? There's nothing in here but a book!'

'Let me see that,' barked Starkey, reaching forward. He plunged his hand inside the sack to see what Marcel had been concealing.

Even in the darkness, he knew instantly what it was. He reeled backwards, dropping the book into the dirt at his feet. 'Alwyn's book. The great Book of Lies,' he breathed as he stared down at it. There was a touch of awe and yes, a hint of fear in the voice of this man who so rarely showed what he was feeling. 'How did you get hold of it?' he demanded.

'I stole it,' Marcel responded, forgetting Bea in his eagerness to impress them all. 'Before I left the orphanage, I crept into the tower and took the book while Lord Alwyn was sleeping.'

Instantly, the Book of Lies responded, its pages fanning wildly as they all watched in dismay. When the pages settled again, the Book lay open at the second-last page and here, close to the bottom, Marcel's words began to appear.

'That means he's lying,' Starkey sneered. 'I knew it. No one could steal such a precious thing from Alwyn.'

Marcel had been caught out, yes, but they soon realised the Book had taken down more than just *his* words. Starkey took a burning twig from the fire and held it over the Book. There, below Marcel's, were his own words, *No one could steal such a precious thing from Alwyn.*

Marcel's hope was that if he told the truth about Bea, Starkey would not demand the rest of the story. 'It was Bea who stole the Book,' he confessed, drawing a reaction from everyone but Hector. 'Lord Alwyn wasn't himself, you see. When he heard the news that Fergus and Nicola had disappeared, the shock made him collapse.'

The Book of Lies closed with a creak and gave off its familiar golden glow.

'So, at last you are telling the truth. That explains how I managed to get you two away so easily,' Starkey said, turning to Nicola and Fergus. 'Alwyn's magic is becoming as weak as his failing body. But I don't like it,' he muttered warily. 'This book reeks of the old wizard and the power he has wielded for so long in this kingdom.' As he spoke, he got to his feet, yanked his sword swiftly from his belt and took aim.

'No, you can't destroy it!' Marcel cried desperately, clinging to the man's arm.

Starkey shrugged him off easily and took aim a second time.

'Wait! You can use it yourself, to know who you can trust.'

'I have my own ways of doing that,' he snarled. The sword was raised again.

This time Marcel threw his whole body in the way and Starkey only managed to check his blade an inch short of Marcel's skull. 'Get out of the way!'

'But it can help you to convince people. With this book laid out before them, they will surely believe what you tell them. You can use it to defeat King Pelham.'

With Marcel thwarting Starkey so doggedly, Hector drew his own sword, ready to strike.

'No!' cried a voice.

It wasn't another anguished plea from Marcel. This cry came from Starkey himself, a command that stopped Hector instantly. And why had Starkey called a halt when only seconds earlier he had been ready to destroy the Book himself? The faint tinge of gold reflected in his face was all the answer Marcel needed.

'You see now? It's true.'

Starkey took one hand from his sword and let his fingers play with the black stubble along his chin, now almost worthy of being called a beard. 'The Book of Lies … sworn to reveal the truth,' he murmured. 'Perhaps this book *can* help me after all.' He put his sword away and nodded to Hector to do the same.

Marcel's heart danced with relief, but Fergus spoke up with his own demands. 'You may have the Book of Lies to help you, Starkey, but you still haven't told us why we are so important. We've come a long way from Fallside. Surely you can tell us who we are now.'

'All in good time,' Starkey replied. He smiled to himself and added, 'When we reach Elstenwyck, I will tell you everything.'

At these words, the Book lost its golden tinge and, to Starkey's dismay, began to buck furiously until it reached the second-last page once more. *When we reach Elstenwyck*, it wrote, but there wasn't enough room to complete what Starkey had said so the paper arched gracefully before their eyes to reveal an unblemished page. It was the last in the Book, apart from the jagged remains where a sheet had been torn away.

But they barely noticed Starkey's lie, as their eyes were drawn to something unnaturally bright on the inside of the back cover.

'What's that?' gasped Nicola. She stretched out her hand, pointing, though she was afraid to touch it. 'Are they words? What do they say?'

Crowding more closely around the Book, they all stared at the darkened leather of the cover itself.

Words, yes, Nicola was right, but they weren't written in the stark black script that crammed the rest of the Book's pages. These letters were large and golden, a dazzling liquid gold that grew brighter as they watched, until the darkness around them was driven back and they could see their own monstrous shadows against the surrounding trees.

This light brought a warmth that was even more heartening than their smoky fire. The glow seemed to penetrate their clothing, until the dampness and cold were gone and they were comfortable for the first time that day.

Marcel tried to gaze at the burning words but his eyes could not bear their intensity. He closed them and turned away, yet to his astonishment he found the words dancing upon the blackness of his eyelids. More than this, they were in his mind and on his tongue, even though he had not read a single one.

When Lords and Ladies quest for fame
A Beast will touch the land with flame
Good men will die, their wives will mourn
While children weep for fathers gone

With swords for teeth and skin of steel
With arrowed claw and poisoned heel
The Beast will grow and spread its wings
Destroying rogues and making Kings

When all my pages fill with lies
Let slip the Beast and see it rise
Till one who understands this verse
Commands the Beast and breaks its curse

He opened his eyes to find Starkey glaring at him suspiciously. But the blazing letters cooled, settling into place on the aged leather in the same way as they had burned into Marcel's eyes, and now they could all read them.

'What is this verse doing in the Book of Lies?' Starkey demanded. Then he answered for himself. 'Perhaps it's not part of Alwyn's magic at all.'

'I thought every word in the Book was a lie,' said Nicola. 'Isn't that what you told me back at the orphanage, Marcel?'

Yes, that was what he had told her.

'But see how the words glow? It's the same gold the Book uses to identify the truth,' said Starkey thoughtfully.

Could words be both truth and lies at the same time?

Starkey's fear of the Book seemed to be slipping away rapidly. He picked it up, opened the back cover and read the golden verse to himself silently.

'Are you going to eat or read from that book all night?' barked Hector, eyeing the untouched food.

The three children turned quickly to claim their meagre rations.

Marcel wolfed down his share then turned back to Starkey, whose portion lay forgotten beside him on the log where he sat with the Book of Lies across his lap.

'What do you think it means?' Marcel asked.

'A Beast with wings … mighty flames … and this line here,' he said, pointing reverently as he repeated it. '*Destroying rogues and making Kings*. What else can it be but a great dragon ready to drive usurpers from the throne?'

He raised his voice so that the others could hear. 'It seems I have misjudged the Book. You were right to stop me when I wanted to destroy it, Marcel. It may well hold the key to this kingdom's future.'

'But a dragon — are there such things?' Fergus called from nearby, where he sat listening to every word.

'Not for many centuries, but the old legends speak of them, one in particular. Its name was Mortregis. It ravaged this land for many years, slaughtering all who dared to stand against it, even the bravest knights.'

'Who killed it, then?' Marcel asked, fighting a growing sense of dread.

'No one. Dragons don't die like other beings.'

'Then why isn't it still roaming the Kingdom today?' asked Nicola.

'It was driven away, or so the ancient legends claim. Driven away by the Master of the Books.'

'Lord Alwyn!' Marcel couldn't believe that a man so frail could ever have defeated a dragon, even if he had once been as powerful as Old Belch had claimed.

'No, not Alwyn.'

'But there are dragons sewn onto his robe.'

'Yes, to recall the first great Master, the one who banished Mortregis. He brought peace to the land by uniting it under one king. Every Master since has worn the dragon's image to remind us of the old stories.'

'So where did this dragon go?'

Starkey fingered his bristly chin, a faraway look in his eyes. 'Nobody knows,' he answered softly.

'Then how could it be called back again?'

'I don't know that either. Not yet,' he said ominously, looking down at the Book.

A harsh wind began to sweep down from the mountain up ahead, until their breath frosted in the firelight. The three children wrapped themselves in their blankets and scrambled for the best position by the fire.

'If you lie tightly together, you will preserve more of your body heat,' Hector suggested.

The idea would have brought a laugh only yesterday. But they were cold, and it was going to be a long and bitter night.

'I'll lie in the middle, then,' Nicola volunteered without hesitation.

The boys quickly saw why. 'You'll be warm on *both* sides,' Marcel complained.

'You could have thought of it first,' she taunted, then relented a little. 'Your turn tomorrow night.'

Marcel didn't remember drifting off to sleep that night, but he did remember the commotion when Nicola rolled over in her sleep and whacked Fergus across the nose. After some angry words, the pair quickly settled again, and before Marcel slipped back into sleep he saw that Starkey was still crouched by the dwindling fire. The last of the flames flickered feverishly on his face as he leaned over the Book of Lies, still open on his lap. He was mumbling quietly to himself as he read those three mysterious verses over and over again.

CHAPTER 10

Journey's End

MARCEL WOKE THE NEXT morning within a forest shrouded in the silver robes of a fine mist. Others might have said it was beautiful the way the wisps of fog clung to the trees. Their eyes might have picked out the moss and lichen that spotted the beech trees so delicately and the thick mats of ferns, their fronds perfectly still and dripping with dew. But the beauty of the forest left Marcel and his companions unmoved. All they could think of was the gruelling day ahead.

'Where is the Book, Starkey?' Marcel asked.

'Don't worry. I have it safe. It's heavy, and you've brought it a long way. I'll carry it today.'

Marcel frowned at this, but he saw the look on Starkey's face and knew that it was not an offer but a command.

They began the new day's trek by crossing the stream, its surface like a mirror until Starkey broke its gentle perfection with his first step. 'If you march hard today,' he told them, 'this will be our last in the high country.' Then it was on into the foothills of the mountain, walking and climbing, for hour after long hour.

The group made slow progress, and when they stopped in a rare patch of open ground to eat a late breakfast of apples stolen from the orphanage orchard and more leathery venison, Nicola groaned and asked, 'Can't we stay here until tomorrow?'

It was just what Marcel would have asked if he'd dared, and Fergus looked as if he agreed too.

Perhaps Starkey noticed this in their faces, because he was more sympathetic than usual in his reply. 'I know you are weary, all of you. But we cannot stop. Lord Alwyn will probably be in Elstenwyck by now, and Pelham will know you are missing. My face is well-known to his soldiers and so are yours. When they don't find us on the high roads, they will scour the forest for the smallest sign. We must stay well ahead of them at all costs.'

'But why are we going this way, Starkey?' Hector asked, equally frustrated. 'Avoiding the roads is one thing, but we've gone past two trails down to the valley already, by my count. If we keep going in this direction, we'll —' He stopped, aware that his complaints were starting to sound like fear. There was no doubting what held his eye, though. It was the mountain that loomed directly ahead.

Starkey had heard the hint of dread and took a moment to consider his reply. 'The route we need is the one Pelham's men won't think to guard. There's a way down into the valley a small distance short of that mountain. Very few know about it and even fewer dare to use it.'

He glanced back in the direction they had come from, and Marcel knew it wasn't just Pelham's soldiers who worried him. Termagant might still be after them too.

At that moment, a danger greater even than Termagant swept down on them. The dappled gloom of the forest had been growing darker as they rested, even though it was still mid-morning. They were all aware of the ebbing sunlight. Suddenly, the darkness could not be ignored. Black and broiling, it was slipping stealthily over the ridge away to their left, blocking the sun and plunging the forest more deeply into shadow as each second passed.

Exposed in the clearing, the travellers soon found themselves peppered by monstrous raindrops. A scything wind drove the drops almost parallel to the ground, their impact stinging like bees. Marcel put his hand up to shield his face and found to his alarm that he had caught one, cold and solid, in his palm.

'Hail!' Starkey shouted. 'Use the trees! Quickly, all of you, pin yourselves against the widest trunk you can find!'

Marcel obeyed without question, pressing himself into the rough bark of a stout pine tree. He saw that only a few steps away Fergus had done the same. Nicola was on his other side, hiding her head beneath her arms but thankfully safe as well. They were just in time, for out in the open spaces where the wind raged freely, hailstones now whistled by like arrows.

Then, as quickly as it had begun, the hail stopped and the cloud scudded away furiously in the direction they had come from. After a few watchful minutes they stepped tentatively from the trees, and were astonished to discover that none of them had suffered more damage than a handful of dampened spots on their clothing.

'What was it?' Nicola breathed, still recovering from shock and fear.

'Magic, most likely,' said Hector.

'No, not magic,' returned Starkey. 'Not Alwyn's, at least. He would have to know where we are to send such a tempest against us. That cloud seemed much too random for his work.'

'Like those wolves yesterday,' agreed Hector. 'Wolves don't attack humans, not a party of us together like this.'

'Yes, these are strange times, right enough,' said Starkey. Reminded of the wolves, he lifted the bandage a little from his hand and winced at what he saw. 'I've heard tell recently of sea monsters fighting fishermen and frogs raining from the sky.'

'I've heard stories like that as well,' Hector murmured, eyeing the mountain, which came closer with every step they took. He shifted the longbow on his shoulder.

Fergus spoke up. 'Starkey, back at the orphanage a whole sky full of bats appeared out of nowhere. Lord Alwyn turned them back using his magic.'

Yes, Marcel thought. It was the old wizard who had confronted the bats and the magic he had conjured to do it had taken all of his strength. Starkey was right, he decided. Lord Alwyn had not created that rogue cloud and sent it spitting an icy breath over the land. But if not Lord Alwyn, then where had it come from?

They travelled on until it was all they could do to place one blistered foot in front of the other. They barely stopped at midday to stuff more of their meagre rations into their mouths. The climbing began in earnest now, as the ground on the mountain's lower slopes became steep and rocky.

As their weary walking continued, Marcel felt a new uneasiness. He couldn't quite throw off the sense that they were being watched.

'Do you feel it?' he asked Fergus, who was walking just ahead of him. 'It's like the forest itself has decided it doesn't want us here any more.'

An anxious glance from Nicola told him she had felt it too. Surely they had lost Termagant by now. Could it be Pelham's soldiers? Maybe they had tracked them down after all.

Finally Marcel noticed Hector staring into the surrounding trees.

'Have you seen something?' Fergus asked uneasily.

'No, but my bones tell me we have company among these trees,' came Hector's foreboding reply. He put an arrow to his bow and looked about warily for a target. Nothing moved, nothing gave out a sound, but it seemed his nerves were screwed tight, for he suddenly wrenched back the string and shot the arrow towards a shadow beneath the trees.

It had barely flown half its course when it was struck down. A second arrow, shorter but much faster, had intercepted it in midair!

Instinctively they all crouched low.

'Who's out there? Is it Pelham's men?' Fergus whispered in dread.

'No ordinary soldier can shoot an arrow like that,' muttered Hector. He was looking back the way they had come, as if he intended fleeing.

'Hold fast, man, or I'll fix your cowardice with this!' his master threatened, brandishing his sword.

Hector stopped his thoughts of retreat but he could not stop his own fear. 'Starkey, you know the stories about that mountain ahead. No human ever goes near.'

'That arrow was fired by one of Pelham's men, I tell you,' Starkey hissed fiercely. 'But he's given himself away now. He's followed us on his own and now he's afraid to take all of us by himself. If he were going to kill us he'd have done it by now. Move, all of you, as quickly as you can. Stay close behind me,' he warned, and then he set off swiftly.

Every footstep was an agony of terror now. If one of Pelham's soldiers had been close enough to shoot at them, there might be others nearby.

An icy wind blew down from the mountain and snow began to fall, obscuring the path Starkey was trying to follow. Their teeth chattered with the cold and they had to wrap their blankets around themselves as they walked.

Late in the afternoon, Starkey announced what they had been longing to hear. 'It's there, just beyond those trees, the pass down from this mountain country. Come on, there's just enough light left if we hurry.'

Soon they had reached the rim of the escarpment, and the huge valley lay stretched out before them, shimmering in the fading light of day. Marcel remembered when he had last seen this view, from the top of the waterfall near Mrs Timmins', and later on Gadfly's back. At last he was about to descend into the valley itself.

'You can't see it yet, but just over the horizon is where our journey ends, in Elstenwyck,' Starkey informed them.

The children soon realised why this path was little used. Starkey and Hector were forced to hack a way through the undergrowth with their swords, but at least the stout bushes offered something to hang on to. In places the edge of the path dropped away into a heart-stopping abyss. When Fergus slipped on the treacherous rocks, he had to dig his fingers into the dirt and grab frantically on to the roots of a gnarled shrub to stop himself from sliding over the precipice. From time to time a loose stone would catapult into their path from above before plunging down the face of the cliff. To avoid another fall, the three children linked hands, forming a human chain. It seemed second nature to them now.

They reached the level ground of the valley just as the sky darkened into evening, sore and exhausted yet relieved.

'I was beginning to think I'd never be warm again,' gasped Marcel, dropping to his haunches to feel the day's heat still lingering in the soil.

Nicola lay full-length on an inviting stretch of grass. 'I'm just glad to stop walking,' she groaned dramatically.

For once Starkey did not turn a deaf ear to their complaints. 'We'll stop here for a little while,' he declared.

Marcel fell into a doze, but he was awoken some time later by the stamping of a horse. He sat up, confused and thinking for a moment that it was

Gadfly and Bea. This horse, though, was not dappled but dark brown from head to toe, with sturdy legs and wide, heavy hooves. This much he could see by the light of a torch Starkey was carrying. Then he noticed she was hitched to a hay wagon.

The questions flew.

'Where did it come from?'

'What do we need so much hay for?'

Starkey laughed at the last one especially. 'Do you see that farmhouse in the distance?' he asked, pointing. 'The farmer there now has more gold coins than he ever hoped to see in his life. As for the hay, you'll see soon enough.'

Yes, they saw that hay at very close range, for the best part of the night. Starkey ordered them into it and under it, checking that not a single part of them was visible, then buried himself beneath the pile as well. 'Hector is the only one who will not be recognised in an instant. He will have to drive the horse. As for the rest of us, we must stay completely out of sight.'

The hay was rough against their skin, and found its way inside their clothes, where it itched and prickled. After the freezing high country, they were now stiflingly hot under the hay. But at least there was no more walking.

They slept fitfully as the night wore on. Every so often they woke as Hector cajoled the horse to keep going, sometimes cursing or even whipping it harshly with a switch he had cut from a tree.

Roosters were beginning to stir when Hector whispered back to Starkey, 'I can see the gates ahead, but they're closed.'

'They'll open at dawn, but wait until others are crowding through on their way to market and the soldiers have no time to search.'

This was how they entered the city, under the very noses of Pelham's soldiers, who were scouring the streets. Marcel couldn't resist stealing a glimpse at the bustling place that had swallowed them up. The activity of the day was already under way, and the streets were alive with shouts and the clattering of cartwheels. Even the air seemed crowded, as houses jostled for space, their upper storeys leaning in over the narrow cobbled lanes. Sheets hung like ghosts from the washing lines strung between them. To a boy who knew only the treacherous forest and the sleepy village of Fallside, these sights and sounds were both frightening and exhilarating.

The cart lumbered on, seeking out the darkest and most deserted streets, until finally Hector turned down a dingy lane in one of the poorer districts and knocked at a nondescript double gate.

An eye appeared at a knothole soon afterwards. 'Who's there?'

The mention of Starkey's name was enough. The gates were opened by a woman who kept herself well hidden from any passers-by. The cart rumbled into a small courtyard and the gates were bolted shut again.

At last Starkey and the children could escape from beneath the hated straw.

'This is Mrs Farjeon,' said Starkey, introducing the woman. 'She's a friend of our cause who will help us while we stay in the city.'

Marcel caught a glimpse of a worried face as she led them across the courtyard. She moved with more grace than Mrs Timmins and her dark blue dress was unpatched and finer than anything that kindly woman would ever wear.

In the light of the doorway, Mrs Farjeon turned again to speak, but before she could say a word her mouth fell open at the sight of the children's faces.

'Yes, they are who you think they are, but they don't know it themselves, thanks to Alwyn's magic,' Starkey informed her. 'Now, is the cellar ready?'

'The cellar, yes, of course, Sir Thomas. Just as you ordered.'

Mrs Farjeon guided them from the courtyard into a modest two-storey house. They found themselves in a gloomy passage, and after only a dozen strides she stopped and bent low to pull up a heavy trap door. She slowly lifted a lighted candle from a bracket on the wall. 'Be careful of the steps,' she warned them, as she began to disappear through the hatchway. The children followed, descending quickly into a cellar much the same size as Mrs Timmins' dining hall, though without any windows. In the sparse light of a single candle, all they could make out was a large, comfortable-looking bed in the corner. It was the most wonderful thing they had seen for days.

'Here you are, children,' Mrs Farjeon said kindly. 'I was only expecting one of you, so you'll have to share a bed, I'm afraid.' She glanced apologetically at Starkey.

They didn't need any more encouragement than that. By the time Marcel had slipped his tortured feet out of his shoes, Nicola had already climbed under the covers. He was luxuriating in the warmth of the bed and falling rapidly towards sleep when Fergus took his place on the other side of Nicola.

Starkey and Mrs Farjeon backed away to the stairs without another word. By the time the trap door was eased into place, Marcel and his two companions were fast asleep.

CHAPTER 11

In a Cellar Beneath the City

MARCEL SLEPT ALL THE rest of the day and finally awoke at dusk to the most delicious smell in the world: bacon and eggs frying in a warm house. For days he had eaten nothing but turnips, carrots and dried meat. The aroma wafting down from above teased his nostrils in a form of delightful torture.

He realised he had been dreaming about Bea and Gadfly. He had thought of Bea many times during the journey, hoping she had arrived safely at the orphanage. Lord Alwyn and his beast must surely have been gone by the time she reached Fallside. Besides, Mrs Timmins would protect her. He didn't need to worry about her, he said over and over again in his mind, but he fretted all the same.

Slowly he became aware of things around him. This was a cellar — he remembered that much — but the room was much gloomier than when he fell asleep. In the morning a chaos of tiny holes and cracks had admitted light through the floorboards above, but now he needed the candle's light to see anything at all. Apart from the bed, the only other furniture was an ornately carved table and four matching chairs with green satin cushions on each seat. They seemed oddly out of place against the rough stone walls and floor.

Fergus was sitting in one of the chairs. 'Do you think that food cooking up there is for us?' he asked when he saw Marcel staring at him.

'I hope so,' said a voice close by. Nicola was awake now and sitting up in the other half of the bed, the pillow supporting her back as she stroked determinedly at her hair. The long journey had turned her brassy tresses into a lank and wind-tossed mess of knots that she battled to untangle.

Then Marcel noticed the fine silver hairbrush she was using. 'Where did you get that?' he asked.

'Mrs Farjeon brought it down while you two were still sleeping. She was very polite, and she *curtsied* when she gave it to me. Can you believe it?'

'She bowed to you!' Marcel laughed as he pictured it. 'Why would she do that?'

Noises at the head of the narrow staircase distracted them.

'Someone's coming,' said Fergus.

Their noses told them more than their eyes. The bacon and eggs *were* for them after all! Here they were, on a tray being carried by that same woman. They had the plates off the tray and began to attack the meal ravenously before they had even reached the table.

'I heard you stirring and thought you must be hungry,' Mrs Farjeon explained. She watched them with a smile until they were nearly finished. 'Would you like some more, Marcel?'

He nodded without even looking up from his plate. 'And you, Edwin?'

The eating stopped instantly. It was obvious whom she was talking to. 'My name! My real name!' exclaimed Fergus.

The woman put her hand to her mouth, but her eyes showed she was mortified by the mistake she had just made. 'I shouldn't have let that slip,' she said, turning hastily towards the stairs.

'Wait!' Fergus cried.

'*I'm* not to tell you anything. Only Sir Thomas,' she retorted, and before any of them could say more, she had scuttled through the trap door and disappeared.

'You know your real name at last,' said Marcel. 'Do you want us to start calling you Edwin now?'

But the question seemed to unsettle Fergus, and he hadn't managed an answer when the trap door was suddenly wrenched open and Starkey's black boots appeared on the staircase. His muddy clothes from the journey were gone, replaced by a fine silk shirt and breeches, and he had shaved off the stubble that had given him a sinister look in recent days. His handsome face was once again revealed as he stood rubbing his forefinger along the line of his jaw.

'You're wide awake at last, I see. Good. You won't be sleeping here tonight.'

'Where are we going?'

'To meet your parents, of course. It is almost time.'

'Time you told us who we are, like you promised,' asserted Marcel, taking the lead.

'I already know my real name,' said Fergus. 'That Mrs Farjeon let it slip by accident.'

'Yes, she told me of her mistake just now. My hand has been forced, I see,' Starkey conceded. 'But no harm has been done. It's time you knew, in any case. If Mrs Farjeon had dared use your full name, she should have addressed you as *Prince* Edwin.'

'Prince!' cried Fergus, scrambling to his feet so quickly his chair toppled backwards.

'The curtsy,' Marcel breathed, as he and Nicola jumped to their feet as well. He stared at the boy he had now come to know, even to like, in a cautious kind of way. But there was so much he wanted to know about himself as well.

'*My* name, Starkey,' he said, slowly, firmly, forcing Starkey to look him in the eye. 'You came halfway across the Kingdom because you had heard it. Why am I so important?'

'And me, Starkey!' Nicola demanded.

Starkey smiled. 'It seems you won't be content until I've told you everything. You'd best sit down, all of you. This story will take some time to tell.'

They settled back into their chairs, though Marcel found it difficult to keep still.

Then Starkey began. 'Before Pelham became King, this land was ruled by Queen Madeleine.' It was a name Marcel had already heard, but it was new to the other two. 'Madeleine had no children of her own, so when she grew old and frail, the people urged her to announce who should succeed her on the throne. I have already told you the names of her rightful heirs. Do you remember them?'

'Damon and Eleanor,' said Marcel, surprised that the names came to him so easily.

'Yes,' replied Starkey, impressed, 'they were niece and nephew to the old Queen. But she turned against them and named Pelham as her successor, even though he has no royal blood at all in his veins.'

'Who is he, then? Why did she choose him?' asked Marcel.

'It was the old wizard's doing. Pelham is no more than a foundling from the streets of Elstenwyck. Alwyn brought him to the palace as a boy and convinced Queen Madeleine to take him in.'

'Are you saying Lord Alwyn used his magic on her?' Fergus asked.

'All three of you have felt his powers. You can decide such things for yourselves.' He paused briefly, as though he needed to steel himself before he could say what came next. 'Surely you can guess what happened,' he continued. 'Alwyn used his magic against you to make sure Pelham stays on the throne. In fact, it was Pelham himself who gave the order. You three were to be taken away and all memory of who you are was to be wiped from your minds.'

'But who *are* we, Starkey?' Nicola urged impatiently. She pushed back her chair petulantly and rose to her feet. '*My* name,' she insisted, slapping her hand to her chest. 'What is *my* real name?'

'Young lady,' he replied, addressing her respectfully, 'you are Princess Catherine.'

Nicola stared at him, dumbfounded for a moment. 'A princess,' was all she managed to say.

Starkey turned. 'And you, Marcel. I can see in your face how much you want to know more.' He leaned back in his chair, taking delight in the delay, it seemed. He swept his arm towards Nicola. 'This girl is your sister.'

'Sister!' It was all too much. Marcel's mind could pick out only one thing at a time, and the first was this: 'Then ... then I am a prince too.'

'Yes, you two are prince and princess — and your mother should be queen. It's the gravest injustice that she is not,' he said solemnly. 'Your mother is Princess Eleanor.'

'Eleanor,' Nicola whispered, letting the name roll over her lips and tongue as though she didn't want to part with it.

The name lay on Marcel's tongue as well. At last he knew. When he had woken up in Mrs Timmins' house, with Robert for a name and little else, he thought he had lost his mother to a fever. Even after that false life was gone from his mind, the sense that his mother was dead had stayed with him, niggling, nagging, impossible to throw off with the rest of Alwyn's thwarted magic.

Now Starkey had told him the truth and he could believe it at last. 'Eleanor,' he said proudly, and if Starkey and Fergus hadn't been present he might even have gone over and hugged his newfound sister.

'And you, Prince Edwin,' said Starkey, turning to Fergus. 'Have you guessed your place in this?'

Each of Starkey's remarkable revelations had plunged Fergus deeper into his own thoughts. He was ready with his answer. 'If I was Princess Eleanor's son, then you would've told me so already. I'd be a brother to these two, but I'm not, am I?' Then, after a brief pause, he pronounced a single name, 'Damon?'

Starkey smiled, offering a simple nod of the head. 'Yes, Prince Damon is your father, and that means you are not a brother to these two, but a second cousin.'

Brother, sister, cousin ... the meaning wouldn't settle easily in any of the three. They were still too full of questions.

Nicola spoke up, careful not to catch Marcel's eyes for the moment, and if he had to be honest, he was glad of it. 'Tell us more,' she urged. 'Marcel and I must have a father and Fergus must have a mother.'

Starkey's features turned sombre. 'I'm sorry, Marcel and Catherine, but your father died fighting for Queen Madeleine. And you, Edwin, I'm afraid your mother is dead also. A fever claimed her some years ago.'

Dead, Marcel murmured to himself. So the false life Alwyn had tried to force upon him was right in one way. His father was dead after all. Just as he had done that first morning with Mrs Timmins, he searched his heart for the sorrow he should feel. He wanted to feel it so desperately, and he was incensed all over again with Lord Alwyn, who had taken even the grief for a dead father from him.

He had to know more. 'Where are they? When can we see our parents?'

'If it were a simple matter, I would have taken you to them this morning.'

'But you said you would reunite us with them. They must be in the city somewhere.'

'Oh, yes. They're here.'

'Then why —'

Starkey held up his hand, as though this would turn back the tide of their pleas. He searched the face of each of them in turn. 'It's time you knew the worst of it, I suppose. Damon and Eleanor are prisoners.'

'Who would dare to keep a prince and a princess in prison?' breathed Nicola.

'A king,' Starkey answered bluntly.

'King Pelham?'

'The usurper,' he snapped. 'Pelham had your parents arrested some time ago, because he fears them as the true and rightful heirs. You children were taken as well, though you can't remember. This is what Lord Alwyn stole from you: not just the memory of who you are, but the memory of this injustice.'

'Why? What threat were we to such a powerful man? We're only young.'

'You will not always be children. Pelham hopes that if you don't know your birthright, then you will never rise up to claim it from him, or from his children after him.'

'The King has children of his own?' Marcel asked.

'Oh, yes. Youngsters still. But they're of no account. When Pelham falls, his brood will fall with him. That's why I have brought you here. Up until now, it has been impossible to release Damon and Eleanor from their prison.'

'You mean there are too many guards?' asked Fergus, as ever the one to think like a soldier.

'No, none at all.'

'Then how —'

Starkey put up his hand again. 'This fiendish kind of prison doesn't need guards or heavy locks. It's magic that keeps it sealed.'

Marcel thought of the strange door into the tower above Mrs Timmins' orphanage, a door with no handle and no lock. 'Lord Alwyn,' he breathed.

Starkey nodded solemnly, then slowly a smile began to curl the corners of his mouth. 'Don't despair, Marcel. You above all should know how magic works. Was there not a way to rid yourself of that ring? Alwyn left a key to your parents' prison, though he never imagined it might be used to free them.'

'A key. Do you have it, Starkey?'

'Oh yes, I have it here in this room with me. Do you understand yet?' he asked, teasing them. 'You three are the key that will free Damon and Eleanor from their prison.'

CHAPTER 12

The True and Rightful Heirs

THE HOUSE HAD GONE ghostly quiet and there was no one to be seen when the four figures stole up through the trap door. Starkey had told them his plan and they were stunned at how simple it seemed, but he had brought them this far without faltering and they would have trusted him with their lives.

'First we have to get you inside the palace grounds. Here, put these on,' Starkey ordered, handing each of them one of the dark cloaks he had ready in the hallway, while clutching a lighted candle in his other hand. 'Pull the hoods over your heads as soon as we're outside.'

'Where is the Book?' Marcel asked.

'It can't help us tonight, but I have it safe, don't you worry, and it will come into its own in the weeks ahead, I'm sure of it.'

They hurried into a large enclosed carriage that waited in the lane beside the house. Hector sat on the driver's box with the reins in his hands. Even his battle-scarred face could not hide his apprehension. They were heading into the very heart of their enemy's lair.

Starkey tapped lightly on the roof and the carriage lurched ahead. The children could see nothing, because heavy curtains shrouded them from any curious eyes that might look into the carriage along the way.

After ten minutes of slow progress they stopped and Starkey ordered them out. Marcel found himself staring beyond the rooftops at a forest of towers and turrets that rose up like spectres.

'The palace,' he breathed in awe.

'Yes, we are still two streets away from the walls. Follow me,' Starkey whispered, taking the lead.

They walked on unnoticed until the palace walls came into sight. There was a small gate silhouetted ahead, not the grand entrance to the palace grounds but a side opening. 'For servants coming to and fro,' Starkey explained.

Beyond the crisscrossed bars they could see the gatekeeper, who was getting on in years, judging by the weary stoop of his shoulders inside his scarlet uniform.

'Now,' Starkey whispered. 'And remember, say only what I've told you to say.'

It had come as a surprise, especially to Nicola, who was the oldest, that only Fergus was to speak to the guard. Starkey had been most insistent about this.

'Good evening, sir,' Fergus called through the bars.

The guard came out of his doze with a start. 'Who's there?'

'There are three of us. You must let us in.'

The old soldier held up his flaming torch but he still couldn't see their faces. 'Aren't you a bit young to be out at this time of night? What business could three children like you possibly have in the palace?'

'You'll know when you see our faces, Joseph.'

These were the words Starkey had told him to use, including the man's name. 'Pretend you know him,' he'd said, 'for he will know you.'

This was the moment. Fergus raised his hands to his hood, turning briefly to see that the others had done the same, then he let it slip from his head so that the light of Joseph's torch flooded his face.

The man stepped back as though he had been slapped. 'Prince Edwin!' he breathed.

Looking behind Fergus, he gasped again. 'Princess Catherine — and Prince Marcel too! But you three were banished into exile. Only the King knows where. What are you doing outside my gate?'

'We've come back to be with my father. Open the gate, Joseph,' Fergus ordered.

Distracted by his own astonishment, the old guard fumbled nervously with the key at his belt until he managed to fit it into the lock and the gate swung open.

Within moments, Starkey emerged silently behind him. With a savage blow to the old gatekeeper's head he sent him crashing to the hard gravel.

'What did you do that for?' Marcel demanded angrily.

'Quiet!' Starkey barked as he picked up the burning torch and unhooked the key from the guard's belt.

'Is he dead?'

'No, he'll recover, but you'd better pray he doesn't wake up until we're long gone from the palace grounds. Quickly, that way,' he commanded, pointing into the darkness. To their left, the palace with its looming towers rose up like a huge beast, overwhelming in its bulk, with some of its windows blinking and still alight.

'Are we going inside there?' Fergus asked.

'No — and keep your faces hidden,' Starkey reminded them harshly.

In the darkness, with the hoods drawn tightly around their heads, the three children could barely see a step in front of them. But their other senses were not as easily blunted, and when the heady scent of roses swam about them they knew they were in a garden of some kind.

'Stop here!' Starkey ordered suddenly. He had seen something up ahead.

'Is it another guard?' Nicola whispered.

Marcel dared a peek over the rose bushes and saw a woman illuminated by the torch she carried. Her head hung low, and from the tiny shudders that racked her shoulders, it was clear she was crying.

'Stay behind me and don't say a word,' Starkey commanded them as he pulled his own hood over his head.

The woman turned as their footsteps crushed the gravel of the narrow path. They could see now that she was standing before a tablet of white marble with a single word carved in the centre.

ASHLERE

'Who's there?' called the woman anxiously.

'Excuse me, My Lady,' said Starkey, holding the hood in place as he bowed. 'I'm escorting these scullery hands to the servants' gate. If I may be so bold, it is very late to be wandering the palace gardens. A guard might mistake you for an intruder.'

'Perhaps you're right. I should go. It's just that the King ordered fresh flowers for ...' She didn't finish, nodding towards the white stone instead as she added in a melancholy voice, 'As if there aren't enough blooms here already.'

She walked slowly away towards the palace itself. Once her forlorn figure had faded into the gloom of the unlit path they hurried on. In his haste, the hood fell back from Fergus's face, letting him see clearly what lay ahead. His gasp made the other two follow his gaze. There it was, a simple stone pavilion standing alone in the darkened gardens, pale yellow light from within escaping in shafts through the narrow windows, like the oars of a grand ship dipping into black waters.

'Do you see?' whispered Starkey. 'There is no sentry at the door. The King and his magician think there is no chance of escape. Come on, it's time to prove them wrong.'

They quickly crossed the last twenty paces to the door of the chamber, which was protected by a small, enclosed alcove. The scent of jasmine drifted gently from the vines that grew in tight webs across the stone. In the centre was a single wooden door with an ornate brass handle on one side. When Starkey held his torch closer they could see an inscription carved into the wood.

> *To common folk this door is locked*
> *But try it if you dare*
> *This gilded cage will only yield*
> *To a true and rightful heir*

Starkey took hold of the handle and pushed down with all his strength, but it wouldn't move. 'Look closely,' he told them. 'There's no space for a key. Lord Alwyn's magic keeps this door shut tight.' He pointed to the inscription. 'Only a true heir to the Crown can open it.'

'But my father,' Fergus blurted out. 'He should be King. Surely he's a true heir to the throne. Why can't he open the door himself?'

'Everyone in the entire Kingdom has asked that same question. They think it means that the cousins are not the true heirs to the throne. But they have all been fooled. No one knows of the cruel trick Lord Alwyn has played on Damon and Eleanor. No one but me.'

'A trick?' asked Marcel tentatively.

Starkey turned to him, his eyes flaming more brightly than the torch he held. 'There is no handle on the inside.'

He turned suddenly and threw his arm wide. 'Look around you, at the palace and these gardens. Each day, as your parents' meals are passed through the windows, they must look out at this beauty, yet the windows are too narrow to allow escape and the door is cruelly locked, as you see. It is all part of their torment, to be so close and know that all they can see is rightfully theirs, if only they could free themselves to claim it. Do you see now what kind of men Pelham and his sorcerer are?'

'But Starkey, you told us *we* could open the door.' Marcel couldn't work it out.

'Don't you see? You three are heirs to the throne through your parents. That's why Pelham had you sent away and had your minds wiped clean by Alwyn's magic. And that's why I stole you back again, from right under his nose, so that you can set them free.'

Fergus was standing closest to the door. Starkey grabbed the boy's arm and pushed his hand onto the cold brass of the lever. 'Any of you can do it. Quickly, open the door.'

With Starkey hovering eagerly behind him and the other two watching and barely able to breathe, Fergus pressed down hard on the handle.

It wouldn't move.

Starkey's eyes widened in horror. 'I don't understand it. The verse is plain. The door should yield to the hand of a true and rightful heir.'

Marcel glanced quickly at Nicola. Was Starkey mad after all? Had they come all this way only to see their plans defeated by a simple door?

But Starkey was made of sterner stuff than this. He swallowed hard, forcing down his panic. 'The rightful heirs,' he muttered to himself, and when he looked up, determination shone in his face again. 'All three of you. Try it again, with all of you touching the handle.'

Marcel reached forward cautiously until his fingers met the cold brass. 'You too, Nicola,' he urged. Her hand joined his, and with one final glance at each other, all three pressed down together.

The handle offered no resistance, as though a feather alone could make it move. The door opened and light from within the chamber flooded out as the children peered inside.

Starkey stepped quickly through the door. 'It's late. They'll be asleep in their beds. Watch for the palace guard while I fetch them. I may be a little time.'

He left the door only an inch open, so that the alcove grew dim. There were voices, low and whispering, punctuated by gasps of disbelief. 'The Prince and Princess!' they heard a woman's voice exclaim. They heard more whispers, but they couldn't make out a single word.

At last there were footsteps. The door opened wide and two astonished faces stared out at them.

One was that of a woman more beautiful than any Marcel had ever seen. She wore a white dress of rich elegance and even in the half-dark of the alcove, her regal poise was unmistakable. She stared at him for a moment, her perfect features swept by doubt, by amazement, and yes, by fear. 'Is it true, Starkey?' she gasped. 'They have no memory of who they truly are?'

'Yes. It is all exactly as I told you. Alwyn's magic has taken everything. They don't even know your faces.'

This seemed enough to convince her. She stepped forward and took Nicola tightly in her arms. But of course it was a different name that she whispered. 'Catherine. Oh Catherine, look at you!' she exclaimed. 'And Marcel!'

Marcel suddenly found himself embraced by those same arms, while close by a man's voice called, 'Edwin, you're alive! I've been desperately worried.'

A tall figure stepped from behind the woman and swept his arms around Fergus's shoulders, hugging the boy to his chest. Damon was as tall as Starkey, with the same regal bearing Marcel had seen in his mother's gracious movements. He was fair-haired, and though the shadows did not allow a proper view of his face, the lines of his chin and nose were strong, as if they had been carved from the stone of his prison.

'There's no time for this!' Starkey barked. 'We have to leave!'

Princess Eleanor loosened her hold. 'Come, give your mother a kiss before we go,' she said to Nicola, who obliged willingly.

Starkey wouldn't have it. 'We *must* go, now!' He had already set out into the darkness of the garden.

The enchanted door gaped open still, light spilling out like gold from a treasure chest. Before he joined the rest, Damon stepped back into the alcove and pulled it shut with the gentlest of clicks.

They bolted back through the garden towards the servants' gate. By now the unfortunate Joseph was moaning weakly and clutching his aching head, but he was in no condition to stop them or even raise the alarm.

Starkey wrenched the gate open and moments later they emerged into the street outside the palace wall. Hector had brought the carriage from the nearby street and now sat holding the reins tightly to keep the skittish horses from pulling away. 'Quickly,' he hissed.

They crowded inside without a care for who was first or who was last, and before the door was even closed the clatter of horses' hooves began to echo along the deserted street. Marcel found himself on one side of his mother, Nicola on the other. Opposite them sat the familiar figure of Starkey, with Prince Damon in the middle and Fergus wedged against the window.

Free of the palace, thought Marcel with relief, but immediately his mind filled with a new worry. 'The city gates ... you told me yourself, Starkey, they're locked until dawn. How can we escape in a carriage like this? The guard will want to look inside, and —'

'Quiet, boy, you'll see soon enough. In a city like Elstenwyck, there is one thing that will make even the most vigilant guard leave his post.'

The menacing hint in Starkey's voice touched Marcel's heart with dread. What was he talking about? What danger, what threat could be feared more than any other?

Only minutes later, Hector reined in the cantering horses in a narrow lane, and brought the carriage to a halt at the entrance to the stables of an inn. Marcel watched through a break in the curtains as Hector jumped down and pretended to unhitch the horses, as though this inn were his journey's end.

They could hear his footsteps on the cobblestones as he moved further up the lane. 'I can see the gate and the guardhouse beside it,' Hector whispered. 'No sign of any soldiers.'

'They will be inside, some of them sleeping no doubt,' Starkey responded sourly. He slipped silently from the carriage towards the stables and for a brief instant Marcel could see out into the night through the open door. It was dark in the courtyard housing the stables, but Marcel glimpsed Starkey fumbling with something in his hands as he darted towards a huge mound of hay. Marcel saw a glint of pale yellow crystal.

'Brimstone!' hissed Prince Damon, who had seen it too.

'What is he going to do?' Fergus asked, as curious as Marcel to know what Starkey had in his hands.

In reply, Damon merely pressed his fingers to his lips. The crease of his brow showed that he had guessed what Starkey was about to do and that it disturbed him. The repeated sound of something hard striking metal had him even more worried.

The old guard, Joseph, might have raised the alarm by now. There could be soldiers galloping towards each of the city gates at that moment, while their carriage sat here, like a ship becalmed at sea.

Starkey leaped back into the carriage, leaving the whinnying of frightened horses in his wake. As the carriage stole further down the curving lane, Marcel pushed back the curtain to take another peek. He saw the sky grow unnaturally bright and heard a muffled crackling noise fill the air. A terrified shout put his worst fears into words.

'Fire! Fire!'

Now, in the still night air, he could hear footsteps on cobbles and doors opening and closing as guests were roused from their beds. A man was bellowing in alarm. 'Quickly, everyone! Man the buckets. The inn is on fire!'

People were beginning to stream out of the inn and surrounding houses, one man stuffing a nightshirt into his breeches, another trying to slip on his shoes as he ran. Some were still red-eyed and staggering after a night's heavy drinking. 'Fire! Fire!' the desperate cry went up. Marcel looked on, appalled.

From this angle Marcel could see the gate and the guardhouse across a cobblestoned square. Two soldiers stood watching the growing panic and a third joined them from the door of the guardhouse, wiping the sleep from his eyes before he slipped a tunic over his head. They conferred only briefly before they broke away to join the rush of bodies hurrying to fight the fire.

'It's working!' Starkey said gleefully to Damon and Eleanor. 'There's only one soldier left to guard the gate now, and if we hold our nerve, soon there will be none.'

Marcel was still looking out into the street as Starkey spoke. He could just see the deadly orange flames licking the inn's rooftop. The harsh light caught the faces of men and women and even children who rushed to fight the fire and he saw in their features the dread of great danger.

'Fire,' he whispered to himself. He knew then what threat Starkey had spoken of. He thought of the many houses he had seen crowded so closely together.

'You started this fire!' he accused him, scarcely believing his own words.

'Of course I did. A fire in one house can destroy a hundred if it isn't put out quickly. Every soul in Elstenwyck knows that, and so they've come running, a bucket in each hand, even the guards from the gate.'

'No!' cried Nicola. 'It's too cruel. That innkeeper will lose everything. And what about all his guests?'

'It's a small price to pay to unseat a false king,' said Eleanor coldly, surprising them with the harshness of her tone.

'But what if someone is trapped inside? They'll be burned to death!' exclaimed Fergus, his voice full of outrage.

'Then let's hope that last soldier runs off in time to save them,' Damon answered, without the faintest echo of Fergus's disgust.

'He's wavering,' Hector called from outside the carriage. 'The last guard, he's ...' The voice paused, while inside the carriage the tension built. 'Yes, he's moving, he's running to help!'

Marcel tried to see for himself but this time Starkey caught him. 'Leave that curtain closed,' he snapped, and so Marcel, like Nicola and Fergus, could only guess at what was happening by the movement and the sounds. The carriage lurched forward, the clip-clop of its horses' hooves barely heard over the shouts of those fighting the fire.

Then they stopped, and the dull scrape of wood against wood told them that the heavy cross beam was being hauled aside. The creak of hinges followed. Seconds later, they were moving rapidly again, through the gate and free of the city.

Princess Eleanor clapped her hands to her chest and let out a relieved sigh.

Damon slapped Starkey on the back. 'A brilliant plan, brilliant!' he proclaimed, all sign of his earlier misgivings gone now that the fire had done its job.

It was dark inside the carriage, so Marcel could not see anyone's faces. He could guess at the expressions he would find on his mother's face and Prince Damon's, from their callous words. But what of Nicola and Fergus? Were they as heart-sick as he felt himself?

On impulse, he parted the curtain again and pushed his head through, staring back towards the city walls. An eerie red glow could easily be seen above the rooftops.

'Marcel, get your head inside before you're seen!' seethed Starkey as he tugged at the boy's shirt.

Marcel resisted long enough to see a vicious tongue of flame shoot above the drifting sparks, then Starkey won the tug of war and he was hauled back through the curtained window.

As he settled miserably into the darkness beside his mother, words began to bubble up to his lips until he could not hold them in. They spilled out soundlessly, just once, but this was all Marcel needed to recognise where they had come from.

When Lord and Ladies quest for fame
A Beast will touch the land with flame

HECTOR MARSHALLED THE STAMINA of their horses skilfully throughout the night. When the first light crept into the carriage, Marcel stirred and looked around him. Everyone was still asleep except for Nicola. She acknowledged him with a nod and a smile, but before he could speak she gestured to him to stay silent. She was inviting him to inspect their mother, as she was doing.

The Princess sat with one hand over the other, resting on her thigh. Even in sleep she managed to hold her shoulders back in a regal pose, as though she were sitting on a throne. The light increased its intensity, catching the shimmering white of her fine silken gown.

Nicola reached up, daring herself to touch the delicate gold chain hung with a single pearl that shone out from beneath the soft, pale brown tresses. And that face was as perfect as they remembered from last night, proud and refined.

As if she sensed their dazzled gazes, Eleanor opened her eyes, and Nicola quickly snatched her hand away. But Eleanor extended hers to stroke the girl's cheek, smiling affectionately. 'Would you like to wear it? Here,' she said, unfastening the catch. 'It's yours.'

Nicola fought back tears as she clipped the chain's clasp behind her neck.

Marcel watched this gift pass between mother and daughter and wondered what she might give *him*. He already knew what he wanted most, to feel the affection towards her that he must have felt once, before Lord Alwyn used his magic. It will come, he assured himself. Be patient. She is my mother and I'll soon learn to love her once more.

Starkey stirred suddenly, and after a brief stretch and a yawn he called to Hector, 'Find a place off the road where we won't be seen.'

Shortly afterwards, the horses slowed and the carriage swayed awkwardly as they bumped their way into a dense thicket of trees. Hector was soon handing a large chest and a sack of supplies down to Starkey from the roof of the carriage. The first held clothing — mostly dresses for the Princess, it seemed. Eleanor took a silver hand-mirror from it and a matching hairbrush which the children recognised from the cellar. She began to brush her hair, and when she was finished she did the same to Nicola, whose face flushed with happiness.

'Girls!' Marcel commented to Fergus. They turned their attention to a breakfast of fruit, cold bacon and freshly baked bread with no turnips or dried venison in sight.

Hector gobbled down a few mouthfuls and wandered off to a nearby clump of trees to catch up on some rest.

As they watched him go, their eyes meandered towards the farmland that stretched unbrokenly to the horizon. The nearest field was planted with shrivelled stalks of corn. The sun was still only halfway into the sky, yet already its heat danced in waves above the ground. A handful of dispirited cattle watched them from a rise not far away, the bones of their ribcages pressing through their scraggy hides.

'Is it always this dry?' Marcel asked Starkey, who shook his head.

'It's never been this bad before. It hasn't rained for a year now. The weather had better change soon or people will starve.'

'It's Pelham's doing,' said Eleanor, interrupting them. 'The land is dying. Isn't it plain to see? It's because this kingdom is in the grip of evil: Alwyn's magic and Pelham's lies. A usurper sits on the throne, and until he is dead the drought will continue.'

Marcel looked out at the parched fields and the sadly withered corn, and realised she was right. Sorcery had done this; there could be no other explanation. Sorcery ... suddenly an idea hit him. Could magic be used to defeat magic?

'Can the Book help us?' he asked Starkey, who had stood silent and solemn while Eleanor spoke.

'What book?' asked the Princess.

Starkey seemed reluctant to answer, so Marcel jumped in ahead of him.

'The Book of Lies,' he said. He hurried to the chest, where he had noticed the leather bag stowed away neatly. 'Here it is!' he cried eagerly as he withdrew the Book from inside. 'Lord Alwyn is weaker without it. You said so yourself, didn't you, Starkey?'

It was hard to judge which of the cousins was more stunned. 'You didn't tell us about this,' snapped Eleanor, her voice rising with every word. She was suddenly very angry.

'There was no time.'

'But the Book of Lies, Starkey. Don't you remember what it did to us?' Damon interjected.

'And to these three, as well,' Starkey responded emphatically. As soon as Damon heard this, whatever he had been going to say died on his lips.

'Bring the Book here, Marcel,' Starkey commanded.

As soon as Marcel held the Book out before him, Starkey spoke to it. 'Lord Alwyn's magic is waning. He won't be Master of the Books for much longer. He would never have let this book fall into our hands if he were still the force he once was.'

The Book of Lies burned brighter than the sun above them. A loud gasp escaped from Eleanor.

'See? It is the truth, just as I suspected,' Starkey declared triumphantly.

'We must talk about this book later, Starkey,' announced Damon. 'Put it away for now. I can't bear to look at it.'

As Starkey did so, Eleanor spoke up. 'Hopefully we won't even need Alwyn's book with what you have planned, Damon.'

'You'll need soldiers, won't you? I can fight for you,' Fergus offered excitedly, looking at his father.

He regretted it, though, when both Damon and Starkey laughed in his face. Humiliated, he went on the attack, 'Where are you going to get these soldiers, then? It'll take a whole army to defeat Pelham.'

'Yes, an army,' Damon replied calmly. 'And that's where we're going now. To join it.'

'You mean you already have an army, waiting for us?' questioned Nicola.

Damon glanced at Starkey and Eleanor. 'Does it matter what they know?' he asked.

'Go ahead, tell them. If Pelham's soldiers catch us before we reach the border we'll all die anyway,' said

Eleanor, alarming the children with her matter-of-factness.

Damon began. 'When I was younger, my mother urged me to test my courage in battle. Elster was at peace, as it has been for so long, so I travelled to Lenoth Crag and fought many battles until Queen Madeleine demanded I return to the palace. But by then I had helped a young chieftain named Zadenwolf to make himself King, the first king the mountain tribes have ever known. They're a savage lot, who dwell in tents rather than towns and have little respect for authority. But they have accepted Zadenwolf as their leader and now they are slowly becoming civilised. It's these men who will knock Pelham off his throne.'

The children could hardly contain their amazement.

Damon hesitated a moment, staring along the road into the far distance. 'We head east from here until we leave Elster and enter the grasslands of Grenvey. Then, when we have travelled far enough, we will climb north into the mountains of Lenoth Crag.'

Hector returned at this point and they set off again, travelling towards the sun until finally it was directly overhead.

The children were beginning to doze when Hector called down urgently from his seat. 'Starkey, there are riders ahead, coming towards us. They're wearing red.'

'Pelham's men!'

Starkey and Damon drew their swords. The ruby-handled dagger appeared in Starkey's left hand.

'Stay inside the carriage,' he snapped at the children. 'Especially you,' he added, with a meaningful glance towards Fergus, who looked almost disappointed. The other two just looked terrified.

'Hold there,' came the call from the leading soldier. 'We're looking for some children missing from the high country.'

'There's only my master and mistress in this carriage,' Hector assured them coolly.

The creak of saddle leather told them that two of the soldiers were dismounting to look for themselves.

'As soon as they open the door ...' whispered Starkey.

He was true to his own order. The unlucky soldier who pulled down on the handle died where he stood, a horrified look on his face and Starkey's dagger through his heart.

Damon followed Starkey out of the carriage and together they rapidly cut down the second soldier with their swords. The two who remained were on horseback still, but the speed and savagery of the attack left them stunned. They were outnumbered as well, now that Hector had jumped down from his seat, also swinging his sword.

'Away!' hollered one of the soldiers. His companion didn't need any more urging. They both turned their horses and fled.

'Stop them!' Damon shouted, but Starkey's legs were no match for the frightened horses.

'We can't let them escape!' Damon raged, his furious roar echoing into the distance.

It had barely died away when a soft *thwang* sounded above their heads. Before they could work out what it was, one of the fleeing soldiers jerked suddenly in his saddle and fell backwards over the horse's rump.

Marcel turned to see Hector with his bow in hand, already fitting a second arrow to the string.

'Again, before the other one gets away!' Damon shouted urgently.

Hector took aim and let the arrow fly. Down, down, it came, on target it seemed, until the point buried itself in the road's surface just paces behind the galloping horse.'

'Try again!' he thundered.

'He's out of range, Your Highness,' Hector replied.

Starkey let forth a savage curse. 'He's heading east, where we have to go. There'll be more of Pelham's men ahead. They'll stop us before we can leave the Kingdom!'

'We can go ahead on foot, staying off the roads, Starkey,' Hector suggested.

'A hundred miles is a long way to walk, and by the time we've covered just one the countryside will be crawling with more of Pelham's soldiers.'

'There is a shorter route,' said Damon in a rather ominous tone, turning to stare over his left shoulder.

Starkey's eyes flashed to meet Damon's, clearly trying to guess what he was talking about. It came to him suddenly, bringing a touch of doubt even to that unflinching gaze. 'Shorter, yes, Your Highness, but impossible. No one has ever reached Lenoth Crag that way.'

'Which is precisely why Pelham will not send his men after us if we follow that route. From my days fighting with Zadenwolf I know of a little-used pass through the mountains into Lenoth Crag.'

Damon and Starkey and finally Eleanor stood staring into the distance. What were they looking at?

'The mountain!' cried Marcel, with sudden realisation. 'But Starkey, don't you remember that arrow? What if it wasn't one of Pelham's men? It might have been some kind of warning, to make sure we didn't go any closer.'

Starkey ignored him. 'Perhaps you're right, Damon. We must go where Pelham's men will never think to look for us. North, through the forest, via the only part of the escarpment that's not too steep to climb.'

'But Starkey,' objected Hector, 'the old stories. There are good reasons why no one has dared go near that mountain for hundreds of years.'

'Superstitions,' he retorted. 'There may be nothing at all to fear on that mountain.'

Eleanor looked along the road where the dust from the fleeing horse had recently settled. 'If we don't take the risk, Pelham will make us prisoners. I'm not going back to the chamber,' she seethed. 'I would rather die.'

'So would I,' said Damon, with equal vehemence.

'That settles the matter, then,' Starkey declared. 'Back into the carriage. Hector, I'll take the reins for a while. We can be at the foot of the mountain by nightfall. Tomorrow, we climb.'

CHAPTER 13

Long Beard

THEY REACHED THE BASE of the great
escarpment just as the sun was setting. It can
be a long, uneasy night when dawn promises
such danger. Marcel might have lain awake through
most of it if the day's journey through the dusty
farmlands had not been so exhausting. But before he
knew it, the sun was stabbing at his eyes and it was
morning.

They hid the carriage as best they could and
released the weary horses from where they were
tethered. The chest would have to be left behind,
though Eleanor insisted upon her silver brush and
mirror and Starkey was hardly going to abandon the
Book of Lies. Their only other luggage was the sack of

provisions, which Hector slung over his shoulder. Of all the wary faces that set off on the climb that morning, his was the most anxious.

The track Starkey found for climbing the cliff face had been made by wandering sheep. For human feet, it was narrow and treacherous. The weary struggle uphill, combined with the nameless dread that had settled on them all, made their trek twice as arduous as the descent three days earlier. Eleanor had exchanged her white gown for one of deep blue velvet, but its hem was quickly soiled. Her face wore an expression of disdain that clearly told them she found this upward toiling unfit for a princess.

Slowly, though, the valley began to recede below them and the air grew cooler, until finally they emerged onto the lower slopes of the mountain itself.

Hector put an arrow to his bow. That same sense that they were being watched took hold of Marcel.

'Careful you don't shoot one of us with that,' Damon scolded him. 'What's so frightening about this place, anyway?'

He soon regretted those words when a rustling noise echoed through the trees. They looked up the steep slope on their left to see a stone, no bigger than a man's fist, tumbling towards them.

A warning.

Soon after this, a second rock came crashing through the undergrowth, closer and more threatening.

Next there was a mighty roar, as frightening as Termagant's growl. It resounded off the trees, so that it was impossible to judge where it had come from. Was it the mountain itself, calling down to them from its invisible summit?

'We have to go back,' asserted Hector, who looked ready to drop his sword and run.

'Hold your ground!' Starkey roared at him.

It was too late to run. The air was suddenly thick with arrows flying in every direction, and all they could do was wait to feel their deadly sting.

Eleanor pressed herself against the trunk of a tree. To her obvious relief, an arrow merely found the wedge of space between her splayed fingers. Another landed in the ground between Fergus's feet. As for Marcel, he heard an arrow lodge in the tree above him. He even felt the faint breeze it created. When he dared reach up and touch it, he discovered that it had missed his scalp by less than an inch. Not one arrow had pierced human flesh.

He jumped with the rest, though, when Starkey called out, 'Listen to me, whoever you are. We mean you no harm. We just want to travel round your mountain, to our allies in the kingdom of Lenoth Crag.'

Silence lingered like a moody ghost in that eerie corner of the forest. No one moved. They did not dare go forward. They would not go back.

Finally, another rock bounced lightly against a tree, rolled a little way then stopped hard up against an exposed root. It seemed like an announcement, and moments later a figure stood up, letting himself be seen in a patch of sunlight. He was no bigger than any of the little girls who lived with Mrs Timmins, although an impressive brown beard sprouted from his chin. His breeches and jacket were dark green — or were they a deep brown? It was hard to tell. Then he shifted slightly and was gone.

A closer rustling noise grabbed Marcel's attention and there, only five feet from his elbow, stood another little figure, just like the first, and behind him another. Now there were three surrounding him, each with a bow in his hands and an arrow ready to fly. All three of those arrows were aimed straight at his heart. His whole body froze, and only his eyes dared to look around at the others. To his terror, he found that they had all been taken prisoner in the same way.

Who were these folk?

Even Eleanor had lost her tongue. So had Starkey and Damon. It was the terrified Hector who mouthed a single, trembling word. 'Elves.'

At this, one of their captors spoke up cheerfully. 'That's right. We're elves and you are trespassing,' he announced, in a voice that was strangely deep for one of his stature. 'Not the first time either, for most of you. I've seen all but two of them before,' he informed his companions.

'Yes, the tall one in black was leading them,' added another. 'On the far side of the mountain, it was.'

Fergus was close enough to Marcel to risk a few whispered words. 'These are the ones who stalked us. But how can they just appear out of nowhere like that?'

Appear out of nowhere! Marcel knew someone else who had the same disconcerting habit. He looked more closely at the elves around him, at their nut-brown skin and wild unkempt hair, and marvelled at how much they reminded him of Bea. Yet for all their similarities, Bea had the gestures and the look of a human being which these elves somehow lacked.

Starkey broke the tension when he asked in his typically blunt style, 'Which of you is leader?'

'Leader!' called an even deeper voice from the shadows. The humans' eyes darted everywhere but they could not see who had spoken. 'I am King of these proud folk, and an honour it is, too,' continued the voice, though the speaker still would not let himself be seen.

'King. Of course. Please accept my apologies, Your Majesty,' Starkey responded deferentially, ending with a gracious bow.

Marcel exchanged a surprised glance with Nicola and Fergus. Humility from Starkey?

'Majesty,' one of the elves whispered jeeringly. Then the word was repeated with a snigger by all of them.

Suddenly a new figure appeared among them. He carried no weapon, not even a sword hanging from his belt, which strained mightily to contain a massive stomach, disconcerting on a frame so small. But the most startling feature of this new arrival was his beard. Thick and uniformly grey, it stretched almost to his knees.

'My name is Long Beard,' he said, observing their stares, 'and this is what makes me King of the Elves,' he added, stroking his impressive growth with a stubby-fingered hand. 'A long beard means I have had many years to grow wise. When I die, the elf with the longest beard will take my place, and my name as well, just as I took it from the King before me. Make no mistake, though: my subjects might laugh when you call me "majesty" but they will riddle you with arrows on one command from me.'

His voice had been light, almost friendly at first, but he ended seriously to show this was no idle threat. Nevertheless, he ordered the intimidating bows lowered. 'Now,' he continued, in the same harsh tone, 'why won't you heed our warnings and leave, the way you came?'

'We can't,' pleaded Starkey. 'We'll be taken prisoner if we go back.'

'That is no concern of ours. We don't want you travelling through our lands.'

'But this is a desperate matter, King Long Beard,' Eleanor urged him. 'It's not just our lives at stake. The kingdom down there in the valley is crying out for help. I am Princess Eleanor and this is Prince Damon.' She motioned to her cousin. 'We are the rightful rulers of

Elster, and are seeking to regain our throne. Justice has deserted the Kingdom. People will die.'

'*People*, yes. It is a matter for human beings alone. We elves are happy and at peace, but only because we have kept ourselves separate from human affairs.'

Long Beard stood with folded arms and a firmly set jaw, waiting impatiently for them to retreat. The situation seemed hopeless.

It was then that a figure came to stand beside the Elf-king, a little figure Marcel recognised instantly.

'Bea!' he cried.

He was running towards her before the echo of his shout had died among the trees. Elves raised their bows in panic and aimed at this crazy human charging towards their king.

'Hold!' Long Beard ordered his warriors.

'Bea, Bea!' Marcel kept yelling, until he stopped only a step away from her and took both of her hands in his.

Marcel was suddenly aware of countless pairs of eyes upon him. His mother and the other adults were staring at him in astonishment. Even Nicola and Fergus were dumbfounded, since they too had not been told of Bea's escape.

'What are you doing here?' Marcel asked Bea excitedly. 'I was sure you went back to Fallside.'

She gave a little laugh and shook her head. 'I couldn't go back to Lord Alwyn! Not with Termagant ready to bite me in half.'

'But when I came back to look for you, you'd disappeared. I thought you were afraid of the forest.'

'Afraid! No. I tried to tell you, Marcel. It was the most beautiful place I had ever seen. I felt alive, at home, for the first time in my life.'

'Then you didn't ride Gadfly back to Mrs Timmins', like Starkey said?'

Starkey's ears pricked up at the sound of his name and he finally understood. 'So this is the little girl you mentioned, Marcel,' and he turned to recount the story to Damon and Eleanor.

In the meantime another thought had occurred to Marcel. 'Bea, Gadfly ... is she still out there, roaming around in the forest?'

'No, she's here, with me. The elves don't have much use for a horse. They wanted to eat her but I told them about ... well, you know,' she concluded with a wink, in case anyone was listening. 'Come on, I'll take you to her now.'

She led the way across the rugged terrain of the mountainside until at last they arrived at a secluded clearing, where they found Gadfly contentedly cropping grass. She fixed Marcel with a look that said, About time you showed up.

He came up and affectionately smoothed her mane. Then he turned back to Bea, able to question her alone at last. 'What happened back there in the forest?'

'I saw them, Marcel. They thought I wouldn't, but I caught them out.'

'Who?'

'Two elves who were hunting a long way from this mountain. They were used to humans who can't see into shadows, but they hadn't counted on me.'

'Bea,' he murmured, barely believing what he was about to say. 'You're one of them. You are an elf.'

'*Part* of her is elfish,' Long Beard interrupted. He had followed them to the clearing on silent feet. 'You are the famous Marcel, is that so? This one has told me a lot about you,' he said warmly, nodding towards Bea. 'It is hard to make her speak of anything else. Cruel wizards, forgotten lives and a boy who saved her from a snarling monster.'

'Oh, but she's braver than me,' Marcel objected. 'Believe me, I know as much about her as you do.'

Long Beard laughed heartily. 'I'm sure you do, but it's time I told you something about Bea that you *don't* know.'

'How she became the way she is?'

'In a manner of speaking.' Long Beard nodded, causing the grey cascade of hair streaming down from his chin to flop against his ample chest. With a glance at Marcel's eager face, he sighed and began his tale.

'I once had a daughter, a beautiful girl, who liked to roam in the forest, much further from this mountain than she should. She would sit and watch humans felling trees. One of these men caught her eye. She thought herself in love and did what no elf should ever do. She showed herself to him. The man took her to his village, where she lived as his wife until a baby was born. Soon after that, the man set out to seek his fortune, leaving my daughter and the little one with his family. But these folk were afraid of her and thought she practised witchcraft. They forced her out of their home and the baby with her. Too ashamed to come home to her own kind in the forest, she strayed from village to village, until at last she was too weak to go on and all she could do was lie down by the side of the road to die.'

He paused, his own throat tight with a father's grief. His next words were heavy with sadness and regret. 'We know this because she was found by elves on a forest track, and before she died, she was able to tell of her trials.'

'The baby,' Marcel breathed. 'The baby wasn't with her?'

'No,' Long Beard answered solemnly. 'All we have ever known about that baby came from my daughter's dying words. A church, she said. She had left her baby at the door of a church.'

Marcel gasped. 'Bea, the story you told me, back in Fallside. You were found on the steps —'

'Yes, of a church,' said Long Beard with a tear clouding one eye. 'You humans called her a foundling. Well, now she has been found by her real family at last.'

'Don't you see, Marcel? He's my grandfather,' said Bea.

Long Beard put his hand lovingly on his granddaughter's shoulder. 'Bea lives with us now, in her true home, here on our mountain and in the forest where you humans are not welcome. So,' he said, putting his hands on his hips, 'shall we return to your friends and see whether they are ready to leave?'

'But Grandfather!' Bea protested. 'Can't you let them pass through the forest?'

'Quiet, Bea. This is no concern of yours.' He led the way back to the party of humans with the other two trailing dejectedly behind, leading Gadfly by the mane.

As they approached they heard a heated argument in full swing.

'No, you can't!' Damon was yelling. 'It's too dangerous!'

'Nonsense!' returned Eleanor. 'It's the only way.' Marcel was astonished to see the Book of Lies clutched tightly to her chest. The book she was so afraid of!

Fergus and Nicola cowered to one side, appalled by their parents' bickering.

'Marcel, the Book!' cried Bea. 'You've still got Lord Alwyn's book!'

'Even here, where humans are not welcome, we know that name,' said Long Beard with a touch of awe. The Book heard him and began to glow in Eleanor's arms, drawing a gasp from the King and the other elves who looked on.

'Sometimes, when humans and elves are hunting in the same part of the forest, we listen to the strange tales they tell one another. That is how we know of this Lord Alwyn. He is said to be a great sorcerer. But what is this strange book?'

Eleanor spoke up. 'King Long Beard, this is the Book of Lies, and it glows whenever the truth is spoken. Let me tell you what kind of man it is we seek to overthrow and perhaps you will understand the urgency of our mission.'

She ignored the angry stares of Damon and Starkey and locked her eyes onto Long Beard's face instead. 'Some months ago, before the entire royal court, King Pelham passed a cup of wine to his Queen, a woman he claimed to love dearly. He stood smiling as she drank it, yet only minutes later she lay dead, her lips turned blue by a deadly poison.'

As they watched, the Book began to glow its familiar gold.

Starkey seemed to recover from his rage and addressed the King forthrightly. 'What do you say now, Long Beard? Will you let us pass?'

Damon had also regained his composure, and added his plea to theirs. 'Would you send us back to a man who murders those he loves?'

The Elf-King was wavering but he still could not quite bring himself to agree.

'Please, Grandfather. Won't you let them pass?' Bea implored, startling all but Marcel why she addressed Long Beard in this way.

Marcel could see how Long Beard doted on his granddaughter, and knew this love was their only hope. The Elf-King's heart was softening before their eyes and it was all because of Bea.

'Very well,' he said at length. 'Since Bea pleads so hard for your cause, I will grant her a special favour. You may have safe passage through our territories. I will even send an elf to guide you.'

The humans breathed a huge sigh of relief. But despite her grandfather's change of heart, Bea still looked unhappy. Her eyes hadn't left Marcel's since she had last spoken. Now she addressed him again. 'Grandfather, I want to go with them.'

The King recoiled as though she had pushed him. 'But you've only just come to live with us. No, Bea, I want you here with me, so that I can watch you grow up among those who love you.' A hint of hostility returned to his elfish eye, to reveal what he thought of human beings.

'You don't understand, Grandfather. If it wasn't for me, Marcel would still be at the orphanage. I'm part of what is happening, whether I like it or not. I have to go.'

After a minute's tense silence, Long Beard spoke again. 'This girl is more stubborn than her mother was,' he told them with a mixture of pride and exasperation. 'I'll let her go with her young friend here,' he said, slapping Marcel good-naturedly on the shoulder, 'but I'm not ready to let her out of my sight so soon. I promised you a guide through the forest. Well, here he is,' he announced, tapping himself on the chest. 'King Long Beard himself.'

CHAPTER 14

Lenoth Crag

THEY SET OFF IMMEDIATELY. Gadfly had permitted Hector to load their provisions onto her back, replenished with extra supplies from the elves.

'Sorry,' Marcel had whispered into Gadfly's ear. 'For the time being, you're our pack horse. Just remember, if we left you behind they might eat you.' She rolled her eyes and snorted her disapproval but let him lead her into the forest all the same. Nicola, Fergus and Bea stayed with them, forming their own troop ten paces behind the adults.

'The forest is a different place now, don't you think?' observed Nicola.

'I know what it is. We're not afraid any more,' said Marcel, and the other two agreed with a smile.

Bea grew excited when she heard these words. 'Do you understand now what I felt when we first arrived in the forest, Marcel, with all those shades of green and the peaceful silence?'

'You'll live here with your grandfather once this is all over, won't you, Bea?'

Marcel couldn't hide the disappointment in his voice. Bea heard it too and the happiness slipped from her face. 'Marcel, it's my home.'

They lapsed into an uncomfortable silence. Marcel's eyes rose to their surroundings instead, first to the trees and then to the snow-capped mountains that ranged tall and imposing, so many miles in the distance.

'How long to Lenoth Crag, King Long Beard?' Fergus called out.

'We should reach the pass through those mountains by nightfall,' he answered.

'But it's so far!' objected Starkey in surprise. 'Surely it's two days' march at least.'

'For humans alone, yes, but elves know ways through the forest you can only dream of.'

If they doubted him, they were soon proved wrong. Long Beard led them along paths that did not go round the many obstacles but effortlessly through them and over them. He charged through thick forest without any need of a track, found stones that led over swollen streams, and guided them along the rim of gaping chasms to where rocks jutted out so that even an elf's short legs could leap across. In her long gown, Eleanor looked just as uncomfortable as she had earlier, but Marcel had to admire her determination not to show it in front of Long Beard.

They began heading uphill, into rockier terrain where stunted trees clung hardily to barren, windswept hillsides. A long day's march brought them to the desolate mountain pass, just as Long Beard had promised.

As they approached they could all see a ghostly finger of grey smoke drifting between the treetops overhead.

Long Beard sniffed. 'There must be some kind of human dwelling up ahead. It hasn't been there long or I would have heard about it.'

Then they emerged into the narrow opening of the pass itself. Two massive granite crags loomed over them, one on either side, their soaring tops whitened by snow. Obstructing the way between the overhanging peaks sat a rough cabin built of stone and fallen logs dragged from the forest.

'So,' observed Damon with surprise, 'Zadenwolf has built an outpost here. Things certainly have changed. Maybe he's had trouble from woodsmen, or perhaps he fears the elves.'

Long Beard gave a quick snort to indicate his lack of concern.

Some horses were tethered on the rough ground nearby — ponies really, their manes and tails long and untidy. 'They make you look pretty,' Marcel teased Gadfly, who pretended to ignore him. Small and unkempt they might be, but they were clearly hardy beasts, bred for a harsh land. They neighed and stamped their feet at the approach of strangers, bringing men from inside the cabin — three, four, and finally a fifth.

'Fighting men,' breathed Fergus, clearly impressed, as the men spilled out into the open. They were dressed for the cold, in heavy fur coats and leather breeches, and each of them was armed with a sword. They advanced towards the group and stopped only a few strides away.

'What's your business here?' asked one who was obviously their commander.

'We wish to enter Lenoth Crag,' Starkey announced imperiously.

'Not unless King Zadenwolf gives his permission, you're not,' was the curt reply.

'It's Zadenwolf we've come to see,' Damon cut in quickly. 'I am Prince Damon of Elster, an old friend. I fought beside him years ago. He'll be glad to see me, I'm sure.'

The men didn't seem ready for this answer. They backed away into a huddle, arguing in hushed tones.

At length their leader spoke again. 'We'll send word to King Zadenwolf immediately. Until we have his answer, I'm afraid you must stay here.'

The cabin was barely large enough for the surly warriors. They helped the travellers get their own fire going then closed the door, leaving them to shelter from the mountain winds beside the cabin wall, much to the disgust of the Prince and Princess. They were all glad to see the sun in the morning and, just before midday, even more pleased to see a dozen riders galloping through the pass.

The soldiers hurried from the warmth of their cabin and bowed to the tallest man among the new arrivals. He dismounted quickly and straightened the axe that hung from his belt. The fur of his coat was thicker than the other men's and his leather boots finer. Much of his face was hidden beneath a black and unruly beard.

'Damon!' he called with genuine feeling, as soon as he sighted his old friend. He strode towards the Prince and they embraced in a manly hug.

'Zadenwolf, it's good to see you again,' Damon responded warmly.

The King broke his hold long enough to bark instructions to the men who had ridden with him. 'Get some tents set up for my friends,' he called to one who led a pack horse weighed down with canvas and poles.

Starkey stepped up to be introduced, but Eleanor held back, gathering the children around her instead. 'This is men's talk. Damon and the King will swap exaggerated stories about the great battles they fought together, but when they get tired of that we want Zadenwolf to meet you. He must see that you are with us now.'

'Why? Does he know us?' asked Fergus.

Eleanor stared at him for a second but her answer came easily enough. 'All sorts of rumours fly from kingdom to kingdom. He may have heard that you three were Pelham's hostages. If he asks you a question, answer him truthfully. This meeting may well decide our kingdom's future.'

The tents were set up, one for Eleanor, her children and Bea, a second for Starkey, Damon and Fergus, a third for Zadenwolf and then two more for Hector and the soldiers. However, the meeting that Eleanor spoke of was held in the open air, where the mountain king seemed most at ease. Long Beard was present, though he assured them he would soon be departing to return to his subjects.

'Here are the children,' said Eleanor, as the three were brought forward and introduced by their real names, Princess Catherine, Prince Edwin and Prince Marcel. Zadenwolf's eyebrows danced eagerly as the names were pronounced.

'Prince Damon has told me of your adventures,' he said to them. 'Tell me, is it true that you forgot who your own parents were?'

Marcel glanced towards his mother, who gave a brief nod. 'Yes, Your Majesty — until Starkey helped us free them from the palace.'

'Yes, you freed Damon and Eleanor from the palace,' he noted with an approving nod. 'Tell me another thing, then,' Zadenwolf asked with more urgency. 'What do you think of Elster's king?'

Before Marcel could reply, Nicola answered for them all.

'He's a usurper!' she cried with all the anger Marcel had wanted to unleash. 'He's stolen the Crown from the rightful heirs,' and in case there was any doubt whom she meant, she turned towards Princess Eleanor and Prince Damon.

But this was nothing compared with what Fergus added. 'Pelham robbed us of our memories and hid us away in an orphanage. I'd *kill* him if I had the chance,' he said furiously.

Zadenwolf broke into an exuberant laugh. 'Royal blood is hot, I see.'

'Yes, truly royal blood is the hottest of all,' said Eleanor vehemently. 'That's what I carry in my veins,' and she pulled back the sleeve of her dress to expose the delicate traces of blue beneath her pale skin. 'Pelham is a usurper who doesn't deserve the Crown. If it weren't for Alwyn's sorcery, he would still be on the streets of Elstenwyck, begging for scraps to eat. This is why you must help us, Zadenwolf. Alwyn had the old Queen under his spell when she named Pelham as her successor.'

Zadenwolf listened intently, but he did not seem moved by her pleas. When Eleanor realised this, she tried a new line of attack. 'Long Beard knows how he treats his own people, even those closest to him.'

She let the dramatic silence that followed do its work. Long Beard took his time, aware of the weight his words would carry. 'It is true,' he said at length. 'Pelham has poisoned his own wife, that much I know.'

Damon and Starkey added arguments of their own. Through it all, Zadenwolf stood with his arms tightly folded across his belly. Finally, he spoke.

'There is one name we have heard for many years in Lenoth Crag. Lord Alwyn. We have sorcerers of our own, but they all tremble at the mention of his name. A wizard more powerful than the mountains, than the clouds and the sky, that is what they tell me. Lord Alwyn's magic has kept the Kings and Queens of Elster safely on their thrones for as long as anyone can remember.'

He paused and ran his thumb gently along the blade of his axe. 'I am King of a warlike people, it is true, but until now they have fought only each other. To fight an army like Pelham's, down there on the plains, would be a great risk ...' He shook his head doubtfully and looked around the faces. 'One army alone would not be enough. I would need an ally to weigh the odds in our favour.'

'An ally?' Damon cried in exasperation. 'But there is no other, not for hundreds of miles!'

The meeting fell silent as Damon's despair infected them all. Marcel sensed Bea at his side. She took his hand in sympathy. Even she could see their chances slipping away as Zadenwolf stood firm. The warmth of her hand in his set Marcel thinking. He could feel it even though he could barely see her. There were many more like her, back there in the forest, just as hard to see. They could put an arrow between a man's fingers or within an inch of his head. Couldn't they just as easily shoot their arrows through a man's heart?

'King Long Beard, would you help us?' he begged. 'Pelham's soldiers would be helpless against an army they couldn't see and bowmen who meet their mark without fail. If you and Zadenwolf joined forces, they'd throw down their weapons and plead for mercy.'

The solemn meeting suddenly erupted into a chorus of eager approval loud enough to win a battle by itself.

'Wait!' called Zadenwolf, raising his hand. 'You are all speaking except the one who matters most. What do *you* have to say, Long Beard? Will you help us overthrow this King Pelham?'

For once, Long Beard did not hesitate. 'You have convinced me that Pelham is a cruel man with an evil heart. But he has done no harm to the elves. If we have lived peacefully around our mountain for a thousand years it is because we do not interfere in the lives of humans.' He shook his head firmly as he beckoned Bea towards him. When she was close enough, he took her hand, just as Marcel had done, and said, 'No, I'm sorry, but the elves will not join your war.'

For just a few moments, an easy victory had seemed theirs. The meeting struggled on as Eleanor, Damon and Starkey clamoured for Zadenwolf's support, but the mountain king would not agree unless Long Beard changed his mind. And there seemed no chance of that.

Eventually it became too much for Eleanor, who fled, in exasperated tears, towards the tent that had been prepared for her.

'We'd better go with her,' muttered Nicola to Marcel. They followed with the slow strides of the dejected until they were only a few paces from the tent's opening. The sounds from inside told them that Eleanor's tears had turned to something more violent. Cautiously they poked their heads inside and there she was, kicking vainly at the sturdy pole in the centre. When this wasn't enough for her rage, she snatched up the silver mirror and hurled it straight at the pole.

'No!' screamed Nicola, as she watched it fly through the air. But her cry came too late. The glass shattered into thousands of glittering diamonds and the heavy silver handle dropped with a thud to the ground.

Nicola's scream had snapped the worst of Eleanor's frenzy, but it had not cooled her anger completely. 'Those cowards!' She sneered in their direction without really seeing them. 'If I were a man, I'd be down in that valley with a sword in my hand, whether I had an army at my back or not.'

Then she seemed to collect herself, and only at this point did she properly take in who was watching. She gave a brief start, before the fury suffused her features once more. 'Leave me,' she snapped.

The pair staggered backwards, appalled. 'Did you see her eyes?' Nicola whispered, when they had moved a little way from the tent.

Oh yes, Marcel had seen those eyes, full of black hatred. 'She's upset,' he said, scrambling frantically for excuses.

'Yes, that's it. Not so hard to understand,' Nicola responded, just as desperate to agree. 'This might be her only chance to win the Kingdom from Pelham. Of course she's angry.'

Angry. It had been more than that. How could their mother's exquisite features burn with such ugliness and rage?

Her tent was cut off to them now. There was no place for them either among the men, who were still arguing, and Bea and Fergus had wandered off somewhere with Long Beard. But just then Eleanor called after them, her voice full of contrition. 'Wait, I'm sorry! Forgive me, both of you. You must be ashamed to see me this way.'

'No, of course not, Mother!' cried Nicola, rushing tearily towards her and accepting the hug offered by her outstretched arms. Marcel was about to do the same when a cry of outrage rose up behind him. He turned instantly to see what had caused it. The circle of men had dispersed, and Damon, Zadenwolf, Fergus and some of the fur-clad soldiers were crowded tightly around something on the ground nearby.

'There, in the trees! After him!' Starkey shouted. He hadn't been standing with the rest, it seemed, and now, with his sword drawn, he was already running into the forest. The others began to charge after him. Only the dimly visible figure of Long Beard remained, kneeling beside something just as hard to see.

Marcel was already running. In a dozen desperate strides he was beside the Elf-King and staring down in horror at a figure that lay motionless, with arms outstretched and eyes closed.

Bea.

Protruding from her shoulder, pointing straight at the sun overhead, was the long, deadly shaft of an arrow.

CHAPTER 15

The Ones You Love Can Be
the First to Die

B EA WAS PICKED UP and carried, groaning, back to her tent and laid on a straw mattress brought from the frontier guards' cabin. Her agony could be heard throughout the camp as the arrow was removed from her flesh.

'Who could have done this? She's just a girl,' Long Beard seethed.

Starkey had returned from the forest by now. 'All I saw was a flash of red. One of Pelham's men must have followed us after all. He was probably aiming for Prince Edwin.'

Zadenwolf and the rest returned an hour later. 'Whoever it was, he has slipped away. I will stay a day or so in case there are others. How is the elf-girl?' Zadenwolf asked.

'She is bleeding badly,' murmured Long Beard, distraught with worry. He came away from the grubby mattress where Bea lay grimacing in pain, and began to pace anxiously from one side of the tent to the other. 'A king who sends his soldiers to kill children,' he muttered bitterly. 'Maybe you *will* have the elves at your side for this struggle after all ...' Then he seemed to make up his mind. 'I tell you, if my granddaughter dies, I will bring my army to fight against this King Pelham. You have my word.'

Eleanor did what she could to staunch the wound, but the bleeding would not stop. 'I'm sorry, Long Beard. She is growing very weak.'

'No!' Marcel cried, sinking to his knees near the girl's head. Nicola crouched beside him but there was nothing either of them could say.

'We have an elf-woman who has learned all the potions to heal such wounds. I will go myself and fetch her,' said Long Beard resolutely, and though the light was fading outside and the chill wind smelled of snow, he set out immediately into the forest.

Eleanor made a broth from the remains of a deer caught by Zadenwolf's soldiers, but Bea was too ill to swallow even a mouthful. Marcel sat up with her as long as he could manage to stay awake, then Nicola took her turn and Fergus too. Bea was still fighting to stay alive in the morning, but each new bandage they applied was quickly soaked in the bright red of her blood.

Then hope. Early that afternoon, the elf-woman arrived. She came alone, with only a light sack over her shoulder, and went straight to Bea's side. 'I am Remora,' she said humbly when they asked her name. Like the other elf-women Marcel had seen on the mountain slopes, her hair was plaited and pinned in a flattened spiral over her ears. The many lines around her eyes and on her forehead told of her age, but despite her hurried journey she was quickly at work on the wound with an energy that swept Eleanor aside.

'Where is Long Beard?' Starkey asked when he came to meet this new arrival.

'He has called all the elves to the mountain for a council. He wants them to be ready — in case they have to go to war.' Remora looked down uneasily at her patient. 'He will send a messenger tomorrow to check on his granddaughter.'

But as each hour passed, it seemed less likely that the elves would have to fight. By nightfall, Bea was sitting up, her eyes open and even the hint of a smile on her colourless lips. Marcel began to spread the word around camp.

When he reached Starkey's tent, he found him with a candle in his hand and his face hovering above the Book of Lies. It was open at the last page. Marcel felt his heart leap when he saw it. The Book had been his once, or so it had seemed. If anyone owned it now, it was Starkey.

But he quickly pushed such doubts aside. 'Bea is getting better! Remora says she's going to live,' he told Starkey joyfully.

'Long Beard will be relieved to hear that,' Starkey replied.

Starkey came back to the tent with Marcel to see Bea's progress for himself. Eleanor was there, of course, doing what she could to help. When she slipped away to eat, Marcel took her place at Remora's side.

'Pass me a handful of that lichenwort,' Remora instructed, pointing to a small bag with pale orange fibres spilling from its mouth.

Marcel had to ask Starkey to step aside so he could do as she asked, then held his palm open while she swept the contents into her cupped hand. She turned away without a thought, but just as quickly turned back. 'Wait. Hold out your hand again,' she whispered with an odd look on her face.

'Why, what have I done?' he asked, offering his hand tentatively.

Remora opened his fingers, and this time she stroked her own palm slowly over his entire hand. 'Magic,' she murmured. 'I feel magic under your skin.'

Marcel relaxed a little. 'That's Lord Alwyn's spell. He used sorcery to take away all memory of who I was.'

Remora considered his answer while she continued to caress his palm, her wrinkled eyes closed this time so that she could concentrate on the feeling alone.

'No, not a spell forced on you by another,' she announced confidently. 'Medicine and magic are two sides of the same coin. I have studied the first mostly, but I know a little of the second. This magic resides *within you*.'

With a start Marcel snatched his hand away and hid it behind his back in case she reached for it again. 'That's a mistake. What you can feel comes from Lord Alwyn,' he assured her. Looking up, he found Starkey's hard eyes staring down at him. 'Isn't that right,' he demanded. 'It's Lord Alwyn's magic, not mine.'

Starkey took a long time to answer, as though his own thoughts had been distracted by what Remora had claimed. 'The old wizard, yes. It must be,' he said finally, but this was no more than a vague denial, not at all what Marcel was expecting.

At that moment Eleanor returned. 'I've made some more broth for Bea,' she declared brightly, passing it down to Remora.

'That's very kind of you,' said the elf-nurse as she accepted the bowl, 'but for now, Bea needs my special tonics. She'll be well enough for your broth in a day or two.'

'Then perhaps you would like it yourself, Remora. You have not eaten since you arrived.'

Remora smiled and nodded graciously.

MARCEL HAD BARELY CLOSED his eyes since the arrow struck Bea's shoulder, but with the patient growing stronger by the hour and Remora to sit by her bed, he slept soundly that night. He woke well after daybreak to find Eleanor feeding Bea the broth she had prepared the night before.

'How is she?' he asked immediately.

'Come and see for yourself.'

It wasn't Eleanor who replied but Bea herself. Marcel threw off his blanket and hurried to her side.

She couldn't say more, because Eleanor had slipped another spoonful of broth into her mouth. But their voices had woken Nicola, who sat up in her bed and asked blearily, 'Where's Remora?'

'She has gone into the forest to collect more ingredients for her potions and ointments,' Eleanor explained. 'In the meantime she wants us to change Bea's bandages and build up her strength with a little food.' She held up the spoon to show that she was following instructions.

With Bea sipping noisily, there was nothing much Marcel could do. He put on his boots and cloak and went outside for some air. It had snowed heavily during the night and the sudden whiteness of the camp site stunned his eyes. He shivered in his worn boots as they sank into the freezing ground. At least it would delay Zadenwolf's departure, and give Eleanor and the rest more time to talk him round.

A clash of swords made him turn sharply, terrified for a moment that Pelham's soldiers had returned. 'I should have known,' he muttered to himself, as the fear subsided instantly. There was Fergus, thirty strides away, wielding a sword against one of Zadenwolf's soldiers, who parried his blows lazily. Three others looked on, cheering each strike and calling out words of encouragement.

'Marcel, come here!' called Fergus, as soon as he spotted him. When Marcel joined them, he thrust the handle of his sword into the boy's hands. 'Feel how light it is,' he crowed proudly. 'Isn't it fantastic? Zadenwolf gave it to me. I showed it to my father and he's promised to have my name engraved along the blade.'

As if mention of his name had summoned him, Damon appeared in the opening of his tent, and instantly Fergus straightened like a soldier. But Damon didn't even look in his son's direction and the boy's face clouded with disappointment. 'I want to fight in the battles against Pelham,' he muttered, swallowing his dismay. 'Father just laughs, but I'll show him what I can do ...'

'There aren't going to be any battles,' said Marcel, before Fergus could get carried away. 'Zadenwolf is afraid of Lord Alwyn, remember? As soon as Bea is better he'll head back into Lenoth Crag and we'll be on our own again, without a single soldier to help us.'

Fergus didn't seem to be listening. He was busy watching Damon cross the short distance from his tent to Zadenwolf's. 'That's the third time he's gone to see the King alone. Old friends from the battlefield, you see,' he added with a knowing smirk. 'If anyone can change Zadenwolf's mind, it's my father.'

Marcel had seen less of Fergus since he'd been sharing a tent with his father and couldn't believe how completely he had come to idolise Damon. For the next hour, Fergus made Marcel reluctantly practise sword drills against him, until their arms ached and the soldiers became bored with watching them. Without an audience Fergus's interest also waned, and only then was Marcel free to return to the tent where Bea lay.

'Bring me another bandage!' he heard Eleanor cry sharply to Nicola as he drew near. He saw his sister's tearful urgency as she hurried to tear off another strip from a discarded sheet.

'What happened?' he demanded as he rushed frantically to Bea's bedside. He had to jump aside as Bea vomited violently then cried out as the convulsions sent pain spearing into her shoulder. The wound had opened again, soaking the bandage with fresh blood. Eleanor sent Nicola scurrying away for a fresh blanket to replace the one Bea had soiled.

'But she was getting better!' Marcel wailed helplessly. 'Where's Remora? Isn't she back yet?'

His mother was too busy to answer him. The answer was plain enough anyway. There was no trace of the elf-nurse.

After a while Bea slipped into a fitful sleep. The bleeding had slowed but not stopped, and the sweat beading on her forehead told them a fever was taking hold of her little body.

Thunder rolled through the mountains, loud and threatening. Marcel couldn't stay still for more than a moment and told his mother he was going outside, hoping to see Remora returning. The clouds were low and dark overhead and their contents were beginning to fall as large, pelting raindrops that slapped noisily onto the canvas and stung his face. They were strangely warm after the crisp chill of the snowy morning.

With no sign of Remora, he returned despondently to the tent. As he entered he just caught a glimpse of his mother hastily slipping a handful of bright-coloured berries into a tiny pouch at her waist.

'Remora *must* come back soon,' he exclaimed. 'What can she find anyway with so much snow covering everything?'

Bea groaned in her sleep. Her face had become deathly pale now. Such a change from earlier, when there had seemed no doubt she would recover!

'She's only small,' he murmured to his mother, fighting back tears. 'She doesn't have much blood to lose. I couldn't bear it if …'

'You care a great deal for your little friend, don't you, Marcel?' Eleanor said in a soothing voice. She put a hand gently on his shoulder and he realised with a start that it was the first time she had touched him since their brief embrace in the door of her prison chamber. 'Many people will risk their lives to bring justice back to Elster. Some of them will die before I am Queen, and the ones you love the most might be the first. I'm sorry, Marcel.'

He stayed by Bea's bed for another hour, but with each passing minute she was slipping closer to death. Where was Remora? He pushed aside the tent flap once more and searched the fringes of the camp with his eyes. No sign of her. Though dark clouds still haunted the mountain pass, the rain had stopped for now, at least. Zadenwolf's soldiers were emerging from the makeshift cabin and the handful of tents and looked as if they were beginning to prepare for departure. A horse whinnied and he turned to see Gadfly among the ponies, water dripping from her shaggy mane.

He stepped out of the tent and discovered that the rain had turned parts of the snow to puddles of muddy soup beneath his feet. He sloshed his way through, avoiding the worst of it, until he reached Gadfly. He knew she was glad to see him even though she feigned indifference. How could you leave me among such creatures? she seemed to complain, nodding disdainfully towards the dishevelled ponies.

'I know, I know. You deserve better than this and I've neglected you badly. I'm sorry, but a lot's been happening over the last couple of days.' Gadfly relented and offered her nose for stroking. He ran the backs of his fingers down the grain of her hair, enjoying its smoothness, until Gadfly snorted suddenly and tossed her head.

He looked up to find Nicola watching him silently from nearby. 'What are you doing out here?' he said, tugging his cloak more tightly around him. 'It's much warmer in the tent.'

She gave a weary shrug. 'Bea's asleep and there's nothing much I can do. I'd rather be out here with you than with ...' She couldn't seem to finish the sentence, as though she was afraid of the final words.

Marcel thought he knew what she meant. 'I can't watch Bea die either,' he agreed wretchedly.

'Bea?' Nicola responded, a little surprised. 'She's not going to die, Marcel. As soon as Remora comes back she'll start to get better again.'

This was what Marcel wanted to hear, more than anything, and it lifted his spirits immediately. But he hadn't forgotten Nicola's unfinished sentence. She would rather be with him, her brother, than ... than whom? The answer was not hard to guess.

'Do you think Eleanor will make a good queen?' he asked tentatively.

'A queen, yes. In a palace with lots of fine clothes and servants taking orders. I can see her with all that. Once it was just what I wanted too.'

'It's what *she* wants more than anything,' Marcel declared, and if the Book of Lies had been sitting across his knees he was certain that its glow would have melted the rest of the snow around them.

'But is she the kind of mother you dreamed of, Marcel?' Nicola asked seriously.

He didn't know how to answer. It had all happened so quickly. He hadn't had time to dream of anything. But Nicola had.

'I've asked her to help me braid my hair three times now,' Nicola went on. 'Each time she makes an excuse. She has to meet with Zadenwolf or Starkey, and then yesterday afternoon, she said she had to pick some berries from the forest. How important can that be?'

'Brushing someone's hair doesn't sound very important either,' said Marcel, before he realised how unkind it would sound.

She rounded on him. 'Boys! You're just as bad as Fergus with his swords and his fighting. Don't you see, Marcel? Brushing a girl's hair is what a mother does, even a queen ... if she loves her daughter. I wonder whether our mother loves anything, except the crown she wants to feel on her head.'

There, the word had been said. Love. It stirred Marcel more than he wanted it to. He had heard that word only recently, and on Eleanor's own lips. 'She told me that the ones you love can be the first to die,' he muttered miserably. 'She was talking about Bea.'

The wind was growing stronger and the first drops of a new rainstorm warned them to find shelter. Brother and sister set off back towards their tent, shoulders hunched and heads down as the rain intensified. Soon Marcel was running, with eyes only for the ground ahead, trying to leap the larger puddles of melted snow, when he collided with a figure running blindly, like himself.

'Fergus! Watch where you're going,' he cried in anger when he saw who it was.

There was no apology from Fergus. In fact, the boy cowered as though Marcel had punched him.

'What's the matter? You're as white as a ghost.'

'I found something,' he said faintly, barely able to look Marcel in the eye. 'At least, I think I did.'

'What? What did you find?'

'I don't want to say,' he muttered, then stood in a daze, letting water pour in a steady stream from his matted hair and down the sides of his face. 'They'll think I'm mad if I drag them out into this storm and it's all a mistake.'

'What are you talking about?' Nicola cried impatiently.

Fergus came awake with a start. 'Come with me, both of you. Then I'll know.'

Tugged away with such force, Marcel could hardly refuse, and Nicola tagged along in bewilderment. Pulling up their hoods against the rain, they followed Fergus away from the camp. Despite their cloaks, they were already soaked to the skin and shivering when Fergus led them off a narrow trail and into the forest, about two hundred paces beyond the perimeter of the camp. 'I was out in the forest patrolling with Zadenwolf's men, but somehow I got lost. Had to find my own way back. I would never have seen it otherwise.'

Marcel still didn't have clue what he was jabbering about. Finally, Fergus found the courage to push his way between two small bushes before stopping again beside a third. 'Here, this is what I found,' he breathed.

Snow had been heaped around and under the bush in a way that seemed unnatural, but the morning's rain had softened it and it was dissolving steadily even as they stood there watching.

'What are we supposed to see?' asked Marcel, still puzzled.

'This,' said Fergus, and pulling the foliage of the bush back a little he revealed something pale and pinkish-brown protruding from the snow. It was a hand, its fingers outstretched and frozen into a grasping claw.

Nicola gasped in horror and took a step backwards. As for Fergus, his courage was returning now that he had company. He fell onto his knees in the melting snow and began to scoop it away, exposing the wrist and then the forearm. Marcel knelt beside him and together they worked towards the shoulder. 'A dress,' said Fergus when he saw the cut of the clothing. 'It's a woman.'

A few more handfuls and finally a face was staring up at them, the eyes open even though they would never see again. Fear and a dreadful pain were frozen in the creased skin of the forehead and around the mouth. With a shock they realised that they knew this face — not well, not as a friend, but they knew her, and the true horror of what they had found suddenly overwhelmed them.

They turned aside to let Nicola see. 'Remora!' she exclaimed, on the verge of tears. 'The poor woman.'

'Who will save Bea now?' Marcel asked, then felt ashamed of himself. Bea was still breathing but Remora was already dead.

'Look at her lips!' cried Nicola suddenly. 'They're blue! She must have been caught out in the snow and frozen to death.'

'A wise old elf-woman like Remora?' said Marcel. 'No, I can't believe it. What if it was one of Pelham's soldiers?' He looked around nervously. 'There could be more ...'

'No, it couldn't be Pelham's men,' said Fergus, interrupting. 'Zadenwolf's soldiers have searched the forest around here for miles. No one's seen a thing.'

Marcel looked again at those lips, unnaturally blue, and a terrible thought came into his mind. 'Remember how Pelham murdered his Queen?' he asked the others. 'Her lips turned *bright blue*. Remora's been poisoned!'

'Poison!' Nicola breathed.

'You know what this means, don't you? It must have been someone in the camp. We have a traitor in our ranks,' said Fergus, touching the handle of his sword where it brushed against his left shoulder.

'A murderer, you mean,' seethed Nicola.

Marcel inspected Remora's body more closely. The initial shock was fading a little and his eyes began to notice how she had been buried. 'She's under the snow,' he murmured.

'You're right,' Fergus agreed. 'Whoever killed her must have piled snow onto her body, to hide it. If the rain hadn't melted it from around her hand I would never have seen it.'

'But there hasn't been any snow since last night,' Marcel pointed out with a frown.

'That doesn't make sense,' said Nicola. 'Remora only left our tent this morning. Mother said so.'

Fergus was taking a closer look now as well. 'See how hard the snow is around her face? No, your mother must be wrong. Remora was killed during the night some time, when the snow was still falling.'

'But she wouldn't have gone out in the dark to look for the things she needed,' Marcel objected. He was becoming uncomfortable with the things they were talking about and the suspicions they seemed to lead to.

'Marcel,' Nicola said cautiously, with an edge to her voice that he didn't like at all, 'Remora had plenty of potions and ointments. I saw them in the bag she brought with her. She didn't need any more, not when she arrived here only yesterday.'

It was clear now what they were suggesting, though neither of them could say it out loud. That job fell to Fergus. 'Are you saying your mother lied to you on purpose? But if she did that, then she must have known what happened to Remora…' It came to him suddenly, what was in the minds of his two cousins. 'You can't think she's the murderer, your own mother?'

Could Eleanor have killed Remora? Marcel dared ask himself. What were those berries he had caught her hiding?

'I don't understand,' confessed Nicola in despair. 'Why would anyone want to kill Remora? She was here to save Bea's life!'

Bea! Marcel's head shot up. 'What did you say?' But he had heard well enough. Ever since they'd uncovered Remora's face, wild ideas had been spinning and swirling around inside his head, too terrifying to make sense. But with those simple words from Nicola he was beginning to guess the truth. And what a monstrous thing it was.

He felt tears behind his eyes, hot and heavy, like the breath in his throat. He forced them back with a painful gulp and pushed out words instead. 'She was warning me this morning. The people you love might be first. She already knows Bea is going to die.'

Though every part of him wanted to fight his own suspicions, Marcel made himself say it out loud. 'That's why she killed Remora. So that Remora couldn't save Bea. She *wants* Bea to die.'

The ideas whirling around each other grew wilder. 'Fergus, when Bea was wounded, did Zadenwolf's men find anything out there in the forest? Any trace at all?'

'I told you. Nothing, not even a footprint. But there must have been someone. Starkey saw a man in red running away through the trees ...'

Fergus didn't finish what he was saying. His eyes widened in shock until he had to blink away the rivers of rainwater that streamed down from his sodden hood. 'You don't think there *was* anyone running away, do you? You think Starkey was lying. But Starkey couldn't have fired that arrow. He was there, with the others, when it happened.'

'Hector,' said Nicola instantly. 'And there's only one man he takes his orders from.' She had been following the trail of suspicions even more closely than Fergus, it seemed.

'I can't work it out,' Fergus moaned in frustration. 'First you think your own mother poisoned Remora and now you accuse Starkey of having Bea shot. Which one is the traitor?'

But Marcel already had an answer for his cousin. 'It must be both of them. Mother couldn't have dragged Remora's body into the forest by herself. She would have needed a man to help her.'

It was all too much for Fergus. 'No, Marcel, this is madness! Starkey tries to kill Bea with an arrow. Your mother kills Remora, so that Bea will die too. Why would they want her dead? She's just a little girl.'

'A little *elf*-girl, Fergus. She's King Long Beard's granddaughter. Don't you remember the vow he made? If she dies, he'll take revenge against Pelham. And if the elves go to war ...'

'Then so will Zadenwolf,' whispered Fergus, understanding at last. He too had begun to feel the horror of such a hideous crime like a weight he couldn't throw off.

'Your own mother ...' he said, staring at first one, then the other, but when he couldn't find words to follow he turned away, afraid to look into their faces any longer.

Marcel looked down at the lifeless body still half-buried beneath the snow. 'They've killed Remora. Now they're sitting back until that wound kills Bea as well.'

The rain fell more heavily than ever now, tumbling straight down on the three children, cascading over their foreheads and cheeks and making watery beards on their chins.

Fergus made a sudden decision. 'We have to tell my father all this. He can make Starkey and Eleanor testify in front of the Book ...'

'No, Fergus,' Marcel replied softly. 'I don't need Lord Alwyn's magic book to be sure. People can hide themselves from you and pretend they're a different kind of person but in the end it gets too much for them and they show their real faces.'

He looked over at Nicola, her cloak so drenched with rain that it stuck to her skin. 'Ask her,' he urged

Fergus, nearly shouting now. 'Ask Nicola what she thinks. We know what Eleanor's really like, both of us, and if she was your mother, you'd know too.'

'He's right, Fergus. Even before this I didn't want to be near her any more.'

'Then it's up to my father. Once he knows what they've done, he'll make sure those two murderers get what they deserve.'

Damon? Marcel wasn't so sure about that, and Fergus wasn't really the best judge of his own father's character. He had fallen under the man's spell from the moment the magical door to that prison had opened.

'I don't know, Fergus. Maybe we should keep this a secret until we know more.'

Fergus's voice developed a hard edge. 'You don't trust my father, do you?'

What could he say? No, he didn't trust Damon, not as much as he needed to. If they ran to him now and poured out their story it would sound wild and ridiculous, and even if Damon was an honest man, he might not believe it. If he wasn't honest, if he was part of the plan to kill Bea ... then all hope was gone.

There in the middle of the waterlogged forest, with the rain beating down relentlessly around them, Marcel couldn't tell Fergus any of this. He needed time to make his own plan, and to gain that time he would have to delay his cousin. 'This is all happening too fast,' he said, feeling his head whirling. 'We have to talk, Nicola and I. Eleanor's our mother, after all, and we're about to accuse her of murder.'

Fergus showed signs of wavering. 'But we're still going to my father, right? You do trust him.'

'All right, we'll show Remora's body to Damon. We'll tell him everything, but not yet, not until Nicola and I have talked it over,' he said, glancing at her bewildered face. 'Give us until this afternoon. After that, it will be up to your father.'

Fergus smiled at this show of trust and started moving off, back to the trail that led to the camp site. 'This afternoon, then.'

'Yes, come to our tent after lunch,' Marcel responded, following after him.

Even as he said it, he knew it was a lie. He couldn't risk telling Damon. And he couldn't just sit back and watch Bea die. Without Remora, what chance did she have? Just look at the way she'd deteriorated since the elf-nurse had disappeared. She'd been so much better last night, but then this morning she'd started bringing up all the broth that Eleanor fed her.

Sudden terror seized his heart. He stopped dead. Behind him, his sister stopped too. 'Nicola,' he said, turning round, 'do you think ... maybe Eleanor isn't just waiting for the bleeding to kill Bea ...'

'What are you talking about, Marcel?'

'Poison!' he yelled, and before he was even aware of what he was doing he had burst through the bushes and was bolting as fast as the slushy ground would let him along the track towards the camp.

He charged past the mystified Fergus, but he could hear Nicola panting behind him, struggling to keep up.

'Wait!' she bellowed, her breath coming in gasps. Finally she caught at his trailing cloak and he was forced to stop. 'You're not going to Damon later, are you, Marcel?'

'What makes you say that?'

'I could tell, the way you were so desperate to convince Fergus.'

Despite his panic, Marcel was impressed. He might as well tell her everything. 'Nicola, I've got to get Bea back to Long Beard, before another drop of that broth touches her lips. There's not a moment to waste!'

'I'm coming with you.'

She wasn't asking him, she was telling him, and though he didn't say so, he was glad. They were brother and sister. Together they had tried to love their mother and together they had come to despise her. He nodded his assent.

'How will we carry her?' she asked briskly.

Marcel answered with a single word. 'Gadfly.'

Nicola managed a brief smile and a nod. 'I'll go and get her. You wrap Bea up as warmly as you can and I'll meet you back here on this trail in a few minutes.' Then she was gone.

With the rain still falling there was no one in sight as he cautiously approached Bea's tent. He listened for sounds of activity within, every nerve strained.

When he entered he was relieved to find Bea alone, sleeping fitfully. He knelt to rouse her, but even as he did so he felt a soft draught against his cheek and heard the gentle *whoosh* of the tent flap being cast aside.

Marcel's heart almost jumped out of his mouth as he turned to find Starkey staring down at him, a strange smile on his face. Clutched to his chest was the familiar leather sack containing the Book of Lies.

'I saw you return from the woods just now, Marcel. I need you to help me with the Book.'

Then, before Marcel had time to reply, the heavy canvas was swept back once more to reveal Eleanor. In her hands she was holding a bowl of steaming broth.

CHAPTER 16

Saving Bea

HOW MARCEL LOATHED THEM both, even his own mother. He wanted to shout at them, to let them hear the hatred in his voice, and tell them he had guessed their dreadful scheme. But these boiling, spitting impulses lasted less than a moment. He had to keep his wits about him if he was going to save Bea.

'Bea is asleep,' he whispered as he came towards his mother, holding a finger to his lips. When he was close enough he tried to take the bowl from her hands, murmuring, 'I'll feed this to her when she's awake.'

'No, wake her now. She needs the broth to build her strength,' insisted Eleanor who would not let go of the bowl.

Marcel knew he must wrest that bowl from her grasp. It was his only chance. Once he had it, he could pretend to trip as he walked towards Bea's bed and let the bowl drop at his feet.

Eleanor looked down at his hands, which clutched the sides of the bowl like her own. 'I'll feed her myself,' she announced, and to show her determination she tried to wrench the bowl free. But Marcel's hands stuck fast. They struggled, mother and son staring into each other's eyes, all pretence of affection now dead.

Then the bowl tipped over and the contents spilled into the dirt.

'You stupid, stupid boy!' Eleanor raged at him. She swept back her hand, ready to slap him across the face for his clumsiness.

But Starkey caught her by the wrist before she could deliver the blow. 'Leave him. Whether the elf-girl lives or dies will mean nothing if we can conjure Mortregis from this book,' he growled, brandishing the leather sack in his other hand. He dragged the Book out of the sack and opened it at the last page.

Starkey's sudden intervention and his imperious tone had clearly aggravated Eleanor. 'This story of a dragon is nonsense!' she snapped. 'Damon thinks so too. I'm just glad we talked you out of telling Zadenwolf your foolish ideas!'

This insult made Starkey furious. 'You might question me now, but you won't call it nonsense when the Book brings us our victory. Come here! Read the verse for yourself. It speaks of a great dragon, one so powerful it can bring down kings and set new ones in their place. It must be Mortregis.'

Eleanor glanced at the verses and swallowed her own fury for the moment. 'Yes, but what is the magic?'

'It seems clear enough. See the last two lines? One who understands the verse will command the beast.'

'Not you though, Starkey. You've been trying to decipher its codes for days now,' said Eleanor, with a mocking edge to her words.

'No, not me,' he said without argument. Instead, his eye came to rest heavily on Marcel.

Marcel's former terror returned. He didn't like the way they were staring at him.

'I know you have some special feel for the Book, Marcel. Those verses were in your mind even before you read them. There is magic in your hands. The elf-woman sensed it. *You* are the one to summon up the dragon.'

'No, not me!' he gasped, dismayed at what Starkey was suggesting. 'I don't feel anything special about this book.'

He should have known. Hadn't he seen the Book of Lies do its work many times before? But lying is an easy habit, the words coming to the tongue before the mind has even realised, and he so desperately wanted to believe the words himself. While the golden verse illuminated the tent, his own words began to appear on the page opposite.

I don't feel anything special about this book.

'See, I'm right!' crowed Starkey. 'You are the key. Here, give me your hand,' and before Marcel could pull away, his arm was seized in the man's steely grip. 'Trace your fingers over the golden letters and let the magic flow.'

Marcel had no choice. The Book had found him out. But he was sure there was no sorcery in him. Perhaps if he did as they asked it would all quickly come to nothing. Then hopefully they would leave him alone, and all he would need was a few moments to pick Bea up in his arms and escape to where Nicola would already be waiting anxiously for him.

He did as Starkey commanded and let his fingers range over the glowing letters. They were strangely warm to his touch, enticing him, urging him to let that warmth flow further into his body and even into his mind, where the simple words of the verse already resided.

This was not what he had expected. He felt himself wanting to give way to the magic, so he could learn the truth it seemed to offer. All he had to do was press his fingers more firmly into the golden letters. But he could not learn the truth unless he let the Book into his mind, and it was this that held him back. He wasn't ready. The Book would surely overpower him.

He tried to lift his fingers from the Book, but it held him there, drawing him down into itself. A book full of lies. No matter what it promised, he couldn't let himself become lost among the Book's pages. He must break free, and if his body seemed to have lost its will he must find another way, before Lord Alwyn's magic claimed him after all.

Free ... there was a different set of words that had once come to him, magically. He fought for them, urgently pushing away his fear until at last he felt them on his tongue.

My fate is my own, my heart remains free

He spoke these words under his breath so that the others would not hear, but in the struggle with the Book they boomed like thunder. What did he know of fate? Was it just what happened to you, like it or not, or could he forge his own way ahead? Could he recover the unknown life that had been stolen from him by Lord Alwyn's magic? No, he decided, he would find his life only when he created it for himself. With this thought, a second line joined the first.

Not magic but wisdom reveals destiny

Where had this come from? Not the Book of Lies, surely, because he had managed to keep it at bay.

Looking down, he saw with relief that his fingers had come free from the golden letters. He worked them up and down and stared about him, blinking like a sleeper just coming awake. Starkey and Eleanor were staring at him, amazed and suspicious.

'Well, did the Book tell you anything?'

'No. I don't know what the verse means any more than before,' he answered.

Since this was true, he was not surprised to see the Book of Lies slam itself shut and glow faintly, but it was not enough for Starkey. 'Did you try? Did you concentrate your mind properly on these words so the meaning would be clear?'

'Answer him,' retorted Eleanor when he hesitated.

'Yes, I felt the magic in my fingers, but ...' He peered into their cold, expectant faces. If he told them what had happened they would make him try again, and this time he would have to let the Book's sorcery flow into him. Those golden letters held a terrible power, an evil he didn't ever want to touch again. Before he knew what he was doing, he launched into a desperate lie.

'I felt the Book's magic but it couldn't tell me the meaning of the verse.'

As soon as they were gone from his mouth he wished he could snatch them back. He had betrayed himself, and any moment now the Book would buck violently back and forth until his lie was recorded.

But to his astonishment, the Book of Lies glowed in Starkey's hands, brighter than he had ever seen it.

'Curse this book!' Starkey roared. 'It's tormenting us with its promises and its magic.'

What had happened? How could he have tricked Lord Alwyn's greatest creation, a magic that could look into a person's heart and know that he was lying? And he *had* lied. *I felt the Book's magic but it couldn't tell me the meaning of the verse.*

Of course it could. It had been eager to do just that.

But wait … *it couldn't tell me* … In one sense, it was true. The Book couldn't tell him because he hadn't let it. He had deceived Starkey and Eleanor and yet told the truth at the same time!

This was becoming more than he could understand. Why had it glowed brighter than ever before? Marcel began to suspect that the Book of Lies had *wanted* him to deceive them. More than that, it had *helped* him to do it!

Starkey's unrelenting gaze bored into Marcel as though he suspected some kind of trick. 'This book has a way to raise Mortregis. It's there in those words. Try again — and this time I shall accept no failure!'

His hand found the hilt of the ruby-encrusted dagger and Marcel's stomach turned sick with fear.

'Princess Eleanor,' came a rough voice from outside the tent. The tension of the moment was instantly shattered.

'Enter,' Eleanor called, and one of Zadenwolf's men appeared before them. 'A messenger has come from Long Beard to ask about the elf-girl. He is waiting in King Zadenwolf's tent.'

Eleanor dismissed him with a wave of her hand. She spoke openly in front of Marcel now, without a care for what he might make of her words. 'What will we do? She's still alive,' she hissed at Starkey, who frowned deeply while his eyes stayed focused on the Book of Lies. She saw this and snapped at him angrily, 'Leave the Book. We don't want it with us when we speak to Long Beard's courier.'

Moments later they were gone, leaving Marcel to wonder whether he should follow them and shout the truth in front of this messenger. No, he decided quickly, Starkey and Eleanor would surely kill the poor fellow, just as they had murdered Remora. He must return to his own plan and get Bea away to safety. They could return at any moment to check on her.

He hurried to Bea's bed and began to pick her up, but she moaned weakly and her body felt so cold and frail that he had to let her fall back onto the mattress. For precious seconds he stared down at his little friend as she struggled for life, and as each of those seconds passed he sensed more strongly that his plan would not work. Bea would probably not survive a journey through the forest, and even if she was still alive when they reached Long Beard, elfish medicine would not save her now. She needed something far more powerful.

With a mixture of hope and the gravest terror, Marcel already knew what he must do. He turned sharply and let his eyes scour the tent for what he knew was there. Yes, the Book of Lies still lay where

Starkey had put it aside. Gadfly was waiting. It was the only way to keep Bea alive.

He put the Book back in the leather sack and looped it over his shoulder, picked up Bea's limp body and stepped out into the rain.

No one challenged him. Zadenwolf's soldiers were still sheltering from the deluge. He hurried towards the forest trail, where Nicola and Gadfly stood shivering.

'What took you so long?' Nicola whispered anxiously. When he hesitated, she pressed him. 'Come on, there's no time to lose.'

'Nicola, where I'm taking Bea, you won't want to come,' he told her.

'What are you talking about?'

Marcel answered solemnly, 'Bea needs more than ointments and potions to survive.' He could barely believe his own words when he said what was in his mind. 'She needs sorcery.'

'You can't mean Lord Alwyn!'

All Marcel cared about was Bea, and if Lord Alwyn was the only one who could keep her alive then he would take her to him. Slipping the leather sack from his shoulder, he held it up for Nicola to see. 'Lord Alwyn would help us if we took his book back to him in return.'

'You're crazy, Marcel. He and Pelham might simply kill us all!'

'If you're afraid, it's not too late to go back to camp.'

'No, I'm with you whatever you do,' she said firmly.

'Then get onto Gadfly's back,' he ordered, and when she had struggled into place he lifted Bea up to sit slumped in front of her.

But Nicola had a sudden thought. 'Marcel, Lord Alwyn will be in Elstenwyck by now. That's days and days away, even with Gadfly to carry us. Bea will never make it.'

Marcel's lips were curling into a wry smile as he began to loop the Book of Lies over Gadfly's head. Instantly she snorted and shimmied, and along her flanks strange lumps began to undulate wildly.

Nicola looked down in astonishment then quickly pulled her feet up out of the way. 'What's happening?' she yelled.

As he swung himself up onto the horse's back in front of Bea, Marcel called out to his sister, 'Nicola, there's something about Gadfly that I never told you ...'

Part Three

CHAPTER 17

Return to the Chamber

THE STEADY BEAT OF Gadfly's wings carried them on towards Elstenwyck. The relentless rain had stung their faces at first, but by the time the dark outline of the elves' great mountain loomed ahead it had eased. They broke over the edge of the steep escarpment to the valley, where rain had not ventured for the past year. The plains below looked parched and their clothes were quickly dry. Farmhouses dotted the patchworked landscape and occasionally they would sweep over a sleepy village nestled in the crook of fields that shimmered and danced in the afternoon heat.

Despite the warm wind that whipped at their hair and their sleeves, Marcel shuddered. Was he leading them all into hands even more evil than the ones they had just escaped?

Behind him, Nicola saw that shudder and guessed the cause. 'We *are* doing the right thing, Marcel. I'm sure of it now.'

Wedged tightly between them so that she would not fall was little Bea, her head slumped onto her chest and closer to death with every minute that passed. 'Come on, Gadfly, faster!' Marcel urged, at the same time secretly dreading their journey's end.

They flew on for another hour. Then two had passed, and finally Nicola cried out, 'There!' and pointed with her arm outstretched. 'The city. Do you see it?'

It was still a long way off, but there was no doubting that their destination was in sight. Soon they could make out the houses inside the city walls, but it was the palace that held their eye. No human being had ever seen it as they saw it now: the round towers planted solidly at each corner, the myriad smaller turrets jutting skyward, each with a column of windows surveying the lush gardens below. With its walls glowing sand-yellow in the afternoon sunlight, the palace didn't seem like the vast dungeon Marcel had imagined when he first set eyes on it at night.

The busy streets below swarmed with townsfolk. Faces turned upwards to see what could have cast such a strange shadow as Gadfly flew overhead. The spectacle left them all open-mouthed, and some scurried along the streets for a closer look.

Agile as a sparrow, Gadfly dipped below the height of the thatched roofs, and with the palace only the length of a street away, she touched down on the cobblestones in a deserted laneway. Marcel jumped down immediately and took Bea in his arms. Nicola was quickly on the ground beside him.

'Pull the leather sack over Gadfly's head,' he instructed her.

As soon as Nicola had removed the sack, those great wings shrivelled and shrank and finally disappeared into Gadfly's speckled flanks.

'Such magic,' she breathed, looking down at the weight in her hands. 'After everything you did to steal it, Marcel, now we've brought the Book of Lies back to Lord Alwyn.'

He nodded with calm determination. 'It's a simple thing. Lord Alwyn can have his precious book in return for Bea's life.'

He turned to look at the palace, so grand and inviting when he had seen it from the air. Now it loomed pitilessly over him once again, the lair of a man he was yet to meet, a man he feared even more than Lord Alwyn, whose name he loathed even more than Eleanor's. King Pelham.

By now, a crowd had found them and gathered a short distance away, staring and whispering.

'They were flying, I saw them. That horse had wings!' cried a flabbergasted woman who clutched a basket of apples from the market.

'Yes, but where have the wings gone now?' asked another.

'Who are those three?'

'Are they witches?' called a bolder, less friendly voice.

Nicola scanned the curious faces. 'We can't stay here like this,' she whispered, and before Marcel could react she started to lead Gadfly along the lane, forcing the crowd to part as they passed through. Just as well, too, for she began to hear a familiar name, uttered with awe and amazement.

'Catherine!'

All too soon it was on everyone's lips. 'It's Princess Catherine!'

'And the boy is Prince Marcel!'

Other names quickly followed, muttered darkly and with an unmistakable edge of alarm and anger. 'Damon ... Eleanor ... houses set on fire ... these two had a hand in it, they say.'

Had the laneway been longer, the seething crowd might have turned on them, but they soon found themselves at the same small gate Starkey had chosen on the night of Damon's and Eleanor's escape. A familiar face stared out at them.

'The young Princess ... and your brother!' he added when Marcel stepped forward. The keys remained untouched at his belt as he came closer to the gate. He glared at them with a confused mixture of resentment, suspicion and something more difficult to place.

'Your name is Joseph, isn't it?' Marcel began tentatively. 'Would you let us through, please, Sir?'

'We want to see the King,' Nicola insisted defiantly.

Joseph raised his eyebrows in surprise. 'I daresay he'll want to see you two, as well. How do you dare to show your faces back here again?' He touched the bandage he still wore on his head.

'We're sorry you were knocked out like that, Joseph. We didn't know our friend would do such a thing.'

'Your friend! They say the culprit was Sir Thomas Starkey himself.'

'Yes, but he's certainly not our friend any more, and he's not here with us now. You have my word. Please believe us, Joseph. We're here because this little girl needs Lord Alwyn's magic. We've come to give ourselves up, as hostages.'

'Hostages? That makes no sense to me,' said the old guard, 'but my poor mind was simple enough before Starkey did his damage.'

Joseph scrambled hastily to fit the key into the lock and at last they were inside. The gate was locked again, though the more brazen of the townsfolk who had followed them along the lane pressed cold, hostile faces against the iron bars to see what would happen. They might have taken matters into their own hands if we'd stayed out there any longer, thought Marcel grimly.

'Where's the other one, your brother?' Joseph asked.

Brother? But before they could ask what he meant, a deep and melodious burp split the air.

'Belch,' Marcel cried as the man himself appeared around the corner of the guardhouse. As soon as Gadfly saw him, she stepped along the path and offered her nose for stroking.

'There's a mad fellow rushing through the palace, shouting about a flying horse. I knew it must be you,' said Belch.

'But what are you doing here?'

'Ah, well someone had to bring Lord Alwyn back to the palace.'

So Lord Alwyn was here, Marcel thought with a mixture of relief and dread. But the sight of Belch stroking Gadfly's nose prompted a lingering guilt, and despite the apprehension that gripped his heart, he turned to the horseman and said, 'I'm sorry, Belch. Gadfly was yours and I stole her from you.'

'Mine! No one can own a horse like this one, Marcel, except perhaps the boy who gives her wings,' he replied, fixing him with a firm stare in case there was any doubt about whom he meant.

'It was not the Prince who gave your horse wings, Belch,' a deep voice called out from behind him. Marcel spun on his heels to find that the stooped figure of Lord Alwyn himself had emerged from the gardens. 'You know the cause as well as I do, Marcel. Now, where is the Book?'

'We have it, Your Lordship. We've stolen it from

Starkey and Eleanor and Damon. We've come here to give it back to you, but in return we beg you to help this girl. She's dying. Please, Lord Alwyn, only magic can keep her alive.' He turned to his sister. 'Nicola, give him the Book.'

This was the moment. They would soon know whether their wild gamble would save Bea. Did Lord Alwyn have any compassion in him? Nicola came forward, holding out the leather sack. As he took it into his hands, the deep lines carved into Lord Alwyn's face seemed to slacken with relief and his ageing frame became a little straighter.

'Let me see the girl,' he said.

Marcel stepped closer, raising Bea's frail body as high as his aching arms would allow. 'She was wounded by an arrow, fired by Starkey's own bowman. See the bandage on her shoulder?'

Lord Alwyn touched her forehead with an unexpected tenderness. 'She is barely alive,' he muttered gravely. 'You are quite right. Only my magic can help her now.'

He paused to think for a moment, looking about the palace grounds as he spoke. 'We must act quickly. Take her to the chamber in the rose garden.'

The chamber! Both children gasped. But what choice did they have? Better to risk becoming Pelham's prisoners than leave Bea to a certain death.

The wizard led the way into the same garden they had once scurried through in darkness. The chamber lay waiting for them, built of the same honey-coloured stone as the palace itself, with only its narrow windows to hint that it had recently been a prison.

When they arrived in the alcove that shaded the entrance, Lord Alwyn read from the inscription carved in the door. '*A true and rightful heir*. Which of you opened this door for Starkey?'

Marcel looked briefly at his sister. 'We did it together, all three of us,' he announced, unafraid.

Marcel's arms were full with Bea's little body, so Lord Alwyn turned to Nicola. 'Your Highness,' he said, 'would you open it for us now?'

As soon as she touched it, the handle yielded, and she opened the door to let Marcel set Bea down gently on a couch, amid a cluster of soft brocade cushions. The room, now that they could see it, was fitted out with every luxury: rich wall hangings, ornate oaken furniture, and heavy velvet drapery adorning the twin beds.

Lord Alwyn knelt stiffly beside Bea, who stirred and fought to open her eyes. 'Let me see the wound.'

Marcel's hands moved quickly, peeling back the bandage, which was completely soaked in Bea's blood. The wizard drew in a sharp breath. 'It will test all my powers to save her,' he murmured. He slipped the heavy sack from his shoulder and put it on the couch at Bea's feet. Closing his eyes, he passed his hand slowly over the ravaged flesh of Bea's shoulder.

'Look, the wound is beginning to heal!' cried Nicola.

As Marcel watched, the blood around that angry wound darkened and became hard. The crusted blood flaked away and new skin began to grow before their eyes. In little more than a minute, all that remained was a scar the size of a silver coin.

Bea's eyes opened at last, the clear dark eyes they all remembered. She was still too weak to sit up or even say a word, but her eyes found Marcel's and her face lit up with happiness. Fighting tears, and despite the danger all round him, Marcel laughed like he never remembered doing before.

A frightened gasp from Nicola broke his joyful thoughts. 'What's wrong?' he asked.

'The door!'

He spun round and saw that Lord Alwyn had deliberately closed the door of the chamber behind them. 'The spell!' he exclaimed, all gratitude draining rapidly away. 'Lord Alwyn, what have you done? We're all locked in here forever now, unless Damon or Eleanor takes pity on us.'

'Damon and Eleanor? I doubt we could expect much pity from those two. Perhaps you have learned that already,' the wizard remarked wryly. He was slumped against the cushions, as though the magic of Bea's recovery had left him without the strength to stand up. 'Certainly I cannot free myself, but for you two it is quite a different matter. By the words of my own magic, you can leave whenever you choose.'

Marcel's face creased into a contemptuous smile. 'No we can't. We know the evil trick you played on Damon and Eleanor. That door has no handle on the inside. Only someone on the outside can open it.'

'Oh, and who told you such a thing?'

Brother and sister glanced sideways to meet each other's eye. What was he hinting at? They had turned back to face him, but now their eyes were drawn to the door again. 'Marcel,' Nicola said in a voice that could barely be heard, 'there's a handle on this side too.'

'Yes, a handle,' said Lord Alwyn, picking up her whisper. 'The door works equally well from inside as well as out. You have my word on the matter.'

His word. With Bea already struggling to sit up, perhaps the old wizard's word was not as worthless as it had once seemed. Nicola rushed over to the door and Marcel saw the handle glide down easily. She let go suddenly without opening the door. 'You try, Marcel,' she urged.

He joined her cautiously, rested his hand on the cold metal and felt it instantly give way. The door swung slowly outwards until he and Nicola were staring into the beautiful garden beyond.

'But it doesn't make sense! Why can we open it when our mother couldn't?'

They turned again towards Lord Alwyn, who had taken the Book of Lies out of its sack on the couch and was rising painfully to his feet. 'She claimed you both as her own, did she? Starkey's idea, no doubt. What of a husband, then? Did she make up a father for you too?'

'He died in battle, for the old Queen,' Marcel responded, not understanding the wizard's words.

'Battle? There've been no battles in this kingdom for as long as anyone can remember. I have made sure of that. No, whatever she told you, Eleanor has never married. Like Damon, she has lived her whole life alone.'

'But she's our mother!' Nicola protested tearfully. 'She even gave me a pearl necklace from around her own neck!'

The Book of Lies lay in the crook of Lord Alwyn's arm, a faint glow already reflected from the dull material of his robe. Glancing down at it long enough to draw the children's attention, he said clearly, 'Eleanor has no daughter. She has no children at all.'

The Book of Lies responded with a steady golden sheen.

This was all too much for Marcel. The Book must be wrong. He started to count off in his mind all the evidence that proved this must be a trick, and before he knew it, he heard these reasons spilling from his own lips.

'But ... but they called us Prince and Princess,' he cried. 'Not just Starkey and Eleanor. That guard, Joseph. He knew Fergus as Prince Edwin, and he called Nicola by her real name, Catherine. Even *you* called her Your Highness.'

'Oh yes, that part is true. You are indeed of royal blood. How else could you be the rightful heirs, with the power to open that door?'

Marcel didn't know what to believe now, but the door stood open and he could see how the Book continued to shine.

'Then, if Eleanor is not our mother ...' he murmured, overwhelmed by what the old wizard was telling him, '... whose children are we?'

Footsteps crunched the gravel of the path leading from a side entrance to the palace, and they spun around quickly to see a man hurrying towards the chamber. He was tall and dark-haired, dressed in the rich red robes of a lord, the edges embroidered in gold. Despite the speed of his approach, he carried himself with regal dignity.

He looked ahead and saw them watching him through the doorway. He threw his arms out towards them. Tears began to stream down his cheeks, heavy tears not of sadness but of joy and relief. 'You're alive after all!' he cried.

But when he was close enough to see their faces clearly, he suddenly stopped dead.

In the uncomfortable silence that followed, Marcel and his sister could only stare, dumbfounded. They had no memory of this man, but they had already guessed who he was.

A name escaped softly from Marcel's lips. 'King Pelham.'

But Nicola stood open-mouthed beside her brother, staring at him, then the King, then back at him again. 'You can't see it, the eyes, the nose ... the two of you look so alike. Marcel, he's our *father*!'

Marcel gazed at this man in the doorway. The King ... his father. Could it really be true?

Pelham too seemed to struggle with himself, his face contorted by confusion. 'Alwyn, what's wrong with them?' he called sharply to the wizard inside the chamber. 'Why do they look so surprised?'

'I did as we agreed, Pelham. I took away all memory of their lives here in the palace, even of you and of each other. Your daughter thinks of herself as Nicola, and if this little girl had not interfered, Marcel would have a different name as well.'

Marcel's head was spinning and he felt a deep dread in his chest. This talk between the two men seemed to confirm what he could barely believe. Pelham *was* his father. He had come here to save Bea's life, prepared to accept whatever fate would befall him, but this!

As he tried to make sense of it, a new thought began to enter his mind. Eleanor was *not* his mother. That must mean that ... He leaned closer to Nicola, whispering his thoughts as this wonderful hope came to life within him. 'If we really are Pelham's children, then the Queen must be our mother.'

He called to the King, 'Our mother, the Queen, is she here in the palace?'

'Yes, she is here.'

He didn't like Pelham's solemn tone, but he brushed this aside. 'Where is she?'

'Don't they know, Alwyn?' Pelham demanded of his sorcerer.

'It is as I told you. They remember nothing. Not joy, not grief.'

'Not even her name?'

'No! Don't say it!' came a wretched cry from Nicola, sending a new chill through Marcel's body. 'I already know her name, and so do you, Marcel.'

'You cannot know it,' Lord Alwyn insisted. 'I swept away all memory of her from your mind.'

'She's out there, isn't she?' Nicola shouted through tears she couldn't hold back any longer. She raised her hand and pointed past the King, into the tranquillity of the rose garden. 'She's under that gravestone.'

Gravestone! Marcel's mind twisted and fought with what he was hearing. He saw again, behind his eyes, their dash through the rose bushes, with Starkey leading the way, until they came across a woman of the court who was weeping before a beautiful tombstone. 'Ashlere,' he murmured, remembering the simple letters carved into the marble.

'Is she right?' he asked, turning towards Lord Alwyn. 'Was Ashlere our mother?'

Before the wizard could answer, Marcel charged through the doorway, with Nicola and the King following him. Brother and sister stood side by side before the grave, while the King stayed back. He seemed unwilling to come any closer to this gravestone among the roses.

'Do you remember, Marcel?' said Nicola in misery. 'Eleanor told us how she died. It wasn't just another of her lies. The Book was there in front of her, so it must be true. Queen Ashlere was poisoned …'

Marcel turned on the King, his father, the words tumbling out in a terrible rage. 'It was you who gave her the cup!' he shouted.

But Pelham was a king and not easily cowed. He thrust off Marcel's savage accusation and called to Lord Alwyn, who was approaching slowly from the chamber. 'Take them up to their quarters and see that a guard is posted outside to watch them day and night.'

And with this command, Pelham charged off towards the palace almost as rapidly as he had arrived.

As Nicola watched him stride away she whispered desolately into her brother's ear. 'Do you see what's happened, Marcel? All we've done is swap a murderous mother for a father who killed his own wife.'

CHAPTER 18

Astounding Truths and Magic Tricks

'I MUST OBEY YOUR father's orders and so must you,' said Lord Alwyn sternly as they saw King Pelham disappear through the distant doorway of the palace. They returned to the chamber, where Lord Alwyn slipped the Book of Lies back into the leather sack and hooked the strap over his shoulder. Bea was still too weak to walk, so Marcel took her up in his arms once more.

Others in the palace had heard of their arrival, it seemed. By the time Marcel and Nicola emerged from the chamber they found dozens of richly dressed courtiers staring at them from the central doorway. Words drifted down to them, as they had done out in the lane. Catherine ... Marcel ... The Princess ... The Prince ...

'You might not remember these faces, but they certainly know you, and they know what has happened,' Lord Alwyn told them gravely.

If these words were not unsettling enough, two armed soldiers now appeared, dressed in the King's scarlet livery, and began to march closely behind them.

The little procession crossed the bridge to the main entrance and the courtiers stood back to let them pass. Among them was the weeping woman from the garden. There were no words of welcome, only silence and grim gazes set against them, though here and there, Marcel found a friendlier face unable to hide genuine affection. One round-faced woman seemed on the point of rushing forward to greet them, but something was holding her back.

Before the palace swallowed them up, Marcel took a final glance upwards at its sombre turrets and half wondered whether he would ever see the sky again. Then the wizard conducted them through the wide doorway and they found themselves inside a glittering antechamber, its ceiling gilded and its walls decorated with magnificent paintings and heraldic friezes. It might have dazzled their eyes if they had been in a mood to notice such grandeur.

Their way ahead was blocked by imposing oak doors that reached halfway to the high ceiling. A splendid marble staircase swept away to the left, and another to the right, with views of twin courtyards beyond. They turned left, and at the top they proceeded along a well-lit corridor, lined with wooden panels carved with scenes of hunting and carnivals. Finally, Lord Alwyn opened a door and ushered them into a large bedroom, leaving the soldiers to stand guard outside.

This room was not as lavish as the antechamber below perhaps, but Marcel looked down, amazed, when he felt his shoes sink into the thick carpet. A wardrobe stood in the corner, and pressed against opposite walls were two splendid beds, both draped in rich brocade. In the middle of one a black cat lay sleeping, and rather than disturb it, Marcel laid Bea's little body on the other bed, beneath a large shield attached to the wall.

'Let her rest for a day or two and she will regain her strength,' Lord Alwyn advised, with a sympathy he seemed to reserve for Bea alone. Meanwhile, the cat had awoken, and after a graceful leap to the floor, it now threaded its way playfully between Marcel's legs.

He barely noticed, since he was staring at Nicola, who was struggling, like him, to take in all that had happened since they stepped inside the palace grounds.

'This must have been our room,' he murmured to her.

'You can tell a boy lives here,' she said, nodding at the shield. 'Was that my bed?' she asked, walking over to where the cat had been sleeping. Both beds boasted ornately carved bedheads, but this one had a chair and writing desk close by, and on the desk were a candle and a quill lying next to a pot of ink. On the other side of the bed stood a bookcase crowded with heavy tomes.

'No, Marcel slept there,' Lord Alwyn replied.

Nicola's face dropped in sullen surprise. But she was not to be disappointed for long.

'You had your own room through there,' the wizard continued, glancing towards a crimson curtain made of the heaviest velvet and trimmed with gold brocade.

'My own room!' exclaimed Nicola, her face coming to life just a little. She had taken three tentative steps towards the curtain before she stopped and turned round slowly. 'Lord Alwyn, if I slept in there, and this bed with all the books was Marcel's, then who slept under the shield?'

'I'm surprised both of you have not guessed already, especially you, Marcel. You were as close as any two boys can be.'

Despite all he had learned, the emptiness inside Marcel's head had never been so unbearable. He looked again at the bed. It was sparse, nothing around it to hint at the person who slept there, except for the shield. The many dents and the ruptured paintwork suggested that it had been well used in tournaments or by knights in training. Whoever had hung it there must have enjoyed such heroics.

It was this thought that pushed a name onto his lips. 'Fergus,' he whispered, bringing a gasp from Nicola. *As close as two boys can be.* Could Lord Alwyn really be suggesting that … 'But why would Fergus live here? He is my cousin, not my … not my brother.'

The old wizard remained silent, though his steady gaze did not leave Marcel's bewildered face. 'It can't be true, it can't,' the boy mumbled, shaking his head vigorously.

Nicola was desperately trying to make sense of this too. 'Wait, Marcel. Do you remember what Joseph said when we came through the gate? He asked where our brother was.'

'But Starkey said that —' Marcel stopped. Everything that Starkey had told them was a lie.

Still his mind rebelled. 'Fergus and I are the same age. How can we be brothers?'

'The same age. Indeed you are. You and Prince Edwin were born on the same day.'

'Are you saying they are twins?' cried Nicola. 'But they don't look the least bit alike.'

'That is true,' Lord Alwyn conceded. 'But what of it? Some twins can barely be told apart, while others are no more alike than two children plucked at random from the street.'

'My brother,' Marcel whispered slowly, still taking it all in. First a sister, then a father; then a mother, tragically dead by her husband's own hand. Now he had discovered a brother. He and Fergus had once been sworn enemies, and even now his devotion to the soldier's life was completely alien to Marcel. He looked at the shield above Bea's sleeping figure. 'My brother,' he said again, as though repeating it like this would make it easier to believe. How close had they been when they lived together in this room?

Nicola struggled with the same disbelief, but her mind wandered even further. 'He's still up there, in the mountains,' she cried with a sister's anguish. 'He still thinks Damon is his father.'

'So it seems, but it was not meant to happen this way,' said Lord Alwyn, his voice strangely free of the ponderous authority it so often carried. 'I should have been more vigilant in my duty to protect you.'

'*Protect us!*' Marcel cried incredulously. Suddenly he was seething with resentment at what this man's sorcery had done to them. 'You sent Termagant after me. If she'd caught me in Old Belch's barn that day, she would have torn me to pieces!'

But Lord Alwyn took them aback with a hearty laugh. 'I sent her to stop you, not to kill you. Only a special command from me would have let her harm you, and I was not about to give it. I had chosen her for that very purpose, because she loves you.'

'Loves me? But she growled and showed her teeth. We were terrified of her.'

'Oh yes, and I'm sure she enjoyed seeing you so frightened.'

'You make it sound as though … as though we knew her before you took us away to Fallside.'

Lord Alwyn nodded. 'Perhaps it is time I told you the truth. Here, Termagant, come to me,' he called.

Marcel gasped at the sound of that dreadful name. Both he and Nicola looked towards the door in terror, expecting the snarling beast to come bounding in to join her master at any moment. But then Marcel realised that Lord Alwyn was not even facing the door, and that he had spoken softly, so that his voice could be heard only inside this room.

As he watched, astonished, the black cat at his feet abandoned him and padded quickly to Lord Alwyn's side. The old wizard took something from the pocket of his robe and, stooping gingerly to one knee, he tied it around the cat's slender throat.

The little cat shook her head, as though a fly buzzed about her ears, and then suddenly her whole body shuddered. Before their eyes, her claws grew rapidly into vicious talons and her front teeth became long, savage fangs. By the time the transformation was complete, the playful bundle of fur had become the terrifying beast they had known in Fallside.

'You named her yourselves, using a word from the fables Queen Ashlere told you. A termagant is a wild and angry woman. Perhaps you had already guessed what secrets lay in her heart.'

'What sort of magic could make this happen?' Nicola asked breathlessly.

'A magic you have already encountered,' was Lord Alwyn's cryptic reply. He was testing them, urging them to guess the answer, as he had done with their brother's bed.

Marcel stared at Termagant's sleek and awesome lines until his eyes fell on the familiar pouch around her neck. 'That pouch. Does it hold something from the Book of Lies?'

'Ah, you have guessed it. A whole page torn from the back of the Book, folded many times to make it fit,' Lord Alwyn announced with a hint of impish delight that astonished them almost as much as Termagant's sudden metamorphosis. 'The Book's power is to know a heart's desire. For men, it can tell when that desire is to deceive, but for animals it is less predictable. In her own mind, your little pet is a great beast, savage and feared by all. She was just the kind of guard I needed with me in Fallside, ferocious to anyone who came near and fearsome enough to make you obey me.'

He waved languidly towards Termagant and she snarled suddenly, sending the children staggering backwards.

'Unfortunately, Marcel, I did not anticipate the courage that you and your little friend would find to defy me.'

At a further nod from her master, Termagant's growl died as quickly as it had appeared and she became calm and docile.

Marcel watched her, his mind still trying to catch up with what his eyes had seen. All the terror this beast had brought him had been for nothing. The claws that he had imagined slicing into his flesh were meant to scare him, not hurt him. Would there be any end to the way his world was turning inside out?

Before Marcel could make sense of his confusion, Nicola challenged the old wizard. 'You said you wanted to protect us. But why did you take so much away from us — our names, who we were, all our memories of life here in the palace?'

'I was only doing what your father wanted, to save you from great harm and misery. Yes, to protect you. That was why he insisted that I go with you to that remote foundling home in the high country. He is a good man who loves you dearly, just as he has been a good king, loved by his people, for his justice most of all.'

Nicola could not bear any more of this. '*His justice!*' she shouted. 'How can you say that? He poisoned our mother, his own wife!'

Lord Alwyn winced at her words. 'There is much still that you do not know — and even more that you can never know, by the terms of my own magic. If you want to know the source of the evil done within this kingdom, then look to Starkey and those two cousins you helped to release from their prison. Is it any wonder that your own father distrusts you? Those two want his throne at any cost, and Starkey is determined to win it for them, so that he can share in their power and its spoils.'

Marcel did not need to be told what drove Starkey or Eleanor, and he had long since guessed that Damon was just the same. What surprised him, though, were the things he was learning about Lord Alwyn. He had feared the man since he first set eyes on him back at the orphanage. He had hated him for almost as long. But much had changed since Gadfly had touched down in Elstenwyck — amazingly, less than an hour ago. Where once Marcel had seen an enemy, now the wizard seemed to offer him the truth.

Both wonderful and shocking, that truth told him that Eleanor, Damon and especially Starkey, whom he had once trusted so completely, were the ones to fear now.

Gazing at Lord Alwyn's ravaged face, Marcel wondered if he dared trust this man instead. What could he find in those eyes? Should he confide in the wizard about what he knew?

'Lord Alwyn,' he began in a faltering voice, 'Damon and Eleanor are in Lenoth Crag, trying to raise an army to take the throne. King Zadenwolf is too cautious to help them, but in these last few days Starkey has spoken of another way. He wants to conjure a great dragon. He even knows its name, Mortregis. He wants to summon it up and use it to defeat King Pelham ... my father,' he added softly, finding the words strange on his tongue.

'Mortregis!' Lord Alwyn responded with a contemptuous snort. 'The beast has been gone for centuries. As Master of the Books, it is my job to see that he never returns.'

'But Starkey is convinced that he can conjure Mortregis from the Book of Lies.'

'Nonsense! The Book of Lies cannot make Mortregis rise up again.'

There was more Marcel could say, but should he? He turned to Nicola, who knew immediately what he was thinking.

'He will find the verses soon enough, whether we tell him or not,' she whispered.

Lord Alwyn had heard her in any case. 'What are you two talking about? Verses?'

There was no going back now, and besides, Nicola was right. It was only a matter of time, whether they trusted Lord Alwyn or not. 'Some strange verses have appeared in the Book,' Marcel answered reluctantly. 'Right before our eyes, in letters of gold. They are still there now.'

At the mention of Mortregis, Lord Alwyn had remained calm, even regaining a little of the disdain that he so often showed for the world around him. But when Marcel spoke of the mysterious verses, he could not hide his distress.

'Show me,' he demanded as he slipped the heavy sack from his shoulder and took out the Book of Lies. Marcel opened the back cover and there were the verses, the letters shining even more brightly than when he had last seen them.

Lord Alwyn's eyes raced urgently over the words, but once he had arrived at the last lines his confidence rapidly returned. 'It is nothing to worry about,' he declared categorically.

Marcel was baffled. Surely the wizard could see the danger threatened in those words. 'But the meaning seems so clear, Your Lordship. Starkey *must* be right. Mortregis is more powerful than any king. There it is on your robe,' he said, nodding at the intricate embroidery that circled the wizard's legs.

'If you understood these verses as I do, Marcel, you would know there is nothing to fear.'

'But Starkey thinks *I* can summon Mortregis,' Marcel confessed. 'He insisted that I had some kind of magic in me.'

Lord Alwyn laughed openly now. 'Your magic was just for show, Marcel.'

His magic! Those simple words, uttered with such condescension, had startled him. 'You mean I *do* have some magic in me?'

'Yes, you dabbled in such things,' Lord Alwyn admitted in the same patronising tone. 'You showed considerable aptitude for the tricks you learned. I wished my apprentices had displayed as much skill for more powerful magic.'

He saw their amazement at the mention of apprentices. 'Yes, I tried to teach many a young man over the years, but they proved a poor lot. In the end I dismissed them all.'

'All of them?'

'None was worthy of the power sorcery bestows. Oh, yes, each of them wanted to become Master of the Royal Books after me, and swore to protect the Kingdom as the Master must do. But they failed the tests I set for them. I could not let any of them take my place.'

He had grown solemn and distant as he told them this, but finding Marcel's eye on him, he permitted himself a tight-lipped smile. 'And I could not let you play too much with sorcery. As a prince, your destiny lay elsewhere.

'I taught you a few tricks, nothing more. That is why you have so many books beside your bed. You borrowed them from me. See this one?' He picked up a volume from the top shelf. 'It is a book of charms and incantations. Simple magic, for entertaining your brother and sister. You can probably still manage the easiest of them. Go ahead, try it.'

'What shall I do?'

Lord Alwyn glanced around the chamber until his eyes settled on Marcel's bookcase itself. 'Those books on their side are untidy. Stand them upright on the shelves. Here, I will find the words for you,' and with a sweep of his hand, the pages of the book began to fan back and forth, reminding Marcel of a far more powerful book close by.

The magic stopped, and on the page that lay open before him, Marcel found a simple couplet.

Lines and angles, flat and bland
Raise these volumes, make them stand

He spoke them under his breath, prompting a gentle rebuke from Lord Alwyn. 'Out loud, boy. The simpler the charm, the louder it must be heard.'

Marcel tried again, with more strength in his voice this time. As he spoke, a strange sensation filled his skull. The words became echoes crashing noisily against his own thoughts, knocking them aside so that they would not distract him. *Concentrate.* That was what the feeling was telling him, and closing his eyes, he began to focus on the bookshelves and nothing else.

Was it working? A gasp from Nicola almost made him open his eyes again, but he sensed the spell would be broken if he did. He could feel an energy leaving his body now, not enough to exhaust him, but sweat was beading on his brow and his breathing had quickened. Without a view of the bookcase, somehow he knew, nonetheless, that one by one the fallen books were righting themselves.

The door to the room opened suddenly and a woman's voice called, 'Your Lordship, I've been sent up with something for the Prince and the Princess to eat.'

Marcel could not block out the sounds and their meaning, trivial though they were. He felt the words inside his head fade instantly, and opening his eyes he was just in time to see book after book rain heavily onto the floor. Only one weighty volume remained stubbornly in place, in the centre of the top shelf.

'Ah, you let the world intrude upon your spell. So like the young and the weak of mind,' Lord Alwyn announced, like a father whose baby son had fallen onto his bottom while learning to walk.

'Just like when he was little, always leaving his books all over the floor for me to pick up,' tut-tutted the plump, motherly maid as she entered and saw the mess Marcel had made. 'Put those things here,' she instructed the other servants who now appeared behind her, carrying a splendid table and three matching chairs. When these were arranged in the centre of the room, the maid placed the steaming tray she bore on the table and stood back.

The delicate fingers of a delicious aroma were already tickling Nicola's nostrils. She inched closer to the table. Despite the wonder of what he had just discovered, Marcel was doing the same. It was now mid-afternoon, and he realised he had not eaten anything since breakfast.

'Your Lordship, the King is waiting for you to join him in the Great Hall,' said the maid.

'I must leave you,' Lord Alwyn said immediately to the children. At a wave of his hand, the fallen books rose, one by one, and returned to their places in Marcel's bookcase. 'But listen to me, both of you. You are not trusted, even if you do not understand why. You must not leave this room.'

'Termagant!' he called as he opened the door and let the maid and the other servants precede him into the corridor. The two soldiers standing on guard saw the creature appear at the old wizard's side and staggered backwards in white-faced terror.

'You may go,' he commanded. 'This beast will guard the children better than any man.' He waved his hand towards Termagant and the creature was instantly more alert, snarling at the children with unmistakable malice. 'She obeys my magic. Once she would not have harmed you, but if you try to leave now, she will ensure you take no more than three paces beyond this door.'

With that, he turned and hurried away as well as his ageing legs would allow towards his appointment with the King.

Termagant's familiar growl had set Marcel's pulse racing. As he closed the door and dragged himself back to the middle of the room, it took a few minutes for his heartbeat to slacken.

He and Nicola gulped down the soup and freshly baked bread then went to check on Bea. They were relieved to find her breathing easily, the colour in her face strengthening with every breath.

'We're the same now, all three of us,' said Nicola, looking down at her with a sigh. 'Our mothers are dead and we have no memory of them, not even a face in our minds or the memory of a hand touching us.'

The melancholy in her voice brought a lump to Marcel's throat. 'Starkey told us we had the same mother, but it's taken that gravestone among the rose bushes to really make us brother and sister.'

Nicola turned to him, letting him see the tears in her eyes. All she could manage in reply was a nod of her head, but she took his hand as well. Once, he would have snatched it away, but not now.

'We know who we truly are now, but we're no better off than when we thought we were orphans, back at Mrs Timmins',' Marcel said bitterly. 'We're still prisoners, with the same terrible guard watching over us, and we still have no idea why.'

'That's what he need to know most of all, Marcel. Why.'

This question, and many others like it, preoccupied them as the afternoon sun waned and slowly gave way to darkness. This had been the longest day either of them could remember, and they did not stay awake late. Nicola slipped through the curtain to her own room and Marcel climbed into his bed among the books, a thousand reflections swirling through his head. It wasn't long, though, before exhaustion overtook him and he fell into a deep and dreamless sleep.

CHAPTER 19

The Tapestry

*M*ARCEL!

The call stirred him from his sleep and made him sit up blearily in bed. He couldn't tell what time it was, but the silence of the palace told him it must be well after midnight.

'Bea, is that you?' he called across the darkened room. No answer.

He threw the bedcovers aside and went to check, but she was sleeping calmly.

Perhaps it was Nicola. He pushed through the heavy curtain and hurried to her bedside, but his sister was fast asleep as well.

Who had called him? The word had been so clear, so loud inside his head. Yes, *inside* his head. Had he really heard it with his ears at all? Very strange. He settled back into the warmth of his bed, hoping to fall back to sleep quickly.

Thump!

He sat up again. It was just a book falling onto its side on the bookcase. He put his head back onto the pillow, only to hear a second book fall. Before he could get out of bed, a third toppled over, then a fourth. By the time he was on his feet, every book on the shelves had landed on the floor.

The feeble moonlight spilling through the window was not enough to see by. He groped his way to the writing desk and lit the candle he had noticed there earlier. Then he discovered something stranger still. Not all of the books on the shelves had fallen after all. There was one that remained upright, the same hefty book that had stayed in place when his rudimentary magic had swept the rest onto the floor earlier.

He reached up, expecting it to stick doggedly to the shelf. But no, when he grasped it the book moved easily. In fact, it felt light in his hand, too light for a tome of this size. He took it to the writing desk to examine it more closely. An impulse he could not explain drove him to turn the pages frantically, ten at a time, until he was a third of the way through the book. Then he stopped, open-mouthed in amazement. The pages of the larger book had been carefully cut away at their centre to create a deep hollow, and sitting inside this hollow was another book, not bound in the aged and wrinkled red leather of the Book of Lies, but with a soft and supple cover stained the colour of the evening sky.

Cautiously, Marcel took this book out of its hiding place and this time he did open the very first page. Only two lines were written there, in the very centre, in a slow and deliberate handwriting.

My fate is my own, my heart remains free
Not magic but wisdom reveals destiny

He turned the page. Spells, enchantments, detailed instructions decorated with meticulous diagrams ... he stared more closely at one illustration where a cat played peacefully with a mouse. There was no doubting which cat it was. Beneath the picture lay the magical words that could make this miracle happen, all in the same sloping script.

He took the quill, dipped it in the inkwell and began to copy the first line of the spell further down on the same page. He managed only three words before the nib ran dry, but by then he knew. The handwriting was identical, and that could only mean he had written everything in this book himself.

Here was proof that he had done more than dabble in the simple tricks that Lord Alwyn had scoffed at. The boy who wrote these words knew more of sorcery's secrets than the old wizard ever imagined.

His eyes were eager for the words, and as he read each rhyme, each incantation, it quickly settled within him, as though he had always known it. Soon he realised he was not just reading this book, his hungry mind was devouring it, page after page. He read on, for many hours, while around him the palace, the city and the entire Kingdom slept.

He became so absorbed that the tiny night-sounds of the palace fell unnoticed on his ears, until he heard a familiar growl that was too much for him to ignore. Someone had surprised Termagant. He heard a deep voice whisper to the beast, expecting obedience. Was it Lord Alwyn?

He left the book on the writing desk and crept to the door, daring himself to press down on the handle. He widened the gap to an inch but no more. There was Termagant, staring down the corridor, which was lit with candles hanging from brackets on the walls. Marcel's eye followed just in time to see a tall figure round the corner at the corridor's end. In that instant, he glimpsed a red robe, fringed in gold.

'The King!' he gasped. But before he could decide whether he was imagining things, Termagant saw him and growled again, warning him not to open the door any wider.

That familiar terror prickled beneath his skin, but he did not close the door immediately. There was something fascinating about Termagant now. He had once drawn a picture of the real Termagant in his book of sorcery. He had not been afraid of her then. Was he afraid of her now? After all, she was no more than a simple cat, made huge and frightening by her own grand dreams and the magic in that pouch around her neck. Marcel had rediscovered a magic of his own in these past hours, from his own book, and as he stood there, peering through the door, he could feel it coursing faintly through his entire body.

What a creature you are, Termagant, he thought in silent conversation. What fantasies must gallop around inside your head.

No greater than yours, came a reply.

Marcel blinked and looked around him. Who had spoken?

Ah, but he already knew. The eyes of the beast upon him confirmed it. The words had come from Termagant herself. She had heard his thoughts, and what was more, he had heard hers in return.

'But how?' he said aloud.

He closed the door and went back to the desk, where the book of magic lay open. He began to study his book again with greater urgency. He quickly realised that much of the magic he had explored had sought out the thoughts of others, even animals.

He tried again, reaching out for Termagant's mind. Yes, it was there within his grasp, a wild and angry vision which he could see through her eyes. He felt the urge to intervene, to lessen her boiling rage, but he held back. He knew it was fear that stopped him. He was afraid of a power he could not remember.

He must know more, he must become stronger, he told himself. But for now he had taken in as much as his mind could absorb. He felt his eyelids drooping and his soft bed beckoned. Just as the sky began to grow lighter, he crawled between the sheets and slept.

THE SUN ROSE SOON afterwards, but Marcel did not see it. He slept on until the motherly maid knocked at the door with their breakfast. He watched from his bed as she entered, white-faced and shaking after passing so close to Termagant. He closed his eyes again while she set the tray noisily on the table and departed.

It took a familiar voice finally to rouse him. 'If you don't come soon I'll eat yours as well as mine.' Sitting up quickly, he found Bea shovelling a fork crowded with bacon into her mouth.

'Bea, you're feeling better!'

He joined her at the table just as the irresistible aroma brought Nicola from beyond the heavy curtain. Between mouthfuls of egg and crusty bread, brother and sister explained to Bea all that had happened while her own life had hung in the balance.

'You *are* still a prince, then, Marcel?' asked Bea, wide-eyed and hesitant, as she struggled to make sense of so many discoveries.

'Yes, and I'm a princess. Just look at my dress!' Nicola cried, standing up suddenly and turning herself around so they could admire the spectacular gown of shimmering gold she had found in her room. 'Isn't it beautiful! Come on, Bea, there are more dresses in here from when I was little. We'll find something for you too.'

Marcel could only watch as Nicola tugged at Bea's hand, dragging her out of her chair and towards the curtain. But his little friend seemed no more interested than he was.

'What's wrong?' Nicola asked when she sensed Bea's resistance.

'I'm sure they're all lovely, Nicola,' said Bea half-heartedly. 'But a dress like yours would make me too easy to see.'

Nicola realised her mistake immediately. 'Of course. I'd forgotten that staying hidden is a part of who you are.' She inspected her own magnificent gown again. The expression on her face showed how much she adored it, but when she looked up she caught Marcel's hard eye on her. 'There are more important things to worry about, aren't there? The things we talked about yesterday afternoon. We *must* find out why our own father is keeping us prisoner.'

'Yes, that's what really matters,' Marcel responded. It was exactly the way he felt too, and her obvious resolve doubled his own determination.

He glanced through the window, judging the strength of the light. 'Look, it's halfway through the morning and no one has come to visit us except the servants who brought our breakfast. They might leave us alone here for days. If we're going to find out anything at all, we'll have to do it ourselves, don't you think?'

'But how are we going to do that?' asked Nicola bluntly. 'We're prisoners, and that's no ordinary guard at the door.'

Marcel had already been thinking about this. 'Bea, are you well enough? Do you think you could …'

'Past Termagant? No, not this time, Marcel. Even Grandfather would have trouble with her so close.'

Marcel's face reflected his frustration as he let his eyes explore the room again, not to inspect its treasures this time, but to find a way out. Nothing seemed to offer any hope of escape … unless …

His eyes had fallen on his own book of magic, from which he had already learned so much. Did he dare?

'Open the door,' he ordered his sister as he stood up from the table.

'Are you mad? You heard Lord Alwyn. Three steps and she'll rip you to pieces.' But her look said she knew he was serious and she did as he asked.

The opening of the door had alerted Termagant, who extended her claws in readiness in case the children tried to rush past her. The click of those deadly talons echoed on the stone floor of the corridor until moments later she stood framed by the doorway. With all the menace they remembered, she snarled at Marcel and bared her savage teeth, while

Nicola and Bea backed away until they felt the cold wall behind them.

Come, stand in front of me, Marcel told Termagant soundlessly.

She paused to think about this, then padded into his view, stopping only an arm's length from his nose. Her sleek features quizzed him, and for the first time the terrible heat in her eyes seemed doused, just a little. But she was not under his control yet.

The old sorcerer is my master. I obey his magic.

I am a sorcerer too. Perhaps you knew that even when I didn't. You and I must have played together many times. Did I practise my magic on you?

Termagant's thoughts hesitated and Marcel saw his chance. He held her eyes with his own, forcing his way into her mind until he heard her recall, *There was a mouse …*

He had her now, he could feel it — so long as he kept his concentration. Termagant's body, huge and frightening though it was, lost the tension that had rippled and danced along its flanks whenever Lord Alwyn commanded her. Marcel was holding her steady with his mind, drawing on the words he chanted over and over again.

Suddenly at the edge of his vision he sensed a shape move. It was Bea. What was she doing? *Go back!* he urged frantically in his mind.

But Bea was not a partner in his thoughts. She kept coming, closer and closer towards Termagant. With a sickening leap of his heart, Marcel understood the terrible risk she was about to take.

'Bea, come back!' Nicola called.

The words broke through to Marcel, disturbing his concentration, and Termagant began to growl deeply. She turned her massive head towards Bea and bared her teeth.

There was no time for Bea to retreat. One well-aimed swipe of those vicious claws and not even Lord Alwyn's magic would save her this time.

Concentrate. The magic lies in the power of my thoughts, Marcel reminded himself. *Lie down, Termagant,* he ordered. *Purr like the cat that you are.*

Slowly, so slowly, Termagant began to settle at Marcel's feet. Now Bea crept bravely towards her and reached out to the tiny pouch that hung from the leather strip around her neck. Bea's nimble fingers worked at the knot that held it in place, prising the leather apart until at last the two ends came free. She backed away with the little pouch in her hands and slipped it into the pocket of her dress.

The transformation began at once. The huge beast, made docile by Marcel's magic, shrank before their eyes. She shuddered, once, twice, and stretched herself out like a cat waking from an afternoon nap, but by the time she stood upright and still on the carpet again, she was a little cat once more.

'How — how did you do it, Marcel?' Nicola blustered, barely able to believe what she had seen.

'I found a book,' he began weakly. He was stunned at how much the magic had taken out of him, but his elation at what he had done helped him recover. 'My own book of magic. You won't believe it. I was a sorcerer, like Alwyn himself.'

But there was no time to show it to them. Their guard was gone and they were free.

'Where do you think we should go, Marcel?' Nicola questioned.

Marcel had his answer ready. 'To get the truth from anyone who can tell it to us. We have to know why our own father is treating us this way.'

'Marcel, do you remember the faces as we entered the palace?' Nicola asked him. 'Some of the courtiers still seem to care about us, even if the King doesn't. Perhaps one of them will tell us what happened. Bea, you scout the way ahead and warn us if anyone is coming.'

Bea crept into the corridor, and with a mischievous wink she vanished before their eyes. Luck travelled with them, and there were no guards about. Moments later Bea waved them on. By the time they reached the top of the sweeping staircase she was already at the bottom, taking refuge behind a suit of armour as two soldiers marched towards them along the length of the antechamber and turned to go out the front entrance.

Down they went, but there were more footsteps coming. 'Quickly, through those doors!' Nicola whispered frantically. She was already running across the intricate marble mosaics set into the floor, heading for the grand oak doors they had noticed yesterday.

They opened one of the doors cautiously, but again no one challenged them, so they bolted through and pushed the heavy door back into place. The echo of its creaking hinges rebounded from the far end of the room, but to their relief the footsteps continued without a pause.

They found themselves in a great hall of breathtaking grandeur. Termagant had come with them from the bedchamber, and she sauntered on ahead, her tail held high as she rounded an ornate throne raised on a low platform at one end of the long hall. There was a large and splendid desk covered with maps of the Kingdom and a pot of ink, and a few chairs were scattered about, but other than this the hall was unfurnished.

Panels on the ceiling were painted the colour of the sky and edged in silver. The banner bearing the royal coat of arms was suspended high above the throne, taking pride of place among rows of colourful pennants. Fastened to the right-hand wall were shields like the one that hung above Fergus's bed, and all manner of weapons: swords, maces and long pikes. They looked as though they had not been used for many years.

Great shafts of sunlight streamed in through a row of windows high up on this side, illuminating a magnificent tapestry that stretched the entire span of the opposite wall. It brushed the floor and rose as high as a man could reach, all but the last two yards crowded with scene after scene, embroidered in rich threads that must surely have been stolen from a rainbow.

Marcel immediately found himself mesmerised by it. One early scene in particular caught his eye. He stretched out his fingers, tracing the stitches. 'Lord Alwyn's robe,' he muttered.

'What is it? What have you found?' Nicola asked, and she hurried to see what had caught his eye. 'The dragon,' she gasped.

'It's Mortregis. Here he's destroying a castle. And look at this,' he went on, touching a different scene. 'A brave knight has challenged him but Mortregis is burning him with his breath.'

'Who's this? Is it Lord Alwyn?' Nicola asked, pointing to a solitary figure in black and deep green. They pushed their faces closer and saw a book in the man's hand.

'No, not Lord Alwyn,' Marcel told her confidently. He could see how long the tapestry was and he had already guessed that the Kingdom's history would unfold as they walked its length. 'These scenes are from long ago. This must be the first Master of the Royal Books. Do you see what this is, Nicola? It's the legend Starkey told us about.'

The story lay depicted in intricate detail before them. The dragon, huge and menacing, became smaller and smaller in the following pictures until it hovered above an open book.

'Do you recognise that symbol?' Marcel asked, excited now that he finally knew its meaning. 'When I first saw it, I thought it was some sort of bat flying beneath the dragon.'

'You've seen it before?'

'Oh, yes, a dragon above an open book. It's the symbol on Lord Alwyn's robes.'

They began to move slowly along the tapestry, their feet finding their own way as their eyes took in each new scene. That same symbol, a rampant dragon caught above an open book, appeared many times, always on the robe of a great wizard, identifying him as Master of the Books in his own time.

At last Marcel pointed to one of the exquisitely embroidered figures whose stance looked familiar. 'There's Lord Alwyn. And this must be the old Queen dying. See her crown?'

Nicola moved impatiently to the next picture, where the crown was on a man's head. She paused before saying his name. 'Pelham.'

They both fell silent now, because beside the crowned figure of the King stood three children. Nicola moved her fingers to touch the woman who completed the group. They traced back through the scenes to where the same woman stood beside their father at an altar, her beautiful name sewn beneath her feet. 'Lady Ashlere. Oh, look how beautiful she was,' Nicola whispered in a voice that would break the hardest heart.

Marcel felt a tug at his sleeve. He and Nicola had

almost forgotten Bea, but she had not forgotten their story. 'You must see this,' she pressed gently, drawing them on to the very last events depicted on the tapestry. One scene showed King Pelham offering a cup to his Queen, Lady Ashlere, and in the picture beside it their mother lay dead, her lips overlaid with bright blue thread.

'The wine was poisoned, just as Eleanor said,' breathed Nicola, aghast.

'Wait! Look at this!' Marcel urged. Above this scene other figures were busy, figures they recognised instantly.

'That's Eleanor. What's she doing?'

'She's grinding berries of some kind. And here,' Marcel continued, stabbing at the cloth, 'Damon is tipping them into the King's wine.'

Before they could say any more, one of the heavy doors began to groan on its hinges. The great shafts of sunlight made them easy to see, and Bea was the only one who had time to hide.

'Who's there?' boomed the newcomer imperiously. 'What are you doing in the Great Hall?'

It was the King!

Through all the twists and revelations that had been thrust upon the children the day before, one thing had not changed. The thought of King Pelham still made them quiver with dread.

When he recognised them, surprise turned to fury. 'What are you doing out of your room?' he roared, as each angry stride brought him closer. Then an odd hint of panic raced briefly across his face. 'How did you get past Alwyn's beast? I saw her there myself.'

He was level with them now, his haggard features contorted with the same anger that tainted his words.

'Then it *was* you who came to our door last night,' said Marcel.

Pelham's rage faltered. 'Last night. Yes, I ... I did come, but the beast ...' He couldn't quite answer in words, and instead he startled them by wiping at a tear that had begun to roll down his cheek.

Tears, from the man they had feared for so long?

He turned to the tapestry and saw the scene they had been inspecting so closely. He touched the image of the dead Ashlere with a tenderness that left brother and sister staring at each other in wide-eyed wonder.

Nicola found the courage to come closer. 'It wasn't you who poisoned our mother, was it? This tapestry tells the true story. It was Eleanor and Damon.'

Pelham dropped his arm suddenly and reeled back as though she had spat at him. 'Yes, the Book found them out. They poisoned the wine, but I can never deny that I was the one who gave her my cup to drink from,' he cried in bitter anguish.

'It was you they were trying to murder,' muttered Marcel, as he felt the full weight of Eleanor's lie settle into the pit of his stomach.

Pelham nodded painfully. 'And every day since then I've wished that they had, if it meant that Ashlere were still alive. If only I hadn't given her the wine, if only I'd taken the first sip myself…'

'Those two,' seethed Marcel through gritted teeth. He saw the face of Remora again, silent and horrible in her icy grave. 'They'd kill anyone who stood in their way. They don't care how many people die, as long as they can sit on that throne.'

But he was still bursting with questions. 'You knew it was those two who poisoned your wine, yet you let them live in that beautiful chamber?'

Pelham turned to his son. 'In any other kingdom they would have paid with their lives, it's true. But I had made a promise. Look here,' he said, turning back to the tapestry. He reached high up to a woman dressed in the finest clothes, a crown proudly on her head, flanked by two others. 'Queen Madeleine. She was the oldest of these three princesses, and when their father lay on his deathbed, he chose her to rule after him. She had no children of her own and only her jealous sisters for company. See? Even the embroiderers have stitched them with sour faces.'

'One of the sisters was Damon's mother and the other Eleanor's,' said Nicola, realising that the story Starkey had told them in the cellar was right about this much at least.

'Yes. Madeleine's sisters were greedy and selfish and so are their children,' Pelham declared with disdain. 'The Queen went through terrible loneliness, until Lord Alwyn brought her a young boy, a foundling, and told her to raise him as her son.' He touched the tip of his finger to one scene where a small bundle was cradled in the wizard's arms.

'You,' said Nicola straightaway.

He nodded with his eyes still on the story that unfolded on the tapestry.

'She loved you,' said Marcel.

'Like I was her own son. But as she grew older, she became afraid for her people. Who would follow her on the throne? Not her sisters, for they had died before her. Eleanor was the elder of the cousins, but Damon was a man, and there are those who prefer to serve a king, not a queen. My mother could foresee great strife between the two, perhaps even war, and more than anything she wanted to spare her people such misery.'

'So she chose you, Father.' Marcel had returned to the picture he had found earlier of the newly crowned King Pelham.

'But what was the promise you made?'

'More than a promise. I took a solemn oath. Damon and Eleanor were afraid of me, or so they told their aunt. They begged her to protect them and finally Madeleine agreed. Lord Alwyn and I pledged before the court and a gathering of the common people that we would never harm either of them.'

'Even when they tried to kill you?'

'It was not something the Queen could have predicted. The best I could do was lock them away, with Alwyn's magic as the key. Your own mother had asked me to build that chamber among the roses, and she would take you children there for your lessons.'

Pelham lapsed into silence, remembering the wife he had lost, while Marcel wished desperately that he could recall anything about her at all — the glimpse of her face, a mother's touch.

He forced his eyes back to the tapestry, to the figure of the woman lying dead at the King's feet. Three more scenes had been stitched into the fabric after it. The first showed Eleanor and Damon being accused by the Book; the second depicted the chamber where they were imprisoned for their crime. But the third! He examined it more closely. Noble men and women stood around, their skilfully rendered faces as grim as they would have appeared in real life, all staring at three smaller figures who were set apart, and whose shoulders were slumped in shame and misery.

'This scene, Father,' he called out, making the others turn towards the tapestry. 'The three of us are being banished. Tell us. What had we done?'

'Done? You hadn't done anything *then*,' the King replied, nodding towards the scene Marcel had found. 'It was what you were *going* to do.'

Brother and sister looked at one another. 'We let Damon and Eleanor out of the chamber, but how could you know we were going to do that?'

The King wrestled with his indecision, his eyes brimming with the affection he longed to lavish on his children. But something was holding him back.

Marcel saw it clearly and felt his father's anguish like a pain in his own heart. 'Tell us, Father.'

Pelham's lips parted to answer them, but before he could speak a deep voice rang through the palace.

'Close the gates! Raise the alarm! The King's children have escaped!'

Moments later the great doors broke open to reveal the stooped figure of Lord Alwyn silhouetted in the entrance, nursing in his arms the familiar shape of the Book of Lies.

CHAPTER 20

A Waning Magic

'PELHAM!' LORD ALWYN CRIED from the doorway. 'Your children ...'

If he was about to say more, the words died on his lips when he found those same children with their father.

He hobbled into the hall, looking frailer than ever, fury and amazement plain to see in each feeble stride. The doors boomed shut behind him. 'Be careful, Your Majesty. They cannot be trusted.'

The Book was awkward in his arms, so as he passed the table strewn with maps he laid it down to free his hands. As soon as he reached them, he turned savagely on Nicola and Marcel. 'How did you escape? And where is Termagant?'

Marcel saw Nicola staring across at him, waiting for him to explain, but she was met only by reluctance.

Before he could stop her, she proclaimed proudly, 'It was Marcel. He tamed Termagant and turned her back into the cat who sleeps on our beds.'

'Tamed her! Nonsense! Your magic was for show and nothing else, Marcel. A game you played to amuse yourself.'

'What are you talking about, Alwyn? What magic?' the King demanded, suddenly suspicious.

'Before you sent Marcel from the palace I'd let him have some of my books so that he could play at being a magician. I never told you, because I knew he was destined to succeed you as King some day, and could never become a wizard like me.'

At that instant, Bea appeared from the shadows with a black cat nestled in her arms. She did not say anything, but the sight of Termagant purring happily was enough.

'It appears you are wrong, Alwyn,' said the King, his eyes following Termagant as she leaped onto the floor and rubbed herself against Marcel's leg. 'Marcel's magic is far from a childish game, it seems.'

Lord Alwyn's mouth fell open and he staggered backwards a step before steadying himself.

Marcel could not stay silent any longer. 'It's true, Father. I found a book of magic hidden in my room. *My own* book. It contains more than simple tricks. It's full of things that frighten even me. And the power to do them has come back into my hands just by reading the words. Before you sent us away, I was a sorcerer, practising in secret and learning all that I could.'

'But Alwyn made you forget who you were.'

'Yes, he wiped away our memories, but his magic could not take what was inside of us. Look at Nicola. She still behaves like a princess. And Fergus, our brother, whom you call Edwin. There's a shield above his bed upstairs, and he is still searching for battles to fight.'

'Don't trust them, Your Majesty!' Alwyn exclaimed. 'They set Damon and Eleanor free from the chamber. What more proof do you need? They have betrayed you, just as it was foretold.'

'Foretold! What is he talking about?' demanded Nicola. 'What happened to make you send us away and have Lord Alwyn work his magic on us? What does that scene on the tapestry mean? Tell us, Father, please.'

The King could bear it no longer. He began to speak. They could see his lips moving, and even his tongue working behind his teeth. But somehow no words came out, at least none that Marcel could hear.

'What is it? What's happening?' Marcel asked.

Nicola's face showed she was just as confused.

'Didn't you hear him?' asked Bea in surprise.

'No, not a word,' said Marcel.

'I couldn't hear anything either,' added Nicola.

'But I could hear,' Bea insisted. 'He told you what the Book of Lies predicted. It's awful, Marcel.' She began to repeat what she had heard, but her voice was silenced, just as the King's had been.

Marcel and Nicola turned bewildered faces towards their father.

'I sent you away,' he explained, 'so you would never know what you were accused of … or of your mother's death. It was too much for children like you to bear, and Alwyn's magic would make sure you never knew.'

'You made us foundlings, just like you were,' said Nicola miserably. 'But we're not, Father. We're your children. We were born to play our part.'

Marcel's mind had leaped ahead. 'If it was Lord Alwyn's spell, then he must have the power to break it,' said Marcel.

'They're right, Alwyn. I can't keep it from them any longer. Lift your spell so that I can tell them everything.'

'But you ordered that they should never know.'

'That time is gone. They are stronger now. Perhaps they were always stronger than I realised.'

The old wizard dismissed this with a wave of his hand. 'They cannot know. It is beyond even my own power to retrieve that magic. You remember that night here in this hall, and so do I. We have it here in our minds,' he said, tapping the side of his head, 'but it will never be in theirs.'

They were thwarted again, and the frustration was too much for Marcel. Only last night he had probed the mind of a creature he had once feared as much as he feared Lord Alwyn. Why could he not use that same magic on a far more powerful subject? What was to stop him from plunging his sorcery, childish and unpractised though it was, into the mind of the great wizard? Then he could take what he so desperately needed: Lord Alwyn's own memory of the night when the entire Kingdom turned against the King's children.

It began before he was even aware he was doing it.

'What's this, Marcel? You dare to challenge me?' said Lord Alwyn contemptuously. He raised a hand and languidly passed it before his face.

Marcel reeled backwards as though he had been struck, but it was no worse than being slapped on the cheek. His own words of sorcery remained firmly in his mind. He straightened, sweeping his own hand in front of his nose. The old wizard's face turned from amusement to concentration. 'What are you doing? You cannot know,' he hissed between gritted teeth.

Words came to Marcel's lips, charms, spells, each one fresh and powerful. The strength he felt throughout every part of his body frightened him, but he had known great terror in these last weeks and it had prepared him for this moment. He wouldn't give way before the guile of the old Master.

Their powers were balanced on a knife edge: Marcel, unsure of himself but determined in a way he never imagined he could be; and Lord Alwyn, armed with every trick, every spell he had ever cast, every irresistible chant he had created during year upon year of sorcery.

For an instant Marcel saw all that the great wizard had done as Master of the Books; it formed a mountain as large and imposing as the elves' domain, towering over the Kingdom. The weight of it would surely send his unskilled magic spinning into oblivion, but as the struggle continued that same weight became a burden pressing down on Lord Alwyn himself.

Marcel felt the memory coming. Now, he whispered urgently to himself. Take it now. And passing his hand before his face again he began to draw out that part of the old wizard's mind and take it into his own.

His eyes were closed yet he could still see. His father, Nicola, even little Bea called to him, wanting to know what was happening, but he was deaf to their demands.

He could hear other voices in the Great Hall now, creating a low rumble of solemn misery. Everyone wore black, and there was the King, sitting on the throne, his robes more sombre than the rest. Off to one side, two women were already stitching the figure of a dead queen onto the tapestry, the thread in their needles the only colour permitted within a palace shrouded in mourning.

Marcel was transfixed by what he saw near the throne: three figures, dressed in black like their father, and among them his own face, that of the boy he had been before he became one of Mrs Timmins' orphans.

Where was Lord Alwyn? Wouldn't he be near the King he served? The eyes Marcel watched through looked down and he saw a flash of darkest green and long, pointed shoes that could not possibly be his. He understood now whose eyes these were, whose robe, whose feet.

'ALWYN,' THE KING'S VOICE *said despondently. 'You've brought the Book, I see. Bring it to me.'*

When it lay in his hands, he went on. 'Must I do this, Alwyn? Isn't it enough that the Book of Lies has found out Damon and Eleanor? Do I need to know the loyalty of my courtiers too?'

Watching through the old wizard's eyes, Marcel looked down at a face gaunt with grief, and saw the feeble movements of a man too weak in spirit to care about the grace of his gestures.

Then words resonated within Marcel's head as Lord Alwyn answered, 'You have to trust the Book, Your Majesty. This is why I created it.'

A bearded adviser, who must be the King's Chancellor, leaned forward from behind the throne, interrupting in an urgent whisper. 'You need to know whether there are other traitors in league with the royal cousins, Sire.'

'Are all my courtiers here?' the King asked.

'All except Sir Thomas. He disappeared as soon as the Book of Lies was called for.'

'He's afraid to speak before it. Was he part of the plot against me, then?'

'It seems so, Your Majesty — and there may be others. That is why you must make all of us account for ourselves, even me.' To show his good faith, the Chancellor took the Book and placed it on a table before the King, speaking boldly in a voice that could be heard throughout the Great Hall. 'I am a loyal subject of King Pelham. I have never done anything to harm him and I never shall.'

The Book of Lies glowed brightly to show it was true, and after that every man and woman of the court clamoured to show their loyalty, many of them copying the Chancellor's very words. Each time the Book of Lies remained silent and still as a gravestone.

'It's done, then,' said the King, relieved. 'Everyone in this room has been tested before the Book.'

For the first time since its arrival in the hall, the Book erupted in a flutter of pages, settling at last with only one leaf left to turn, and here it wrote his words.

'What's this? Has someone held back? Who is it?'

But the Chancellor had kept a record. 'No, Your Majesty. Every member of the court has spoken … Wait, I see why the Book wrote down your words. Your children are here but they have not been tested.'

This sent a ripple of stunned and disapproving murmurs echoing through the hall. 'Not the children … no need … love their father …' were some of the fragments that rose above the din.

'Your children don't need to show their loyalty,' said the Chancellor firmly.

'Wait!' cried Nicola. 'We should do it just as everyone else has.' Stepping forward, she placed her hand gently upon the Book. 'I love my father deeply and hope he lives a long life as ruler of this kingdom.'

The Book closed and glowed for all to see. Marcel followed, copying her words, because there was no better way to say what he felt.

But when it was their brother's turn, he chose his own words. 'I swear to protect the Kingdom from its enemies and carry on the work of the King. I will never do my father any harm.'

To the horror of all gathered in the Great Hall, the Book of Lies jumped suddenly and flung open its cover. None was more alarmed than Fergus himself as his words were recorded on the second-last page.

'No!' he shouted, staring at the Book in disbelief. 'I would never do anything like Damon and Eleanor have done! I would never want to kill my own father!'

Again his words were written on the page and all around him grim faces hardened against him.

In a final desperate appeal, he tried again. 'They are in prison, a magical prison, with Lord Alwyn's sorcery as the lock and key. They can't do anything unless they are freed, and I would never do it. I won't ever set them free.'

This time the Book closed with a thud and began to glow.

'That much is true, at least,' Pelham muttered. The hall had become so quiet that his words were easily heard. 'And how can those two challenge me unless they are released from their prison?'

The dark and hooded eyes of the more suspicious moved to the Princess and Marcel beside her. Nicola again took the lead and said clearly, 'I would never set Damon or Eleanor free from that chamber.'

Watching through Lord Alwyn's eyes, Marcel wanted to shout at her, to stop her. 'Don't say the words! You don't know what tragedy they will bring!' But he realised that even for magic some things are impossible.

The Book began to buck and unfurl its pages, and when they settled her words appeared on the open page. There seemed no doubt this time.

'Traitor!' a voice called from behind the King.

'No!' she yelled. 'It can't be true!'

But even her own father had to believe it this time.

Marcel was made to swear that he, too, would never release the murderous cousins from their chamber, and when the Book reacted in the same way he stood accused just like his sister.

'All three of you!' wailed the King.

'It can't be true, Father. The Book is lying!' Nicola pleaded. But they had all witnessed its damning response.

'That's enough!' her father wailed, tears soaking his eyes. 'Take them up to their rooms!'

Before they had gone, he cried out again. 'All of you, leave me! Get out and take this accursed book with you.'

There was a brief hesitation, but when the King's face darkened even more, the courtiers began to drift through the oaken doors, the Chancellor pausing reluctantly to lift the Book from the table before the throne.

'Not you, Alwyn,' came Pelham's voice. 'Stay with me.'

When they were all gone and the doors hastily closed, he turned a stricken face towards the wizard. 'What do you make of this? Could the Book itself be lying?'

'Impossible, Pelham. It was created to identify truth and it will always do so.'

'But you heard what happened. My children will betray me. One of my own sons will try to kill me.'

Although he was confined within Lord Alwyn's mind, Marcel yelled out, 'No, Father! Don't believe it! The Book of Lies must be wrong! Fergus will never harm you, not once he knows who he really is!'

He couldn't be heard, of course, and instead his father's voice began again.

'Is there any way to avoid such a fate, Alwyn? I have heard it from their own mouths, but they are only children still.'

The King stood up suddenly and roamed down the hall, searching the tapestry for some clue, some way out. 'I will send them away, to the high country, where no one knows their faces. Let them lead a simple life, as farmers and a farmer's wife. Let them be orphans, as I was, but in the home of a woman with a loving heart to care for them, as Madeleine cared for me.'

'But the high country is not so far away. They could still return to betray you.'

'Use your magic, then. What can it do?'

'I can make them forget their lives here in this palace and the prophecy of my book.'

'Yes, it's the only choice, Alwyn. See that they never know of this day, and make sure no one can ever tell them of the betrayal the Book promises. Send them separately and unnamed, so that none will suspect who they are.'

Lord Alwyn turned away, leaving Marcel without a view of his father, but halfway to the huge doors the King called him back. The harshness of his ordeal fell away and he was not a king but a father. 'I can't bear to think of them let loose up there to fend for themselves. Go with them, Alwyn. Watch over them until they are settled into their new lives, away from treachery and murder, where they won't have to grieve for their mother as they do now.'

A SUDDEN SURGE OF noise in his ears told Marcel the magic was ended. He opened his eyes and found Bea and Nicola staring at him in wonder. He looked quickly for Lord Alwyn and saw him slumped in a chair beside the large desk, with the King kneeling at his side.

'What happened? What did you do?' Nicola asked him urgently.

'I saw ...' he said tentatively, still trying to understand what had happened. Then he was speaking, telling his sister all that he had witnessed through Lord Alwyn's eyes. This time, she heard every word.

Pelham heard it too. 'Alwyn's spell has been broken,' he exclaimed in astonishment. He rose from where he had been tending to his sorcerer, who looked close to collapse, one of his arms spread limply across an open map of the Kingdom.

'Such powers, my son ...'

But Marcel could not think about that now. The shocking vision of what had happened here in this hall was still too vivid in his mind. What a terrible thing. They had been accused of betraying their father, and not by a human witness. They had been accused by the Book of Lies itself.

'I don't understand it,' he cried in frustration. 'The Book of Lies must always show the truth. But what it showed about us was a lie!'

Lord Alwyn recovered enough of his strength to sit upright in the chair. 'No, not a lie!' he spat. 'The Book will always seek the truth. My magic demands it.'

'What good is that?' Nicola snapped. 'Eleanor used the truth to trick us! She told us that Pelham had poisoned his own Queen. Her words were true but it was still a despicable lie, and the Book must have known it.'

'Yes,' Marcel asserted. 'It looks into a person's mind and knows what he is thinking. It looks into our hearts too and knows what we barely know ourselves. It *must* have known she was lying.'

Not just Eleanor, either, he saw now. He appealed to the King, knowing that he was the one who must understand. 'I've even done it myself, Father. I tricked Starkey. I could feel the Book reach inside me. It knew I was lying and it helped me do it.

'Evil ...' he murmured, remembering what he had sensed when his fingers were pressed against the Book. 'I've felt it with my own hand, a sly and patient kind of evil, just like Eleanor's lies. The Book has learned how to deceive, even as people are telling the truth.'

'That's right!' Nicola shouted, coming to realisations of her own. 'That's what happened here in this hall, to make you think we would betray you. We would never have let Damon and Eleanor out of the chamber if Lord Alwyn's magic hadn't been worked on us. Don't you see, Father? The Book made it happen. It has found a way to create evil out of the truth!'

'Nonsense!' roared Lord Alwyn, with what little force he could muster. 'My magic would never allow it!'

Marcel saw the indecision in his father's face and knew he must convince him somehow. There was worse to fear from the Book's predictions. Far worse.

He moved close enough to touch the Book of Lies, which had lain all this time on the map table. 'But what about the verses that have appeared in the Book?' he insisted. 'You must tell my father about the dragon, Lord Alwyn. There is real danger, and you can't ignore it any longer.'

'Verses? A dragon? What is my son talking about, Alwyn?'

Before the wizard could answer, Marcel opened the Book at the back cover, where the words were still emblazoned for all to see. The steely glare he fixed on Lord Alwyn demanded an answer.

'These verses are nothing to worry about, Sire,' Alwyn said hastily. 'Some lines have appeared in the Book of Lies. Here, see for yourself.' He tapped the leather where the words were now exposed. 'Starkey believes they describe a dragon. He has convinced himself it is the great dragon of legend.' All eyes followed as Alwyn swept his arm towards the tapestry, to the scene where Mortregis was tamed by the first Master of the Books.

The wizard's face broke into a knowing smile. 'Starkey's a fool. He has even tried to conjure Mortregis from the words of this strange verse. But you know as well as I do, Pelham, that Mortregis is not a dragon at all.'

The King nodded. 'I know what Mortregis is,' he conceded.

'Do you see now why there is no need to be afraid of this verse?' Lord Alwyn continued. 'The key lies in the last two lines:

Till one who understands this verse
Controls the Beast and breaks its curse.'

The wizard addressed Marcel in the patronising tone that adults reserve for ignorant children. 'Look closely at the tapestry, Marcel, and you might come to understand as well.'

Marcel backed away towards the tapestry, desperate to solve this strange puzzle, while behind him the King stooped again and pored over the verses, conferring with his sorcerer in quiet murmurs.

Marcel could see his father still trusted the old wizard, who knew so much that he was yet to learn. He must earn his father's respect by discovering what Mortregis was for himself. For a moment he considered trying another spell, but something held him back: the words from the rhyme that began his own book of sorcery. *Not magic but wisdom* ...

He found the embroidered figure of the dragon and began to examine it again. Nicola and Bea were soon at his side.

'Help me,' he begged them both in a whisper. 'I have to understand what Mortregis really is. My father won't listen to me until I know.'

'It *was* a dragon. Can't they see that?' said Nicola hotly, tracing her fingers over the creature's teeth.

'Shaped like swords,' muttered Marcel, remembering the verse. He noticed the vicious claws ending in triangular tips like arrows — again, just how the poem described them.

Bea was gone from beside him and he saw that she had moved to inspect the scenes before Mortregis first appeared. When he joined her, he found soldiers fighting one another with real swords, long pikes raised against galloping horsemen and the sky above them filled with an arc of deadly arrows. The death and misery of battle were stitched into each of the dreadful images, the fine needlework capturing every wound, every drop of blood. At the margins, widowed mothers and their children waited anxiously for men who would never come home.

'The horror of battle,' he said softly. He began to walk slowly beside the tapestry, checking every picture sewn into the fabric.

'What are you looking for?' asked Nicola as she followed him, perplexed.

'Soldiers. Fighting. More scenes like the ones back there, at the start of the tapestry.'

Slowly an idea was growing inside him, and by the time they reached the most recent part of the Kingdom's history, he knew.

'War!' he breathed. At last he understood.

He strode back to Lord Alwyn and the King, who straightened to his full height to hear what his son had to say.

'The Master's magic is meant to protect your people, isn't it, Father, and the greatest evil is Mortregis. I saw it in the tapestry. Mortregis is war, and it has risen up again, after all these years, as though it truly were a dragon, to tear your kingdom apart. If the prophecy is right, Starkey and Damon and Eleanor must have convinced the elves and the men of Lenoth Crag to join them after all. Their armies are marching towards Elstenwyck right now!'

The King's face lost every trace of colour. 'Alwyn, could this be true? You are Master of the Books, the Kingdom's sorcerer. It is your job to keep Mortregis at bay, just as each of the Masters has done before you.'

'Don't listen to him, Your Majesty, he's just a boy!' cried Lord Alwyn as he fought his way awkwardly out of the chair. 'My magic, the magic of the Book of Lies, has protected this kingdom from the scourge of war since before you were born.'

Marcel couldn't bear the anguish in the old wizard's face, but he went on. He must make his father see the truth. 'The Book of Lies has broken free of your magic, Lord Alwyn,' he announced boldly. 'It is so full of lies that they have begun to overwhelm the sorcery that brought it to life.'

Marcel could see his father was torn between the old man he had trusted all his life and the son he loved, in spite of all. But as King, he must make a choice. 'Could your book be corrupt, Alwyn?'

'The Book of Lies contains my greatest magic. You may trust it as you trust me. It would never deceive you.'

No sooner had he spoken than his own words began to appear opposite the verses, on the final page of the Book. Marcel saw them first, then the

King, father and son staring down in disbelief as each letter looped and curled onto the brittle paper. Only then did Lord Alwyn follow their gaze, and his own eyes widened in terror as he realised what was happening.

'Your own Book denies it, Alwyn. What does this mean?' the King demanded.

For once, Lord Alwyn had no ready answer. He was too stunned by his precious creation's astonishing response.

Looking up at the King, he pleaded, 'I have never lied to you, Pelham.'

At this, the Book of Lies heaved all of its pages over until the front cover appeared, and once it had closed its golden sheen glowed in competition with the very sunlight that streamed in through the high windows.

Marcel could see his father's heart reach out to the man, wanting to believe him. But in his own heart he knew the real truth, and though his words would strike Lord Alwyn like the cruellest stones, he kept up his attack.

'No, you've never lied to my father. You lied to yourself instead,' he said harshly. 'Your book can tell when any of the King's subjects is lying, even to themselves, but you've never turned it on yourself — not until now. *You* are the greatest liar of all, Lord Alwyn. I listened to the story you told us of your apprentices, but I don't believe what you said. You *wanted* them to fail the tests you set for them. You deceived yourself when you decided that the only one worthy of sorcery's power was you.'

But still Lord Alwyn was not daunted. Summoning every last ounce of his strength, he insisted doggedly, 'All lies. My magic is still strong. I will drive back Mortregis. There is nothing to fear.'

Now the Book of Lies went wild, fanning furiously from first page to last and back again. It jumped and shuddered so vigorously on the table that it upset the pot of ink that sat on the open map. It toppled over, spilling its contents across the Kingdom, starting in the mountains of the high country and spreading rapidly across the forest to the wide valley, gathering in slow rivulets that made their way steadily towards Elstenwyck.

The spreading stain seemed like an indictment of Lord Alwyn himself. In a panic, he tried to stop the ink with his bare hands, which were soon blackened indelibly with the colour of death. But even this could not turn back the tide.

The Book had stopped its frenzy and lay open again at the final page, where the wizard's last words were beginning to appear.

My magic is still strong. I will drive back Mortregis ...

Marcel looked down at the ruined map, where the ink formed rivers that washed relentlessly towards

Elstenwyck. 'You have no one to follow you,' he said to the wizard, 'and now your magic is dying. The Book has just confirmed it. You have let evil seep into the Kingdom — constant drought that has left the people starving, animals behaving strangely. Do you remember the bats, Your Lordship, how they came screeching and flapping down from the mountains, a great horde like the ink across that map?'

'I turned them back as I have always done.'

'But you cannot turn back Mortregis. Not this time. You have left the Kingdom without a magic strong enough to protect it.'

Lord Alwyn rose up as tall as his frail body would let him, and with his eyes locked on Pelham's, he gasped, 'I would never betray this kingdom.'

It was the solemn oath of a man desperate to believe his own words. But his own creation would not spare him. The Book of Lies bucked with a kind of glee, flipping its pages in a final taunt, and when it had settled again at the last page, it wrote his words at the very end.

I would never betray this kingdom.

The King and his children stared down in horror at the damning words. Lord Alwyn could deny the truth no longer. Finally, the wizard turned his eyes to the page and found his own words among the last that would ever be written in his great Book of Lies.

'But I have lived my life for this kingdom! For you, Pelham, for Queen Madeleine who adopted you and for her father before that. I must go on,' he panted.

He stooped over the map of the Kingdom, so much of it already claimed by the invading ink. 'Back, back into your bottle!' he commanded, as he swept his left hand over the stain.

The ink remained.

He tried again with his right hand but the result was the same. He turned his palms towards himself and saw only the same black that had enveloped the landscape from the mountains almost to the gates of Elstenwyck.

'Gone,' he whispered. 'My magic is dead.'

His eyes widened in agony and he took a sudden breath. He released it moments later in a stifled sigh that echoed softly through the hall. That faint sound was quickly followed by another: the dull thud of flesh falling against hard marble.

'Alwyn!' the King cried out as he rushed to where his Master of the Books lay in a crumpled heap amid his black and green robes. Pelham called to him again, and when those deep-set eyes remained closed he took the man's wizened hand in his own.

But already it was growing cold.

CHAPTER 21

Sparks in the Darkness

ON THE DAY AFTER Lord Alwyn's death, the royal court gathered to farewell their Master of the Books. The Great Hall, so solitary and deserted when Marcel, Nicola and Bea had first peeked inside it, was crowded with every nobleman and dignitary of the Kingdom: grand lords and generals, knights with swords at their belts and beside them ladies of the court, their dark gowns brushing the marble floor. The King, seated on his throne, was dressed in deepest black and so were his children, welcome at last to stand at his side.

'Lord Alwyn was the most brilliant sorcerer of his age and a faithful servant of us all,' the King told them, his trembling voice barely able to mask his grief. 'For countless years, his magic has protected this kingdom and kept it at peace.'

Out of the deepest respect, Pelham did not tell them that Lord Alwyn had died leaving no one to take his place.

The Book of Lies was there, set to one side. The King could not bring himself to destroy the greatest creation of his dead sorcerer, but he was wary of its deceit. He had ordered it sealed inside a glass case where it could not hear a single word.

Marcel listened sadly, with Nicola and Bea at his side.

When the King finished his speech, Lord Alwyn's body was carried solemnly out through the tall oak doors and the courtiers shuffled mournfully into line behind it.

Only Pelham and the children remained in the hall when the bearded Chancellor reappeared suddenly in that same doorway, red-faced and anxious.

'Your Majesty, a farmer has just arrived all the way from his village near the border with Grenvey. You must hear his news.'

'Bring him in,' Pelham ordered, and within moments a shabbily dressed man coated in fine dust was helped into the Great Hall by two soldiers.

'Forgive me ... Your Majesty,' he spluttered, fighting for breath and almost falling to the floor as he tried to bow. 'I have been riding for hours ... as fast as my horse would carry me.'

A chair was brought for him by one of the soldiers.

'What is your news?' Pelham asked anxiously. 'Tell me what has happened.'

'This morning ... soon after dawn ...' the exhausted messenger began, though he could manage only a few words at a time between rasping breaths. 'A band of tribesmen ... forty of them ... down from the high country north of Grenvey. They looted our village and ... and set it on fire. Then they set up camp nearby to wait for the rest.'

'The rest!' cried Pelham, aghast. 'How many?'

'I saw at least six hundred, and still they were coming. A thousand or more. Brutal savages, every one of them. They ... they slaughtered all the men of my village,' he cried in anguish, close to collapse. 'All but me.'

'How did you escape?'

'I didn't. They gave me a horse ... and set me free, with a note for you, Your Majesty.'

He opened his jerkin and withdrew a scroll of paper. Pelham took it and read:

> *We have your son. Surrender the throne to Eleanor and Damon and he will go free.*
> *If you send your army against us, the boy's throat will be cut.*

As the soldiers helped the stricken farmer from the Great Hall, Marcel pictured Starkey's ruby-handled dagger in his mind. 'Fergus! Father, you must save him!'

'Save him? How, boy?' demanded the Chancellor, who deliberately refused to address Marcel by his royal title.

'I don't know,' he replied helplessly.

'Father, you must do *something*!' cried Nicola, aghast.

Pelham slumped wretchedly back into his throne without answering her. The Chancellor came closer and began to give his own advice. 'Your Majesty, this must seem like a great shock to you, but in fact it is not a true threat at all.'

'What do you mean?' the King asked warily.

'You know the Book's prophecy as well as I do, Sire. It has already been proved right. Your own children betrayed you when they released your enemies from their prison.' His frosty gaze fell on Nicola and Marcel as he spoke these words. 'Prince Edwin is still with them, perhaps planning even more treachery. Starkey's note might simply be another of his tricks. Remember what the Book foretold. The boy is determined to kill his own father. Need I explain what that means?'

Marcel watched his father's careworn face and saw the tiny movement of muscles in his cheeks and jaw. 'What are you suggesting, then?'

'Ignore this threat, Pelham,' the man urged him, lowering his voice as he became more familiar. 'Let

Starkey kill the boy and you will thwart the most dire warnings of the Book. How can a son kill his father if his own throat is cut first?'

Marcel sprang forward, pushing the bearded adviser aside. 'No, don't listen to him, Father! All the lies in that book have overpowered Lord Alwyn's magic, just as I did. It has deceived us all, especially you.'

Nicola was quickly at his side. 'You can't let them kill your own son!'

'If he is not an accomplice in this evil, then he may already be dead,' argued the Chancellor, drawing a gasp from Marcel and Nicola.

Before either could reply, Pelham took command. 'Quiet, all of you! This matter does not concern the Book or its predictions, or even whether it can deceive us by telling the truth. My son is a hostage and they are determined to kill him.'

'He will only be the first of many to die,' the Chancellor reminded him, in defiance of his order to be silent. When he saw the look on the royal faces around him he flinched, but he would not back down. 'I'm sorry, Your Majesty, but a terrible war is descending upon us. Hundreds, even thousands will die, and in the end even the life of your own son will count for little. We must defeat these invaders or the Kingdom will be plunged into darkness.'

'Surely you can't be so heartless!' Nicola shouted in outrage, but again Pelham would not listen to her.

'The Chancellor is right,' he conceded miserably. 'I am a father, yes, but I am also a king. If those two cousins replace me on this throne, justice will die and peace will become a thing of the past. I cannot betray the trust Queen Madeleine placed in me, even to save my own son.'

'Can't your men at least try to rescue him?' Nicola begged.

'What could they do? As soon as I attack the enemy camp, Starkey will kill your brother.'

Before Nicola could respond, the Chancellor spoke to Pelham. 'Your Majesty, there are urgent matters of war to discuss. Your generals are waiting.'

'I'm afraid you're right again,' said the King, rising from the throne. And without another word the two men departed from the Great Hall.

Nicola could hold in her rage no longer. 'We can't just sit back and wait for Fergus to die! And the Chancellor's right: what if they *don't* wait until they reach Elstenwyck to kill him? Something has to be done *now*. If our father refuses to get Fergus out of the camp, it's up to the three of us ...' She thought fast. 'Bea, you could sneak into the camp without being seen. If you explained the truth to Fergus, he might escape with you. Would you do it?'

Bea stepped into the sunlight that streamed in towards the tapestry, letting them see her clearly. 'Of course,' she said without hesitation.

'But they could be anywhere by now!' Marcel

objected. 'We'll never track them down, even if we can find horses to carry us.'

'There's one horse that could track them down,' Nicola answered with a daring and determined edge to her words. She ran to the glass casket that encased the Book of Lies.

'No, the Book cannot be trusted!' exclaimed Marcel, appalled by what his sister was suggesting.

'But it can still give Gadfly her wings, can't it? That's all we need it to do.'

'But the evil inside it has made it unpredictable. We can't be sure what it will do, especially now that Lord Alwyn is dead and there's no magic to control it.'

'No magic! What about you, Marcel? You *defeated* Lord Alwyn's magic yesterday. And I saw the candle alight in your room last night, long after the rest of us had gone to bed. You've learned even more, haven't you?'

It was true. But there had been nothing in his own book of sorcery that gave him the powers of Lord Alwyn's creation. The Book was dangerous and unstable. Most of all, he was convinced that it was eager to create even more mischief.

'No,' he said firmly. 'I'm still not sure that I can control the Book's powers. The risk is too —'

'The risk!' called a voice in disbelief. But it was not Nicola's. For the first time in their brief friendship, Bea turned an angry eye on Marcel. 'We have taken risks before. Why are you so afraid now when your own brother's life is at stake?'

The risk certainly didn't seem to worry Nicola either. She had already set off towards the wall opposite the tapestry.

'What are you doing?' cried Bea, going after her.

'One of these is what I need,' she muttered. Before either of them could ask what she meant, she unhooked a rusting mace from where it had hung unused for a hundred years or more and tested the weight of it in her hands. It was little more than a rough, spiked ball of iron with a stout handle protruding from its centre. A primitive weapon for battle, perhaps, but just right for what she had in mind.

'Stand back,' she called to the others, and swinging the mace awkwardly over her shoulder, she advanced on the glass case. At the last moment she closed her eyes, but this wasn't enough to ruin her aim. The case exploded with a deafening crack, followed by the tinkling of shattered glass raining upon the floor.

Nicola opened her eyes and they widened in amazement at the destruction she had caused. She put down the mace and stepped gingerly through the shards to pick up the Book of Lies. After a quick shake to dislodge any specks of glass, she strode over and handed it to Bea.

'Quick, someone might have heard the glass smash! I'll find Old Belch and ask him to let me ride Gadfly around the gardens. That sounds like something a princess might do. You find a bag to hang round her neck. All right?'

Bea nodded, and together they rushed towards the enormous doors, without seeming to give Marcel another thought.

They were heading towards such danger, yet neither of them appeared the least bit worried. Marcel felt suddenly ashamed of himself, watching them set off alone, all because he was afraid to test the strange powers he had found inside himself.

'Wait!' he called.

They turned and stayed where they were until he caught up to them, their eyes searching his face questioningly.

'All right. I'll come with you too,' he sighed.

Bea's face shone brightly even though there was no sunlight picking out her features. 'I knew you would.'

But when they arrived at the stables, Old Belch guessed what they were up to immediately.

'You're going to make her fly again, aren't you?' he demanded, but there was a sly gleam in his eye. 'I'd like to have another look at those wings. And you *are* a prince and princess, after all. I must obey your commands,' he added with a wink, to show that such things mattered little to him. 'But tell me first: where are you going that you need wings to get there?'

'To save a life,' Marcel answered, all trace of his earlier reluctance now gone, 'and perhaps a kingdom too!'

Old Belch gave them another feedbag to carry the Book around Gadfly's neck. Minutes later, she rose majestically into the sky above Elstenwyck with the three children clinging tightly to her back. The townsfolk gaped and pointed, but they were soon left behind.

GADFLY FLEW ON FOR hours over the drought-ravaged wheat fields and dusty, desolate farms. In the west the sun was closing its eye behind the distant mountains, as though it did not want to see what the night would bring. They were glad to see it go; their plan could work only in darkness.

Another hour passed, then two. They had never travelled this way, so there was nothing they could use to give them a bearing, yet somehow Gadfly found the way ahead. Perhaps she used the stars, as mariners did.

'What's that?' Nicola cried into the roaring wind. Amid the blackness below, a bright speck of gold appeared. The closer they flew, the more it separated out into earthbound stars, until they realised they were approaching the dying embers of a village. As they flew directly overhead, a roof gave way and crashed in on the burned-out walls of the cottage below. A shower of sparks erupted into the night sky and a few eager flames went scavenging among what remained.

To their right, perhaps two miles away, they could make out more pinpoints of light. 'There's the camp! Gadfly, take us down quickly, away from their sentries,' Nicola shouted into the horse's ear.

Once on the ground, they found a thicket of trees that could serve as a hiding place of sorts while Bea crept in among the tents to find Fergus.

'What if they catch you?' Marcel worried all over again.

'They won't catch me,' she sniffed dismissively. 'It's dark. I could wander round their camp for hours and they'd never know I was there.'

'Bea, you will be careful, won't you?' he whispered, but there was no answer. She was already gone.

The next twenty minutes were a torment for Marcel. 'Do you think she's found him?' he asked Nicola. He let two more minutes go by then asked the question again. When he spoke a third time, she turned on him in frustration.

'I'm nervous enough without you going on like this,' she said heatedly.

What would they do if Bea were captured? They were too far from the rebel camp to see or hear, in any case. All they could do was wait impatiently and take turns checking on Gadfly, who was hidden well back in the trees, her wings folded against her body, ready to take flight again at a moment's notice.

After ten more minutes of silence, Marcel couldn't help himself and was about to ask another impatient question when a stone landed in the fine dust near his feet. 'It's Bea. It must be. She's signalling us.'

'So you don't get a fright,' said a soft voice at his elbow, and there was Bea among them again.

'Did you bring Fergus?'

'Yes, but Marcel —'

Before she could explain, something stirred in the trees around them.

'Who's there?'

A low bough was pushed aside at the edge of the thicket, admitting a dark figure to their hiding place. 'Marcel?'

Relief flowed into Marcel's tensed muscles. It was a voice he remembered only too well. 'Fergus! Over here.'

The figure came closer, the handle of a sword jutting from his side. The shadowy outline could only be their brother. He stopped a dozen paces short of them, obviously reluctant to come too close.

'What's wrong, Fergus? Didn't Bea explain?'

'Yes, she told me what you sent her to say.'

'Then you know who we really are. None of us belongs to those murdering cousins at all. King Pelham is the father of all three of us, and you're not my cousin, you're my twin brother.'

'It's more lies,' Fergus answered coldly.

'No! Why would we lie to you now?'

'You did before, when we found Remora. You told me you trusted Damon and that we'd tell him together, but it was a lie. You just wanted a chance to sneak away. I don't believe this story of yours. It's a trick to get me away from Damon.'

Marcel tried to close the gap between them, but Fergus backed away sharply, drawing the sword from his waist.

'Listen to me,' Marcel urged. 'Damon is as bad as Eleanor. He helped her to murder Queen Ashlere. Do you remember the gravestone among the roses in the palace gardens? It's our mother under that stone, Fergus, yours as well as Nicola's and mine. She was the first to die, and if we don't stop this war thousands more will die with her, just so those two can sit on the throne. We can't let it happen. Pelham is a good king and the people love him. *He's* the true and rightful heir.'

'I don't believe you. I don't believe any of this. I'm going back to camp. I won't give you away, but you'd better leave before Zadenwolf's soldiers find you here.'

Fergus turned away. Any moment now he would be gone into the darkness, their last hope disappearing with him.

'Wait!' Nicola called. 'If we tell you all this before the Book of Lies, will you believe us?'

'Nicola, what are you saying?' Marcel asked, mystified. 'You know the Book can't be trusted. The evil is too strong.'

'For Lord Alwyn, yes, but he was sick and dying. You're stronger than he was now, and whatever evil lies inside the Book, it must still make that golden glow if what we tell it is true. Everything the Book said about *him* yesterday was true, wasn't it? What do you say, Fergus? You know how the Book works.'

'Where is it? If this is just another trick to make me come with you to Elstenwyck ...'

'No, we have it here with us,' said Nicola, and as she spoke she raced into the trees, returning quickly with the Book of Lies, which she had retrieved from the bag around Gadfly's neck.

Marcel took it from her. He focused every part of his mind on it, sensing immediately the foulness of its lies, sniping and feuding, battling the feeble magic that had once kept them in check, determined to escape his control. But slowly he managed to push them down as though they were autumn leaves under his feet, until he could feel them crushed and still. 'Now, Nicola,' he whispered. 'Speak now.'

She closed her eyes, took a breath and began. 'I am truly a princess, the daughter of King Pelham and Queen Ashlere,' she said solemnly. When she dared open her eyes, she found the Book glowing gently.

Fergus's hard glare began to soften and he took a step closer.

'Now me,' said Marcel. 'I am Prince Marcel, the true son of King Pelham.' He felt the Book's glow even before he saw it amid the darkness.

'Watch the Book, Fergus,' he pressed, 'and you will finally know who you are.' Marcel said clearly, 'You are the son of King Pelham, just as I am. You are not my cousin but my brother and my twin.'

He stood waiting for the Book to glow a third time. But instead, his face creased in horror when it opened suddenly, startling him so that he dropped it into the dirt at his feet. There, the pages began to fan wildly until the last page lay exposed. Though it was too dark to see clearly, there was no doubt that his words had been written down.

'There!' Fergus cried triumphantly. 'It's not true. I'm not Pelham's son and I'm not your twin, either.'

Marcel was too shocked to make sense of what had happened. 'But my magic took charge of the Book! I know it. It can't deceive us, not now!'

'You sound like Lord Alwyn,' Nicola said scathingly.

What had happened? Marcel stared down in shock at the Book of Lies, but for Fergus the Book's response only confirmed what he believed. He pushed Marcel and Nicola aside and picked it up, holding it across his hands just as Marcel had done. 'I am the son of Prince Damon,' he declared, and instantly the Book closed with a snap and began to illuminate the dense thicket around them with its golden glow, as bright as they had ever seen it.

'I don't understand,' Marcel mumbled.

But he did not have long to ponder what had gone wrong. The heavy tread of a boot disturbed the fallen leaves and he dropped the Book from his hands. None but Bea had time to hide.

Soon they could just make out a fur-clad soldier, who entered the clearing and stopped rather deliberately with a hand on the hilt of his sword, as though he were waiting for a signal. The children quickly knew why when a second man stepped out of the darkness, followed by several more. Finally, Damon himself appeared, brandishing a torch that lit up the surrounding trees.

'Check behind those bushes. See if any of Pelham's men have come with them,' he ordered. One of the soldiers ran forward and soon returned leading Gadfly by the mane.

Damon gestured towards the children. 'Take them,' he called to the soldiers.

Nicola was quickly wrenched off her feet. She kicked frantically, but there was little she could do against the strength of a full-grown man. Bea crept out of her hiding place to help her, and even though the soldier could barely see her, he grabbed her as well and passed her to one of his companions.

'Get the boy,' barked Damon, but before a soldier could capture him, Marcel snatched Fergus's sword from his belt and backed away into the centre of the clearing. When one of the men approached, Marcel wielded the sword fiercely and only an agile leap saved the soldier from injury.

'Stay back!' Marcel shouted as he lunged at a second man who tried to disarm him.

'What's the matter with you all?' Damon growled at them. 'He's just a boy. Seize him!'

Nicola wrestled with her captor, but when he wouldn't succumb to her kicks and scratches she shouted at Damon instead. 'You lied to us! Eleanor's not our mother.'

'No,' he said calmly. 'But we needed you to believe it so you would open the door of the chamber. After that we kept you around in case we needed you as hostages. Starkey had his dagger ready for the day you were no longer of any use to us.'

'Yes, you needed *us* to open that chamber. *We're* the rightful —'

'Silence her!' Damon roared, and the soldier clamped his hand over Nicola's mouth.

'Is it true, Father? Was Starkey going to kill them?' Fergus asked as he came to stand beside Damon.

'As long as they live, these two will claim the throne. To be a king, you must dispose of your rivals.' He took his own sword from his belt, and handing it to Fergus, he nodded towards Marcel, who stood surrounded by soldiers in the middle of the clearing.

'Kill him.'

Marcel saw Fergus's face pale at this command, though in the dim light no one else could tell. He weighed the sword in his hand as the cowardly soldiers backed away, leaving Marcel alone. Fergus took a tighter grip and attacked.

Marcel was forced back as he fended off the first savage blow. Sparks flew from their blades, lighting their faces for an instant as the sharp clash of steel against steel rang out in the night air, strike after strike. Stay on your feet, stay on your feet, Marcel urged himself, remembering the wolves and the lessons Fergus himself had taught him.

How long could he defend himself against such blows? Three times, four times Fergus struck, and he threw back each blow valiantly, but he was not as strong as Fergus and his arms seemed ready to drop from sheer exhaustion. *His* skills lay in magic, not sword play. If the fighting stopped for just a moment he might be able to conjure a spell to save himself. But Fergus was relentless.

Three more brutal sweeps of Fergus's blade sent Marcel retreating, until his foot caught against a tree root and he fell. Before he could scramble to his feet Fergus was on him, and only an urgent parry stopped the blow from slicing his head open. The next jarred the sword from his hands, leaving him helpless. Fergus raised his arms again and paused with the sword balanced above his head, as if he were mustering all his remaining strength.

Then his shoulders slipped and his elbows drooped almost to his sides. He held the sword still, the blade in front of his eyes as he stared at it, as though unsure of what it was. Suddenly his body convulsed and he threw the sword away and staggered backwards. 'I can't,' he said quietly. 'I can't do it, Father, not even for you.'

'Grab them both!' Damon ordered his soldiers angrily when he saw that the battle was over.

Marcel was hauled to his feet, while a second pair of men took hold of Fergus, who was still bent over in shame.

He was startled to find himself manhandled with the rest. 'Father, what's happened?'

'You're a fool, boy, and now you're a hostage like your brother and sister. Unless Pelham surrenders, you'll die with them as well.'

Fergus gazed at the man he had thought of for so long as his father. Slowly, understanding began to spread across his face and he turned desperately to Marcel. With a mighty surge of his shoulders, he threw off the hands that held him and lunged for the sword he'd discarded. But before he could pick it up a black leather boot stamped down on the blade and he found himself looking up into a pair of cold and sneering eyes.

'There'll be no more fighting from you, young prince,' snarled Starkey, who had appeared suddenly out of the darkness, with Hector's ravaged face at his shoulder. Starkey grabbed Fergus roughly by the arm and returned him to his captors.

'They've brought you a present, Starkey,' Damon told him with mild derision.

Starkey did not understand at first. When Damon nodded towards the ground in the centre of the clearing, he turned with little interest.

'Don't you see it?' Damon teased him. 'I thought you'd cut your own throat the day they stole it from you. Now they've brought it back. That silly book you prize so highly. It's there in the dirt, waiting for you.'

Starkey didn't pause to hear more. He rushed to reclaim the Book of Lies, clutching it to his chest like a child with his most cherished toy. Then he turned back to Damon. 'What was that fighting I heard?'

'I'd hoped one of Pelham's brats would dispose of the other,' Damon explained casually.

'Both of them! Is Marcel injured?' he asked anxiously.

'See for yourself. He's still breathing.'

'Count us all lucky, then,' Starkey responded. He turned away towards the camp. 'Bring them,' he growled at the soldiers. 'Their lives aren't worth a farthing, but before he dies that one will decide the victor in this battle.'

At these words, the Book of Lies began to glow in his arms like a searing sun amid the blackness of night.

CHAPTER 22

Let Slip the Beast

THE FOUR CAPTIVES WERE tied up hand and foot and allowed a few hours of fitful sleep in a tent crowded with the paraphernalia of war. It was only in the weak light of dawn, when they were dragged into the open, that they could take a proper look at the surly warriors of Lenoth Crag, all of them clearly hungry for battle. The rough furs that kept them warm in the mountains seemed out of place here and made them look like wolves that had strayed far from their forest homes.

After a breakfast of scraps left unwanted by the soldiers, they were tied up again, this time with a single long rope around their waists, the loose end pulled along by a cold-eyed sergeant on horseback.

'Stay on your feet or I'll drag you all the way to Elstenwyck on your bellies,' he warned menacingly.

The long hours that followed were cruel. Hot and sweating under the same merciless sun that had parched the farmland of Elster, they marched all day. Their mouths became so dry they could barely speak.

Nicola moistened her lips and tongue enough to whisper to Marcel, 'Can you get us free?'

She meant his magic, of course. But with so many guards around, there was no sorcery that would help.

Only Bea gave them hope. 'Marcel, look what I have in my pocket! I'd forgotten all about it.'

He looked down and found her holding the little leather pouch that had once dangled around Termagant's neck. 'If it worked the magic of the Book on Termagant, it might be enough to give Gadfly her wings ...'

Perhaps it would, but the rope held them tight, and they had seen Gadfly earlier, weighed down with weapons and supplies. Her disgruntled snorts had shown what she thought of this cruel treatment.

Marcel looked around for her again, and that was when he saw what was happening behind them. They all turned, until the rope was tugged and they were forced to trudge forward again, but that glimpse had been enough. As the army marched relentlessly towards Elstenwyck, the withered fields of wheat and corn they passed were being set alight. The fire spread easily in the hot, dry air.

'*A Beast will touch the land with flame,*' Marcel murmured, remembering the fire back in Elstenwyck, and what they had seen last night.

Just before sundown, the walls of the city appeared in the distance. 'Make camp!' came the call. Then Zadenwolf himself moved among his troops, bellowing an instruction that sent a chill through Marcel. 'Don't spend too much time on it. Tomorrow night you'll be sleeping on the soft mattresses of Elstenwyck.'

Towards midnight, Hector found the exhausted children asleep in the open and kicked them awake. 'Starkey wants you.' He untied their ropes but took hold of Bea so that she did not fade away unnoticed into the night. Then he led them between the fires and the tents to Starkey's quarters. Few of the men were sleeping. Some sharpened the blades of their axes and swords. Others simply stared silently into the flames, wondering perhaps whether they would be alive at sundown tomorrow.

The Book of Lies lay on a table in the middle of Starkey's tent. When they were assembled opposite him, he opened it at the very last page. '*When all my pages fill with lies,*' he quoted from the verse he knew by heart. 'There's barely a line left on this page. It's time for Mortregis to return,' he insisted, looking pointedly at Marcel.

He turned as Eleanor and Damon entered and came to lean over the Book. 'Do you still believe in this sorcery?' sneered Damon, revealing his contempt for such things.

'Quiet! You'll both change your tune soon enough.' Eleanor turned towards the children. 'These are more valuable to us than that book. Pelham will surely give himself up now that we have all three of his brats.'

'No, Marcel and the girl came alone, to rescue their brother, it seems. Pelham cares more for his kingdom than he does for his own children.'

Eleanor eyed the sullen figures huddled against the side of the tent. 'Then they are worthless as hostages. Why wait until tomorrow to kill them?'

Starkey turned his intense gaze to the table before him. 'Because I still need them,' he said, without looking up. 'The verses in this book hold a clear promise.

> 'The Beast will grow and spread its wings
> Destroying rogues and making Kings

'Do you hear it, from a book that can only tell the truth? It has victory hidden in its magic, I tell you.'

'You're wasting your time,' barked Damon. 'You would need the skill of Alwyn himself to perform such tricks, and if your spies are right the old fool is dead.'

Starkey's hand found its way to his chin, letting the fingers work at the lengthening stubble. He had not shaved in some time, and his handsome face had become haggard and wolf-like as it had been in the forest. 'Yes, I have my spies,' he said as he turned his glowering eyes on Marcel. 'You were in the palace with Alwyn before he died. You told him about these verses, didn't you, Marcel? Did he teach you how Mortregis can be conjured?'

Marcel stammered a terrified denial, but Starkey was in no mood to believe him. 'He did, didn't he!' He strode to the other side of the table, thrusting that hated face so close to the boy's nose that he could smell the sweat as it trickled onto the despicable man's brow.

'Leave him, Starkey,' said Damon angrily. 'That dragon is no more than a childish legend. We have our own forces now. Even if the elves do not join us after all, Zadenwolf's army will cut Pelham's men to pieces.'

'So we will,' replied a deep voice from the entrance to the tent. They all turned in surprise to find Zadenwolf himself in the opening. 'Elster's army has not fought a battle in centuries. It will be no match for my war hardened warriors, now that the old wizard is dead,' he assured them.

Zadenwolf knew little about the Book of Lies so he barely noticed when a hint of golden light filled the tent, emanating from the table before Starkey. But the others saw it, and it brought a gleeful smile to some faces and dread to others.

Suddenly Fergus was talking. He had remained withdrawn and ashamed all through that desolate day, but now he seemed consumed by anger and bursting to speak his mind. He took two resolute paces towards Damon. 'You think Zadenwolf alone can bring you victory, don't you?' he sneered. 'Have you told Eleanor about the secret meetings you had with him? Yes, I've overheard you, begging him to turn against your cousin, so that once Pelham is gone you will rule alone.'

Fergus dodged a savage blow from Damon, shouting, 'He's planning to kill you, Eleanor!' before Hector clamped a sweaty hand over his mouth.

He had managed to arouse Eleanor's suspicions, though. 'What's he saying, Damon? Are you plotting to betray me?' When Damon hesitated, she demanded hotly, 'Swear it now, in front of the Book of Lies.'

The tent fell silent as they waited for his answer. 'No,' he said finally. 'I'm a prince and soon to be King. I'll not have my loyalty tested like a common subject.'

Marcel had quickly realised what Fergus was trying to do. If they could get these two squabbling, then their true natures would be revealed. Perhaps Zadenwolf would grow frustrated and abandon them. It was a slim hope, but they had no other.

His sister must have caught on as well. She called out to Damon. 'You're a fool to trust Eleanor, too! She doesn't want to share the throne any more than you do. She has her poisons ready. You'll have to watch everything you drink, every mouthful of food.'

Eleanor took Nicola's arm, her face a picture of fury, and began to push her roughly out of the tent, but Nicola just continued her attack. 'Think of my own mother, Damon. You'll suffer the same fate as Queen Ashlere.'

'Wait!' shouted Damon, his face suddenly pale with fear. He took hold of Eleanor's wrist and made her release the girl. 'Is it true? Would you poison your own cousin?'

'Make her swear before the Book,' Nicola urged.

Eleanor eyed the Book of Lies haughtily. 'I won't be tested by Alwyn's book either. I am the rightful heir, born before you, Damon. If anyone is to rule alone, it should be me.'

Already unsettled by Nicola's suggestion, now Damon was incensed. 'I am the male heir! A kingdom should have a king, not a queen with a woman's weakness.'

'Weakness! I had the strength to poison Pelham, when you were too frightened to act.'

'You wouldn't pour it into his wine. That part you left to me.'

'What about Starkey?' Fergus said cunningly. 'If he can make the Book's prophecy come true, do you really think he'll let either of you rule?'

Eleanor and Damon turned narrowed eyes away from each other to focus the full force of their distrust on Starkey.

But Starkey himself was not fooled by these tricks.

'Enough!' he thundered. 'Don't you see how these children have put us all at each other's throats? Our plan remains the same. You will rule together, with me as your Chancellor — once Zadenwolf's army has defeated Pelham,' he added, with a nod towards the King, who watched stony-faced and silent near the entrance.

The shameful tale of how the cousins had tried to poison Pelham had left Zadenwolf unmoved. But stony-faced? No, not quite, Marcel saw. His eyes had wandered to Zadenwolf's grim features while Starkey and the cousins made their spiteful claims and he had discovered something unexpected. Zadenwolf's lips might be hidden beneath the thick hair of his beard, but hadn't they curled into the faintest hint of a smile? Yes, Marcel was sure of it, though as he searched for it again that fleeting smile had vanished. In its place he found a venomous stare fixed on Starkey, like that of a snake inspecting its unsuspecting prey.

Fergus and Nicola had shown the way, and now it was Marcel's turn, not with magic but with the same weapon that his brother and sister had used. 'Do you trust King Zadenwolf, Starkey?' he began cautiously, hoping that if he kept his voice low and reasonable, almost friendly, then the man would hear him out.

'What do you mean?' snarled Starkey, glancing uneasily towards Zadenwolf.

Marcel continued quickly now, knowing he would have only one chance to get this right. 'The King has brought his great army into Elster to kill my father, but will he really go back to the mountains and leave it all to you?'

'Foolish boy!' he retorted. 'We've already promised Zadenwolf a part of the Kingdom, in the high country adjoining his borders.'

'Cold and remote, like Lenoth Crag,' said Marcel. 'This valley is warmer than where he comes from. And more fertile too, in spite of the drought. Why would he be content with a bit of forest when he could have everything? How can you be sure he hasn't come to take the throne for himself?'

At an angry nod from Starkey, Hector strode across the tent, and with a vicious flick of his hand he silenced the boy's mouth at last.

Sickening colours blundered into one another behind Marcel's eyes as Nicola helped him to his feet again. Now the tent had become deathly silent. Zadenwolf had not said a word and the expression on Starkey's face had begun to change from sly confidence to a raw and nervous doubt.

'Won't you deny it, then?' Fergus taunted Zadenwolf, taking up the attack.

Nicola joined in. 'Is it true? Have you played all three of them for fools?'

At last the reluctant King spoke up. 'It is all as we agreed. You three will be the powers in this land. I will not betray you.'

It was what Starkey and the royal cousins had longed to hear. But even as they tried to pretend that they had never doubted, the Book of Lies erupted. The cover flew open and the pages began to fan rapidly, inevitably, until the last page lay revealed. Close to the bottom edge of the paper, words began to appear, Zadenwolf's words.

It is all as we agreed.

The unseen quill reached the end of the line and began the next. It would certainly be the last, because no more words would fit on the page after this. The magical script looped and coiled, repeating the King's words, proving them to be a lie.

You three will be the powers in this land.

Finally, there was less than half a line left, with precisely the right number of words to fill it. They were written into place, and at last the Book of Lies was full, with the last words recorded on its pages forming the most wicked lie of all.

I will not betray you.

Zadenwolf himself knew nothing of how this strange book worked, and it was only the shocked response of the others that warned of how he had been exposed.

Eleanor's eyes grew round and wild. She fixed them on him with a fury that might have sent a lesser man lurching backwards in dismay.

'He's tricked us!' cried Starkey, enraged.

Damon drew his sword, but Zadenwolf was ready for him. His own weapon flashed in the candlelight, knocking Damon's from his hand before he could attack.

'Sergeant!' he roared, and before Hector or Starkey could lunge at the treacherous King, three burly soldiers burst into the tent. 'Take their weapons,' he ordered sharply, and when it was done, 'Set up a guard around this tent. These three are my prisoners, and the children and Starkey's bowman too. If they show their faces outside this tent tonight, kill them.'

'You can't do this!' Eleanor stormed. 'This kingdom is mine by right!'

This was the first of a dozen frenzied accusations from her and Damon, each more vehement than the last.

Zadenwolf dismissed them all with contempt. 'You were fools, both of you, and you as well, Starkey. Did you truly think I would risk my army against Pelham's in return for a scrap of land fit only for elves to live in? These children here have more sense than the three of you.'

'What will you do with us?' asked Nicola fearfully from where she stood huddled with Marcel, Fergus and Bea.

'Haven't you guessed?' he goaded them. 'Tomorrow I do battle with Pelham, with the elves as my allies, but what is the use of killing one king if there are still others alive who can claim his throne?'

With this cruel announcement still ringing in his captives' ears, Zadenwolf swept through the open doorway, a gloating smile on his face. His soldiers followed, leaving the prisoners alone, though the squeak of leather and the clink of metal all around the tent told them that they were well guarded.

'This is outrageous! We can't just wait here to die!' Damon snarled.

'You heard him,' snapped Eleanor. 'One step outside and you'll die tonight instead of tomorrow.'

Then she turned on him. 'It's all your fault, you know! *You* persuaded us to trust him!'

Damon had no answer to this and his brief defiance quickly foundered. He turned away from the rest, nursing his wretchedness in private. Seeing this, Eleanor's courage failed as well. She slumped in a corner of the tent and began to weep tears of self-pity.

Marcel was stunned to see them turn so rapidly from indignation to cowardly, snivelling despair. He found himself quickly losing heart as well, and there seemed little comfort in the downcast faces of his brother and sister. Not even Bea, for all her courage, could force the defeat from her gaze. They would all die in the morning; and after them, who could say how many others, some wearing the alien attire of Zadenwolf's army, the rest in the red livery of his father, the true King. As Marcel stared around the tent, full of desolate and hopeless figures, he saw that the real enemy was not

Zadenwolf at all. It was Mortregis himself, returned from his sleep.

His thoughts were interrupted by a voice he had come to loathe more than any other: Starkey's. What had he said? Others in the silent tent had not listened either, but every face was turned towards him as he spoke a second time. 'Our only hope now is the Book.'

'What are you talking about?' Marcel responded furiously. 'If it weren't for the Book this evil would never have entered the Kingdom. You should destroy it now. See? Its last page is full. Its magic is finished.'

'Yes, the Book is full, Marcel. It is free at last to create its *greatest* magic, the magic promised by the verses,' he declared, becoming excited in a way that repelled the children. He stabbed his finger at one of its golden lines. '*When all my pages fill with lies,*' he quoted. 'Say it, Marcel. You know the verses by heart, just as I do. Say the next line.'

'*Let slip the Beast and see it rise,*' Marcel muttered, though in the confines of the tent they could all hear him clearly.

'All we need is one who understands the verse,' Starkey went on, poking his finger now at the final two lines. 'You, Marcel. You understand it. You will help me conjure Mortregis from his sleep and then I will deal with these kings, Pelham and Zadenwolf both.'

'No. I can't do it.'

'Can't!' shouted Starkey. 'You won't, that's what you mean. Alwyn left the secret in your hands and you know that it will defeat your father.'

'No, you don't understand! You can't have what the verses promise!'

'We'll soon change that.' Starkey swept aside his cape to reveal the ruby-handled dagger, overlooked when Zadenwolf's soldiers disarmed them earlier. He snatched it from his belt, and grabbing Nicola from Marcel's side, he held its deadly blade to her throat.

'Don't help him, Marcel!' she gasped, her voice determined but her eyes betraying her fear.

Eleanor looked on, unconcerned, as Nicola's fate hung in the balance. 'No, Starkey. Try the elf-girl. He's even more devoted to her than to his sister.'

Bea stood brave and unflinching as Starkey came at her with his deadly blade, his teasing sneer replaced by a grim mask that sent a chill through Marcel.

'Please don't hurt her!' he begged.

'Her life is entirely in your hands. Turn your mind to the Book and show me what Alwyn taught you. You understand these verses, I know you do. *Let slip the Beast*,' Starkey quoted, 'and your little friend will go free.'

Fergus threw himself at Starkey, but before he could grab at the knife Hector hauled him away. Fergus appealed to Damon, the man he had once trusted with a son's blind loyalty. 'Don't let him do this.'

'What does it matter if the girl dies? We'll all be dead in the morning if your brother holds back his magic.'

My magic, thought Marcel. It had been enough to overwhelm Lord Alwyn, but the old wizard had been close to death, his powers weakened and almost gone. What did Marcel really know of his own magic — a single book, so much of it confusing and only half-learned? There was only one page of it that was truly part of him. It had survived even when Lord Alwyn took away everything else that he was and everything that he had taught himself. The words that began his own book of sorcery.

> *My fate is my own, my heart remains free*
> *Not magic but wisdom reveals destiny*

Wisdom — all that he had come to know and all that he knew to be true. He had already used it to unmask Zadenwolf. But what did he know of the Book of Lies? More perhaps than even its creator, he saw now. He looked up at Starkey, whose expectant face somehow grew more grotesque and distorted each time he saw it. 'There *is* no dragon,' he told him plainly. 'The Book has deceived you, just as it tricked my father and Lord Alwyn himself.'

'You're lying!' Starkey thundered. 'What else could the verses speak of but Mortregis? The beast's very name means "Death of a King".'

'Yes, it's Mortregis, but he's not what you think he is. You've already conjured this dragon, Starkey.'

'What are you talking about?'

'Look outside this tent, if you dare. We're surrounded by soldiers ready for battle. They are armed with swords and arrows, just like in the poem.

> *'With swords for teeth and skin of steel*
> *With arrowed claw and poisoned heel*

'And you yourself set fire to the land we passed through today. You see?

> *'A Beast will touch the land with flame*

'Every line in the verses is the truth, but at the same time a lie. Don't you understand?' He stepped forward suddenly and pressed his hand down on the cover of the Book. 'Mortregis is the war you've brought on us all.'

Marcel did not need to look down. He could feel the warmth of the Book's glow on his open palm. He also sensed a cruel pleasure rising from it. The evil on its pages was delighted with the mayhem it had brought to the world of its creator.

But Starkey's darting, desperate eyes *were* drawn inevitably towards it. 'No!' he roared, and with a savage lunge he pushed Marcel away and placed his own hands on the Book. 'The dragon is real!'

With even greater delight, it seemed to Marcel, the Book of Lies responded immediately. It writhed in an endless frenzy, streaming through its pages from one cover to the other, then reversing itself as it searched in vain for a space to record just one more lie. The flapping and fanning became hysterical laughter that seemed to mock them, Starkey most of all.

'No, it hasn't betrayed me! I won't believe it! There's a dragon to be conjured up from these pages still.'

At first he tried to close the cover, but the Book's urge to find a place for his words was more powerful than human hands could resist. When he realised his attempts were futile, Starkey picked up the Book and hugged the open covers to his chest, like a father with an infant child. 'It promised me the power of a dragon,' he cried demonically, hugging it even more tightly against his heart. 'I can feel its heat in my bones. *I must have the power of that dragon!*'

None of them could quite believe what happened next. With the open Book still thrashing against his chest, Starkey began to rise up, huge and repulsive beyond all description. His feet grew into massive claws; his skin gave way to scales the size of a knight's heavy shield. That sharp and angular face took on a new form, his mouth and nose shaping themselves into a hideous snout as his mane of black hair hardened into a row of vicious spines ranged down the back of his elongated neck. The emerging creature was too much for the tent, which became a shroud over its head until, with a sweep of its vicious tail, the canvas was ripped aside.

Marcel and the others were forced back by the sheer size of the monster, now as tall as ten men stacked on each other's shoulders. In its claws, once Starkey's human hands, the Book of Lies writhed chaotically, the white of its crowded pages standing out starkly against the dragon's dark and steely hide.

The bravest of Zadenwolf's soldiers took aim, but their arrows were no match for those scales. Wings spread out ominously from behind the beast's shoulders, and with a surge that blew many of the fleeing soldiers off their feet, it rose into the air, hovering above them and picking them out with its devilish eyes. To their terror, the dragon began to fill its lungs, leaving no doubt about what was to come.

Zadenwolf suddenly appeared and tried to rally his terrified troops. The beast's eye fell on him, alone in the circle of deserted tents, a sword in his hand as he shouted orders that no man would stop to obey. The dragon contorted its wrinkled neck and, when the aim was perfect, opened its jaws like a snake about to strike. Flames poured from its throat, a long, deadly tongue of the brightest fire. There was no time for Zadenwolf to run, and no hiding place that could save him. The flames struck his face and chest, searing the fur from his collar and the hair from his head. Even the metal of the sword that remained clutched in his hand began to melt. By the time the flames subsided, there was nothing left but a charred skeleton and the echo of a blood-curdling scream.

The dragon took another breath and looked about for others who deserved its vengeful wrath. It found Marcel, with Nicola and Fergus beside him. They knew that when the dragon breathed out again, a sheet of flame would char the flesh from their bones, just as it had done to Zadenwolf. The three of them would all die together. The creature's snout lunged towards them so it would make no mistake with its aim, its massive belly heaving, its neck distended.

Then a distraction. Something flew wildly about the dragon's head, stealing its attention.

Gadfly! But how could she fly without the Book?

Marcel saw the answer instantly. The little pouch was tied around her neck, and yes, when he took a closer look he could make out the tiny shape of Bea herself, clutching fearlessly onto the untidy mane. Gadfly beat her wings, swerving and dipping like the insect she was named after, and miraculously the dragon's head swerved away from the helpless children below. But Gadfly and Bea were in grave danger themselves now, as the beast focused its fury on them alone.

'Get behind him!' Marcel shouted desperately to Bea, though whether he could be heard amid the soldiers' screams and the dragon's mighty roar there was no way to tell. But at the last moment, the horse ducked sharply, just as the terrible flames shot out into the night. On the ground below, the children felt the fire's heat, but it was so high above their heads that it died harmlessly in the night air.

'Run!' cried Nicola urgently, and they began to flee as fast as they could before the dragon could take another breath. All except Fergus. Starkey's dagger still lay where he had dropped it, and holding it by the blade Fergus took aim and sent it spinning towards the beast.

Marcel watched in awe as the dagger tumbled end over end and then struck not one of the impregnable scales, but the fleshy back of the creature's claw. A bellow of rage split the night air, and in that same terrifying moment the Book of Lies fell from the dragon's grasp. The Book dropped heavily to the ground only a few strides from Marcel and Fergus, but by then the beast was already breathing in again.

'Come on!' Fergus turned, certain that his brother would follow on his heels.

But Marcel did not move. He wasn't looking at the horror above him. He was more concerned with what he could hear. Voices, a dozen, no, a hundred, or was it a thousand? All speaking at once and all coming from the Book of Lies. He knew what they were. Every lie the Book had ever heard, all the deceit that had corrupted it, was trying to escape before it could be destroyed by the fiery breath of the dragon it had unleashed.

Lord Alwyn was gone and there was no Master of the Books to take his place. There was only a young prince who had taught himself the sorcerer's arts. He had no robes of black and green embroidered with a rampant dragon above an open book, but Marcel knew he was the only one who could take Lord Alwyn's place. It was that symbol which told him what to do now.

The magic of the Book of Lies was Lord Alwyn's magic. For all the dragon's power, it was part of a waning sorcery, which Marcel knew was doomed to die as Lord Alwyn had done. The Kingdom's fate lay in new and untried hands.

Marcel raised his arm towards the beast and felt his untested magic touch its fiery skin. He reached further, right into that surging chest, and found the creature's evil and tormented heart. He took hold and let the camp around him fade away, until the sensation of power that surged through him was enough to make him cry out. His mind lost all connection with his body. All that existed for him now was the dragon hovering over the open Book.

A bone-crushing roar filled his head, a cry of anguish loud enough to drive the dead from their graves. Towering over him, the grotesque figure of Starkey, transformed into the image of his own heart's desire, no longer held any fear for him. His magic had taken hold of this creature's heart and slowly, relentlessly, he drove its evil strength away into the night, out towards the distant mountains, out of his father's kingdom.

Instantly, the beast began to change, to shrink, not into its human form but into a swirling cloud. The Book of Lies fanned its pages all the more frantically, and as Marcel watched, fascinated, the cloud was sucked down between its covers. When it was gone, a burst of flame erupted from within the Book, burning fiercely as the voices of a thousand liars slowly died.

MARCEL STOOD ALONE FOR many minutes until Bea brought Gadfly gently to the ground, close enough for him to stroke her nose. His brother and sister came back to stand at his side. Nicola whispered in amazement, 'You saved us all, Marcel. Your magic destroyed Mortregis.'

'No, Mortregis cannot be destroyed. All I've done is drive him out of the Kingdom.'

Zadenwolf's soldiers could be seen fleeing into the night, not even stopping to grab their weapons. Their leader had died a horrible death and the dragon's single breath of flame had also set fire to much of the camp. The invading army was scattered in every direction across the scorched landscape, all thought of conquest forgotten, hoping only for a safe return to the mountains of Lenoth Crag.

At dawn, Long Beard and his elfish army arrived to join a battle that would never take place, and King Pelham emerged with a small party of soldiers from behind the city walls. Both kings found that the only occupants of the enemy camp were the four exhausted children. They were sitting in a circle around a pile of white and smouldering ashes. This was all that remained of the great Book of Lies.

Epilogue

MARCEL STOOD BEFORE THE grave of his mother, with his father beside him and his sister a pace in front. 'I wish I had some memory of her at least, as you do,' he said to the King. In those tumultuous hours in the Great Hall, he had taken part of Lord Alwyn's memory for himself. But it would be wrong to steal the memory of his mother from his own father's mind, no matter how much he longed to conjure up the image of her face.

He looked for Fergus, who lingered behind them, uncomfortably quiet as he had been ever since their return to the palace two days before. Memory or not, these four now shared a common grief.

'Is there any news of Damon?' Fergus asked his father.

'He is still at large,' came the reply.

Marcel knew, as they all did, that Damon had managed to escape amid the fear and confusion created by the rampant dragon. Eleanor had not been so lucky. Abandoned by her cousin, her blue gown had stood out among the many roughly dressed soldiers fleeing towards the high country. Some disgruntled villagers had dragged her, weeping, before the King. 'Don't put me back in that prison!' she'd pleaded in anguish. 'I couldn't bear it!'

But Pelham had turned away unmoved and sent her back to the chamber only ten paces from where they now stood. Eleanor had not been a prisoner there for long, however.

'Have they discovered how she did it?' Nicola asked.

'Some berries were found in a small bag beside her body. The apothecary says they are the same poison that killed your mother.'

'The kind of death she deserved, then,' said Nicola, her voice as cold as her mother's gravestone. 'We won't mourn for her.'

Marcel had to agree. Did he still hate Eleanor, even now? Ever since his first day with Mrs Timmins, his heart had rolled about inside his chest like a fishing boat in an angry storm. He wasn't sure whether Eleanor's death had taken him to the crest of a wave or down to the deepest trough. He closed his eyes for a moment, hoping for calm, but it wouldn't come to him. Not yet.

They walked through the rose garden and back towards the main entrance to the palace. Once inside, the King joined his advisers in the Great Hall, leaving the children to return to their rooms. When Nicola slipped through the heavy velvet curtain, the two boys were left to themselves, and each went to his bed and lay flat on his back, hands behind his head. For Marcel this was difficult, as Termagant instantly jumped onto his chest and sat there like a triumphant soldier who had conquered the castle.

'Marcel —' Fergus called tentatively, but before he could continue his brother cut him off.

'There's no need to say it again. I know you're sorry about the fight. I've told you a hundred times, you didn't know the truth.'

'No, it's not that,' Fergus responded, rolling onto his side. 'I've been thinking about what happened before then. Do you remember what I said to the Book of Lies? "I am the son of Prince Damon", that's what I said, and it glowed so brightly I could barely look at it.'

'It couldn't resist the evil inside it. It was trying to deceive, like it did in the Great Hall all those months ago, when Father tested our loyalty. It was so full of lies it wanted to cause havoc.'

This was what Marcel told his brother, but secretly he hadn't been able to brush aside the same nagging uneasiness.

Perhaps it was something in his voice, or maybe Fergus was better at detecting his brother's moods than Marcel was aware. 'You've been thinking about it too. You used your own magic that night, didn't you? You made the Book of Lies keep to the truth; not just what was in my heart, but every kind of truth, like it was supposed to do.'

There had been too many lies for Marcel to deny it. He nodded slowly and without a word. He *had* forced the Book of Lies to do its job faithfully, as Lord Alwyn had created it to do, and yet it had not written down Fergus's words. *I am the son of Prince Damon.*

Fergus grimaced and moved to the window, where he could look out again at their mother's grave and the chamber where the cousins had been kept prisoner. 'I've thought of something else that doesn't make sense. Do you remember the night we came to rescue Damon and Eleanor from down there?' He waved at the view through the window, prompting his brother to join him. 'You and Nicola were too slow, so I tried to open the door on my own. The handle wouldn't budge, Marcel. The door wouldn't open for me any more than it would for Starkey.'

Marcel did remember, but this was the first time he had thought about it and he found himself only more confused. 'What does it mean? You're a true and rightful heir, the same as Nicola and me.' There was so much about the sorcerer's arts that he was still to learn.

A knock at the door interrupted them. Marcel opened it to Bea, who let herself be seen clearly.

'Marcel, my grandfather and his soldiers want to be on their way. It's time to say goodbye.' She paused. 'I'd better give you this before I go,' she added, and plunging her hand into her pocket, she pulled out the pouch containing the folded page from the Book of Lies.

'Could I look at it?' Fergus asked, and Bea held it out for him to take.

Marcel barely noticed. He was too preoccupied by the thought that Bea was about to leave. He wished he had found a spell that could calm the emotions that swirled within his chest. 'Nicola will want to see you off as well,' he mumbled, to mask his discomfort.

Bea rushed through the curtain to tell Nicola the news, but once the girls had joined the two boys outside the door, Fergus broke away. 'I'll come down in a minute. There's something I need first,' he said quickly, and strode away in the opposite direction, with considerable purpose.

'Are you sure you want to go back to the mountain?' Marcel asked Bea as they headed towards the marble staircase.

'I have to spend some time with my grandfather, Marcel. He thought I was dead!'

'But you don't have to stay with him forever.'

Bea didn't bother with an answer, but let out a heavy sigh instead.

Nicola heard it and turned on him. 'Leave her alone, Marcel. Of course she wants to live with Long Beard and the elves. They're the only family she has.'

Marcel didn't feel that was quite true any more, and when Bea looked up, her face suddenly serious, he knew she was thinking the same thing. 'Don't worry. I'll live in the human world again, you'll see. What about you, Marcel? You have magic in your hands now and a sorcerer's book of your own.'

'It's not quite the Book of Lies, though,' he said, out of respect for Lord Alwyn. For all the evil that had crept into the land in his dying days, that old man had kept the Kingdom safe for more years than anyone could remember. It sent a shudder through Marcel's body to think of one person taking on such a burden.

Termagant led them down the grand staircase, her tail held vertical and rigid like a flagpole.

'I've heard rumours,' Nicola said to her brother as they followed the cat. 'Father wants you to be the new Master of the Royal Books.'

'He's talked to me about it,' Marcel replied, without giving anything away. In fact, he and the King had spent much of last night talking about it, and some time after midnight, when everyone else in the palace was safely asleep, Marcel had said yes. He had agreed to take Lord Alwyn's place, and the very thought of it twisted his stomach into a knot.

They emerged into the courtyard at the front of the palace under a low sky that had already delivered a steady, nourishing rain through much of the morning. It had stopped for now, as though the clouds were granting them a respite for their farewells. King Pelham was there with Long Beard, who called his granddaughter over to join him. Her friends went with her.

After they had stumbled awkwardly over the painful words of goodbye, Nicola leaned forward and hugged Bea tightly. Then it was Marcel's turn. They held each other for a long time, and when they finally stepped back, Bea's face was flushed and red.

'Glowing like a candle,' her grandfather teased her, 'and that's not such a good thing for an elf in the forest.' But he was laughing as he said it.

With handshakes, then a final lingering wave from the palace gates, Bea, her grandfather and the troop of elfish soldiers headed out into the city. Marcel stood watching, but they didn't want to be gaped at by the crowds, and within moments they had all found the shadows where they were impossible to see.

'Where's Fergus?' Nicola asked all of a sudden, looking about her. He hadn't come down from the palace as he'd said he would. 'He should have come to say goodbye; we might not see Bea again for a long time,' she complained in a forthright tone.

Marcel had heard her speak firmly like this a number of times in the past two days. He quietly hoped that he would not come to resent it in the years ahead.

Mind you, *he* was annoyed with Fergus too.

A commotion in the courtyard made him spin round and angry voices erupted from the stables away to his left. That was Old Belch's voice, surely. Then the clatter of hooves on the paving stones signalled the appearance of a horse and rider. As they broke free of the stables, Marcel saw that it wasn't just any horse, but Gadfly. And on her back was not some insolent soldier, but Fergus himself, with a sword hanging from his belt!

'What are you doing?' Marcel yelled as he ran towards Fergus, aghast.

Fergus ignored Marcel as he leaned forward over the restless horse's mane. He had looped something around Gadfly's neck and now he was tying it into a hasty knot.

Marcel knew instantly what it was. Already the magic was at work on the mare's flanks. Before anyone could stop him, Fergus urged Gadfly forward into a canter, then a steady gallop, and when her wings were free, a wild and desperate charge. The horse launched herself into the air, Fergus afraid but grimly determined as he grasped at her mane. Up and over the palace wall they climbed, towards the grey clouds, growing smaller in the distance with every beat of those wings.

'Stop him, Marcel!' cried the King.

Perhaps Marcel's magic *could* have done it. But he kept his hands by his side.

'Where's he going?' Pelham demanded.

'After Damon,' Marcel answered immediately.

'But why? I have half an army searching for him. What can Fergus do?'

Marcel didn't want to reply. He didn't even want to guess, though he could hardly stop his mind from jumping ahead. 'The Book of Lies,' he mouthed under his breath. It was gone, a puff of ashes scattered on the wind, but as he watched Fergus finally disappear towards the high country, Marcel couldn't stop the whisper in his mind.

We're not free of it yet.

The End

Acknowledgments

I WOULD LIKE TO thank my wife, Kate, other family
members and friends, and particularly Margaret
Connolly, all of whom have given me valuable advice
and support during the long gestation of *The Book of
Lies*. I would also like to acknowledge the hard-
working team at HarperCollins, especially Emma
Kelso, who has helped to guide this story for so long.

James Moloney